SUBVERSION

SUBVERSION

BOOK ONE OF SUBVERSION TRILOGY

RUHI PARIKH

Edited by Amy Vrana
Cover Art by Ebook Launch
Layout by Vellum

Printed by Amazon KDP

Disclaimer: This book includes intense action, violence, and language. Please read with caution.

This is for those who cower in a world ridden in nothing but malicious intent.
Just hold on tight, and light will give way.
I promise it will be worth it.

SUB·VER·SION

a systematic attempt to overthrow or undermine a government
or political system by persons working secretly from within

EMPTY

November 4, 2064
11:20 a.m.

A COOL BREEZE SIFTS into the dark and lanky room, making shivers run up my spine.

I sigh, plopping onto the hard mattress as my back hits the rigid and rock-like surface. I wince as soon as unbearable pain shoots through me, almost like lightning striking a tree. Finally, I roll over on one side and take a deep breath in, my eyes settling onto the cracked and barren wall.

This is my room.

Well, our room, actually . . . my mother, father, little sister, and mine.

Since we're Poor, all we own is a one-story home, which isn't much of a home to begin with, since it consists of a scrawny living room, a small bedroom, and a bathroom that holds a toilet and a shower that barely function themselves.

I know it may not sound like much, but trust me, it is.

This is the life we are accustomed to, and there isn't much we can do about it. I mean, we can complain to the government and demand for a better life, which would end immediately with execution. But at least we wouldn't have to suffer.

A frown grows on my lips, but I cannot exactly tell if that is from sadness or anger. Is it sadness that I have built up in my eyes, ready to be plunged out in waterfalls of tears? Or is it anger that I have conjured up in my chest, willing to pounce out of my lungs like violent flames?

Only God knows why I'm frowning.

My cold and numb fingers dig into my palm, my nails etching red marks on my sensitive skin. I bite my lip, almost to the point where I feel sweet blood seeping out. *What is this life? What am I even doing here, wasting my life away, laboring for this stupid country and having no future set for me?*

My thoughts are interrupted when I hear a short knock on the beaten door. I unlatch my nails from my skin and swivel my head around, making eye contact with Emilia, my little sister.

Her petite frame lingers in the doorway, her dark hair sticking up in various places. She lets her soft voice filter into the room like an aroma. "B? Mama says it's almost time to go."

I let out a breath, sitting up on the edge of the concrete mattress. "I know, Em. I know."

She presses her lips together into a thin line and sits beside me, placing her hand on my thigh. "It'll be all right. Everything will be all right."

I bite the inside of my cheek. *Will it? Will it, really?*

Ignoring all intrusive thoughts, I bring her closer, wrapping my arms around her shoulders and pressing her face into my chest. "Thanks, Em. I love you."

I feel her grin forming against my ribs. "I love you too, B," she mumbles out, "but I can't really breathe right now."

"Oh." I laugh, letting her go as she lets in a deep breath. "I'm sorry."

"It's okay," she says, smiling softly.

Silence fills the room like an amorphous liquid. Em starts to fiddle with her fingers as she murmurs, "Will we be all right? I mean, Mama and Papa have been upset lately, so does that mean that we're not going to be okay? Please, B, tell me if we're going to—"

"Em." I look down at her, her chocolate eyes eerily reflecting my mother's. "Don't think about it too much, all right? Whatever happens will be for the best . . . even if the government hates us." My words are desperate to not only console her, but me, too.

She twiddles with a string that she pulled out from her pocket. I furrow my eyebrows. "What's that?"

Em holds it up to me. "I came here to ask if you could do my hair. Mama seemed too busy . . ."

"Yes, of course," I say. I signal for her to sit on my lap, which she obediently does. My fingers rake through her knotty hair, separating it into three parts. Then, I make a braid effortlessly, tightly pleating and enclosing it with a cute little bow. I tap her back lightly. "Done."

She squeals and runs her fingers through her braid. "B, I love it!" Her arms wrap around me, her face pressing into the nook of my neck. "Thank you!"

Suddenly, I notice from the corner of my eye that someone stands by the front of the door. Em and I whirl our heads around to meet our mama's frame, covered in a light blue dress that barely seems to hold itself together at this point. Her dark hair is tied into a low bun, accentuating her mature and sunken features. My mama is very beautiful, but the stress of being a mother during these times has seemed to overcome her natural features.

She suddenly runs over to Em's braid and exclaims, *"Mira vos! Te ves bello!"*

My mama starts to ramble in Spanish about how beautiful her little *hija* is. She is Argentinian and acts like one as well with her booming voice and dominant personality. However, she has lived in the States for her entire life and was born here as well, yet her parents have taught her everything there is to know about our native country.

Before the Dark Ages during the 2030s, my mama—Marianna Gonzalez—was a very refined woman pursuing a degree in education. But once the tensions between the Rich and the Poor began to rise . . . Well, it was unfortunately that time Mother was struggling with her bills, and she was placed into the Poor category because anyone who earned below the designated salary range was immediately named as a "Poor."

When battles formed in America, due to the tight financial situation, my mother had met my American father, David Cohen. He was a rich and successful businessman that was well-known in the country until one of his friends started blackmailing him to do certain things that involved his money, and my father, being the loyal and caring friend that he is, went along with *every* word his friends said.

It was a short road to bankruptcy and begging on the streets. He still recounts to this day that he had wished he was Poor at any other time in the country. Hell, he even mentioned that the First Great Depression would've been better for him.

Yeah. The 2030s were *that* bad.

I don't know much about the 2030s because I wasn't born until more than a decade later. When I try to bring up the economic crisis that led to the divergence of the Rich and the Poor, my parents dodge it and berate me for even bringing up the mere notion of it. Sometimes my mother would give in and explain little to me, but that is with great persuasion. It seems like a sensitive topic for them because they resided in a time and world where one's financial status determined whether they would be deemed a worthy person or not. And their offspring would live the same life their parents did. It was all based on the family's economical situation to alleviate the long-lasting Second Great Depression.

My parents were and forever will be disheartened by the unfortunate circumstances they were put into. And to this day, I can still see the sadness etched into their eyes whenever they walk by me. My rage and hatred for the government has been growing because of that.

The government, encompassing a board of Rich men and women, makes us labor and break our backs for them while the Rich just stare at us in pity and erupt into laughter.

And thirty years later, in the fiery pits of hell, otherwise known as Washington, D.C. . . . The president is being inaugurated.

Tobias Remington's second inauguration.

The hatred I have for that man is indecipherable and going to see him inaugurated at the Capital Center *again* makes me want to vomit. He has done *nothing* for us. All he has done is favor the Rich, and that is it.

When are we going to get freedom? Justice? When will we stop being treated like slaves? When?

"Blaire?"

My mind hovers back to reality as my mom and my little sister stare at me in confusion. "Are you okay, B?" Em whispers, poking my arm with her finger.

"Yeah, I'm fine," I mutter, shaking my head. "Just zoned out, I guess."

Unfortunately, my lie doesn't seem to convince my mom as her eyebrows thread back with realization. She taps Em's back, her eyes emanating concern. "Go give Papa some company. I need to speak to Blaire in private."

"Okay, Mama." Em smiles. Her doll-like legs soon tread out the door, which leads to dust shooting out of the frame—almost like fireworks.

Silence fills in between us as I look up into my mom's soft brown eyes. "What's wrong, *hermosa*?"

I let out a sigh, my body deflating. "Mama . . . Do we really have to go see Remington get sworn in as president? Do we really have to put ourselves through that torture yet again?"

Her lips press together as she places her soft yet ragged hand on top of mine. Her thumb brushes over my rough calluses due to me mining all day long yesterday. My body aches, my muscles feel like lead, and my head pounds due to a mini migraine that I know is on its way to burden me. I *barely* got any sleep last night—just as usual—considering all four of us sleep on our puny little mattress.

"Blaire," she says, her voice tightening. "This is the world we are living in. Who are we to change it? We can't decide whether we should go or not. You know the consequences of us not attending the inauguration, right?"

Yes, I think. *If our names are not checked off at the inspection station, then we would be immediately executed.*

My silence seems to have answered her question. "That's what I thought," she whispers.

"But Mama," I whine, "don't you feel at least a little bit of hatred toward these . . . Rich people? They make our lives miserable!"

"I do feel hatred, *mija,*" my mom whispers harshly. "When my parents died in the war . . . It broke a part of me and made me feel miserable." She pauses, her eyebrows suddenly pushed up. "Blaire, I know you feel hatred. We all do. But if we even dared to speak our thoughts or opinions . . . It's over for us. All of us."

My face slackens with defeat as the truth dawns upon me. She's right. No matter how hard we try to retaliate against the rich and powerful, we will never be able to win. Never be able to capture our freedom and escape this place known as hell. It's just how it is, and it's just how it's going to be.

"I'm just . . . *so* tired of laboring all the time." My eyebrows press together with frustration as I lift my hands up. "Look at my hands, Mama! No nineteen-year-old should ever go through this. And it burdens me to even think that sweet and innocent Emilia is going to go through this once she becomes an adult. It's unfair."

My mom presses both of her hands on my cheeks and rubs her thumb against my cheekbone, sending warmth through my body. I would've never been able to survive this world without my mom. Through my anger and frustration, she's the one that calms me down. She's the one who makes me feel like I'm at home, even though this place can never be called home.

"I admire your fiery spirit, *mija*, I always have. You are just like your father because you both have this fire running through your veins. I admire it so much. But . . . You know what this world is like, Blaire. You know how our president is. And you know what the Rich are like. There is simply little to nothing we can do to change this place." She sighs. "You know that, right?"

All I do is stare back at her with a blank expression, her deep and thoughtful words echoing into my mind.

She kisses my forehead, mumbling that she loves me.

I lay there in her arms. "Me too, Mama." Even though she only embraces me for three seconds, it feels much longer, as if time has just ceased.

The aura radiating from my mother's presence makes me realize just how wise she is. Me and my sister were lucky enough to have parents who were educated before the war, before this place succumbed to utter misery. And from a very young age, my mom taught me all there is to know about the world.

Out of everything, I was enthralled by the English language and the mysterious ways it worked, so I often sneaked into my mom's tiny library in our closet, dusted off some classic literature, and spent the entire night huddled in there, reading every single page of *Night* by Elie Wiesel. That is when my vocabulary shot through the roof, and my mother always used to joke that my speaking skills were so established to the point where I could easily disguise myself as a Rich person.

A year later, Emilia was born, and my mom moved on to home school her when she grew up, teaching her the same things she had taught me. Emilia wasn't so keen on the English language, and as a growing twelve-year-old, she still struggles to keep up with the language. So, I assist my mother in educating her sometimes. We all are in the same boat, undergoing the same issues, so we secretly help each other out in hopes of a Guard not finding out about our secret schooling.

Eventually, it is time to leave. My mama takes my rough hands and leads me out the door. I look ahead to study her timid appearance, my walking starting to slow.

She turns around, noticing the foreign look on my face. "Everything okay, *mija*?"

I nod my head, reassuring her with the lie that slips out of my mouth with eventual regret. "Yes, everything's fine, Mama. I promise."

Her lips curl into a smile. "That's great, Blaire." Her grip tightens on my hand as my stomach churns. "Let's get going then."

2

HATRED

November 4, 2064
11:55 a.m.

I LEAN AGAINST THE corner of the living room wall. My sage- colored jean jacket is slung over my shoulders, and once I start to feel the cool air swarming around me, I decide to give in by wearing it. I finally find myself feeling warm in this cold and desolate place.

I look ahead and see Mama and Papa in our tiny and tattered kitchen. The lamp light flickers every now and then, the walls in the kitchen are covered in bits of expired food, and I swear I just saw a rat scurry by.

This place is not ideal. But it's our home, so complaining about it isn't going to get me far.

My papa's apprehensive eyes land on me, and he walks over, his bruised hands pushed into his ripped jeans. His tired green eyes, like mine, brush over my outfit. "Are you ready, darling?"

"Yeah," I murmur.

He raises his eyebrows and purses his lips together in

thought. "This won't last too long, I promise. But we have to go to the inauguration."

"I don't want to, though." I speak with a low volume, my head thumping against the cracked walls repeatedly.

"Blaire." His hands escape from his pocket and grasp my shoulders, squeezing them reassuringly. "It'll only last for two hours. We just have to get past the inspection station, stay in a single file line as we sit in our seats, and act like considerate citizens when the president and his family appear."

"I know how the inauguration works, Papa." I scowl but immediately feel guilty as soon as my father's face falls. "I'm sorry. I didn't mean to let my anger out on you. I'm just really upset about this."

"So are—" my papa starts, but the door suddenly bursts open.

Em gasps as she runs over to Mama and buries her face into her torso. I stand there beside my father, watching with wide eyes as huge spurts of dust swirl in the air. The outside light peers inside like a ghost, suddenly revealing three distinct figures. *Guards.*

They are dressed head to toe in navy blue uniforms with huge rifles slung over their shoulders. Massive masks cover their faces, and all I can regard from them is the stormy and furious ambiance in their eyes.

"Is this the Cohen Family, Rank 2899 in *Poor?*" A dark and dominant voice erupts out of one of them.

My dad's cheeks flush as he blurts out, "Yes."

The Guard nods his head once, and the other two start to walk off. "Follow me," he growls, "and stay in a single file line if you don't want your heads blown off."

A tiny whimper comes out of Em, and I can almost feel her clutching onto my mom, who has a forlorn look on her face.

I take a final look at our tiny shack as I close the door behind us. It feels as if I am closing the door to peace and safety, and now I am entering a world that I know I am not safe in.

No one is safe out here.

12:01 p.m.

The sounds of our footsteps resound into my ears, creating a rhythmic noise that I find myself getting sick of. And what irritates me the most is that my foot seems to be slipping out of my combat boots due to the soles being torn apart.

Suddenly, I hear a woman screaming from my left side, and I swirl my head around to see a Guard clubbing her back. Blood surges out of her bruised skin like a waterfall, and her screams drowning in agony reverberate into the melancholy atmosphere. I would be horrified by the sight my eyes landed upon, but I have grown accustomed to this—the daily beatings of Poor men and women that do nothing to harm others. My eyes stray to the ground, and my stomach immediately churns in disgust as I unconsciously pull Em closer to me. Her body seems to be trembling with fear.

"Shh, it's okay." I continue to walk behind her as her chest heaves with silent cries. "Just don't look over there."

"Why are they hitting her?" she whimpers.

"I don't know, Em. Just please don't look there," I add hurriedly. She murmurs an *okay*, sniffles, and we continue to walk in a single file line.

The Poor sector is not so far away from the Capital Center, otherwise known as the gathering area in front of the White House. The White House, also, is known as where the president and his family reside. *Damn him and his family.*

Every single part of me wants to jump out of this stupid single file line, take down all three of the Guards, grab my family, and *run* toward the Midwest—never looking back. No

Poor person ever wants to live here because the Rich people have taken *everything* away from us, including our money, will to live, and the passion and ambition we buried into our souls. But they snatched it away. Of course they had to snatch it away.

A deep feeling of hatred and frustration settles in me as I see us nearing the inspection station. The Poor settle in lines as I hear the raucous laughter and cheer of the Rich, cradling wine in their hands and seeming engrossed in moronic Rich people conversations. They slip past the inspection station since they apparently don't need to get checked in, and they take their seats at a nice seating arrangement where white linen tables line the ground, waiters coming over to assist them and classical music playing elegantly.

Well, on our side . . . It's a completely different story.

On our side are creaky and neutral-toned chairs with no tables lining the ground, no waiters assisting us, and no classical music playing elegantly. It is just a depressing atmosphere with Guards present at every corner, rifles cocked and ready to shoot at some innocent Poor person.

The White House stands before us, its smooth white walls glowing against the gray contrast of the sky. Every single other place is cast in ruins in D.C., but the White House and several other Rich people's mansions are built elegantly, as if not a single scratch had even encountered them. The utmost reformation of the buildings must have undergone since the Rich people highly believe in preserving what is "worthy."

In front of the White House is the Capital Center. The entire Center itself is majestic and massive. Lights cover the entire expanse and shine most of them on the stage, where a white marble ground covers the entire area.

I feel shivers run down my spine as the cool air rushes back and forth around us. Unconsciously wrapping my arms around myself, I grit my teeth as my dark hair flies around me like a bird that wants to be cast away. My eyes set upon the sky, clouds covering every inch of the bright blue-sky underneath.

Our line inches forward as women seated at the inspection tables grab the forearms of each person, take a small laser, and painfully sear the laser through their skin. This is to inflict a Tag on each Poor person, so if a Poor person were to *behave poorly*, the Guards would have to shoot them dead. Tags usually fade away every quadrennial inauguration, as I can see faded away on me.

When Remington was elected four years ago, I screamed at the top of my lungs when the shock of the laser incised into my skin. It hurt for not even a second, but at that time, I thought it was the most painful thing in the entire world.

But now? I'm not so scared of it anymore.

My mother and father quickly get Tagged, and I see it newly engraved into their olive skin. Em is up next, but she immediately steps back into me, distress on her face. Em was eight years old at her first inauguration, but any child below the age of twelve is not allowed to attend one. She instead was pried away from our family and was forced to stay at a "home" for Poor kids until their families came back from the inauguration —the same home children stay when the adults are at work. The children were considered lucky if their families came back in the first place.

"You got this, Em," I whisper into her ear.

She at first struggles to listen to my encouragement, but as soon as I reassuringly pat her shoulders, her tightened body slowly loosens as she reluctantly juts her arm forward.

With great hesitation, she turns to a red-haired woman dressed in white. "Give me your arm," the woman declares, and Em extends her arm out. The lady's thumb grazes over her forearm, takes the wand-like laser, and presses the metal surface onto Em's skin. A small flicker of electricity appears from the wand, and she screeches, reeling away from the woman.

Em begins to tear up, and as I start to comfort her, Mama comes rushing in and whispers, "I got her. You just do your thing."

Slowly agreeing to my mother's wishes, I watch my family sit by the front row of chairs. I close my eyes for a moment and open them just to see the red-haired woman staring at me as if I was taking up all the time in the world. "Are you ready?" she asks monotonously.

I nod my head and thrust my forearm out at her. She presses the wand against my forearm and the pain is over before I can even wince. A burning feeling grows on my skin as my fingers graze over the tattooed area. **COHEN, BLAIRE. 19. 08/14/2045. RANK #2899.** It's etched in very tiny and dark letters, and before I can even take it in, the lady yells, "Goddammit, we don't have all day here!"

My cheeks flush red as I scamper past the stations. All the people in the line behind me move up one, pitiful looks plastered on their faces.

Once I see my family, I breathe out a sigh of relief. Meandering past the overwhelming crowds and intimidating Guards, I sit beside my mom, Em in the middle, and Dad on the other side. When I notice that she is still trembling, I reach over and say to her, "It will be okay, Em. The pain will go away."

Minutes later, when Em's emotions stabilize and everyone becomes seated, a baritone voice erupts into the air.

"Welcome to the Presidential Inauguration." The voice resounds into my bones and through the surrounding speakers —so loud and so daunting. "It has been a tradition for us Americans to recount every single pursuit this country has granted us, dating all the way back to July 4th, 1776, when our founding fathers granted the Declaration of Independence. Now, almost three centuries later, we have persevered through several discrepancies and proved that we are strong Americans united by blood and passion.

"We have been through numerous issues, ranging from societal and economical setbacks. But they insinuate that we are brave, and we have proved to our past presidents that we can get through this. And all 3,000 citizens of the United States *will* get through this."

3,000 citizens of the United States? I scoff. What happened to the other 4,030 of us?

"When the Second Great Depression hit in the 2030s," the hypnotizing voice states, "America was left with a tough interface. Millions of Americans all over the country died due to famine, dehydration, and a lack of willpower. Tensions rose in this country, and those who dared to retaliate against the powerful and the worthy . . . were punished." Pause. "But those who dared to endure it all are successful, are proud, and are grateful for what God has granted us.

"Although, there was one man that guided us plentifully, and without him, we would've been left to the wolves. This man is our true savior—the true hero of this country." The deafening silence makes my ears ring and invisible knives seem to be prodding at my skin as I wait in anticipation.

"May I please re-introduce to you, the man who guided us, the man who dared to lead us through dark and mysterious times, and the man who will continue to fight for each and every one of us . . . President Tobias Remington!"

3

GRAY

November 4, 2064
12:22 p.m.

FOOTSTEPS POUND AGAINST THE stage.

Anger forms inside of me as Tobias Remington smiles broadly at the Center. A six-feet tall man with attractive features yet a distasteful personality perfectly describes our president for the past four years, and unfortunately, four more. As thunderous applause spreads throughout the Center, he straightens his red tie and states "thank you" multiple times. The wide screens adjusted on the White House walls turn on and zoom into Remington's face, exhibiting his confident and arrogant expressions.

The cameras start to show the rest of the Center, which is filled with thousands of people. There are a lot more Poor people than Rich, so much more to the point where some of them spread out to the sides. And even though there are a lot more of us, the Rich are still more powerful. Sometimes, I wonder if their ostensible brutality is fabricated through their own insecurities.

The shiny smile depicted on Remington's face makes flames crackle in my body, ready to be hurled out in complete ire. This is the man that has been making our lives miserable for the past few years. And this is the man that will continue to make our lives a living hell.

"How are you holding up, *mija?*" my mom whispers in my ear.

Without looking at her, I murmur, "I think you know the answer to that question, Mama."

She sighs, taking my hand and squeezing it. A breath of relief escapes out of me. *Just what I needed.*

"Good afternoon, America!" Remington takes a breath in and studies the crowd. "Serving as president for four years made me realize how astounding it is to be in this position again, no matter how difficult it may seem. And I will admit, the past thirty years have been difficult for this country too, but we have prevailed through those hardships that placed us in a questionable area. Many countries during those times dealt with the hunger crisis too, but they had managed to resolve it in a matter of time. Unfortunately, our country was not able to because we had another issue as well . . . social divisions.

"America had the best military, education, and freedom in the world, yet some mindless creatures counteracted those amazing opportunities and fought for something they couldn't have—wealth. Now, money, as we all know, is a very valuable object, and it determines your place in society. It also determines your strength. Your intelligence. Your ambitious needs. And your virtuousness. *Those* attributes are what define your presence in this country. And those who lack those attributes are placed in their truthful social hierarchies.

"This country encountered many changes—just like this inauguration. Ever since 1937, America has followed its traditional values for the Presidential Inauguration—all on January 20th. But we had laid down new rules, such as voting processes initiated since June and the actual inauguration replacing the election date. All of this was placed on May 6th, 2039, as you all might be aware of.

"Now, to this day, I will serve as the 56th President. I will make sure to represent all those worthy individuals of this country and those that have sacrificed themselves for the furtherance of this country—otherwise known as our remarkable presidents. This is only the beginning, citizens! Thank you!"

A couple seconds of silence encompasses, and I swear I can hear a pin drop in the Center. But suddenly, a huge roar of applause unleashes in the air, slashing its murderous fangs at those who dared to object. Tobias grins—almost sadistically.

He speaks once the Center quietens. "However, I would not be here without the people who support me: the wonderful vice president, the impressive government, my friends that stuck with me since day one, and . . . my lovely wife."

He pauses.

"So, may I please have the honor of welcoming Isabelle Remington onto the stage?"

Light applause enters the Center, and my curious eyes trail over to the side of the White House, where a woman emerges. She is a dainty woman wearing a red-striped coat dress and pointy black heels and walks up to the stage, a gracious smile forming on her thin lips.

She speaks, her prose just as distinguished yet poisonous as her husband's. The way her words filter into everyone's minds is just as hypnotizing as an enchanter would be. If she wasn't associated with such a sanctimonious creature, then I would admire her.

Once the First Lady finishes, Tobias says into the microphone, "Last but not least, may I please have the honor to present on stage my brilliant and incredible son, Jax Remington?"

And that is when he steps onto stage, his jaw clenched as the heels of his dress shoes pound against the marble. I have only seen Jax in person four years ago, when his father was first inaugurated. But now?

He's a man. A powerful man that seems to share a story of his own, not just of a president's son.

His confident steps lead him to the front of the stage, allowing the camera to move onto his chiseled and clean-shaven face and dark hair, his determined gray eyes settling over the crowd. "Good afternoon, everyone." His deep and commanding voice booms into the speakers, making me immediately snap out of my thoughts. And it seems as if those three words alone were enough to shut up the entire Center.

"I am honored to stand on this noble stage." His lips are parted as he takes a deep breath in. "And my family and I are especially honored to be a part of this again as my father continues to make sure everyone rightfully gets equal rights." *Did he just say* everyone *getting equal rights? Bullshit.*

"I have absolute certainty and trust in my father that he will make this country a better place." Jax's voice falters, his thoughts suddenly seeming to trail off. I furrow my brows in confusion. What is he doing?

"And"—he clears his throat—"I-I hope you have a great day. God bless America." He murmurs the last line to himself and goes to stand on the far back side of the stage, his lips pressed together into a thin line. No one else seems to be bothered by his sudden detour in his speech—instead, they are focused on what Tobias and Isabelle are saying now.

But I can't help but study his movements and facial features—the way he's looking anywhere but the audience. A certain faraway look is cast on his silver eyes that shine against the bright stage lights. It seems as if he feels out of place.

My eyes scan the huge screens as one of them is currently

focused on Jax's faraway look, and I study the thin line that runs along his right cheekbone. *Is that a scar?*

"Have a wonderful day, America!" Tobias exclaims as cheers erupt across the floor. I bring my hands together and slow clap, my eyes trailing over to Jax, who suspiciously slips out the back.

November 5, 2064
1:29 a.m.

My eyes snap open, my breathing erratic. I am covered in sweat as I lay in bed. Em has her arms wrapped around my waist, but as soon as I sit up, she grumbles to herself and turns to the other side, wrapping her arms around Papa's waist now.

I still can't seem to understand how the hell we all fit onto this mattress, which is big enough to fit all four of us, but it gets so claustrophobic to the point where I even wake up in the middle of the night and find trouble falling back asleep.

Just like right now.

My black tank top clings to my chest as I fan myself. I crane my neck toward my family, who are sound asleep, soft snores erupting out of them. No matter how much hell we go through, sleeping will always be a peaceful exit from this horrendous world that makes us mine by the forests until the moon rises.

And we do that every single day, droning on like obedient creatures.

Since Em is not eighteen years old, she is not allowed to labor yet because, as horrible as this place is, it's just not horrible enough to the point where they endorse child labor. So, Em stays at the home the government sends kids under the age of twelve during the inauguration. They claim to house them amiably, but the skeptical side of me disagrees with that statement.

I take a deep breath in and look over to the door, which is

cracked open. I need to get fresh air. This sweaty environment is making me feel uncomfortable.

Since I am in the middle, it's going to be difficult for me to get out of bed. So, I wrap my small blanket around myself—we all sleep in separate blankets—because it's going to be cold outside, crawl onto the foot of the bed, and set my feet gently onto the wooden floor. It creaks slightly, and I wince, darting a panicked look toward my family. Nobody seems to stir. *Still sound asleep,* I note with a sense of relief.

I slip out of the door and enter the main room. Then, I take in my surroundings.

The entire room is dark, the tiny kitchen and the tiny living room—only having one tattered couch and a small boxy TV—barely visible. I press my lips together as I look toward the front door, which is closed. *I just need fresh air. Once I am refreshed, I can go back to sleep.*

My hand traces the doorknob and I pull it back. *I must be very quiet.* Once the door opens, I slip out into the cool air and close the door gently. A weight seems to lift off my shoulders as I step onto our small patio.

A Guard stands on the other end of the road, his back to me. My movements are precise, each foot forward marked with the utmost thoroughness. It is imperative that no sound is made; otherwise, I *will* be shot and killed.

Once I feel as if it is safe, I sit by the corner of the patio, hidden by the large pole, and bring my knees to my chest as my teeth chatter to the point where that's all I can hear. I wrap the blanket around myself even tighter and recline against the exterior wall, my senses watchful, hoping no random bullet is lodged into my skull.

Whenever I think about a Guard possibly shooting me, I don't even think about the possible pain I'll endure. Instead, I think about the misery my family is going to be put through, thinking that their daughter is gone.

They already lost one of their kids.

My chest heaves as I silently sob, every single part of me falling apart. I feel my heart plunging to the ground, its remnants shattering into isolated pieces. I feel lost, worthless, and miserable in this world that I still fail to call home. How can I even call it home if I get treated like scum every day?

Ever since I turned eighteen and started laboring, one single thought ran in my mind, and that was to leave this shitty place and trek to the Midwest with my family. Nothing else.

But instead, I'm stuck here. And as hard it is to realize this . . . there's nothing I can do. Nothing.

I wipe my tears away, and it takes every part of me to bring myself up to my feet. Though, I don't know whether that's from the cold air that bites into my skin or my oppressive anxiety that never seems to unlatch its fingers around my veins.

The wind dances around me, and I hear the trees swaying in the distance, its heavy branches swinging seeming like monsters against the night. I tighten my blanket around me, and as soon as I start to place my hand on the doorknob, I feel a cloth latch onto my lips.

A foul taste seeps into my mouth as my muffled screams erupt into the suffocating fabric, and someone's hands— covered in leather—grasp my skin so tightly that I feel the pain spreading like a bacterium. I scream until my lungs ache, I fight until my muscles ache, and I cry with such anger that my eyes ache.

But that is until my eyelids start to droop, my body numb with the uneasiness that overtakes my beaten mind.

4

DARK

November 5, 2064
3:43 a.m.

SIRENS PIERCE THROUGH THE *empty air, and I sob, my tiny hands tightening their grasp around my mom's wrist. "Mama, what is happening? Why are they taking him away?"*

I look up to see my mom, who has endless tears running down her cheeks—yet her face remains as solemn as ever. "I don't know why, mija. I don't know why."

"What does that mean?" I gasp when the vehicles start to drive away, and I scream, tugging on my mom's sleeves. "He's gone! We need him back!"

"Blaire, hermosa, there's nothing we can do. Nothing at all."

I shake my head, refusing to acknowledge what my mother had said.

He sits in the car, bruises running along his body like pinpoints on a map. He looks beaten. Lost. Confused. And his silence speaks like harsh words, almost like a slap in the face as he is pushed into the van.

I watch him go away; his fate is etched into the sky with no remorse. I scream until my lungs give out, and all that is left of me is my hoarse voice and me and my mom, watching my brother disappear into the midst of the city . . .

My eyes snap open, my body jerking awake.

Sweat clings to me as ragged breaths escape out of my dry mouth. All I can see is complete and utter darkness as I feel my body restricted to one area.

I can't feel anything.

But I realize that I am tied up to a creaky chair, my arms slung and tied behind me, my feet pinned to the legs of the chair, and a wide piece of duct tape attached to my mouth.

I try to release an ear-splitting scream, anything to get me out of this foreign area and get me back home. My wails resonate against the black atmosphere, echoing into the night pitifully, and I try again, but all that continues to come out are useless, muffled cries.

Where am I? My eyes dart around to different areas of this foreign room, but all I can make out is darkness. No furniture, no people, no exit—*nothing.*

I move back and forth against the chair, trying to wring my feet out of the clips that dig into my black leggings, and my arms are bound together so tightly that the ropes scratch into my delicate skin. How did I get here? I can't even remember anything.

Tap. My breath hitches in my throat as I try to figure out where the sound came from. *Tap.* I furrow my brows and I murmur to myself. *Tap, tap, tap.* The sounds become more frenetic, louder, and vivacious.

Two figures emerge from the dark and mysterious mist. All I can make of these figures is that they are covered head to toe in black and their faces are hidden underneath a black mask, which only reveals their eyes. One of the figures seems to have a strong, masculine build with dark skin appearing on the exposed sides and brown eyes concealed with a dominating presence. The other figure has a more feminine build with a lighter skin tone and lighter brown eyes, but they still hold the same tall and dominating presence as the other.

Who are these people? Thousands of other questions form in my mind, and I try to wriggle out of the ropes and the cuffs, whimpering like a lost puppy. I need to get the hell out of here.

"You might want to stop that." A sultry and assertive female voice rings out into the intense air as something presses against my skull. *A gun?* My heartbeat screeches to a halt.

"If you dare to move one more inch, then this will happen." As elegantly as ever, the person brings their finger to their trigger, presses it back, and a deafening *click* rings into the air. I gulp. *I'm not scared of a stupid gun.*

But, to my alarm, they start to press against the trigger again.

I shriek, squirming and wriggling around, but they raise the gun to the ceiling, and an even more thunderous sound pierces through the air. *Boom!* The shell clangs to the ground, giving way to a vociferous silence. A lump grows in my throat, making it hard for me to breathe.

"Except"—the person hisses, leaning down until their light brown eyes are mere inches away from mine—"that bullet will plunge into your brain instead. Understand?"

Before I can respond, their hand suddenly comes to the tape stuck to my mouth and rips it off me. I scream for a split second, but the person immediately clamps their hand against my mouth. "No running away, no fighting, and especially no screaming. Do you understand?"

I nod desperately, my eyes blurring with tears.

"Good." The person sighs and stands up. "You got this?" They turn to the buff individual beside them.

The larger person eventually stands in front of me, their build, almost like a skyscraper, outreaching my cowering self. They clear their throat. "Blaire Cohen. Nineteen years old. Born on August 14th, 2045. Rank number 2899. Am I correct?"

My jaw slacks and my eyes widen. "How did you know that?"

The person chuckles. "Guess I was." They clear their throat and lean down to hold the arms of the chair I am tied to, their face very close to mine. Their pupils swarm with anger—anger built up inside of them. "All right. Now, you must be wondering why you are here, tied up to this puny little chair, and you might also be wondering if me and my lovely friend here are going to kill you."

A few seconds pass.

"We are not going to kill you."

I look down at the ground and breathe out a sigh of relief. "Okay, so . . . Why *am* I here? I-I don't even remember what happened. I think I was on my balcony, and suddenly I-I passed out and—"

"Shh, shh." The person tries to soothe me. "I know you have questions, and I promise we will answer them all. But you must answer the questions I am going to ask you now, understand?"

I glare at them in anger. "No! I deserve to know *now!*"

"Wow, he didn't tell us she was a feisty one," the buff person says, and the other person laughs. *He?*

Their dark brown eyes bore into me. "We will answer every question you need to ask us. Be patient."

I accept my fate and sigh, nodding my head slowly. "Fine, I guess. Ask me questions."

They take a deep breath, and I dare to lock eyes with them. "Say, Ms. Cohen, have you ever heard of the word *subversion?*"

"Yeah," I mutter. *All thanks to my intense love for literature.*

"And do you know what its Latin root is?"

I breathe in, clenching my hands into fists. "I don't know."

"It is *subvertere,*" the feminine figure says. "Meaning to overthrow."

I cock my head in confusion, and the larger person sighs.

"You are here on a very important mission. Known as the Subversion Act."

"The Subversion Act?" I question out loud, but the gears in my mind begin to click, like pieces of a puzzle finally interlocking together. "Oh. This mission involves overthrowing the government?"

"Finally figured it out, huh?"

I press my lips together. "But I'm still confused. Why this? Why now? Why me? Why—"

"Shh," the feminine figure says. "We told you we would answer your questions—"

"Then answer them!"

"—if you follow us."

I look at them in confusion. "Follow you? Where?"

"You're going to have to trust us," one of them whisper.

"How?" I scoff. "You guys kidnapped me and brought me to this shady place. You could kill me for all I know."

"Didn't we say that we wouldn't?" Their cocoa eyes seduce me into surrender. "So, trust us on that. We didn't bring you here for the hell of it. We brought you here for a reason."

"And what is that reason?"

"See, again with the questions." The feminine figure chuckles. "I can't believe he forgot to mention how much of a questioner you are." Who is this *he* they keep mentioning?

I decide to keep my mouth shut. A plan to overthrow the government, huh? Fine by me. I've been planning to destroy them since I was a kid anyway. Besides, what exactly do I have to lose, except my family? Maybe we will prevail in the end, and I'll be able to escape with them to the Midwest, like I've been dreaming anyway. And if we can't escape to the Midwest, then we'll go north. Or south. Anywhere except D.C., honestly.

This will be worth it. And the passionate looks on the puzzling individuals has me thinking that maybe I should take the risk.

I jut my chin and look at the large figure dead in the eye. "Fine. I'll go with you, but only if you answer this quick question of mine."

Their fists tighten. "Shoot."

I gulp. "Who is this *he* you're talking about?"

Their taut postures suddenly loosen as they exchange worried glances to each other. A few excruciating moments later, one of them comes forward and barely audibly says, "Someone you'll know of very soon."

Suddenly, the two people come forward and start to untie me. The ropes circling around my wrists loosen, and I breathe out a sigh of relief as the pain digging into my skin dissipates. Finally, they lean down and undo the latches covering my ankles, and I wiggle them out, closing my eyes in satisfaction.

Before I can relish any further in my physical freedom, I feel rough and large hands encircle around my red wrists and pull me up to my feet. My feet wobble as my torn combat boots pound against the concrete floor, and my dark hair flows onto my back as the large person pulls me forward. Their companion lingers behind me, their light brown eyes watching my every move.

The darkness in the room that I was so used to seems to transition into a much more visible atmosphere, and a dark door seems to appear in my sight. The person dragging me lunges it open and urges me toward a black van that seems to blend into the murky night.

Every part of me wants to rebel and unleash my wrath upon these people that stole me away from my home, but as of now, I want to stay alive. *Only for my family.*

The person's hands press onto my back as I lift my feet up onto the floor of the van, and scorching tears that had failed to come out before suddenly fall down my cheeks. My vision hazes as I sit down on a soft leather seat, my breath ragged, and the two people close the door before slipping into the front.

My tears suddenly come to an end, and I sniffle as I drag my hand across my face, taking a deep breath in. *Just breathe, Blaire. Just breathe.*

The van jerks to a start, the engine lights turning on. The buff person, who is in the driver's seat, looks back as the car reverses out of the dark alley. I look out the window and try to see where I was kidnapped, but all I can make out is a small torn-up building and not much else because the fogginess on the windows seems to impair my vision. I try to analyze the situation I am in and make sense of this enigmatic night, but the person next to the driver suddenly clears their throat.

I lock eyes with them as their piercing brown eyes move across my face. My heart beats erratically, and I clench my fists so hard I can feel my calluses turning red.

"Are you ready to destroy the government with us?"

5

UNKNOWN

November 5, 2064
4:23 a.m.

MY CHIN RESTS ON the van door, my head bobbing up and down as the van drives through the bumpy roads. I notice that we have left the city far behind due to the grimy suburbs transforming into an area engulfed in half-dead nature. The reason our world is so ugly now is because of our bold initiatives to hurl our anger for each other onto the trees and the animals. Swarms of fire, smoke bombs, firecrackers, hurtling bullets—you name it. The humans back then just couldn't control themselves and at least attempt to fix their issues in a more diplomatic way.

That is why the government exploits the Poor as the laborers and environment cleaners, picking up after the trash the Rich themselves left off. They were the reason the deadly civil war happened. Because of a Great Depression that was, in no way, our fault—but the wealthy and haughty still found a way to blame it on us, that our inability to pay off our debts was why America was submerging into an inevitable economic hell.

There are, unsurprisingly, thousands of questions running through my mind, and all I want to do is shoot questions at the two inscrutable yet intimidating people sitting in the front with rapid-fire speed. However, the logical side of me decides that bombarding these two strangers with questions is probably the last thing I should do.

The sound of gravel against the tires crunches and resounds against my ears, and I look over to the left side as I analyze the forest sodden with dead trees. There is a small path leading into the eye of the jungle, and the van swerves to the left.

We are surrounded by mounds of trees towering over us like creepy monsters in the night. And, as if it wasn't dark enough already, the impervious atmosphere engulfs us even more as we travel farther into the belly of this secluded forest. The van spins right, and I notice that there is a small clearing of grass among the looming trees ahead of us. The van drives onto the grass, the tires rolling over the soft ground, and it finally staggers to a stop.

"We're here," one of them says.

I look around, seeing nothing but open space. "Um . . . Are you sure about that?"

The femininely built person looks over to the other person, and they sigh. Finally, they lean forward on the dashboard and press a glowing red button. The gears in the van shift and rotate, and I furrow my brows in confusion as I mumble frantically, "What's going on?"

They ignore my question. Just as suspected.

Suddenly, the grass lifts above our heads, and I realize the van is sinking into the ground. I hold my breath in anticipation, lost for words, as I gaze at the sight above, the ground engulfing us as we plunge into complete and utter darkness.

And then that obscurity transforms into a beam of luster.

I see two to three vehicles parked beside us with the same build and color as ours: black and large. Then, I look ahead and see two gigantic doors embedded beneath towering tan walls that gleam against the pouring luminescence.

More questions rack up in my mind, and before I can even attack the people with them, they are already out of their seats and rushing to my side, hauling the van door open. "Welcome to our home." The feminine person offers me their gloved hand.

I press my lips together as I take their hand and step onto the pavement. Just this morning I was watching the inauguration with my family, and now here I am with these two menacing kidnappers, leading me into their home which seems to be several feet underground.

One of the people swings the doors open, leading me inside. I am greeted with a large wine-colored couch wrapping around the middle of the living room, and in front of it is a glass coffee table with intrinsic decorations on top. A wide screen television is mounted above a fireplace with flames flickering and crackling beneath the lined fence.

My curiosity leads me to the other side of the massive expanse, where a beautiful kitchen lies. On the other side is a large hallway that I believe leads to other rooms, and as I start to go over there, a rough hand, not covered in leather anymore, encircles around my wrist.

"I know you are eager to receive a house tour, but I promise that in due time, you will."

I turn around at the clear voice, eye-to-eye with an overwhelmingly tall dark-skinned man with a smile playing on his full lips. His large hands, now pushed into the pocket of his military jeans, are covered in veins.

I raise my eyebrows in shock. "Were you the guy who kidnapped me?"

"The very one," he says and chuckles, extending his hand out. "The name's Jeremiah Morgan, ex-Guard."

I reluctantly shake his hand. "What do you mean by that?"

"What I mean is that I used to be a Guard—someone every

single Poor person despised." Jeremiah takes a seat on the sofa. "Everyone knows that our main job is to hold the Poor people in line, and if they even breathed wrong, then we would have to hold them at gunpoint. I had a wife and a newborn at home, and I loved them with all my heart. The only reason I carried on with that stupid job was to keep my family financially pleased. But, one day"—he pauses—"I was done with the job when I was supposed to execute a Poor old lady. I couldn't do it. So, right then and there, I dropped the gun and ran until I was shot right here."

He goes and pulls up his left pant leg up, revealing a prosthetic. "It hit my calf, and I couldn't walk. I could barely stand with this injured leg. So, I carried myself to the hospital, hoping the others wouldn't catch up to me, and the doctors concluded that I had to get my leg replaced with a prosthetic. I spent a good majority of my time in the hospital learning how to walk with this thing on me. However, days later, my old coworkers swarmed into the hospital and ordered for me to show myself to them. I knew they were going to kill me on sight, so I sneaked out and ran away. I couldn't go back to D.C.; it would be too dangerous. So I had to fend for myself."

I stand there, speechless, reeling in what Jeremiah told me. It has not even been minutes since we have met, and yet this stranger is pouring his heart-wrenching story to me with the littlest of hesitation. I can tell he is a good man.

"What made this situation worse is that I wasn't even allowed to see my beautiful wife and my baby girl anymore. And that shit happened three years ago."

My jaw hangs open. "You haven't seen your family in three years?"

"Yeah." His voice breaks. "And I hate the government with all my heart, for separating me and my girls."

I swallow hard. Yet again, I'm speechless.

He clears his throat as his dark brown eyes shift into anger.

"My number one goal now is to destroy the government until they are a bloody pulp. Especially that son of a bitch that walks around as if he is engraved out of gold itself."

"Don't worry, Jeremiah. We will."

A familiar voice rings out from the kitchen, and I turn around to see a tall and gorgeous woman with pale skin and light brown eyes, leaning against the fridge and putting an apple to her mouth. I raise my eyebrows as I notice her hair, wildly colored blue, red, and purple. A septum piercing glistens against the lights as she walks over here, her entire presence intimidating yet intriguing at the same time.

I notice a line of tattoos starting from her neck and running down her left arm, tattoos that seem too detailed and intricate to examine with my naked eye. "Did he share his sad story with you?" A hint of amusement resounds from her voice as she wraps an arm around Jeremiah's shoulder.

He lets out a chuckle, swatting her arm away. "Vi, no one wants to hear your attitude right now."

She chucks her half-eaten apple at him. "Shut it, dude."

Jeremiah scowls as he throws the apple back at her. She lets out a hearty laugh.

When their exchange dies down, the slim girl takes a deep breath and brings out her inked arm. "My name is Vienna Powers—everyone calls me Vi, though—and I am a cool white *and* Asian chick with amazing kidnapping and apple-eating skills." She winks as she takes another omnivorous bite out of her apple.

I shake her hand, noticing how her hard and remorseless brown eyes back when she kidnapped me evolved into soft and amused ones.

"If you want to hear a story from her too," Jeremiah says as he makes his way over to the fireplace, "then prepare to be disappointed."

"Why?" I blurt out, suddenly intrigued.

"Because it's none of your business." She scoffs, taking her hand away from mine.

Suddenly alarmed by her change in behavior, Jeremiah looks over at Vi in a scolding manner. "There was no need to get all crabby at the girl like that. How would she know?"

"Whatever," she says. "It's not her business, that's all."

Confusion grows in me. First, this woman was so nice to me, shaking my hand and joking around, and ever since Vi's background was brought up . . . something really bad in her seemed to have clicked.

Jeremiah lets out an exaggerated sigh beside me. "Don't be alarmed by her, she's just someone who would rather talk about anything but her past." Before I can answer, he looks at the hallway. "Mallory! Dylan! We have a visitor!"

A few seconds of silence pass by, and two people walk out from the hallway frame. My eyes first latch onto a slender and tall guy with black-rimmed glasses and floppy brown hair. He tumbles out of the hallway, sending me a bewildered look, but then his eyes widen with realization. Meanwhile, the pretty and petite blonde beside him fixates her blue eyes on me, and then they both share perplexed looks with each other.

"Are you Blaire Cohen?" the guy, or I'm assuming *Dylan*, questions.

I let out a mumble that they hopefully receive as a *yes*.

"Whoa," Mallory whispers, walking closer to me. "We've been tracking you down for *days* since you are famous in this household."

Her fingers run through my hair as Dylan comes up and swats her hand away. "Stop being so creepy, you're going to scare her off!" Mallory frowns and Dylan sends me an apologetic look. "I'm sorry about her, but she's right," he says with a sigh. "You're very well-known here."

And that is when I find my voice.

"I'm sorry, but my patience is wearing out at this very

moment because I have been kidnapped by you people and I have no goddamn clue what's going on." I let out a nervous chuckle. "So, please, for the sake of me and my family, can someone explain to me why the hell I'm here?"

Silence. Nothing but heavy silence.

The taps of Vi's feet thump against the hardwood floor, and she stops right in front of me until our faces are very close, her height several inches more than mine. I try my best to make eye contact with her, but the intensity from her eyes makes me want to sink to the ground. *That's* how intimidating she is.

"We promised you answers, right?" she whispers, her voice eerily leveled. "And so, we will give you answers."

"But Vi, it's almost five o' clock," Dylan protests, gesturing toward the hallway.

"It's all right." She brings up a hand. "It's not like we get much sleep anyway." Her eyes land on me. "You are an important guest in this household, so we will treat you however you wish."

A breath of relief escapes out of me. "Thank you."

"Don't mention it." Vi attempts to smile.

The others are already seated on the wine-colored sofa, and Mallory looks at me with a broad grin. I smile back at her, but it doesn't quite reach my eyes.

And so, I sit on the leather-padded armchair as everyone else piles up on the sofa. This is the group I'm part of now—whether I like it or not—so I need to be more trustworthy of these people as we take down the government.

"Let's begin," Vi breathes out, her hardened eyes drilling into me.

6

SURREAL

November 5, 2064
4:42 a.m.

"THERE WAS A VERY powerful man." Vi's voice shakes throughout the premises like a shattering earthquake. "He was like any other ordinary Poor person because he simply wanted to get rid of the government and establish a better environment for everyone. But what held him apart from the other Poor people is that he dared to make sacrifices to get him one step closer to what he wanted . . . . freedom."

I hold my breath, nothing but the sound of enunciated silence reverberating into my soul. Here is the snarky and intimidating Vienna Powers explaining to me about the place I am in and how the hell I ended up here, and I gaze at her with the utmost concentration as if my damned life depends on it, and it honestly does.

"And so, he formed this alliance known as the Subversives, simply known as a pact of people determined to destroy this wretched government. He recruited us because he spent months researching us, making sure that we were truly fit to take on this job. However, it's difficult to find people willing to take on this complicated task, so he had to make do with us." She gestures to them all. "And no one even dares to fight against the government because we all know what the unfortunate outcome of our bold actions is."

"And that is what makes this situation even worse." Jeremiah clenches his jaw. "The Rich people stand with the government, and vice versa. And who stands with us? Nobody."

"This is why we need to stick together," Vi says, "and that's why we need you, Blaire."

My eyes widen. "But why *me*, though? Out of all the people in D.C.?"

"Well, you are—" Dylan starts to blurt out, but Jeremiah clamps his hand against Dylan's mouth.

"Not yet, bud," he hisses.

My mouth opens in confusion, and I look over at Vi. "What was he about to say?"

Vi stands up at the speed of lightning. "Now, how about that house tour? I bet you're dying to get a look around here!"

"But—"

Mallory gets up and grabs my arm, urging me forward. "I can't wait to show you all the rooms!" she squeals.

"Wait." I clear my throat. They all stop in their tracks. "I just want to know *why* I'm here. What do I have to do with this? Yeah, I do hate the government with every single part of me, but doesn't every Poor person feel the same?"

A surreal feeling infiltrates into the stiff air. "Now, that is the one question that will be answered, but not with my words." Vi's lips curl slightly. "Instead, it will be answered with time and patience." Her words remain hung up in the air as Mallory escorts me farther into the place that I now must call home . . . willingly or unwillingly.

4:49 a.m.

"This is the gym." Mallory opens the door and reveals an economically sized room.

I raise my eyebrows as I take in everything. "Who works out here?"

"It's usually Jeremiah and Vi that do, but Dylan and I sometimes join—whenever we feel like it," she adds.

"But we are supposed to remain fit in order to even take down the government *physically*, right?"

"Well, it depends how we take down the government."

"Yeah, if only I knew how we were," I murmur.

She sighs as we walk out into the hallway. "I know you're frustrated about not knowing what's going on, but you *will* find out soon. And I know that it's not fair that we tore you away from your family like that."

"Can I even contact them?" I ask. "My family is going to freak out when they see that I'm not there. And they can't even contact the government because there's no way in hell they are going to help a Poor family."

"I understand what you're trying to say here, but if we let them know you're here, then that's a major risk, Blaire. However, we will decide when we'll tell them because they will know one day."

Our footsteps echo into the hallway as Mallory leads me to the next room. "Thanks for trying to calm me down. And I'm sorry if I was a bit too much on you guys . . . I'm just really confused. I want to be here—of course I do—but I can't seem to understand what's going on."

She places a reassuring hand on my shoulder. "Y'know, I was in the same position as you are."

"Really?"

"Yeah." She lets out a short laugh. "Vi and Jeremiah were the only ones that weren't kidnapped; they actually had a choice."

"How come?"

"Well, that's their story to tell, not mine. But anyway, the rest of us were kidnapped. *He* was so desperate for someone that it was literally impossible for us to get out of this situation." She pauses. "I remember when I was kidnapped, which was about a month or two ago, and I was not compliant at all. I tried to fight out of their grips, screamed for a way out, and even punched Vi in the face." She chuckles, and I grin. "I didn't understand it then, but the reason why they make us go through the whole traumatic kidnapping process is to emphasize the severity of the situation. If they amicably invited us in their home then we would not have taken our positions seriously.

"So, yeah, it definitely took me a while to get adjusted to this new environment. Heck, it's been a while since I've lived here, and I'm *still* not used to it. But I don't miss my place at all—that's for sure."

I look at her worriedly. "How is that?"

"Why have you guys been standing here for the past twenty minutes?" Dylan's voice pierces through the air, and I almost jump back in shock.

"Dylan!" Mallory shrieks and punches him.

He winces and clutches his arm, sending her a deathly look. "The hell was that for?"

"That was for scaring the living daylights out of us," Mallory snarls.

He rolls his eyes. "Whatever. I was just wondering why you've been standing outside my room like that."

"Your room?"

Mallory shakes her head. "It's *not* his room."

"But this room does belong to me, though." Dylan smirks as he opens the oak doors, revealing a massive room with dozens of computer monitors, four black office chairs, and other electronic components that scurry in and out of the room. Astonished, I begin to take in everything around me.

"I'm guessing you like technology?"

"Well, that is a bit of an understatement." He grins, sitting at the front console where cameras of what I'm assuming the Capital Center is cornered on. There is no one standing there, the entire area remaining desolate as the gray-scale cameras depict a solemn outlook of the beating heart of the city.

"I am a computer genius, not to brag," Dylan says.

"He is," Mallory concedes. "And this dude is an actual genius itself, considering the fact that he's smarter than Einstein."

"And I have an IQ that is twenty points higher than his, not to brag again."

As Dylan continues to boast his intelligence, I take a seat beside him, and my jaw practically unhinges as I look at the cameras. "How did you manage to break into a premise that the *government* owns?"

"Sorry, but a magician never reveals their secrets." He looks over at me amusingly as he zeroes in on another camera layout.

My eyes widen even more. "You can look into the *White House?*"

"Yeah, I sure can." He leans back in his office chair. "Took me at least twenty-three consecutive hours to do so, but it was well worth it—as you can see here."

"I'm amazed," I mutter as I see several Guards go in and out of the White House. I never saw the interior of the White House because it is a very private area where the president and his family would reside. Only a few Rich people are allowed to view the inside beauty of this palace, so seeing the majestic interior of this place itself makes me swallow a dose of thrill that I've never tasted before.

I narrow my eyes as dozens of rooms of the White House show up in front of me, and I try to notice every single detail of every room, but there are just so *many.* My heart pounds as I look over at Dylan, who stares at the cameras triumphantly.

Few minutes later, Mallory escorts me out of the room,

leaving the masterminded Dylan to his wonderful creations. "That dude may be the most annoying person I have ever dealt with in my entire life, but my-oh-my is he smart."

We manage to go through a short and narrow hallway where certain doors align the tan-colored walls. Two rooms are completed, and now it seems like we have three more left.

"This one here is the bathroom," she begins to say as it is revealed right in front of me. I breathe out a sigh of relief as I notice the cleanliness. By the far right, there seems to be a line of showers with curtains separating each one. This is much better than the bathroom at home, which was grim and had a repulsive odor.

Once we view the bathroom, Mallory leads me to the second to last room, which is the boys' room. She opens the door to reveal Jeremiah. "Hey, Jeremiah," Mallory singsongs.

He grins at her. "Are you giving Blaire the house tour?"

"I sure am." She smiles.

"What do you think about it?" He asks me.

"I think it's amazing so far," I say, but then I notice there are five beds placed in the small room, so close to each other where there is very little leg room present. "Why are there five beds when it's only you and Dylan?"

"Because *he* had thought that more men would be recruited," Jeremiah says. I open my mouth to speak, but he interrupts me. "And no, I can't tell you who *he* is. Sorry."

"It's all right. I've established at this point that all I have to do is be patient now."

"Atta girl."

I whirl around and see Vi behind me, her rainbow hair tied up into a messy bun. She seems to be wearing a satin-like and wine-colored nightgown. "C'mon, I'll show the girls' room to you really quickly." She gestures toward Jeremiah. "G'night, Jeremiah! Sweet dreams!"

"You too, Vi!" He grins, and we leave him be.

The door closes behind us and Vi leads me to the girls' room, which is directly across the boys' room, with Mallory trailing behind us. The light flickers on as we enter the room, where five beds are present as well. It's the same space and outlook as the boys' room, and I immediately cast my eyes upon the bed in the far corner.

"I see you've already made your pick." Mallory chuckles, and I grin as I sit down on the foot of it. I decide to lay down, and I feel all the pain seeping away from my body, all the exhaust that has clung onto my shoulders dispersing into thin air.

"I think it's best if we pass out now," Vi announces, sitting on her bed, which is the farthest away from mine. Once she turns off the lights, Mallory sits in the mere middle. Silence fills in the room as I bring the thin-clothed blanket up to my chin, the warm material smelling like sandalwood. My dark hair, which probably looks like a tornado has spun through it, clings to my back as I adjust it. And my body reeks of sweat and the built-up agony of the whole day. I make a note to myself that the first thing I'm going to do in the morning is shower.

Looking up at the ceiling, I acknowledge just how different this room is compared to mine back home. The floorboards don't seem to creak every time I step on them. There aren't random noises occurring. And there is no inconsistency in the indoor temperature.

Because you are in a different place now, Blaire. Of course things are going to be different here.

Different scares me, though. Only because I live in a world where changes in society often lead to worse outcomes. That's why whenever change is involved, I feel uneasy.

But this type of change is different. This is the type of change I've been longing for my entire life. And, because this change is different, I think I will be able to cope with it.

I don't know how much longer I stay up, pondering against the darkness. But eventually, I find myself falling asleep. Somehow, I do.

7

DESTROY

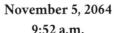

November 5, 2064
9:52 a.m.

I STIR AWAKE, THE soft blanket clinging to my body as a loud yawn erupts out of me. I expect to see sunlight peering in from the windows, my parents engulfing me in hugs and kisses, and going out to the living room to enjoy breakfast with my family. But instead, I remind myself that I am in a secret underground home with people that plan to destroy the government.

I sit up. My arms feel like lead as I draw them across my chest, sweat clinging to my body as my nose scrunches up in disgust. First things first . . . I *must* shower.

My eyes wander over the room, seeing that I am the only one in here. As I start to walk out the door, someone else saunters in and I jump back in shock. *Vi.*

She sends me an acknowledging glance. "Good morning, Blaire. I just wanted to let you know that I left some clothes for you in the bathroom. I assumed that you're probably going to want to shower after last night."

"Thanks." I try to smile.

"Don't mention it." She pulls her colored hair back. I notice she's wearing a black leather jacket with a white tank top underneath, ripped jeans on the bottom, and stain-free combat boots. "Also, don't take too long in there because your waffles are getting cold." *Waffles? What are those?* Before I can even ask what she meant, Vi is already out of sight. I sigh and start to tread over to the bathroom.

I swing the door open and notice the neat pile of clothes sitting on one of the counters. My mouth drops as I pull them apart, feeling the soft fabric and cleanliness of these items: navy green shirt, black jeans, sneakers, soft socks—alongside a cotton padded bra—underwear, a hair tie, and a blue comb.

I bring all my items over to one of the showers and place them on the rack outside. When I see the coast is clear, I quickly strip off my dirty clothes and throw them in the empty laundry basket in the far corner. Then, I walk inside the shower, closing the curtain behind me, and turn the silver knob up until cold water splashes onto my skin.

A gasp escapes my mouth as the freezing water hits my body like icicles, and I bring the knob down to the left as the water simmers to room-temperature. My body relaxes as I pile all my dark hair up in my hands and relish in the soothing warm water.

After I shower, I bring the knob to the bottom right, the water completely coming to a stop, and I take a deep breath in. My mind feels so empty—in a good way—and I feel as if a considerable amount of weight is lifted off my body.

I grab the towel folded on the racks and wrap it around me. Once I dry myself, I wear my comfortable clothes and struggle to comb through my knotty hair. After a considerable amount of time spent behind that, I find my sight fixated on the girl behind the mirror who seems reticent, her inscrutable eyes wavering.

My skinny body in contrast to my five-foot-seven self makes

me realize how deprived I really look: I barely eat in general, so I appear to be skinny—not deathly skinny, but enough to the point where I may come off as underweight. My breasts aren't too small or large either, but I can say they come in the way whenever I mine in the caves. And speaking of mining, my arms seem to be a bit muscular yet roughed out due to my endless hours of working.

My face seems to grasp the same facial features as both my mother and father. My eyes, of course, are familiar to my father's—dark green, and appearing to be so dark they come off as black sometimes. And my facial structure is almost the same as his—angular, challenging, and sharp.

On the other hand, my nose and my lips are the exact copy as my mother's. Our noses are small, stooping down to a low angle and perking up just a little bit. But our lips are lavish and naturally a pinkish-red color, and they seem to be a bit larger than average—portrayed with a cupid's bow and the lower lip dipping to a significant angle.

I wrap the dark hair-tie around my wrist and escape out of the bathroom. I walk out into the living room and see everyone seated by the oak-colored dining table.

Dylan spots me by the corner. "Hey, Blaire!"

Everyone begins to call me over. I send them a half-smile as I sit at the empty chair situated between Mallory and Jeremiah. Vi and Dylan sit on the other side with an empty chair on the left. In front of me is a seemingly cold plate of the so-called *waffles* Vi told me about.

"Told you your waffle got cold," Vi says, taking a hefty bite out of hers.

"Do you want me to warm it up?" Jeremiah asks me.

I look over to him and shake my head. "No, it's fine. I don't even know how to eat this, honestly speaking."

"Vi, you didn't explain to her what a waffle is?" Mallory hisses at her.

47

She nonchalantly engulfs the food with some sort of syrup. "Well, I'm here to explain now."

"Ooh, wait!" Dylan frantically waves his hand at her. "Can I do it?"

Vi merely glances at him and smiles for only a split second. It's definitely rare to see her smile. "Go for it, Mr. Faulkner."

Dylan's face brightens as he leans over to teach me. After a few minutes of him educating me on how to eat this foreign meal, I finally get the gist of it. Everyone watches me excitedly as I prop the torn-off waffle piece into my mouth. The syrupy flavor oozes into my mouth as I beam at the others. "This is delicious!"

"Thanks, I made it." Mallory grins, and everyone nods their heads like delighted little kids.

After we finish eating breakfast, we clean the kitchen and sit in the living room. Everyone looks over at me, and that is when the realization dawns upon me. *They're about to explain their plan.*

My attention grows as I shoot a glance over at Vi, who says, "Well, this is the moment you've been waiting for."

A few seconds of uncomfortable silence forms in the air like a toxic chemical, making it hard for me to breathe. Vi looks over at Dylan while he picks up a remote in his hand and presses a red button on it, making the television flicker on. My eyes widen as I notice certain colors and visuals appearing on the screen like magic. The TV settles on a scale of the White House and the Capital Center. I see a small scene play out in front of me: five people marching into the Center with huge rifles raised, ambushing those who dare to walk in front of them. Finally, they go past the White House entrance and force the members of the government to either surrender with their words or their lives. That's when a speed-play occurs of the five people gathering everyone in the city to reform and create a unified society.

"It's as simple as that," Vi says, leaning forward as she points at the massive screen. "Since we're playing on the offensive, it is imperative to stand our ground and demand for the government to step down."

"It may seem impossible since their numbers easily outrank ours," Jeremiah adds, "but with enough planning and determination, we should be able to form a solid idea."

My shoulders are tense. "How did you guys manage to get all of this?"

"We didn't." Mallory raises her eyebrows. "*He* did."

"Ah, you mean the super secretive person you all refuse to tell me about?" I remark sarcastically.

"Yes," Vi deadpans. "But anyway, enough about that, we are here to talk to you about this plan." Pause. "On December 31st, we will gather all of our weapons and gear. We will drive into the Center and set rank. Since it is New Year's Eve, not that many Guards will be patrolling outside, especially in the Rich sector too, so that will give us some leeway. After we set ourselves onto the platform, we will expect some Guards to come over and see what all the chaos is about.

"Since we are heavily armed with the best weapons, they will obviously not be dumb enough to kill us because we will kill them too," she snarls. "But our main plan is to hold our stance in the middle of the Center until they back down, and we won't back down until we get what we want—which is a confrontation with the government, comprised of stubborn and simple-minded Rich people that will take a hell of a lot of force and persuasion for them to surrender."

"And what if they don't?" I ask.

Vi studies her nails. "Oh, they will." Her eyes then slither onto me. "But, worst case scenario, if odds are truly *not* in our favor, then we're going to have to, I don't know, kill them. But we want to avoid the violent route as much as possible since we are all for peace and prosperity."

A few seconds of silence passes again. I feel so much more

confident compared to me yesterday because I have actual hope filled up in me now. I want to be a part of this—hell, more than *anything.* This is what I've wanted since day one, a shot at a life I've wanted to share with my family. There is hope. And I want to partake in any risk for that hope.

"That sounds wonderful." I exclaim. "I'm in!"

"Yes, Blaire is on the train!" Dylan cheers. Everyone else grins with excitement.

I feel my heart bursting with happiness, realizing that I am about to accomplish something that I've been dying to do for my entire life: make the government perish into nothing but dust.

But something pops into my mind, my heart-rate slowing, and my pulse pounds into my ear—so hard to the point where that is all I can hear.

My mouth drops open slowly as my fingers dance around with overwhelming anticipation. *Where did I get this sudden notion from? Are they going to like it?*

Vi looks at me cautiously. "Um, Blaire? You good?"

I glance at the others, my body clenching in surprise. "I have an idea."

"What is it?" Jeremiah asks.

"Well, um, let's think about it like this," I start off. "Who is the main root of all these problems?"

"Uh . . . the Rich people?" Mallory says.

"Yes—and no. There is someone even more of a problem than the Rich. Can anyone guess who?"

Jeremiah decides to answer this time. "Tobias Remington?"

I grin. "Bingo."

"I don't understand what you're trying to say here," Dylan stammers.

I take a deep breath in as I tuck a few strands of hair behind my ear. "We all know that Tobias is the main root of all these problems. If he didn't exist, then who would the Poor people follow? The government?" Everyone starts to look a little less confused. "It's not the government we should be trying to destroy here. It should be the president."

"Wait." Vi scoffs. "Are you trying to say here that we should change our plan?"

"No." I shake my head almost immediately. "This is just an alternative. Just hear me out, okay?" Vi nods her head hesitantly, and I carry on. "Anyway, we need to get under the president's skin. He is obviously the main issue here, so we need to destroy *him* instead. However, it won't be that easy, and luckily for us, we have the perfect method to get us one step closer to Tobias."

"And what is that?" Mallory questions again, her blue eyes widening in astonishment.

I lean forward in my seat and meet everyone's gazes. *Here goes nothing.* "Well, how about we kidnap the president's son?"

8

KIDNAP

November 5, 2064
10:27 a.m.

"WAIT." VI PAUSES AND looks at me in utter disbelief. "You are telling me that you want to kidnap Jax Remington?" She starts laughing. "Is this a joke?"

"Look, just listen, please," I beg. "I know this seems to be the most bizarre thing you ever heard—"

"Damn right."

"—but it will make sense once you hear me out. Please?"

She closes her eyes for a second, breathes in and out, and opens them again. "Fine," she says. "Have at it."

My hands begin to tremble. "When I was at the inauguration yesterday morning, I saw something that made me think. A lot, in fact." The look on Vi's face makes my voice waver too. "Jax seemed to look out of place there. He even seemed disinterested in his speech and barely said anything. I may be overthinking this, but I really think that he wouldn't mind if he had a getaway from his life and his parents, specifically his father."

"So, you basically just want to help Rich Boy, huh?" Vi narrows her eyes at me. "Help him escape his household?"

"No." I shake my head desperately. "I'm just saying that to possibly convince you that maybe kidnapping him won't seem so out-of-nowhere because there is a viable reason why. We can either force Jax to reveal sacred information about his father to us, or we can blackmail Tobias by saying that in order to return Jax to him, he must step down from his platform. Maybe we can do both." I let out an overwhelming breath. "I know that he won't like it if we kidnap him. Hell, no one likes to be torn away from their life like that. But maybe it won't be that difficult to kidnap Jax because, judging by how he acted yesterday morning, maybe my idea could work out."

Vi shakes her head twice, chuckling humorlessly. "Sorry to break it to you, but we're sticking to our idea, the one that we thought of for *months* and spent endless time on."

A sense of defeat takes over me as I murmur, "Okay."

She sighs and looks over at the others. "We're here to work as a team, right, guys?" Everyone seems to agree. "We cannot risk any sort of last-minute ideas right now."

Silence forms around us, and my sudden idea slowly disappears into thin air. Maybe she's right. I shouldn't have randomly brought up that idea because it's completely out of the vicinity and completely unapproachable. I mean, how are we to kidnap the president's son? Jax Remington, the most unfathomable and emotionless man to ever exist. Hell, Vi *is* right.

However, somebody starts to speak.

"Wait, Vi? I think Blaire might be onto something."

I whirl my head around to see Mallory desperately looking at her.

"What the hell are you talking about, Mal?" Vi's eyebrows push together like tectonic plates colliding.

"I—" she clears her throat. "I just believe that maybe we should switch to Blaire's idea instead."

Vi snorts and shakes her head. "Go on, indulge us. Why are you saying that you want to follow her plan instead, who *just* now joined our team?"

Mallory looks over at me and sends me a reassuring smile. A grin grows on me, but I find myself wondering why she jumped to my rescue suddenly.

"You guys don't know about this," she begins to explain, "but I used to be Rich."

My eyes widen at Mallory's statement, and I look over at the others hurriedly and see that they seem to be equally just as surprised.

She presses her lips together, her eyes windows to her soft soul. "I don't like to talk about my past much because I don't like reminding myself that I used to be part of the worst group of people alive. My parents are snobby Rich people that are extremely close friends with the Remingtons, which also means that I am, or was, close friends with Jax as well.

"Blaire is right: Jax *despises* his family and the Rich. He's always wanted to leave the city behind and start somewhere new." *Just like me.* "He never fit in with the Rich, and neither did I. We both wanted to escape our treacherous lifestyles." She frowns. "I harbored feelings for him, but I don't know if he ever felt the same. I didn't want to risk our friendship, though, because he was the only person I had—the only person that understood me. So, I decided to hide my feelings and pretend that I never liked him like that.

"We continued to be friends, and I eventually lost all romantic feelings for him. However, at the same time, I started to become rebellious. I began insulting the Rich right in front of my parents. I never attended family meetings. I never managed to make myself look presentable. And my rebellious attitude led to me willingly leaving my home." I notice Mallory's face hardens, her eyes prickling with tears. "I remember those miserable weeks I endured, becoming the

Poor. I understood their hardships and how terrible the Rich treated them. I understood how truly difficult it is to live here in D.C. during this time and day. Those few weeks were exhausting, demeaning, and made me feel worthless. But suddenly these guys came to my rescue." She gestures toward Vi and Jeremiah. "They picked me up at my worst times and led me to a much better life. I am truly so thankful for you guys."

Jeremiah gets up immediately and hugs Mallory as she sobs into his arm. "We will always be here for you, Mal. Right, Vi?"

Vi sighs as all anger starts to leave her face. She goes and pats Mallory's head, trying to console her. "We will. Don't worry."

Dylan grins from his seat.

Mallory sniffs as everyone sits back down. I look over at her, who smiles at me. "So, I obviously see where you're coming from, Blaire. I do think that we should kidnap Jax, as horrendous as that truly sounds." She glances over at Vi, who seems to be in an internal struggle with herself. "We'll only go through with the plan if everyone else agrees too."

"I'm definitely in," Dylan says. "I know this plan was out of the blue, but I see where Blaire comes from, and Mallory as well."

"Count me in too." Jeremiah winks.

As everyone agrees, we are then left with one person. Everyone looks over at Vi as she takes a deep breath in. "I don't know what to think right now," she murmurs. "I mean, we had such a stable plan! Everything was going so smoothly."

"But think about it, Vi," Dylan says. "Nothing is ever going to go smoothly in this screwed up world. So, it'll be worth a shot."

Vi sighs and presses her lips together. After a few torturous moments later, she says, "Shit—*fine*, we'll go through with Blaire's plan."

Everyone starts to whoop and holler, but Vi suddenly says,

"But if this plan doesn't work out"—her cold eyes land on me —"then I will break every single one of your fingers."

My lungs constrict. "Got it."

Once our intense discussion finishes, everyone disperses into different directions. I decide to roam around, hoping to get a closer look at this place.

As I wander through the hallways, I start to think about Mallory's disheartening story. She started off with such a stable and pleasing life filled with nobility, importance, and wealth, but then decreased to nothing but a wallowing figure. And it must've been very difficult for her to deal with that change. Also, I wonder if her parents are still on the lookout for her, or if they don't even care about her in the first place. Only the universe would know.

My fingers graze along the walls of the hallway as I sit on the white armchair situated in the far corner. My back hits the soft material as I close my eyes and ponder, but then my heart twists and turns with angst as I think about how distressed my family must be right now, finding out that their daughter is gone—and there's nothing they can do about it. The helplessness they must be feeling . . . It makes my heart shrivel.

But, in the end, I'm gone for a good reason. I'm here to create a better life for the Poor, which I've been wanting to do for the longest time. And I will achieve it with these people.

Starting now.

10:51 a.m

I find myself wandering over to the technology room. Dylan is sitting on one of the chairs, stretching as a wailing yawn escapes out of him. A soft smile creeps upon my lips as I knock on the door. "Dylan?"

He spins around, and his eyes brighten when he sees me. "Ah, Blaire! Come on in."

I continue to grin as I sit on one of the black chairs beside him. He takes a deep breath in and gestures toward the massive security cameras encased on the television screens. "Just doing my daily job."

"I see." I chuckle, studying the movement on the cameras.

There is much more activity present now than at midnight as I see dozens of Guards walking in and out of the Center. They seem to be pulling a man toward the door of a black van, and when he jolts and tries to wriggle out of their grips, one of the Guards decides to throw him to the ground and pulls out his gun.

Before I can even process what happens next, he shoots the man. "What the hell?" My hands fly to my mouth.

Dylan winces as we watch the Guards carry the man, now shot and limp in their arms, over to the black van. "Hate to say it, but this is pretty much what I see every day from the security cameras. Just innocent Poor people getting shot daily . . ." He shakes his head. "It's terrible."

I feel my heart squelching in disappointment as the van drives away into the distance. There are no sounds appearing from either of the cameras, which I am thankful for because I can't bear to hear the earth-shattering screams of the man and the egregious *boom* of the gun.

The screen interchanges into the grand entrance of the White House, where a news crew seems to interview Tobias, Isabelle, and Jax.

"Does the sound work?" I ask.

"Yeah, it does. Give me a second." Dylan flicks one of the many switches on the console board upwards, a light emitting from it. I suddenly hear voices from the screen, and I begin to analyze their faces and conversation.

"—so glad to see that you are having a fine day on this beautiful Wednesday morning," one of the crew members says to Tobias while Isabelle and Jax stand on the side. "I mean, compared to yesterday, we can definitely say the weather is much livelier now."

"Definitely." Tobias grins and gestures toward the blue sky. "Although, I am upset that the weather decided to be gloomy during my inauguration, but I guess we can't always get what we want, correct, Natalie?"

Natalie chuckles. "Unfortunately, that is. However, I have some questions I'd like to ask you all, if you don't mind."

Tobias shakes his head, gleaming as his slithery gray eyes latch onto the camera. "Of course I don't, Natalie. Go right ahead."

"All right." She pauses. "So, it's been almost twenty-four hours since you've been re-elected as President. How do you feel?"

He answers almost immediately, adjusting his red tie. "Well, I feel fantastic! I do believe that the next four years are going to be splendid for us, also considering how well the past four years have been for our nation." *Lies.* "I hope to continue on with my current efforts and help our country become number one since it was demolished around the war." His face morphs into a sad expression, as if he is trying to depict his false perturbation.

"Yes, our country did not prosper during the Dark Ages, unfortunately." Natalie frowns. "How exactly do you hope to move our country to the top of the ladder?"

"I think that maybe we should focus more on the financial aspects of this country. We have lifted our spirits and souls from the bottom and managed to bring it to the heavens, so I know our country can react the same way as well—and I intend to accomplish that ideal by making sure everyone in this country benefits our flourishing economy. And if I see any Poor people scurrying about"—he snarls at the camera—"then our government will make sure they will be rightfully punished for their doings."

Anger rages inside of me as I gnaw at my lip. "I hate him."

Dylan whispers beside me, "Me too."

Natalie moves her blazing red hair to the side as she tugs at her coat. "Speaking of the Poor people! I have been informed that there was a Poor man shot by a Guard just a few minutes ago. Do you have anything to comment about that?"

"Yes, that man was being very disrespectful and insulted a Guard right to his face. When we were about to *peacefully* lug him into the van and interrogate him there, he just kept on fighting against his restraints. One of the Guards decided to shoot him, which I believe was the right thing to do. If one is not going to comply with our well-established rules, then there must be blood involved." He looks toward his wife and his son. "You two must be getting bored with all of this jibber jabber. Would you like to go inside?"

"Actually," Natalie interjects, "we want to pursue a conversation with them as well. That's why we specifically asked for them."

"Oh." Tobias clears his throat, his graying hair shimmering against the camera lights. "Well, carry on, then."

The red-headed interrogator sends a gracious smile toward Isabelle. "So, Mrs. Remington . . . since your husband is reigning as president for two terms, I believe you must be feeling quite happy for him."

"Yes, I am." She beams, adjusting her dark hair as her lips contort into a glorious grin. "I really think Tobias here will be one of the best presidents this country has ever had, again." She chuckles. "But in all honesty, he has great plans set for our citizens!"

"Oh, really?" Natalie's eyes widen. "Such as?"

"Well, we hope to donate a thousand dollars to our wonderful educational institutions for all students!" *Of course the snobby Rich folk get a benefit from their endeavors.* "The younger generation deserves the best education out there since they are going to be our future leaders. And my son will be tutoring younger kids."

"Is that so, Mr. Remington?" Natalie gestures toward Jax.

He adjusts his jet-black hair and looks at the camera, forming a forced smile. "Yes. I have been tutoring some kids in American history and informing them of our remarkable past. It is essential in my part to enlighten the young children of this because it does shape this country's future alongside their own."

"I am astonished to hear that!" Natalie beams at him. "Now, while your father manages the country, what are you going to bring to this country as well?"

He takes a deep breath in and pushes his hands into the pockets of his leather jacket. Jax's gray eyes fixate onto the camera as his smile slips away, but his voice seems to be attached with the same tone as before. "Whenever I'm not tutoring children, I assist my father in his duties and prepare to take over his platform when my time arrives."

"That's excellent! It is definitely encouraged to start preparing as soon as time allows, correct?"

"Yes," Jax murmurs, his eyes deferring away from the screens. His parents continue to engage with the interview, but Jax on the other hand seems to be like a foreign creature that manages to make his way through this unwelcoming world.

What Mallory told us this morning rings into my ears: *Jax despises his family and the Rich as well . . . wanted to leave the city behind . . . start somewhere new . . .* I gulp, thinking that maybe—just maybe—Jax would be an excellent addition to the team.

"You're right," Dylan murmurs beside me. "It really seems like he doesn't belong there, judging by his actions. And the way his voice just trailed off . . ." He looks over at me as he shuts the camera down, the screen turning black. "You're a genius, Blaire."

I start to blush. "No, I'm not. It was just a random thought."

"A random thought?" Dylan scoffs. "No, that was your amazing analyzing skills right there! Your plan is definitely going to work out—I mean, think about how much Jax knows of his father and the dirty secrets he hides!"

"That's exactly what I mean," I say excitedly. "He lives with Tobias. He knows possibly everything there is to do with him, even his dirty little secrets. It may be hard to persuade Jax to join our team, but what other choice does he have? He's obviously outnumbered, and we will threaten to torture him if he doesn't manage to cough up information. Either way, he will be a great help because he's the *president's son*. The information he knows could help us big time."

"What's going on?" Mal shrieks as she, Vi, and Jeremiah burst into the room. "We heard some ruckus happening here."

I shoot a glance toward Dylan, whose eyes flicker with imminent excitement. Finally, I look toward the others and say, "We have something to show you guys."

9

INHUMAN

November 5, 2064
12:53 p.m.

I PLOP ONTO THE couch, exhausted due to the strenuous day. The remote on my side ends up in my hand as I press the *up-arrow* button, leading to a news channel. I narrow my eyes as I see red headlines running on the bottom of the screen with infuriating words portrayed.

SHOULD POOR PEOPLE CONTINUE TO LIVE THE LIFE THEY ARE GRANTED? OR SHOULD EVEN MORE RESTRICTIVE LAWS BE PLACED ON THESE REMORSELESS CREATURES?

My insides fill with anger that broils in my chest. *Remorseless creatures? What the actual hell?*

The man and the woman above the headline sit at clear desks, their backs straight as rulers, and their hair done with the utmost precision where not even a single strand is out of place.

It almost seems as if they aren't real, regarding their minimal imperfections.

They introduce themselves as Nathan and Wendy, and as they run through the daily spiel and counteract upon the various things that occurred in the past few days, my thoughts start to run wild.

I think about this place—this sad and meaningless place that was once filled with a prospering environment and astounding feats. No matter how rough one's life was, they knew that they could at least survive because they had a roof above their heads, they had endless supplies of food and water, and they had at least some sort of hope available for them.

But as the 2030s approached, the nation succumbed to the Dark Ages. It had nothing to do with the environment; in fact, the reason this country plunged to its doom was because of the people. The Second Great Depression occurred, and the wealthy believed that those who were in poverty were the reason for it, when in reality, it was because the stock market had crashed. It was unfortunate that anyone who looked to be in poverty was immediately pounded to death by the wealthy because they thought of them as inhuman. Unworthy.

To make matters worse, the government did absolutely nothing to protect the poor from the upper class's wrath. It was the rich they only cared about because they believed maybe they could help America get through the economic crisis. And, according to what my mother had told me, the government did attempt to eradicate every single "poor" person back then—in hopes to get the nation back on track. However, it was pretty unsuccessful to pinpoint them all because there were just *so many*. The population was also rapidly dwindling due to the shortages in food and water, the daily battles that were a part of a large civil war, and a higher suicide rate because people were financially and socially displeased.

I heard the last moments of the war was when the government in D.C. claimed that they were the last remaining city. It was just a quiet yet eerie land submerged in corpses, destroyed lands, and burnt buildings.

2038 was when a new society was formed in D.C., consisting of just 3,000 people. Boundaries were placed, dividing everyone up into the Rich and the Poor—based solely on how much an adult earned during that time—and a grim era began.

To this day, the same gray cloud that hovered over everyone during the Dark Ages still remains, haunting and reminding us of why we are here. While the Rich people thrive and have minimal things to worry about, us Poor people carry unbearable weights on our beaten backs, laboring for a world that doesn't even want to support us. That's why I've always wanted to get out of here. Escape out of this steel-wrapped bubble that has encased me for what seems like forever. Escape out of the latches of this heart- wrenching world that deters me and escape out into a world that will be different but for my own good. Because I need to leave.

But here I am now, in this sudden change that submerged out of nowhere and trapped me for however long. Although, I don't even feel trapped anymore; I feel like I've managed to find light at the end of the tunnel. And I need to now reach toward it like my life depends on it. Because it really does.

"Just this very morning, there was news that a Poor man was shot by a Guard."

I snap back to reality, my back ramrod straight. The television continues to play, but the sentence that escapes out of Wendy's mouth makes all my never-ending thoughts halt.

The screen transforms into a slow-motion video of the Poor man wrangling out of the Guard's grip. It begins by the Guard throwing him onto the ground as if he were a doll, bringing out a gun, and firing at him. Blood pools out of his chest as all the Guards carry the limp body away, leaving nothing but the stain of the man's blood expanding on the ground. The scene plays again, but in real- time speed, and that is when I realize that this was the same Poor man I saw getting shot on Dylan's camera.

The video stops as the screen shifts onto Wendy and Nathan. Wendy takes a deep breath in as she still portrays her bright grin at the screen. "There were controversial attitudes formed around this video, such as one side claiming that the Guard had no right to shoot the man—that it was just an act of defense," Wendy says. "Although, some other people disagree with those statements, declaring that the Guard had the utmost right to shoot the man because he, of course, is lower than us. Obviously, this is a two- sided argument between people who agree with either empathy or practicality." She turns to Nathan. "Let's see what people have to say about this."

The screen flickers into a live video of a middle-aged man and woman, who are dressed completely in formal wear. They stand in front of a huge mansion, their faces strict and their postures taut.

"Mr. and Mrs. Karnowski, what would you like to say about the controversy that sprouted this morning?" The interviewer behind the screen asks.

Mr. Karnowski clears his throat. "Well, I believe that the Guard made the best decision. Poor people are considered as low individuals compared to us fine folks—no doubt about that. I am speaking this from the country's point of view, in hopes to abolish any thoughts or ideas of rebellion. America has been through enough, and any person that dares to fight against our well-formed nation should be punished for it. That man was fighting against the Guard, and the Guard had every right to shoot him because it was for self-defense."

Penetrating disgust fills up in my chest as his wife speaks. "I agree with my husband. As a woman in this country, it feels very unsafe to walk at night, and seeing a man like that get what he deserves . . . Well, it makes me feel safe." She chuckles. "I am glad to see that America is standing up for herself. God bless America!"

The screen becomes black for a split second. Finally, it shifts into another Rich family, except there is a young lady with her son, who seems to be a teenager. They wear burly coats with huge scarfs, and their pale skin glistens against the November air. The son holds an expression that reflects the fact that he doesn't want to be there, interviewed beside his mother.

"Hello, D.C. News!" the interviewer behind the camera exclaims. "I have here with me Senator Leanna Cromwell. And, next to her is her son, Liam Cromwell."

Leanna smiles at the cameras graciously. Meanwhile, Liam sends a small smile our way—one that doesn't reach his eyes. I lean forward, intrigued by this boy's behavior.

"What do you have to say about the Poor man getting shot by that Guard? Remember to give your honest opinion."

Leanna sighs and purses her lips together. "Well, if I'm being completely honest . . . That disgusting old man deserved to get shot."

I suddenly feel the urge to ram my fist into the screen. "And why is that, Ms. Cromwell?"

"Because Poor people do not even deserve to breathe in the same area as us," she snarls, her eyes widening crazily at the screen. "Hell, I don't even know why they are still here! They should be killed! Every single one of them!"

"Mom!" Liam screeches.

Leanna's face falls as she glares at him. "What the hell are you doing?"

"Just stop it, Mom!" he shrieks again. "What you're saying is wrong! I am so tired of you talking about Poor people as if they are animals. They are humans too! And just because they earn less money than us doesn't mean they aren't worthy to breathe in the same air as us!"

"Liam, just stop speaking!" she yelps, and her widened eyes land on the cameras. "Cut the cameras, right now!"

The screen turns pitch-black, and I notice the screen is switched to Nathan and Wendy again. "Well . . ." Nathan clears his throat awkwardly. "As we saw here, everyone holds different opinions on the shooting."

As Nathan and Wendy continue to engage in discourse, I think about Liam and how he stood up for the Poor—for *us*. It made me feel a bit more hopeful. Just a bit more hopeful for our future.

Suddenly, I hear footsteps behind me. I crane my neck around to see Vi. "Should we add him to the team too?"

I chuckle as I mute the TV. "Were you here the entire time?"

"Well," she starts off, sitting on the far-end of the sofa, "I was here long enough to see that teenage boy standing up to his bratty Rich mother."

"Can you believe he did that? I was shocked."

"So was I." Vi rubs the back of her neck. "It's really rare to see Rich people show some sort of sympathy for us."

"Yeah," I whisper, "It really is. And it makes me so mad. I wish I could just get out there right now and do what I've been wanting to do for a while—take all of those bastards down."

"We will," Vi says, her brown eyes gleaming with an unknown energy. For a second, I think she's going to yell at me, or worse, threaten to break another one of my limbs. But instead, she adjusts herself in her seat and quietly says, "And you know what, Blaire? Each second goes by, and I think that maybe your plan is better than mine."

"Seriously?" This might be the first time I've received a compliment from her. *Progress.*

"Hell yeah." She snorts, clearly not comfortable of talking in a friendly manner. "It sounded very absurd to me at first, but the more I thought about it, the more I realized that it wasn't as far-fetched as I believed it to be. I mean, kidnapping Jax

Remington? Of course it's going to be difficult . . . but it's definitely not impossible."

"Exactly. And at this point, I'm desperate for anything, or even anyone. I just—I just want us to get the life we deserve. I want to step forward and claim victory for everyone, that's all."

Vi leans back. "Well, that's why we brought you here, right?"

"Right," I whisper, smiling.

And to my surprise, she smiles too. Vi is a beautiful woman equipped with a rigid personality, but the smile on her face is enough to melt away my first impression of her. Even though she has a past that seems to be so horrible to the point that she refuses to bring up, I believe that she is still a courageous person. And I am curious and determined to know of her upbringing.

Suddenly, the great moment ends when she clears her throat and wipes her grin away. Vi immediately gets up to her feet and gestures to the hallway. "Well. I'm going to go now." She stuffs her hands into her pockets. "Uh, let me know if you need anything, I guess."

Before I can say anything else, she leaves.

I furrow my brows as I am left alone, leaving me to think about what the hell just happened. But instead, I swallow hard and sit back down on the couch, grabbing the remote and jabbing the unmute button as Nathan and Wendy start to speak again.

10

HIDDEN

November 5, 2064
1:10 p.m.

I TAKE A DEEP breath in and get up from the couch, my feet aching from either sitting all day or not sitting enough. Either way, I just want to get up and move around.

Once I shut the TV off, I walk around the expanse, yearning for some sunlight, or something to do with nature. I look around the room, noticing the intricate designs and engravings carved against the walls. My fingers run along them, my mouth gaping in awe as I still cannot seem to wrap my mind around the fact that this is not just any ordinary home; this is a home that seems to have been constructed from the Gods themselves, every single detail and inch crafted with the utmost delicacy, as if it were made of precious glass itself.

As I stand here, reveling in the luxury, I just can't help but wonder . . . who built this place? Who is the mastermind behind this organization? And most importantly, who is this *he?*

As I sit down on the armchair, trying to connect the missing pieces, I see everybody emerge from the hallway. "Follow us," Vi says.

I look at her in confusion, getting out of the chair slowly. "Um, where?"

"Oh, you'll see." Mallory grins mischievously.

Confused yet intrigued, I walk toward them, my hands pushing into the back pocket of my jeans. "I thought you guys already showed me everything about this house. What else could be left?"

Jeremiah smiles ambiguously. "Something really amazing." He gestures toward Vi, who lowers herself to the ground. What is she doing?

My eyes widen with curiosity, watching Vi lift a huge chunk of the ground, revealing a dark and vast hole below. The hinges creak, and my insides spin with puzzlement. I investigate it, seeing the complete darkness below, and I turn my head around to look at them. "What is this?"

They ignore my question while Vi latches her foot onto the side of the hole. As I narrow my eyes at where she placed her foot, I notice that there's a ladder hung on the side of it.

Once Vi slings herself onto the ladder, she climbs down quickly, her body vanishing into the emptiness. I watch with bated breath as Jeremiah climbs down next, which I am honestly flabbergasted by how quickly he goes down due to his prosthetic leg. Once he brings himself into the darkness, Dylan goes next and then Mallory. With extreme hesitation, yet the dying urge to follow them, I eventually decide to bring myself toward the ladder.

I grab the floor as my leg reaches down to the hole, cool air from below hitting my ankles. I bring my leg to the fifth rung of the ladder. Then, I climb down the ladder slowly and carefully, my body clinging onto it as heavy breaths escape out of me.

Several seconds later, I see a little bit of light appearing as my feet land on the hard pavement. I let go of the ladder, whirling around and seeing dim lighting exhibited on different glass cases. The rest of the group stands by a large table, and I gaze at the area in utter awe.

"Wow," I mutter, my fingers grazing the hard glass cases that encase the most prestigious of weapons. The weapons range from small handguns to rifles that can possibly kill a person in seconds. As I continue to stare at the firearms like a child gazing at candy, I feel a light tap on my shoulder.

"You like it?" Dylan grins at me.

"I mean . . . yeah! Where did you guys get this stuff? These are the types of weapons I see Guards with. How did you guys even—"

"Just sit here." Vi guides me as her hand collides against my back. She leads me to the huge meeting table where black office chairs crowd around the oblong-sized glass table that has a huge map of the Capital Center portrayed on it. In front is a flat-screen TV, and on the shelves around us are books that have very interesting titles engraved on the sides. Some I have read, such as *1984* and *Animal Farm* by George Orwell, *Fahrenheit 451* by Rad Bradbury, *A Clockwork Orange* by Anthony Burgess, and so many more.

I sit down on one of the office chairs. Once everyone gathers around the table, Vi begins to speak. "This is the secret underground room. While the house is secretive itself, this room is even more secretive because it contains the most precious materials. And not only that, but this is where we hold the most precarious meetings in which we discuss life-or-death situations." Her eyes narrow on me. "You are privileged to see this room because—trust me—we have recruited enough members, but they did not pass the obstacle in order to see this."

"So, if they didn't pass, where are they now?" I ask.

Realization settles in my stomach as I see the conflicted looks on everyone's faces. *Oh.*

"Anyway," Vi mumbles, "I hope you realize what value this

room holds. As little and decoration-deprived it may be, the elements that are portrayed boldly here display the goal of the Subversives—taking down the government. But now, our motives are to solely take down the president for now. It will be difficult to accomplish our task since there's so very little of us, but, if we kidnap Jax successfully, then we can begin getting under Tobias's skin.

"I am considering keeping Jax here in this room for a couple of days and force him to reveal information about his father. Physical force may need to be applied." She sends Jeremiah a knowing glance. "Or if we are truly not able to succeed, then we can blackmail Tobias to step down from his platform by threatening him with Jax's life, just like Blaire said.

"But I'm getting ahead of myself. We first need to fully prepare to kidnap Jax and bring him on our side. We are already halfway there because Jax's mindset itself revolves around escaping the Rich as Mal brought up. This propels us to a much better standing." She places her hands on the table, her posture ramrod straight. "This is our one chance to achieve freedom, so let's use it wisely."

Seconds later, everyone starts to applaud. Vi playfully rolls her eyes, failing to hide her small grin.

Once we talk about the rest of our plan and finalize it, we decide to wrap things up. I get out of the chair and follow everyone up the ladder, lunging myself forward as I climb my way to the top.

The dark and dim atmosphere changes into the illuminated aura that I thought did not offer enough brightness in the first place. I lift myself up to my feet, dusting myself off as I set my eyes forward. Then, I look behind me as Vi closes the portion of the floor that was lifted, placing it back down onto the ground.

I start to see everyone go their own ways, and I sigh, wondering where to go next. But, as I start to walk into the hallway, I see from my peripheral view that Mallory stands next to me. I turn toward her with a shy smile on my face, for she smiles back. "You want to hang out with me for a bit?"

"Of course." I grin, and she leads me into the hallway.

We sit in the technology room, where no one seems to present. A massive array of cameras tower over us with different perspectives of the Capital Center depicted in gray-scale.

"This will give us the perfect opportunity to brainstorm ways to kidnap Jax," Mal says. "First I was thinking that maybe we should find some way to sneak into the White House since that's where Jax and his family live."

"But isn't the White House heavily guarded? If we even set foot in that place, then we're going to get shot on sight."

"That's why Dylan hacked into the White House security system, so we can have a better approach if we ever felt the need to go to extreme measures. We first weren't going to lay a finger on the White House because our first plan consisted of just the Center. But the new plan consists of the White House now, so we need to be prepared for this."

Her words sink into my mind. I look toward the White House cameras, where they spiral into the view of the grand staircases into a few hallways. The hallways themselves are crowded with dozens of Guards, ready to shoot a person dead in a millisecond.

"This has to go perfectly well," I mutter into my hands.

"It will." Mallory rubs my shoulder reassuringly.

I look away from the cameras. "I just want us to take these bastards down. Ever since I was kid, I always wanted to hurt every single Rich person out there And the person I've wanted to hurt the most is Tobias Remington."

"Well, this is your perfect opportunity to fulfill those dreams because now you have us." She beams, her cupid-shaped lips curving upwards. "And trust me, I feel your hatred. I despised being treated like royalty, knowing that there were people in this place that weren't even able to eat three meals a day. It sucks to see that, and it sucks to see this country spiral toward its doom. This country would have prospered if everyone just got along and didn't separate into two divisions. But instead, the entire country is deserted. All because of the civil war that took place. And the only place present is D.C. Who knows, maybe there's some other place out there. But for now, it's just us. Just us in this screwed up world."

Warmth fills in my veins. "I hope there's more Rich people like you, Mallory, because I know that in order to properly take down this government, we're going to need powerful people."

"Exactly. That's why we need all the help we can get." Mallory beams. "Also, call me Mal instead."

"Okay." I smile. "And yeah, we will be successful, if we continue to work hard toward our goals."

With that said, I look at the camera. One peculiar segment of it piques my attention as I lean forward with curiosity.

"Is that . . . ?" Mal whispers, leaning forward as well.

She doesn't even have to finish her sentence because we know damn well who I just spotted in the camera.

Jax Remington walks in the hallway, clutching papers in his hands as his long legs stride forward. His eyebrows are pushed up alarmingly as he runs his free hand through his hair. Then, my keen eyes zero in on the very thin scar that runs along his cheek, the same scar that I managed to pick out during the Inauguration.

Mal plays with her hair. "Even when we were kids, he'd *always* look stressed. I can't blame him, though; his parents are horrible."

I frown. "I can only imagine."

Once Jax disappears out of the frame, I take a deep breath as I look toward Mal. "Well, looks like we're really going to have to step on it if we want our plan to be completely fool-proof."

"Yeah, you're right." She crosses her arms over her chest. "It's going to be hard to make our plan completely fool-proof though because this is Jax Remington we're thinking of kidnapping here. I don't know how we're going to make it work—" Mal gasps as she brings her hand to her mouth, looking at me with widened eyes. "Blaire!"

"Yes, what happened?" I ask hurriedly.

"Oh my gosh . . ." she mumbles, pushing herself up to the huge control panel as she types on the keyboard of the desktop placed in the corner. The screen is suddenly filled with words, and when I look at it closer, I see short written passages from Rich people, speaking of what they do every second of their lives.

I scoff derisively. *How the hell do people say what they do every second of their lives? Do people even care about that shit?*

"This is the D.C. blog page, where Rich people would recount their daily lives." She scoffs. "My parents were highly associated with social media and posted about their lives almost every single day because they believed that since they were 'people of worth and acknowledgment' that everybody else wanted to join in on their shenanigans too. Seeing this stuff now disgusts me."

I frown. "Seeing this stuff disgusts me, too."

Mal sulks, lifelessly scrolling through the feed. "Now you know what I mean by me not being born in the right place. I just didn't belong there." And then, she gasps again as she jabs her finger at the screen. "Holy crap, Blaire! Look at this!"

I inch toward her, rearing my head forward as I try to decrypt the words on the screen. Once I do, my heart stops.

Jax Remington (@JaxRemington13) 09:01am:
Good morning, everyone. I have great news . . .

On November 14th at six in the evening, I am hosting a party at Governor's Central! I am doing this to celebrate my father recently being re-elected as president. This will definitely be a night to remember.

I love you all! Long live America!

Sincerely, Jax Remington

11

DEVISE

November 5, 2064
1:31 p.m.

"COME HERE, EVERYBODY! YOU have to see this!" Mal bellows. In just a few seconds, the rest of the group filters into the room, wondering what all the commotion is about.

"What is that?" Dylan points toward the screen.

"Just read it," I say.

A few moments later, a slightly audible gasp escapes from Vi's mouth. "Is this real? Or are you just shitting me?"

"No, we swear it's real," Mal says desperately.

"So, let me get this straight." Jeremiah begins to pace around the room. "Jax Remington is going to throw a party on the 14th? And all of D.C. is invited?"

"Well, it's not *all* of D.C.," Mal says. "Poor people aren't allowed to do many things, let alone party. So, if everyone's on the same page here . . ."

". . . We're going to have to be disguised as Rich people," I finish off.

"Mal, you used to be a Rich person," Vi says. "Did you ever go to one of Jax's parties or any other Rich people's parties?"

"Yeah, I went to a lot, especially Jax's. But the reason why he ever throws parties in the first place is to please his parents. I bet he was forced to throw this party—even posting that message on the blog page too."

"So, his parents literally force him to engage in society?" My words are filled with disgust. "That's terrible."

"I know." Mal sighs, blonde locks effortlessly falling onto her face. "That's why doing this for him—bringing him into a much better life—makes me feel satisfied. I used to be pretty good friends with him, but I don't know if his thinking changed. Maybe he adjusted to the Rich life and rarely thinks of a life outside. Or maybe he genuinely wants to follow in his father's footsteps and conquer the nation with his presence, but the Jax I knew was the complete opposite, that's for sure."

Silence fills the air like a gust of foreign wind, and Mal breaks it by clearing her throat. "Anyway, if we plan to kidnap Jax at his party, then we're going to have to plan this very precisely."

"I agree with you on that," Vi says. "But let's start with the basics, all right? Since the party begins around six, we will have to arrive at Governor's Central around quarter to six so we can memorize the layout of the place itself because it may come in handy at some point."

"Wait, what's Governor's Central?" Dylan asks, adjusting his black-rimmed glasses.

"It's like a hangout place for the Rich people," Mal answers, "and it's also where all of the important meetings, parties, and events are held, especially for political members. I guess Jax was allowed to host his party there because he, of course, is part of the most illustrious family in D.C. itself."

Dylan raises his eyebrows, registering her words.

Jeremiah takes over now. "We have black SUVs available to

us—the same exact ones that the government utilizes. This will come in handy because we can seem like important and young members of society since we will obviously be incognito as Rich people."

"In simple terms," Vi says, "we are basically going to have to dress up in bright and flashy clothes and act like the world revolves around us."

"And will that also mean we have fake identities?" Dylan asks.

"Correct." She cracks her knuckles. "We will be disguised as different people, and we will not draw much attention to ourselves. If Jax were to approach any of us, then we must converse as little as possible. We cannot act like we don't belong there; in fact, we have to act like we belong there more than him," Vi emphasizes. "This is probably the riskiest thing we will ever indulge ourselves in, so please, do *not* screw this up."

My heart thuds.

Vi takes a deep breath as she studies every one of us. Her eyes then stop on Jeremiah. "You are not Jeremiah Morgan anymore. You are instead Henry McCall, a workout instructor for Rich people. You got it?" Jeremiah nods his head, averting his eyes to the ground.

She then makes heavy eye contact with Dylan, who drums his finger onto the edge of the console. "You are not Dylan Faulkner anymore. You are instead Brandon Garfield, a Rich teenage boy who aspires to be a part of the government. Understand?"

Dylan grins. "I got it."

Then, she narrows her eyes onto Mal. "Ah, Mal, you must be the most disguised here, even to the point where your hair and eye color is different too because Jax actually knows you." Vi ponders for a moment, but then she gasps. "All right. You are now a model named Victoria James, someone who hopes to spread her name around D.C. You have red hair with the most beautiful green eyes, and most people seem to find you alluring."

Mal asks, "Will I have to wear a wig and contact lenses?" When Vi nods her head, she murmurs to herself, "Well, this is going to be interesting."

Finally, my heart lurches in my throat as Vi's deep brown eyes latch onto mine. "Ms. Cohen, the latest addition to the gang. You are also important since you are the one who raised this thought- provoking idea in the first place. So, forget all about your life. . ." She raises a finger to her lips in thought. "You are now Marie Davis, an architect with huge morals, and all you are there to do is study the amazing work of art known as Governor's Central. Do you copy, Miss Marie Davis?"

"Yes," I murmur while trying to absorb all this information getting thrown at me.

Vi smiles satisfyingly. "And I will be Georgia Adams, a Rich woman who plans to study law."

"I love these new roles we're doing." Dylan chuckles.

"I love them too, but we have to be serious about this as well." Vi raises her eyebrows at him while he sinks into his chair. "This is going to be one of our most important missions because we're kidnapping a well-known individual in society. And if we truly want to find out the deep dark secrets of the president, then we must execute this plan with little to no flaws. Everyone understand?"

We let out a simultaneous "yes."

"Perfect. Let's get some rest today, and you guys can get used to your roles and work them out for next Friday." Suddenly, she pauses and looks at all of us. "What we're doing is what no one in this world even dares to do. We are fighting for equal rights here: equal rights for not only us, but for our people and family as well.

"This is what we've been yearning for, and we will only prevail if we stick to our plan and not be distracted. This depends on us. We need to be the new faces of this world, the ones where people will now look up to when we take that dirty son of a bitch down. Tobias Remington is a cruel man, and I just know that if we bring Jax on our side, then we will be unstoppable."

And with that statement running around in my mind, I think that this is the beginning of an era. The beginning of a new chapter, each flipping page leading to new revelations and opportunities. And I know that if we bring Jax Remington on our side, we will indeed be unstoppable.

That is when Marie Davis comes in handy for the party—for the kidnapping. And the president's son won't have a clue about the hell that's about to unravel for him.

12

UNUSUAL

November 14, 2064
5:47 p.m.

MY DARK LOCKS FALL against my bare shoulders as I look in the mirror in front of me, admiring my hair, which never looked as healthy and voluminous as now.

"Took a while to get rid of your tangles." Vi snorts behind me. For the past hour, she has been helping me get ready for tonight, and I have to admit, a lot of effort was made to make me look at least quasi-presentable. And unfortunately for Vi, she was stuck with me, especially when we had to get through my hair that was pretty much impossible to fix. However, due to her perseverance and secret knack for fashion, we got through it quite earlier than expected.

My eyes travel down the blazing strapless black dress wrapped around my body, embellishing the same obscurity that my dark green eyes do. On the bottom I wear black stilettos that dig into the back of my heels, and I wonder how the hell I am going to wear these for the rest of the night. For just a quick moment I am grateful that I am Poor and don't have to partake in such an excessively luxurious lifestyle.

Vi's words make me snap out of my trance. "Is there anything you want to add to your makeup?"

That is when I study my face. My skin is caked with foundation as all the blemishes that first appeared on my face are now flawless—just my revamped olive skin is portrayed. And my full lips are emblazoned with maroon-colored lipstick that brings out the gleam in my eyes that are flourished in dark eye-shadow with golden glitter adorning it.

"No, I think I look good," I say perhaps for the first time in my life.

Vi reacts by patting my shoulder. "Good. Confidence is key."

I notice how Vi's colorful and vivacious hair is wrapped up in a low bun, which highlights her mystifying features. Her makeup is fiery, just like her. She wears a white blazer with nothing underneath and on the bottom she wears tight dress pants and high-class shoes. I have admitted this before, and I will admit it again, but she is absolutely gorgeous. So gorgeous to the point that I begin to question whether she's human.

I've been here for almost two weeks, and I think I have formed an acquaintance with Vi. Sure, she may send me scornful looks every now and then and refuse to smile more than three times a day, but it's the progress that counts. And in comparison to the day I first got here, I can say quite confidently that me and Vi are slowly getting on the same page. As long as I don't bring her past up.

Once Vi and I get ready, we walk outside of the girls' room and go where the others stand. They are all spread out across the room, and I am not even able to recognize them because they look so *different*.

Jeremiah adjusts his navy-blue blazer as his eyes glaze over us, a grin inflicting on him. Dylan, on the other hand, wears a black and white suit with shiny black dress shoes that seem to glint against the white lights. Both look incredibly handsome, and I start to think that they are impersonating their Rich personas a bit too well.

And finally, Mal emerges from the kitchen, her silver heels clacking against the floor as her long and luscious red hair—which is not really her hair to begin with—falls in waves against her back. The front of her dress, however, covers her entire torso with a red exterior, falling to her thighs as it curves around her body. Her lips are covered in bright red lipstick and her fake green eyes are accentuated due to the white eye-shadow that covers her eyelids.

We start to walk toward the huge double doors that lead to the garage of where all the black SUVs are. The doors close behind us, and we find ourselves climbing into the SUVs—Jeremiah drives while Vi takes shotgun, and the rest of us climb into the back.

The engine hums to life as the interior lights of the vehicle flicker on. A female robotic voice erupts from the car. "Good morning, Jeremiah Morgan. It is currently fifty degrees Fahrenheit outside. It is partly cloudy, and chances of rain are predominant early in the morning. I advise you to invest in a rain jacket if it were to pour at dawn."

The robotic voice continues to spew information about the day, a quaint whirring sound reverberating in the air as the car ascends to the top. The floor above us creates an orifice in the middle, and I gape out the window, seeing the orange sky gleaming above us. The car lurches onto the ground as it closes again.

Once the ground closes beneath us, the car drives forward, treading along the road silently. I press my lips together as I watch the trees sway against the wind, blurring and blending almost like an obscure portrait. The sky appears to be a contrast of a blood red color, a sunset orange, and then an ominous dark blue. I think about how beautiful this world is, how aesthetic it is and how much it provides to us . . .

Except us humans decided to wreak havoc and exact our hatred for each other onto our world, which did not deserve our end of the wrath at all. It's a very disheartening factor to acknowledge, knowing that the world is ruined because of *us*. And there's no coming back now.

The quiet humming of the engine continues to drone in the heavy silence as I blurt out, "Wouldn't the Guards notice us being out here?"

"I mean, of course." Vi scoffs and glances back at me. "Why do you think we dressed up as Rich people?"

The answer forms in my mind. "Oh . . ."

She looks back at the front. "Don't worry—we thought about every single scenario that might occur. That's why we stuffed Mallory with the heaviest disguise." Vi pauses to herself, her eyes narrowing in thought. "Though we should still remain careful and hold an incognito presence among everyone tonight."

"And when we enter D.C.," Jeremiah starts to say, "the Guards will most likely roam around us and question who we are. Since Rich people are the only ones to obtain a vehicle like this, they won't question us as much."

"Oh," I murmur. "That makes a lot more sense now."

After ten minutes of heavy silence and gazing at the rising moon, the earthy ground molds into the outskirts of the city, beaten buildings and ruins scattered around us. The war had unleashed its wrath upon the entire nation, and every single Rich and Poor person latched their claws into the opposing end, and unfortunately, our cities and towns were the victims of it. Nothing is left of America, nothing except D.C. with a society that barely functions. This is the result of our chaos, our violence, and our hatred—and we must live with it.

The desolate ruins delineate a lack of longevity in the city, trails of litter speckled around the fissured roads, and buildings with cracked walls and broken roofs stand despondently. The outskirts of the city are known as the Poor sector, where every single Poor person resides. Where we are now is amid different pawn shops that have cracked windows and people loitering on the sides, their feet probably aching from walking long distances.

Once the bleak shops disappear, villages start to appear. Seeing the villages makes me think of my family and what despair they must be going through right now. My parents mine alone everyday now, living their lives without two of their children now. And it takes every part of me to not jump out of this car and reach out to my parents, lend my aching hand toward them so hopefully their warm touch will spread abundance throughout my sore heart— but I can't. Because I am here, on a mission with other people who share the same hatred and desires as me, and I can't leave them.

A dark blue color fully ascends upon the partly cloudy sky and the Poor sector diminishes. A small opening on the path is imminent, and a huge line of Guards stand ramrod straight along the opening, highlighting the obvious distinction between the Rich and Poor sector. When we went to the inauguration, this division was not prominent because Poor people were allowed to enter the Capital Center. But now it is an ordinary day in D.C. during the year 2064, meaning that our tiny nation is divided again.

The SUV rolls to a stop as the engine purrs out a sound. A few Guards come toiling over, huge rifles cocked in their hands and dressed head-to-toe in navy blue uniforms. One Guard knocks on the window as Jeremiah allows it to be rolled down.

"Welcome to Washington, D.C.," the Guard's deep voice booms. "May I have your ID?"

I narrow my eyes onto Jeremiah's frighteningly calm expression, nonchalantly reaching into his pocket and pulling out a fake ID of him. From here, I notice his dark-skinned face on the card with bold words etched next to him. **HENRY MCCALL. Sex: M. Age: 32. Height: 6ft 6in. Weight: 230 lbs. Rich #39.**

An inaudible breath of relief releases from me as Jeremiah hands him his fake ID. The Guard's hand, covered in a navy-blue glove, reaches to grab it. His glassy eyes run along the words, seeming to scrutinize every detail of it. He then hands it back to Jeremiah. "You may carry on, Mr. McCall." Jeremiah sets the car forward, closing the car window simultaneously.

"The Guard asked for Jeremiah's ID as you saw there," Vi states, turning around to look at us. "They will make sure that whoever is driving has to be a Rich person, in order to enter the Rich sector of the city."

"Why didn't they ask for ours?" Dylan ponders.

"Because there's no way in hell a Rich person would be seen with Poor people," I say, pressing my lips together in thought. My words vibrate into the air, letting the others take note of it.

We drive toward the city, the cracked and barren roads seeming to alter into smooth ones. The pawn shops that lack life and have people loitering on the sides now form into a city filled with enormous buildings, shiny and shimmering cars roaming around, and people either engrossed in their conversations with others or on the phone with somebody. Only Rich people can have these so- called telecommunication devices— able to say that they love someone in an instant. I wish I had that privilege. I wish I could grab my device and call my parents in just a few seconds and pour my heart out to them.

People are smiling. People are laughing. And people are seeming stress-free . . . because they have money. Money that seems to be built from air itself, considering how everyone was on the brink of poverty during the Dark Ages consisting of the Second Great Depression. I wonder sometimes how they were able to acquire money and, most importantly of all, effortlessly build the remnants of D.C. back up. And they were reconstructed so effortlessly to the point that no scratch, let alone speck of dust seems to encounter it.

Meanwhile, in the Poor sector . . . It is basically the replica of Hell. The car continues to drive through the city, and the huge Capital Center stands out in the middle, exhibiting its beautiful white exterior. There were talks around the nation that the original Capitol building was tremendously destroyed with no origin point found, only because of the terrifying mass riots that ensued, so the government built a renowned Capitol right in front of the White House and named it as the Capital Center. This was meant for government-issued events such as the quadrennial election or inauguration.

Rich people crowd around the Center, just like always. And just as inferred, Poor people are not allowed to set foot in the beating heart of D.C., let alone gaze at the Capital Center. Only the inauguration is when they are allowed to—and obviously not the fabricated election that is, in reality, complete control of the Rich—meaning that is the only time we are *allowed* to be laughed at by the Rich people. Only for having less money than them.

The car swerves into the Rich suburbs of the city. Beautiful mansions stretch out to the sky with gorgeous engravings and decorations portrayed. This is where the significant figures of society reside because they—of course—make the most of the entire nation. There are also 7,030 residents in D.C., and at least 3,000 of them make up to be Rich. The rest are the Poor, but our numbers continue to decrease because many of us die every day due to two reasons: starvation or a Guard killing us.

Suddenly, an enormous and architecturally-advanced building stands out in front of us. It is covered in alabaster-colored walls that stretch out to the sky, each brick and shilling seeming to have been implemented with the greatest efforts. Hundreds of the Rich stand by the entrance, dressed in their expensive outfits and engaged in colloquial approaches.

The car parks by the left, and we exit immediately. I continue to gaze at the view to the right, where the massive Governor's Central stands out among the other man-made Rich buildings.

I stare at the view wordlessly as I notice the massive amount of Rich people crowded at the beautiful entrance of the Governor's Central. There are two columns stretching from the left and right sides of the entrance with large engravings carved upon them. We walk farther, and I feel a jabbing pain immediately at the sides of my feet. I wince as I rush to regain myself.

We reach the entrance, and Jeremiah whispers to us, "I'm guessing Jax has already arrived because everyone's starting to go inside."

"Isn't Tobias and Isabelle going to be here as well?" I ask.

"No, because this is a party held by their son," Dylan answers as we huddle into a group, making sure our words are not heard by the others and not look suspicious as well. "I don't know if you noticed, but only people our age are here."

I look around the area, seeing that Dylan is correct. The area is swarming with young adults, talking wildly and laughing loudly. Their immature and fervent conversations are already beginning to bother me.

"Well, we should start going inside too," Mal says. We all verbally agree.

This is our first mission here: kidnap Jax, bring him to the underground home, and enforce strict ideals on him so we can accomplish our number one goal. I take a deep breath as I notice the five of us walking together, our faces expressionless, and we continue to walk forward as I try to ignore the jabbing feeling at my toes. *Damn high heels.*

VIBRANT

November 14, 2064
8:34 p.m.

LOUD MUSIC BOOMS AROUND us as we are engulfed within the colorful atmosphere. My eyes dance around as I interpret just how vibrant this place is.

We continue to walk through the crowds while getting ambushed by people dawdling in the middle. I try to force myself to understand the environment I am thrown in: people dressed in expensive clothing, holding expensive drinks while conversing loudly. Music playing so deafeningly, reverberating into my ears until that is all I can hear. And fumes of smoke suddenly swarming around me like a silent fog as I try to stifle a cough.

"What the hell is that?" I murmur.

"Marijuana." Vi looks at me mischievously.

My eyebrows pinch together. "And what the hell is *that?*"

"A mind-bending drug that can possibly screw you over," she says, and as I open my mouth up to speak, I watch as she suddenly grabs a cigarette from a random person, props it in her mouth, and elegantly blows it out, long lines of smoke forming from her lips.

My eyes burn as a harsh smell wisps around me. "That's so strong."

"Exactly." She sports a half-witty grin while adding a small cough afterwards. "Which is why I advise you to not do it."

That leaves me in confusion, thinking of how nonchalantly she smoked someone else's cigarette. We continue to walk alongside the others, but Vi sends a look toward Jeremiah as he then nods his head. Everyone seems to receive this cryptic memo that I have no idea of as we disperse into a secluded hallway at the left.

Once we disappear into a closet here, Jeremiah snarls, "I can't believe you grabbed that person's joint!"

"Hey, what did I say before we left? We have to make ourselves like the Rich." Vi's hands dance around, and it seems as if this *marijuana* is really loosening her up. "Act greedy and super narcissistic. I had to blend in by *acting* like them. So, that is why I stole their joint and smoked. And did I miss a good ol' smoke."

Mal furrows her brows. "Okay, it's fine. You can smoke, I guess. But . . . now what? Do we just roam around and hope to run into Jax?"

"Sweetie, why do you think I rammed us up in here?" Vi glares at her.

We huddle into the tiny closet where there seems to be no one but—well, *us.* Faint music thumps from the outside, creating a distinct sound as I hone myself for the group's discussion.

"All right, so I brought everyone here because we need to discuss the final part of tonight's plan—the actual kidnapping. Jax is obviously roaming around this place, and he is most definitely not going to be alone because, well, he is the host of the party. That makes our plan even more difficult—but there's no need to worry because I have it all planned out.

"First of all, remember how I said that we should refrain from engaging in a conversation with Jax? Well, that remains true . . . except for one person."

Vi glances over at Jeremiah, who scrunches his face up in confusion. "Me?"

"Yes, *Mr. McCall*. Your main goal tonight is to talk to Mr. Remington purposefully. Do you remember your profession?"

"Yes, I'm a workout instructor."

"Correct." Vi snaps her fingers. "Now, Jax is a man who seems to have a fit and muscular body. Obviously, he works out." She gestures to Jeremiah. "And that is when you step in. Since you are a workout instructor, you will bring this to him"—Vi pauses to hand Jeremiah a small white card—"and explain that you can be his workout instructor. Basically, just spew information about working out and keeping a perfect diet and blah, blah, blah." From here, I can see that the card holds a fake phone number, Jeremiah's credentials, and a fake address.

"Once you keep his attention, the rest of us will find a small room to prepare the kidnapping. But don't fret because we have the entire map of the place right in my hands." Vi reaches into the pocket of her dress pants and brings out a piece of paper folded up several times. She unravels it as the paper grows to a larger length and width. The paper turns out to be an intricate map of the Governor's Central, dark lines expressing the different rooms and sectors of the place.

"With a little help from someone, we managed to obtain the map of the Governor's Central." Vi nods once at Dylan. "Thank you."

He kindly brushes her off. "No problem."

My eyes begin to rake over the paper, making note of the many markings made on it. The first thing I notice is the marking of the entrance, which notes a huge space marked *the center*.

The center runs off into many directions, sporting many different hallways that start from the main area. The first floor holds four different hallways, and in each hallway are three rooms with a bathroom in each one. One of the rooms holds an emergency exit. On the other hand, the second floor consists of two hallways, much bigger than the hallways downstairs because the two rooms in those hallways are suites. There are no emergency exits by those rooms.

"I'm guessing that we kidnap Jax in the room that has an emergency exit?" I ask Vi.

"Bingo." Vi smiles for the second time tonight. "As we can see here"—her finger lands on the marking that indicates the room I pointed out—"there is only one place where there is an emergency exit, which is in the room. The other emergency exits are in the public, and the only private emergency exit is in the first-floor room. That means that, once *Henry* manages to hold Jax in his grip—not literally, of course—the rest of us will prepare for the kidnapping. And here is how we will do it.

"I will fetch the SUV at the front of the building and bring it to the back." Her fingers trace the drawn road on the map, but then her finger dances around to the back of the building, right beside the room with the emergency exit. "We are lucky that there is a small gravel path in the back, which means I will bring the SUV there with no issues, such as cameras watching us."

"But *wouldn't* the cameras be watching us, regardless?" Mal asks, her eyebrows raising with concern.

"That's when our computer extraordinaire comes in handy." Vi looks over at Dylan. "Do you know how to hack into the server?"

"Of course," he says, and that is when he brings out a small black device from his pocket.

I watch astonishingly as he presses onto the device and

light emits from the screen immediately. The light transmits from the device and brings out a three-dimensional view of it. That is when I see a detailed transcript of all the cameras placed around us, even where the hidden corners are—which we are lucky we are in the closet, since there doesn't seem to be any here. Dylan places his fingers at the three-dimensional view as he quickly does his magic right in front of us, numbers and words popping and going as I continue to watch with surprise.

Moments later, a green light emanates from the display. "The cameras are disabled, and the console panel will have absolutely no way to trace where our bug came from." Dylan turns to us. "We're good to go."

Vi sends him a grateful look. "Now that we got that finished, this is when *Marie Davis* and *Victoria James* come in handy." Her brown eyes land on me and Mallory, and I feel my ears piquing with interest. "When Jeremiah manages to bring Jax to the secluded room, he will quickly bring Jax to the room, but not knock him out. We need him to be awake."

Jeremiah frowns. "Goddammit."

She continues, "That is when Blaire and Mal will come into the room. Jax will obviously be fighting against Jeremiah's grip, so Blaire or Mal will sedate him with a special drug in our sterilizer. This will knock him out for a good hour. By that time, the three of you guys will go out the emergency exit where I will be in the car, waiting for you all. Then, we will drive off and, at that time, there will be less Guards on the road because not many Guards patrol the Rich sector at midnight. Everyone got it?"

"Wait," Mal interjects, "won't people notice that he's gone?"

"Yes." Vi suddenly has a sadistic look on her face. "We want people to freak out at his disappearance. This will cause a blunder in society because everyone is now going to be focused on Jax suddenly disappearing. This will allow us for more of an advantage of truly taking down Tobias because everyone will be too focused on Jax and we can blackmail Tobias too, if needed."

Mal's face registers a sense of calmness as she then nods her head. "I'm just really nervous about this plan. I hope it goes well."

"All we can do is hope for the best," I say. "We've definitely worked hard since the plan was initiated, so hopefully our hard work will pay off."

"It will," Dylan says, sending me a kind and motivating glance. "And we definitely should not screw up."

Jeremiah barks out a laugh. "Screwing up is a no-go for now."

Everyone concedes in light laughter, but I can still feel the tense atmosphere around us because we are all a part of the biggest heist induced in a while. And this heist is not an ordinary one because this is not a valued object we're stealing: it is actually one of the most valued individuals in D.C.

Jeremiah was right . . . screwing up is *definitely* a no-go.

9:02 p.m.

We eventually conclude that it is best if we go our own ways since sticking to each other like glue will raise suspicions of us. We must stay in eye-range of each other, just in case Jeremiah decides to initiate his conversation with Jax. He was told to talk to him around ten because we plan to escape the parameters around midnight when the Guards aren't really around.

So, in those thirty minutes that have passed, I'e sat by the bar, where a bartender asks me every five minutes if I want a drink or not. And every time, I shake my head.

I run my fingers over my black dress, still not seeming to understand that I am in the middle of a heist right now while being in the Rich sector of society. Not only that, but I'm wearing flashy clothing that I still feel uncomfortable in—not to mention the heels that continue to jab at my feet like wood-peckers pecking their beaks into tree bark. Part of me cannot wait until this night is over, so we can move on to the next part of our plan.

But the other part of me feels so astonished to be at this party, observing the many movements and conversations around me. I've always wondered what it's like to be at a party because in all the books I've read from my mom's library, there was always a party scene. And the atmosphere of a party described in a book always felt full of delight and liveliness.

So why the hell do I feel so stressed right now?

I lean back against the counter while swiveling around on the bar-stool, my feet dangling. From the corner of my eye, I watch two men eye me down, specifically my cleavage, and I feel my cheeks warming up as I snap my eyes down to my chest. I pull my dress up quickly as I try to conceal it as much as possi-ble, and I turn around in the chair, feeling embarrassed from the encounter. Do Rich men have no shame? Watching a woman like a mere object? I feel more of an urge to leave this place.

I sigh, my dark locks falling onto my face. I push them back as I gruffly get off my seat. Even in the vibrating music and resonating voices, I can hear my heels clicking and clacking against the hardwood floor as I make my way into the bathroom on the first floor. *I need peace and quiet—fresh air of some sort, at least.*

I push my way into the ladies' room, the colorful and radi-ating lights transforming into bright white lights. A long line of mirrors stand in front of me, alongside a row of tiny cubicles where toilets seem to be in them. I stand in front of the sink and thank the universe there's no one in here.

"C'mon, Blaire," I say to myself. "Why are you acting like this?"

Words rupture into my mind. *Because I'm scared of what's*

outside. This is a place I've never been to, and being here in front of these Rich people while pretending to be one . . . It's a lot to take in. And I'm nervous. Mortified. Unable to move.

I let out a shaky breath as I notice myself in the mirror—notice how different I look. My eyes have never looked this bold before. My skin and lips have never looked so beautiful before. I myself have never looked so beautiful before.

My body straightens up as I admire my physique. I run my fingers up my body, feeling a smile tickle my lips. This is me. This is who I am right now. Not Blaire Cohen . . . *Marie Davis.*

I exit out of the bathroom. But suddenly, I feel a presence behind me that makes me stop in my tracks.

No way.

From the corner of my eye, I feel him lingering—a man of great height, build, and authority. I gulp as I continue to walk down the hall. *Do not make conversation, Blaire. Refrain from talking, just like Vi said.*

But as soon as I start to exit the hallway, he says, "I promise I won't bite." His voice is mixed with humor, almost an amused tone.

And with that, I force myself to turn around. It is too late now. I cannot ignore him anymore.

I look up at the silver eyes I've noticed on television screens for so many years. The complex and enigmatic man I've wondered about for so many years.

Jax.

14

UNFORGETTABLE

November 14, 2064
9:10 p.m.

A HUGE LUMP GROWS in my throat as I see the president's son standing in front of me. His jaw is hinged closed as his eyes study me intently, and I feel my mouth getting drier by the second.

I don't know if it is the atmosphere of the night or Jax's intense gaze on me, but I feel my cheeks reddening by the second. I look at the floor, hoping he will just disappear out of my sight.

But, to my unfortunate disavowal, he doesn't.

Instead, he steps closer. I try to move—believe me—but my feet remain stuck to the ground like magnets. This is the same man I see on television, smiling valiantly and creating a noble image of himself. And here he is, right in front of me in the flesh.

He clears his throat. "Mind if I ask how your evening is going?" *Goddamn, why does he have to be so polite?* I decide standing here like an idiot while continuing to stare at the ground isn't the best decision, so I instead bring my eyes up to him. My breath hitches as I notice the beauty of his face, just how painfully beautiful he is.

"It's going well," I say barely audibly.

He leans in closer to me until our torsos are merely a foot apart. "I'm sorry, could you repeat that for me?" His voice is deep, husky, and resonates like birds calling into the wind.

"I said it's going well—what about you?" I repeat, my eyebrows raising.

A smirk tugs at his lips. "Same for me. I felt suffocated over there, so I decided to be by myself for a while. However"—he pauses—"I don't mind having company now."

I feel my cheeks burn like hell. How can I ever forget? This is Jax Remington, who flirts with every girl his gray eyes lay upon.

Silence falls over us, and that is when I plan to mutter out words that lead to my departure, but instead, this son of a bitch carries on the conversation. "So, what's your name? Someone as beautiful as you must have a beautiful name as well."

I draw my lips into a straight line, fighting the urge to run off in a panic. "Marie Davis. I believe you are Jax Remington, correct?" I joke.

A deep laugh rumbles out of him as he stretches his hand out. "Yes, I am him." Before I can think of what I'm doing, I accept his hand, engaging in a friendly handshake. His hand is firm and rough yet soft at the same time.

"I am glad to run into you, Miss Davis. I hope you don't mind me calling you miss because, judging by the absence of a ring on your ring finger"—he glances down to my hands—"I decided to go with my intuition."

"That's all right." My ability to speak English is suddenly disappearing. "I-I love the party so far."

He smiles, dimples creasing into his cheeks. "Thank you. I always throw these huge banquets whenever there's a huge cele-bration in town, such as my father's inauguration."

"That's wonderful," I reply, but saying the next sentence makes bile rise in the back of my throat. "I'm glad your father was inaugurated, purely for the betterment of this country."

"I'm grateful to hear that." He grins, but there seems to be a lack of excitement present in his swarming gray eyes that hasn't left my face at all. This makes me think of what Mal told us about Jax, how he secretly hopes to leave his privileged life behind. And I can see it in him right now—nothing will truly be as convincing as his expression that speaks more words than he can say himself.

Another bubble of silence encloses over us, and I try to pop it by finding the quickest way out of this conversation. "Thanks for talking to me; I feel very honored to be standing here with you. But unfortunately, I must leave because my friends are expecting me."

"You really must go?" He frowns.

For a split second I feel awful, but I quickly brush any impostor emotions off me. "Yes, I must."

He lets out a disappointed chuckle. "I understand, friends must come above all else."

"Correct." I nod my head. He nods his head as well, his eyes delirious. Something about this makes me feel uneasy, knowing that he has no idea what's to come. But I need to go through with this because not only is this the group's idea, but it's also mine. I need to follow through, no matter who or what tries to stop me. Even Jax Remington, who is talking to me as if I were any other normal Rich person. This is the man who I've watched on the screens for many years, and he's front and present at this very moment . . .

And with that said, I turn around, brushing off the incoming images of Jax's dazzling face, how he stands out amongst the huge crowds—not only because of his social status but his looks as well. If social standards did not exist in this society, then hell would I make a move on him.

Blaire, what the hell is going on with you? Snap out of it!

As I start to walk away, I hear him shouting behind me. "Hey, Marie!"

I take a heaving breath in. What now?

I turn around reluctantly and am startled as I see Jax is inches away from me now, his torso almost digging into my chest. The dim flashing lights and the pounding music makes my breathing slow, my heartbeat quickening as his animated eyes study me like a sculpture. His body is way too close to mine, yet I don't seem to make any efforts to move. He makes me feel paralyzed from every inch and part of my bones—and I don't like it at all.

Jax's eyes brush over my lips. "I couldn't seem to shake off a gorgeous woman like you, so . . . Meet me on the second floor at midnight, okay?"

My heart throbs as his eyes search my face for an answer. *Shit, what do I say?* My mouth twitches as I realize that my answer is going to be nonessential either way. So, for the hell of it, I say, "Of course, handsome."

This time, I see his cheeks redden as he tucks his chin into his chest. "Okay," he whispers. That's when I notice the gray suit over his light blue shirt that is buttoned to the very top, excluding the last few buttons he left unbuttoned. His long legs are covered in the same gray color as his suit, which resembles his silver eyes. He screams dominance, authority, and power, and it makes me feel undermined.

Suddenly, his hand grabs my hand—very softly indeed. He brings it to his lips, placing a light kiss that makes my insides churn. Even seconds after, I can still feel his touch lingering on my knuckles. And what's scary is that I don't know what to feel about it.

And to my liking, he lets me go. It feels weird to not be enamored and consumed in his presence, but I know it is for my own good because I need to keep myself incognito and especially away from Jax, now that I am acknowledged by his eyes.

No other words are spoken as I walk away from him, my heels clicking and clacking onto the hard ground. Even though I know his presence still lingers behind me, my heated gaze transforms into a hard glare as I feel a wave of dedication rush over me. This is when my mark begins. This is when *it* begins.

And Jax is right—I will see him at midnight. Just not in the same way he intends.

9:19 p.m.

I run up the flight of stairs, my feet aching as I slide down the wall, sitting on the carpeted ground. Music continues to pound downstairs, causing the place where I'm sitting to vibrate. I sigh, trying to make do of the conversation that happened just a few minutes ago.

What just happened?

My head thuds against the wall. *Thud, thud, thud.* I let out an exasperated breath as I stretch out my aching legs, tearing my heels off my poor feet. I feel a wave of relief wash over me as I realize that my feet can finally breathe. How do Rich women even bother to wear these torture devices?

And so, I sit here, barefoot and head banging against the wall, waiting for the night to pass by as the continuous music plays downstairs. I wait and wait and wait—

"Blaire? The hell are you doing here?"

I see very familiar figures peek out from the stairs since I am seated by the front corner of the hallway. No other soul seems to be up here.

Obviously, no other than me, Mal, and Vi.

"Oh, hey," I murmur. They exchange glances and then walk over toward me.

Mal sits to the right of me as Vi sits in front of me. "Are you guys enjoying the party?" I try to change the subject.

"Yes, I am, to my utter surprise." Mal's green eyes emanate with excitement. "The food is just spectacular! Not to mention the cute guy I kind of flirted with. Oh! And—" Vi clears her throat as Mal's face flushes red. "Uh—Blaire! How dare you try to change the subject!"

"Yeah, so answer our question first." Vi cocks her head. "Why are you up here, sitting on the ground so depressingly?"

"Well—uh—because you told me to not exchange in any conversations, so I decided to be up here to make sure I do just that." I let out a nervous chuckle. Vi still seems to not be convinced by my statement at all. *Well, shit.*

I decide to let down my guard. I take a deep breath in, preparing to let out words that might be the trigger to the bomb. "Okay, so, don't be upset, but . . . Jax and I talked."

Mal and Vi's eyes both widen at the same time.

"*I* didn't start up the conversation, though."

"Still." Vi scoffs, and I am suddenly surprised that she didn't rip my head off. "The whole point was to be out of his sight, so we don't make ourselves known in his eyes."

"Look, just listen to me, all right?" I whisper. Vi sighs and halfheartedly lets me go on. "I had to go to the bathroom, and when I came out, he was standing there. I started to walk off, but then he started talking to me. It would seem weird if I ran off like an idiot because, at that point, I had to speak to him too. And worst of all, he asked for my name. I, of course, said my name was Marie."

"Well, in that case," Mal says, her red locks falling over her shoulder, "I see why you had to talk to him."

Vi studies me. "What did you guys talk about?"

My heart-rate increases as I recount the flirtatious conversation I had with Jax. Once I finish, I fidget as I watch Mal's eyes light up mischievously. "Quite interesting."

"Oh, stop." I snort. "He's Jax Remington! There's no way I'd want to be with him."

"Maybe not in this situation." Mal shrugs. "But be completely honest with me, though—would you ever be with him *if* the Rich and the Poor didn't exist?"

My cheeks flush red as my eyes simmer onto the ground. "Uh . . . I don't know. What about you?"

She scoffs. "Younger me would've said yes in a heartbeat. But I am completely over him now because he didn't reciprocate what I felt. So, I thought, what's the point in waiting for him?"

"Yes, exactly." I grin. "You deserve better than him."

"Thanks, Blaire." Mal blushes. "But just because I am over him, doesn't mean I don't think he's attractive anymore—because that boy is *beautiful!*"

I let out a laugh. "Okay, I'll agree with you there too."

Once our conversation dies down, we suddenly hear the voice of a very familiar man downstairs. My eyes widen as I send a hurried look at Vi and Mal. Then, we stumble to our feet as we go to the railing and peer over into the center of the Governor's Central.

Everyone looks toward Jax Remington, who is standing at a podium.

He stands with a purpose, his hands grasping the microphone as he runs his fingers through his luscious hair. Everyone crowding around him cheers on as he speaks again. "Thank you for coming here! It means a lot to me, seeing my wonderful supporters gathered at the Governor's Central celebrating not only my father's inauguration, but the progress of this country as well. It honors me, once again, to see the presence of you all. I promise this night will continue to be unforgettable as we embark through the night with drinks, laughter, and fun! Again, thank you so much! God bless America!"

"God bless America!" the crowd roars, the entire room drowning in applause. I notice throughout the entire time that he nears the edge of the stage, seeming like he feels the urgent need to be anywhere else but *there*. There are so many signs present about him not feeling comfortable around the Rich, and at this point, the kidnapping has to occur.

"Guys, what time is it?" Mal whispers.

"It should be around half past nine," I say.

Vi speaks beside me. "Is everyone thinking what I'm thinking?" We all nod our heads. "Okay." She curls her hands into fists, her eyes trained on Jax. "I'll try to find Jeremiah and tell him to begin the conversation with him whenever Jax is alone. You guys find Dylan and stay together by the first-floor hallway on the right but try not to make your presence known."

"We got it," Mal and I both say at the same time.

"Good," Vi says. "I hope this plan doesn't go to shit."

"It won't." Determination clings to my voice. "We just got to stick to the plan and not stray off, all right? Let's do this."

And with that said, we trample down the stairs, tension and adrenaline bursting through our veins.

The plan is now initiated.

15

INITIATE

November 14, 2064
11:58 p.m.

TICK, TOCK. TICK, TOCK.

I watch the hands on the clock attached to the wall move gradually. *Any time now.*

Beside me, Mal paces back and forth, gnawing at her nail. "What's taking him so long?"

"I don't know," I say, leaning against the wall.

We separated from Vi almost two hours ago because she went off to find Jeremiah and tell him to begin the conversation with Jax. Meanwhile, Dylan, Mal, and I were standing in the hallway, but we then told Dylan to venture off to find Jeremiah and eavesdrop on him if he was conversing with Jax. So, Mal and I have been standing here for the past thirty minutes.

Just as I start to complain about Dylan's long departure, he emerges from the corner and prances to us, spewing information out of his mouth.

"About ten minutes ago, I spotted Jeremiah talking to Jax, so I hid behind some wall and managed to hear what they were saying. Jax seemed pretty engaged in the conversation, and there were no people—especially women—climbing over him like hungry ass animals, so he had no distractions." Dylan sucks in a sharp and concise breath. "To sum it all up, incognito Henry McCall is still talking to Jax and he should be pulling in the bastard at any moment now."

We hurriedly make our way to the room. The door creaks open, revealing a majestic room with two beds, a nightstand imposed in the middle, another door adjacent to the bed which I'm guessing leads to the bathroom, a vanity in the front with a dresser beside it, and a heavy door in the far area of the room with the hefty words EMERGENCY EXIT engraved on the top of it. The entire aura of the room is dark and desolate, with its navy green walls and carpet that almost resembles the color black.

"Give me the tools we need," Mal whispers to Dylan. I close the door, make sure to lock it, and my eyes trail over to Dylan, who hands over a rag, a small syringe, and ropes. This is what we need to control Jax when Jeremiah brings him here because there is no doubt he will fight against us.

I sit on the soft bed, feeling the mattress sink beneath me as Mal spreads out the materials in front of us. I feel the warm material of the rag, the thick cotton rubbing against my fingers. I can just picture Jax tied up in front of us, struggling to breathe as I tighten the rag against his mouth. Sweat beads will trickle down his face as he fights against his restraints. All the suffering and pain his father inflicted on us will be transferred to his son so he knows the hell we went through. The hell his father put us through.

"Blaire?"

I snap back to reality as Dylan looks at me with concern, standing in front of me. "Is everything okay?"

"Yeah, I'm fine," I lie, placing the rag next to the other materials. "I'm just thinking about this whole thing we're doing. Is it really going to work?"

"All we can do is hope," Mal answers, sitting by me on the bed. "Once Jeremiah brings Jax in, then we have to *immediately* stick to the plan. Once we do that, then every single one of us will carry him out where Vi should be standing by the emergency exit."

"I'm so nervous," Dylan says, his brown eyes trained to the carpet. "This is *Jax Remington* we're kidnapping here."

"The boy I used to be friends with," Mal murmurs. "Hell, it's so difficult for me to even process the fact that I'm going to meet him again. Will he even remember me?" She shakes her head. "I doubt he will. I mean, he *is* such a high class man. The man is too good for me. Probably why he never liked me back."

I jump to console her, but Dylan speaks before I can. "Look, Mal." He sits beside her, his knee grazing hers. "Jax would be a fool if he didn't remember an amazing woman like you. If anything, you deserve better than him."

Mal's pale cheeks flushes to a deep red color as she pats his shoulder. "Thanks, Dylan."

He smiles. "Of course."

Silence starts to establish amidst us, and that is when I find myself drowning in my thoughts. Here I am now, attempting to kidnap the president's son, when not so long ago I was living a tedious lifestyle. Day and night, I endured an endless cycle of work, and I yearned for a change in my life. I yearned to take down this dreaded government, establish a much better and benevolent system that benefits *everyone* because I know how it feels like to be the lesser-known person. To be the hated. To be the solemn. To be the looked-down-upon. To be the Poor. And for years and years, I dreamed of leaving D.C. with my family, getting past all the Guards and everyone else.

I feel my heart cracking as I reminisce about my brother, Nicolas Cohen. He was tall, lean, had kind eyes, and was my getaway from this disgusting world. We always talked about leaving this place and forming a better environment for everyone because we held very similar thoughts. He was just like me, except older and male. I loved him like nobody else, and I miss him very dearly.

The pain I felt, watching the Guards take away my beloved brother, was so unbearable. I remember clinging onto my mom's arm, tears streaming down my cheeks, barely able to breathe. That burden—that pain—still holds on to me like a leech, and no matter how hard I try, I can't seem to shake it off. I want to take revenge on those stupid Guards by decapitating every single one of them.

Nico was being hauled away for a reason I still am not aware of to this day. Mama and Papa told me that he was taunting one of the Guards and he was being jailed for an unknown amount of time. My younger self was too busy being upset about my older brother instead of comprehending the foreign words my parents spat out. And at that time Em was a tiny baby, so I held onto her very tightly from that point forward. I don't want her to leave, like Nico did. And neither do I want my parents to ever leave me too because they are truly all that I have left.

Knock, knock!

My throat tightens up as we send each other hurried looks. "Is that Jeremiah?"

"Probably!" Dylan exclaims, rushing to open the door. Mal rushes to grab the sterilizer while I grab the rag, my heart pounding so overwhelmingly fast. *Bring it on.*

The door swings open. Silence.

Few moments later, two men stumble into the room. Arms, legs, and chests strike each other. Loud grunts and roars erupt around us.

I loop around them just so I can lock the door because I don't think someone's going to be very pleased when they waltz

109

in here and see a large ex-Guard and the president's son wrestling each other.

Jeremiah's giant paw is on Jax's mouth as he tries to squirm out of his grasp, kicking and punching him. Jax's coat is thrown to the ground as Mal picks it up and slings it over her shoulder. *Smart move.*

Meanwhile, the rest of us stand in panic as Jeremiah snarls, clinging onto Jax as he pushes him onto the bed, his hand still against his mouth. But he lets out a bloodcurdling scream as Jax gnashes his teeth down on his hand.

"This bastard bit me!" Jeremiah yells.

Before their fight can progress any further, Mal storms over to the men, her red hair swaying against her pale shoulders. And before I can even process what happens next, she leans beside Jeremiah and stabs Jax with the sterilizer into the side of his neck. He lets out a yell, his stormy gray eyes flickering over to Mallory with no recognition, but instead with hatred. She frowns, her eyes shifting to the ground as she pushes the needle even farther into his neck.

Jax's fights and protests cease as his body becomes limp underneath Jeremiah, his eyelids shutting. His mouth gapes open, and I take that opportunity to go by the other bed and wrap the cloth around him once Mal has taken the needle out. I feel his soft skin against my hand, his gaping lips grazing over my arm. I brush off any unwanted feelings by tying the rag together tightly, his entire lower part of his face covered in the cloth.

So here we are, in front of Jax, who is wearing fancy clothes and is hosting probably one of the biggest functions D.C.'s ever had.

Except he is also knocked out and half-dead.

We start to pick him up, which is a bit difficult, but we manage to carry him to the emergency exit in no time—probably because of Jeremiah. I sling my hand across his leg as Dylan pushes the heavy emergency exit door open. Cool air rushes in as I spot Vi parked in front of us. Silently, she calls us forward as we rush toward the trunk of the SUV.

Everything happens in a blur.

Stuffing Jax into the trunk, his eyes closed and his breathing uneven.

Shutting the trunk very softly.

Quietly settling in the car, thick silence suffocating us.

Vi revving out of the back and driving onto the D.C. roads.

The movement of the car causing Jax's head to thump against the trunk constantly.

Exiting the Rich sector and venturing to the outskirts.

Seeing the villages and reminiscing over my family.

Mal holding me while Dylan cracks a joke in hopes of lifting the depressing atmosphere.

And finally arriving home. What a wonderful yet rare word that is.

Once the ground consumes us and the SUV is perched on the platform, we climb out of the car—not one word spoken—but the silence buzzing as loudly as ever.

Stealthily, Jeremiah picks up Jax, his body slung over him as he bobs up and down due to his heavy steps. We follow behind, my heart still racing.

The double doors slide open as we walk into our underground home. Jeremiah leads a still-slung-over Jax to the dining table chair that Dylan quickly brought over to the middle of the living room and drops him onto there. His head dips back while the rest of his body is strewn out in different directions, snores erupting out of him.

"What now?" I whisper into the darkness.

"Now, we tie the man up," Vi says. She fetches the ropes from Mal, who runs her fingers along her red wig nervously. Then, Vi's heavy footsteps echo into the large home as she goes up to Jax, eyeing him as she ties him up—his hands bound together very tightly, his legs tied back to the legs of the chair, and a larger tying around his torso just in case if he came up with any clever ideas.

"Mal, how much dosage was there in the sterilizer?" Vi asks.

"Enough to knock him out," Mal says, sending her a smug look.

"Well, we can attest to that." Vi looks over at Jeremiah, who has a cup of water in his hand. She grabs the cup, and before I can even blink, she splashes every droplet of water onto Jax's face, the rag soaking wet. Immediately, his eyes open to the size of saucers, wandering around the foreign environment and the strangers around him.

We stand here, our presence overlooking the cowering privileged boy, whose eyes hold frustration yet agonizing fear at the same time. And for once, we feel powerful in front of the Rich.

Even if it's for a single moment.

16

RAGE

November 15, 2064
1:01 a.m.

JAX'S EYES TRAIL OVER to us and then slowly over to me, radiating with anger. He's realized that precious little Marie is not who he sought to be. That is when he growls and tries to speak against the rag, so all that comes out are muffled cries. Vi groans and runs over to rip it off him.

He heaves in a deep breath and bellows, "Who the hell are you people?"

"We are called the Subversives, and we want your father to step down from his platform." I shrug. "It's as simple as that."

Jax leans forward in his seat, eyeing me down with extreme resentment. "*You. Marie Davis.*"

I look over at Vi, who sends me an acknowledging glance. Then, I look back at Jax, who has a perplexed expression plastered on him. "Actually, the name's Blaire Cohen, and I'm Poor."

Jeremiah and Dylan introduce themselves, allowing Vi to speak next. "My name's Vienna Powers, and everyone calls me

Vi, except *you* can't call me Vi. You haven't gained privileges for that yet, Rich boy." She narrows her eyes at him.

Finally, we all glance toward Mal, who has already peeled her red wig off and green-eyed contacts, resorting back to her blonde hair and blue eyes. She purses her lips, her body filled with fear. "And I'm Mallory Reaves."

He knits his eyebrows together, his silver eyes gleaming with recognition while his face slackens. "Mallory? What are you doing here? We were looking for you *forever* when you disappeared! And this is what you were doing when you were gone, huh? Hanging out with these good-for-nothing Poor people and planning to go against your own—"

"Shut up," she hisses, her blue eyes flashing at him with bitter anger. I can feel her pain that screams from the rooftops. "Don't talk about my friends like that."

"Friends?" Jax scowls.

"Yeah. They are my friends." Her eyes rake over us, bathing in happiness. But as soon as she fixes her vision on Jax, they become cold and furious. "Now, if you want to live, I suggest you listen to us very carefully because you are going to be living with us whether you like it or not." Then, she mutters underneath her breath, "Or whether *we* like it or not."

She turns away from him, closing her eyes and opening them with ease. Finally, her eyes trail over me. "Blaire, would you care to explain to Jax here everything he needs to know?"

My lungs deflate as I look around desperately. Vi nods her head, and so does Jeremiah and Dylan. Jax, however, creases his brows together in irritation.

I release a breath I didn't know I was holding. "Okay. I will."

I step toward him, my body towering over his. I pull my arms behind me and press my lips together. "You see, me and you . . . We're very similar, Mr. Remington. You are kidnapped. I was kidnapped by these people too. You're probably distraught, scared out of your mind, wondering how you got here. Above all else, you are most definitely pissed off. You probably want to slit all our throats—and honestly, I felt the exact same way as you.

"However, while we are similar in those aspects, we are also quite different. You are the son of Tobias Remington, the most privileged man in D.C. You don't have to worry about anything. But me? *Us?*" I gesture toward everyone. "Us Poor people constantly worry about whether we are able to eat three meals a day. We endure laborious periods, and even if we unintentionally or intentionally piss someone off, then it's *goodbye* for us. It sucks, Mr. Remington. It sucks more than anything in this entire dreadful world.

"So, that is when this group was formed, named the Subversives. We follow the Subversion Act, and the word subversion itself means to attempt to take down a higher authority. Think you can connect the dots from there?"

Jax narrows his eyes at me, his expression livid and distraught. "So, let me get this straight. You people decided to kidnap me because you want to take down the government?" He lets out a laugh that holds no trace of humor. "How the hell am I going to be a good help to you guys? I am the last person you'd want to be kidnapping right now."

"You didn't let me finish, dumbass," I snarl, stepping up to him until our bodies are almost close. I see his chest rising in and out with every heavy breath he takes, and I kneel to him, my eyes latched onto his like glue. My challenging gaze eventually has him rolling his eyes, which he then trains on the ground.

"As I was saying . . . We *first* planned to take down the government. The plan these people presented to me was amazing. However, I eventually raised the idea of kidnapping you because I decided to shift our focus from the government onto your father. If he crumbles down, then so will the government, then so will the Rich people. Those who want to be on our side, they are more than welcome to. We just want to take down your father, Jax. So, us kidnapping you will help us achieve our goals."

He grins, shaking his head and laughing. "Again, even if I wanted to I still wouldn't be of much help. I just do whatever I please."

"Oh, are you sure about that?"

I whirl my head around to Vi, who drums her fingers on her chin in mocking thought. "Because a little birdie told me that you despise your father."

Jax narrows his eyes onto Mal. "What is this I'm hearing?"

"Just the truth," she says nonchalantly. I get up from my position and walk back to where I was. Jax exchanges a glance with me, which holds nothing but seething silence.

"What exactly did you tell them?"

"That you wish to run away, since you despise every single bit of your father." Mal smiles.

To our surprise, he suddenly growls, ramming his body against the chair he is tied down to. "Get me out of here! Please! I don't belong here!"

"Shut it," Mal says, her words drenched with anger. "I know you want to be here. I know you want to take down your father. I know you want to be a part of the Subversives so you can pursue the dreams you've always wanted to. I know you do."

"No, I don't." He frowns, continuing to fight against the ropes tied around his body. "I belong with my father. I belong with the Rich, like I always have. I don't know where you're getting this bullshit from because—"

Mal goes and slaps him, a loud crack resonating into the air. I hold my hand up to my mouth, and I see from the corner of my eye that everyone else seems to be equally shocked as me.

"Don't lie to me, you bastard. I remember you telling me that when we were hanging out in the garden that day. Our parents were in a business meeting, and they told us to play outside. We walked around the garden, and we delved into one of our many conversations about running away. We both hated our parents and the Rich in general—you *know* that, Jax. I know that, too.

"Now, it is your choice. You can continue to be a nightmare, whine, or scream and shout or whatever, but that won't change anything. And if you even dare to leave, then Jeremiah won't hesitate to strangle you to death."

Jeremiah cracks his knuckles while sending him a death glare.

"And I sure won't hesitate to kill you," Mal says. "You are here now, whether you like it or not. I know you're privileged, so you're used to getting whatever you want, but in this case . . . You're not. And I think you can deal with that."

She walks away, her heels pounding against the floor as they decrease in sound. Her body disappears into the dark hallway, and I hear a distant closing of a door.

Silence.

Dylan clears his throat. "That was . . . something else."

"Yeah, I agree with you there," Jeremiah whispers. "Vi, what now?"

She seems to be speechless after everything that happened too. "I don't know. I guess we take him away to the underground room. I already have the place set up." Vi looks at Jeremiah. "You got the handcuffs?"

He nods his head, pulling them out of his pocket.

"Good," Vi says. "You will be watching Jax first. Then it'll be me, then Blaire, then . . ." She winces. "Maybe not Mallory today. So I guess we will wrap the night up with you, Dylan."

The idea of monitoring him has bile rising at the back of my throat. For one whole hour I will be watching *Jax*? The smug look on his face does nothing to appease my increasing hatred for him.

Once the shifts get finalized, Jeremiah goes over to the secret underground entrance, pulls open that segment of the floor, for which Jax exclaims, "Damn, what the hell? Did you just . . . lift that up and . . ." He rubs his forehead. "Please tell me this is just some big nightmare."

As he continues to ramble, Jeremiah walks over to the back of Jax's chair, grabs both of his hands and loosens the ropes interlinking and connecting around Jax. They all fall from the ground as he rises to his feet. He stumbles around, his eyes opening and closing animatedly, but then his balance revels once Jeremiah grabs his wrist and pulls him forward. Jax doesn't say a single word the entire time, his expression completely ambiguous. And for the remainder of his time here, however long that may be, I am determined to make him crack. To solve the puzzle known as his emotions. And help us advance toward victory.

"Climb down here." Jeremiah points down the hole, grasping his wrist tightly.

Jax leans over, gets a good look of the vast darkness, and shakes his head. "I'd rather not."

"You don't have a choice in this matter."

"Well, yeah, um"—he chuckles—"God knows what you people are keeping down there."

Jeremiah clenches his jaw as the grasp on Jax's wrist visibly tightens. He winces. "Whoa, what the hell, man?"

"Do you want me to throw you down there instead?" The ex-Guard threatens. "Just to have your body be a disgusting pile of guts at the very bottom?"

Jax's eyebrows get pushed up to his forehead. "Okay, okay, wait—*fine*, I'll go." He glances down to Jeremiah's large and strong hand encircling him. "Only when you relax on my wrist." Reluctantly, he loosens his grip, and Jax says, "Finally. Jesus, I'm pretty sure I heard my bones cracking."

Moments later, Jax begins to climb down the ladder, and Jeremiah follows behind him, right before stuffing the handcuffs in his pockets. I feel horribly bad for Jeremiah since he's the first one to deal with our annoying detainee.

The rest of us, afterwards, set to go to sleep for the little time we can, and that is when I realize that from here on out, everything we do is in our hands. We need to be cautious because embarking on the wrong path will lead to chaos . . . which can also lead to death.

17

DETAINEE

November 15, 2064
4:59 a.m.

I WAKE UP AND look around the darkened room consuming me in its presence. While I lay here, gazing at the ceiling, I feel the soothing fabric of the blanket coil around me, protecting me from the dangers outside.

I turn around to the other side, where I see Mal sound asleep. I think back to what happened tonight when Mal chastised Jax. She left him in order to find herself, and there she was, yelling at her childhood friend. I found it weirdly empowering, not just for her, but for me as well.

Because now I am about to go monitor the human and male form of Hell.

I peel the blanket off me and place my feet on the carpet. I try not to disturb the others, especially Vi, who just came in and slept, and tiptoe toward the marginally opened door.

The cool air from the vents hit my skin as I walk into the hallway. The lights are dim, and I curl my arms around me as I shiver. Wearing a flimsy little black tank top with gray shorts was not the wisest decision.

Once I reach the living room, I kneel by the specific segment of the floor and pull it up, roars of arctic air whisking into the environment. I sling my foot onto the ladder and slowly bring my body down into the engulfing darkness.

Several moments later, I step onto the hard concrete ground and turn around.

In front of me is Jax, staring at the books showcased around the large meeting table. I am first alarmed, seeing that the weapons are in full-view of him on the other end of the room and that he can easily grab one and shoot up the whole place, but I immediately remember that they are all encased within bullet-proof and possibly *atomic bomb* proof glass. So, I breathe out in great relief.

I slowly walk toward him, studying his puzzling manner, how his hand-cuffed hands are resting against his chest. How his torso is stiff and straight, not even seeming to twitch in any directions. How he just stands there in one place, so still to the point that I question whether he's alive.

I clear my throat. At that, Jax turns around, visibly surprised at my appearance. From this distance, I can see his face change into a distasteful expression. "Oh, it's you." He scoffs and turns around.

Sighing and praying to God that this unfortunate encounter ends as soon as possible, I walk toward him, each step marked deliberately. I want to let him know that I'm not afraid of him. That his quips and immoral manners don't faze me.

I'm only here to monitor him.

I decide that if I'm going to be here for a full sixty minutes, then I might as well start some sort of conversation with him. So, I say, "Have you gotten any sleep?"

Jax turns around again and chuckles. "Do you honestly think I'm going to be able to sleep in a place like *this*?" He looks around the entire room, bathed in dark concrete walls and flooring. "And I've got to say, the interior designing is horrible. I mean, if you're going to house me here, might as well make it a bit more visually pleasing."

I clench my fists in order to stop myself from knocking his teeth out. "I don't care about your opinions."

"Didn't you ask me if I got any sleep?" He raises one eyebrow. "Sounds like you care about my opinions to me."

"I only did that to make conversation."

"Okay, well, if we're just making conversation here"—Jax sits down at the head of the table abruptly—"then let's make conversation."

"Are you kidding me—"

"Why did you say your name is Marie Davis?" He cocks his head. "When, in reality, it's not?"

I grumble underneath my breath and reluctantly sit at the other end of him. All we have between is a large slab of the oblong table. "Look, I had to do that."

"No, you did not." Jax scowls. "You could've just told me your actual name instead. There was no point in developing a persona if you were just going to kidnap me in the end."

"Well—okay, I apologize for that." I let out an exasperated breath.

"Why, thank you." He snorts. "You know, I hate to say it, but you may be the nicest person I've encountered yet."

I lean forward. "What do you mean?"

"Well, the first one, or the really scary dude, threatened to push me down this goddamn place. Thank God I complied in the end because otherwise I wouldn't exactly be intact right now. And, just when that really scary dude left, another scary person came in, except it was this woman that was extraordinarily more terrifying than the first one. I mean, just look at this shit." He suddenly points to a huge bruise on his jaw that I had not seen before. "She punched me in the freaking jaw when I said that I wanted water! Last time I checked, wanting to be hydrated is not a crime."

The words seem to flow out of his mouth so effortlessly, every gesture and expression he makes completely animated. I just sit here in awe, hearing this man go on and on about his rights as a human being to have a mere sip of water. It appalls me that even in this situation he still finds a way to make everything about himself. What a classic Rich person move.

Once he finishes, he takes a deep breath and leans back against his chair, his gray eyes landing on me. The emptying pits of his pupils tear me down, scrutinizing every inch of me. His strong jaw is clenched, the scar on his cheek shining against the dim lights, and his hands cuffed together scrape to the side. That is when I notice the dress shirt he had on for the party, except it's mildly torn and damaged. His hair is unkempt, one strand inching down his forehead. And as I study this man, I still can't seem to swallow the fact that he's right in front of me. In the goddamn flesh.

I pinch myself just to make sure this isn't some horrendous nightmare.

Moments later, he clears his throat. "So, what is the plan for tonight? Are we just going to keep on staring at each other like this?"

My fists uncurl, preparing to jump out of my seat and strangle him, but I eventually decide to compose myself. "No. You are actually going to sleep now."

"I'm telling you, I absolutely cannot sleep in a place like this." Jax scrunches his nose. "Besides, I am probably slightly drunk as well, so sleep is definitely out of the question."

"You're drunk?" I cock my head. Probably explains why he's talking so much.

"Yeah," he says, looking at me as if I'm the dumbest person in the world. "Who the hell goes to, or let alone *hosts* a party just to not get drunk in the end?"

"Well, I wouldn't know." My voice is pricked with revulsion. "Your father doesn't really allow our people to do much, let alone live in peace."

At that, Jax lets out a short laugh. "I knew this was coming."

"What?"

"You bringing up my father." He looks down at the table. "You're now going to bring up every single thing he's done in hopes to miraculously bring me on your side, aren't you?"

"No, I'm not—"

"Or that you think I'm easily going to reveal all his secrets to you and let you guys live in peace and harmony?" He pauses. "Do you really think it's going to work that way? Because it's not."

"Look, you are not going to give me your attitude," I say, my voice rising in both pitch and volume.

He looks amused. "Is that your attempt to seem scary? Because it's not really working. Maybe try working on your posture? You kind of shaking doesn't really terrify me."

That's it.

I scramble from my chair, charge over to him, nothing except the intent to hurt him *very* badly appearing in my mind.

He suddenly jumps up from his chair and looks concerned yet charmed at the same time. "What are you doing?"

"About to kill you," I huff, charging at him. He looks so much like Tobias. And I hate it. I hate *him*.

I run up to him and barricade him with my body against the concrete wall next to the library. My chest digs into his hard torso, and he looks down at me, clearly not amused with my determination to murder him, and probably not affected by my vicious look either.

He smiles. "Is this supposed to be scary too?"

"God, can you please just shut up!" I yell. "Everything you do is just so . . ."

"Irritating?"

"Yes!" I grumble.

Jax chuckles. "Well, if it makes you feel any better, I'll probably be a lot more easier to deal with once the alcohol in me subsides."

Silence.

I sigh and cross my arms over my chest, defeat washing over me. "You're really not going to sleep, are you?"

He shakes his head. "Nope."

I curse underneath my breath and notice the way he looks and feels and seems to be different compared to when I see him on television. On television he's so distinguished and put-together, every step and movement he takes laced with purpose. But now? He's overwhelmingly messy. Disconcerting. Quite obnoxious. And just thinking of the fact that he flirted with me just a few hours ago, our bodies so close to each other and his breath tickling my skin . . . It makes me feel queasy. That I even allowed a man like him to talk to me like that. Someone associated with the enemy.

"So, what *is* the plan for tomorrow?"

I snap out of my thoughts. Jax pushes his eyebrows up, still pressed against the wall and still finding this whole situation to be humorous.

"For us it's just going to be a normal day. But for you?" I pretend to think. "You will be interrogated the entire day."

"Yeah, in hopes to get some information out of me?" He snorts. "Not going to happen."

"You really don't have a choice in this matter, you know that, right?"

"Oh, I think I'm aware of that now. I just have absolutely nothing to say."

Confusion is all I feel. "What do you mean?"

Suddenly, his expression isn't light-hearted anymore; instead, it's masked with solemn and regret. "Um . . . Forget about it."

I look up at him. "Why?"

"Just forget about it." There's an urge to his voice as he tries to push past me, but I hold him back, my eyes desperate for some answers.

"What are you talking about?"

"God, you're such a nosy woman," he says, rolling his eyes.

"Answer my damn question—"

"Also, why are you pressing me up against the wall like this?" He smirks. "If you wanted me then you could've just told me, Cohen."

Heat unexpectedly creeps up my neck, surprised at his nickname for me. "No, I-I *don't* want you. No. Not at all." I pause in hopes to compose myself. "Just . . . Answer my question. Why should I forget about it?"

He adjusts his jaw. "Because it's none of your business, okay? My personal life is *personal* for a reason."

"Not in this situation."

And what he does next scares me to the core.

Jax veers his head down to me, his face alarmingly close to mine. Besides his unlikable personality, his features are absolutely flawless. Narrow, masculine eyes. Sharp jaw that can slice through paper. Clear and radiant tan skin. A facial structure that eerily seems to be carved like a Greek sculpture itself. Even though he's definitely real—definitely in my presence—his face is the only part of him that doesn't seem real. There's no way a face like that can be made from mere humans. It had to be made in a laboratory.

The sudden curl to his lip is frightening, and the way he tears me down with his threatening eyes . . . It makes me cast my eyes down to the ground.

"Listen here, Cohen." His voice is low, barely a whisper. "I didn't ask to be here. I was just innocently partying until you guys kidnapped me. Obviously I don't want to talk to you. Obviously I don't want to talk to *anyone* here. I think you can understand why." Jax then leans down to my ear, his mouth so near—needlessly and terrifyingly near. "And I do have something I could share with you guys. But I won't."

I dare to look at him. "Say it."

He shakes his head. "It is something I truly cannot say."

"Why?" My voice comes out as a choke, so desperate for information. Something to help us destroy Tobias.

Jax looks at me, his eyes an inventory of buried secrets and pain. I can see it in him. He's transparent. And what he says next almost solidifies what Mal told us about him.

"Because he would kill me if I did."

18

FIERCE

November 15, 2064
8:03 a.m.

EVERYONE GATHERS AROUND THE oblong table in the underground room—as if we weren't underground enough. Vi's at the head of the table, her slender face masked in contemplation. Jax is next to her, still handcuffed and significantly quieter. Mal is in front of him, sipping green tea in her mug and avoiding eye contact with her ex-best friend. Jeremiah is next to her, barely able to fit in the chair due to his massive size. Dylan is next to him, drumming his fingers against the coffee table and seeming just as concerned as us.

And next to Jeremiah is me, still thinking about last night.

I was in great shock when Jax almost revealed to me his life at home and especially how his father perceives him. It seems as if his loopy state of mind allowed some unwanted sayings to slip from his mouth, which is why I'm grateful for Jax being slightly drunk. But, as soon as the words came out, he refused to say more. I was so *close* to knowing something we can use against Tobias, but it just ended up slipping from my fingers. And because of that, we might just have to resort to other methods to put Jax to great use.

After my frustrating encounter with him, we eventually separated and went to the opposite sides of the room. I stood by the books, analyzing all of the preserved works and counting which ones I've read; Jax went to the far corner on the far side and attempted to fall asleep, but he ended up failing and decided to pace back and forth, murmuring to himself for possibly the remainder of my stay there.

Once my shift ended, I left and embarked to find Dylan since his shift is right after mine. I also told him that Jax was going to be annoying. The look he sent me was hysterical.

But now, as I look over at Jax, I see that he hasn't spoken a word since we all climbed down here. Without a word he went to the table, sat himself, and has been extraordinarily obedient for the time being. And this is in great contrast to last night, when he talked my ear off due to his unnecessary comments and remarks.

I guess Jax was right. He *is* less annoying once the alcohol wears off.

We are all sitting here currently, ready to begin round one of Jax's interrogation. God knows how many days or weeks this whole process is going to take, but hopefully he complies and it doesn't take too long so we can get into motion at least before the end of the month. We just want to start off with a slow and simple process, and if things don't seem to work, then we will have to make the interrogation increasingly more difficult for him.

But one step at a time, right?

Silence falls through the air, and Mal disposes of it by saying, "Good morning, everyone. How did you guys sleep last night?"

"Wondrously." Dylan grins.

"I agree too," Vi says. "How about you, Blaire?"

I nod my head once. "It was good." Everyone else pitches in their answer, except one person.

"How about you, Jax?" Jeremiah says.

He sighs and leans back. "Should I tell the truth or lie?"

"The truth," I blurt out.

"Okay." He sets his lips into a straight line. "To be honest, I've slept terribly. Why—did you expect me to sleep like a baby?"

"We never said that," Jeremiah says. "We just want to check in on you. Mental health goes above all else, and you are a part of us now—whether you like it or not." I can tell he is struggling to be nice to him.

Jax laughs. "Says the guy who threatened to throw me down a hole last night."

He clenches his jaw. "We were frustrated with you at that time. We now hope to talk amicably with you."

"Only because you want to interrogate me." Jax looks at Jeremiah in great humor. "You believe that in order to get the best and unbiased answers from me, you want to baby me and make sure I don't get irritated."

"Congratulations, you figured it out, smart-ass," Vi growls, her patience running very thin. "But you do not have the authority to talk to us like that. Not here, at least. So why don't you zip your mouth shut before I shoot your balls off?"

Surprisingly, he casts his eyes to the ground, his face reddening. Five excruciatingly long seconds later, Mal says, "All right, well . . . Now that everyone has answered my question, I guess we better start off with the interrogation." She looks at Vi. "Shall we begin?"

Vi nods. Then, she looks over at Jax in one swift motion. "In this interrogation session, you have three simple rules." She holds one finger up. "Number one, the most important rule of all, don't talk back to me. Obviously. Number two"—another one goes up—"I don't want to hear your sarcastic or irritating remarks. And lastly . . ." She brings one last finger up, her eyes narrowed at him. "You must answer every question truthfully. And if you do not follow these rules, then you will be interrogated more, except each session will be increasingly worse. That's why I advise you to enjoy your luxury now, in case you were to screw it up for yourself."

"What are you going to do if I mess up?" Jax says in a bored tone.

"Bad things."

He chuckles. "Thanks for that totally specific answer."

"Rule number two, broken." At the speed of lightning, Vi leans over the corner of the table and wraps her hand around Jax's neck. His eyes are widened as she squeezes tightly, her face completely neutral. "There's one thing you should know about me, Rich boy. I never lie. If I say something, I mean it. It's as simple as that." She arches her eyebrow, satisfyingly watching his face turn bright red. "Nod if you understand."

He nods his head rapidly. She lets go, and he intakes large gulps of air, clinging onto the table.

Vi says, "Are you ready to begin now? And do you take into consideration the rules and the consequences if you do not adhere?"

Jax adjusts his positioning, his taut muscles clinging to the dirty dress shirt on him. "I do," he says reluctantly, clearing his throat afterwards.

"Good," she says. "Let's begin." She leans back in her seat, looking up at the ceiling. "What plans does your father have for D.C.?"

He laughs. "Damn, you're just jumping right in, huh—"

She glares at him, curling her fists tightly. We all look at each other, worried about how this could possibly go.

Jax immediately restates his answer. "U-um . . . He just wants to better the environment. And provide guidance for everyone."

Vi raises her eyebrows.

"Okay, maybe not everyone," he rephrases. "Just the Rich."

"Why is that?"

"Because he believes Poor people are not as good as the Rich."

"And what's his reasoning behind that?"

"Well, he never really told me, so I'm just going to assume it's because the Poor earn less than the Rich."

The intensity from Vi's eyes is enough to make a man cower to the ground. "Now, tell me why the Poor earn less than the Rich."

"Uh . . ." He adjusts himself. "Because they just do?"

"Okay, this is where things don't make sense." Vi's eyebrows furrow. "Statistically, the Poor work more than the Rich. They are the laborers. They, in actuality, are the ones keeping this country together. Not the Rich. You people just sit around, sipping expensive wine from your even more expensive glasses and expect the world to fall at your feet. So things don't really seem to add up here. How is it that the ones who work significantly more than the others earn less?"

Jax's face is neutral, but his eyes are wavering around in question. I can't tell whether he's finally understanding our situation, or if he's known from before but forced himself to stomach certain lies about society. And considering what Mal said as well, how she and Jax used to share everything together, I feel as if those same feelings are still swarming around in his mind, but he's trained himself to shove it all away and deal with the life he has now. And I believe, with enough interrogation and persuasion, we can bring those buried notions out.

Vi continues on. "Do you know why I believe your father only helps the Rich? It's because he's a self-conceited and discriminatory asshole that is way too worried about his reputation. And you're just like him, you know that, right? You worry about your reputation too. If you didn't, you would've at least been like Mallory, who had the actual balls to stand her ground. That's why you're just like your father. You both are a bunch of cowards."

"Okay, I get it, all right?" Jax chuckles lowly. "I am a big fat coward for not standing up against my father. I totally get it. But what impact do I really have, huh? I'm only his son. If I say anything, I'll either be ignored or completely criticized. I don't want to deal with that shit. I'd rather just keep my mouth shut and go on with life."

"At least you have the luxury to do that," Vi says. "Many Poor people die everyday from just *breathing* wrong. There are kids out there who don't have a single family member left alive and they've had to fend for themselves ever since." Her voice cracks for a split second, but she immediately clears her throat, straightening her posture. "Accept your privilege, Rich boy. Know that you are lucky to be born as a Rich, not as a Poor."

Jax sighs and looks at the table, his face hues of conflicted emotions. Sweat bathes on his forehead, and unruly strands of hair stretch onto his eyes, his gray eyes that are layered in inescapable and groundbreaking revelations. His muscles constrict beneath his collared shirt, veins appearing on his forearms as his fingers writhe. It's as if I'm analyzing an unknown creature, someone of bewildering movements. Everything he does or says is puzzling. Does he agree with us? Wants to agree with us, but can't? Or he genuinely doesn't give two shits about us? I don't know anything anymore.

Mal breaks the silence yet again. "Are there any more questions you'd like to ask him, Vi?"

She bites her lip, colored hair framing her pale face. "Sure, why not?" She looks over at him, contemplates, and then says, "Was it true?"

He breaks from his trance. "What?"

"What Mallory told us about you?"

Jax immediately scoffs and shakes his head to himself. "Can't answer."

"Yes, you can," Mal grumbles.

"Actually, I can't." Jax winces. "Sorry to burst your bubble."

She looks at him for the first time today. "Why do you have to be so difficult? Just answer her question."

"And don't forget rule number three." Vi cracks her neck.

"Screw your rules," Jax growls, but his body language points toward the fact that he's scared out of his mind. "If I am not comfortable answering a question, then I am not going to answer."

"All right." Vi slowly gets up from her seat and looks at Jax. The look on her face makes my throat tighten. "Get up."

He narrows his eyes, mutters to himself, and slowly gets up. My face freezes up as I notice his body slowly angling to the other side of the room. I am immediately alarmed.

At that, Jeremiah shouts, "Vi, watch out!"

As soon as those words escape from his mouth, Jax makes a run for the weaponry showcased in the bullet-proof glasses. He clenches his fists and rams his back into the glass, but the glass makes a dull sound—not budging a damn bit—and Jax crumbles to the ground, wincing to himself.

Slowly, but so intimidatingly, Vi strides over to a fallen Jax, who stares at her in fear. As he scrambles up to his feet, desperate to not be in her wrath, she brings up a hand and says, "If you move, then I will pluck each and every single one of your eyelashes out."

His chest rises in and out as he stills, not even daring to blink.

Once Vi reaches him, she gestures for him to get up. The cold glare in her eyes is hypnotizing as he wordlessly gets up, humiliation smeared all over him.

And then, in the fraction of a second, she kicks him in the crotch.

He doubles over to the ground with a resounding *thud* and, with a pained tone, he yells, "What the f—"

"Today at seven in the evening," Vi says, her face as hard as stone, "I expect you to be in much better behavior for your second interrogation. And since you did not comply with my rules, horrible punishment will be waiting for you."

Silence. "Jeremiah?"

He shoots up from his seat. "Yes?"

Vi gestures to Jax. "Take him to the shower upstairs and freshen him up. It's okay if you take his handcuffs off; as long as he's clean and acts like an obedient person. After he's done, he should be back here, alone, and thinking about his actions. I hope to not encounter many issues with you for the second round. If I do, then things are just going to keep getting worse for you."

She walks away, goes to the ladder, slings her foot to the first leg, and says, "And make sure you shower well. You look terrible."

TORMENT

November 15, 2064
6:55 p.m.

"YOU READY TO SEE how this goes?" Mal nudges me.

"Oh, I'm so ready," I say, looking down into the gaping hole. "This interrogation could honestly go either really smoothly or really badly."

"With no in between, right?"

"Yep." I chuckle. "We'll just have to see how Mr. Remington acts today."

"My intuition tells me he's going to act like a bitch," Jeremiah says suddenly, kneeling next to us. "Not really surprised, though. When I was monitoring him last night, I had to tune him out in order to not go insane. The dude was talking way too much."

I snort. "Because he was drunk."

"He was?" Jeremiah and Mal both ask simultaneously.

"Yeah, he told me that. I first found his talkative and loopy personality very annoying and very unnecessary, but he started to open up to me and almost told me about his father's—"

"Are you guys ready to go now?"

Vi stands near the opening, followed by a grinning Dylan. Compared to the rest of us, he's very excited to see how this encounter goes with Vi and Jax, considering how she beautifully kicked him where it hurt the most and left him alone in his own pain and misery. We all then climbed upstairs afterwards, both astounded yet entertained by what occurred.

For the time being, we oversaw D.C. news, and obviously everyone is in great shock over Jax's disappearance. There are already thousands of missing posters lining the city, and the whole situation is so traumatizing to the Rich that they've already started to propose theories as to why and how the beloved Jax Remington could ever vanish.

Which is why we need to get a move on with this interrogation so we can focus on Tobias himself—instead of his disobedient and ignorant son.

It takes us a couple of minutes for everyone to climb down the ladder, and once we do, we are shocked by what we see.

Jax is hunched over in the far corner, huddled into a ball as he murmurs to himself. As his blank gray eyes land on us, he immediately scrambles to his feet and sets his shoulders back. I notice that he's changed out of his formal clothes into a loose black shirt, gray sweatpants, and is now completely barefoot. His face looks much cleaner compared to when we last saw him, and his hair is somewhat neatly combed. The only thing that hasn't changed is the fact that his handcuffs are still on.

Until Vi says, "Jeremiah is going to take your handcuffs off now."

Jeremiah looks at her alarmingly. "What? Why?"

"Just trust me."

In the end, he always listens to Vi. So, he takes a deep breath in and reluctantly goes up to Jax, fishing for the key in his pocket. He brings it up in his large paw and takes Jax's wrists roughly. A few moments later, he manages to release the handcuffs from him, for which he breathes out in relief.

Then, Vi walks forward, sets the equipment on the oblong table, places a wooden chair in the middle of the room, and slowly looks at him. "Come to me."

I can hear Jax gulping from here as he trudges to her. His hands seem to be shaking as his eyes are locked to the ground in fear, which I don't exactly blame him for since the most terrifying person in the world is in front of him.

Vi shoves her hands into her pockets, narrows her eyes at him, and takes a deep breath in.

"Take your shirt off."

His eyes are lit with amusement.

"Oh, get your head out of your ass. I'd rather eat live cockroaches than have anything to do with you."

As she waits for him to do what she said, he grumbles and lifts his shirt up over his head, revealing his strong and hard body. I attempt to stray my eyes away, but his tan and meticulously carved chest makes it very impossible to do so. His muscles move in gracious ways as he lets his shirt fall to the floor, his body towering over Vi—but not too much. I'm guessing Jax must be four inches taller than Vi and seven in comparison to me.

Finally, she points to the chair. "Sit there."

Without a word, he walks over to the chair and sits himself. His chest rises in and out as he clenches his fists, terrified for what's to come.

Vi looks over at us. "Dylan?"

He pushes his glasses up. "Yes?"

"Give me the ropes. And Mal?"

"Yes, Vi?"

"Grab the equipment."

As the two of them venture for their designated items, Jeremiah comes over to me, confusion etched in his eyes. "Hey, Blaire?"

"Yeah?"

"What did you mean by him revealing something to you? When we were up there?"

"Oh." I take a deep breath in. "Well, he was about to reveal something to me about his father before he caught himself. I guess he didn't let his intoxication get the best of him."

"Damn." Jeremiah crosses his arms. "You were so close."

"I know," I say. "Let's just hope Vi's technique brings out what he was going to say."

"Yeah." He sighs. "What do you think the torture technique is going to be?"

"I don't know," I say, confused as to why Vi refused to tell us about it. "Hopefully it's effective."

"Yep." He clicks his tongue. "Hopefully."

We walk over to the others, and I watch in awe as Vi effortlessly ties Jax's hands to the arms of the chair with the ropes Dylan brought over for her. Finally, she goes and ties his ankles to the legs of the chair, and I watch Jax, how he hangs his head low and refuses to look at any one of us. Not only is he not aware of what's to come, but we aren't either. This night can end in so many different ways—either in Jax finally being a truthful human being and allying with us, or him refusing to say a single word, leading to even more torture.

I sure do wonder what Vi's torture technique is.

My breathing evens out as Mal gives a handheld black machine to Vi. She holds it in her hands, adjusting the three gray knobs on it. Then, she grabs a bunch of wires from the table, unravels them all, and attaches two of them to Jax's temples and three on his naked torso. Large white dots grasping his skin transpire into the thin black wires that are soon plugged into the black machine.

Once she sets everything up, she steps back, clutching the device in her hand. "Shall we begin, everyone?"

We all say a simultaneous "yes."

"Wonderful." Vi almost grins. "This is how the interrogation is going to work. So listen closely.

"I am going to ask you a series of questions. However, if you lie for any of them, the machine will detect it and immediately electrocute you through the wires and the nodes attached to your body. Every question you get wrong will lead to an increase of pain. In the beginning, it will be a tiny zap. But as time goes on, you may end up being dead." She shrugs. "Who knows.

"And, if I were you, I would let my ego subside and focus on staying alive—which I know you want to. The decision is all yours, but make sure to choose wisely." Her lips press together. "Say that you understand."

"I understand." His deep voice cracks very slightly, and his chest constricts as I see lines forming on his forehead. I can tell he's scared for his life.

"All right." She pauses, her expression dangerous. "Your interrogation begins now."

The air is immediately thick with silence. Jax's mouth is agape, his eyes narrowed in thought as his breathing becomes steady. I can tell he's forcing himself to remain calm because this machine can probably detect the slightest of hesitation. And getting electrocuted? I never heard of a torture technique like that because the Guards only kill people on the spot with their guns; they don't feel the need to torture—unless it's a truly heinous wrongdoing. So I have no idea of how this is going to go—how torturous this machine really is.

Vi takes a deep breath and tucks a few strands of hair behind her ears. "Let's start with something nice and easy—just to warm you up. Why did you throw the party at Governor's Central?"

Jax presses his lips together, contemplating what to say. "Because my father got inaugurated."

Nothing happens.

"Were you told to throw this party? Or did you do it of your free will?"

Long, strenuous seconds of silence pass. Jax closes his eyes and slings his head back against the neck of the chair. "I was told to."

I involuntarily move forward, so close and so determined to cracking the code. To solving the puzzle. To pursuing pure happiness.

"Why were you told to?"

"My parents require me to be engaged in my father's political life. They say it'll help me prepare for when I become president."

"And do you want to become president?"

He squares his shoulders, leering his jaw to the side. His gray eyes shine against the dim lights, landing on an object in the far distance. He contemplates what to say, probably weighing the consequences over his dignity.

Finally, he says, "Yes."

It all happens in a matter of seconds.

Veins appear on his forearms and reach up to his neck, and he grits his teeth, squeezing his eyes shut as he lets out a strained growl. Lines of electricity seem to be traveling into his skin, and his entire chest is erratically rising in and out, carved muscles bulging as he squeezes his fists in great torment.

And the entire time, Vi looks at Jax satisfyingly, her eyes shimmering in delight.

Seconds later, she switches the knob off. He lets out a long and heavy sigh, strands of his dark wet hair clinging to his forehead. His eyes are begging for mercy, and his lips open and close, no sound or words seeming to come out.

She cocks her head. "You want to try that again?"

Jax rolls his neck, attempting to compose himself. It seems as if he's in an internal battle with himself as he struggles to say, "N-no. I don't . . . d-don't want to be president."

She leans forward, clearly riveted. "Why?"

"Because, uh . . ." He bites his lip. "It's not for me. I-I have no desire to be president."

"So why don't you just tell your parents that?"

There is a long pause. I bring my hands together and hold them up to my lips, praying that Jax will just out himself already. Prevent any pain for himself. Accept who he is and move on.

There has to be a damn good reason why he's struggling so much to tell the truth.

His hands shake just as much as his voice does. "I . . . can't. Because my parents expect me to follow every s-single word they say. If I don't . . . Then I w-will be known as a disappoint-ment." He looks down at the ground. "T-they already think of me a-as one."

"Why?" Vi demands again.

"Because I'm not the p-perfect and ideal son they want me to be! Th-that's why I am struggling to do this. That's why I buried my . . . bad thoughts away."

"So let's get onto the question we left off on then. Was what Mallory said about you true?"

He closes his eyes at the same time Mal looks at him. She is desperate too. She is irredeemably willing to prove herself right.

Jax opens his eyes, and they land on her. His body slackens as he says, "Yes."

My heart mends and prospers at the same time. *Finally.*

Vi taps her finger against the metal body of the black machine. "And do those thoughts still apply to you?"

"Jesus, this sucks."

"No commentary," she scolds him. "Just answer the damn question. Do you still hate the Rich and your father, more specifically?"

He sucks in a sharp breath. He taps his foot against the hard concrete floor, his jaw sharp, and the scar on his cheek glinting. The history behind that scar is unknown too. Pretty much everything about him is unknown.

Jax doesn't say anything for a good ten seconds. The wait is so excruciating, so harrowing to the point that I begin to lose my patience. Vi especially does too as she snarls, "I don't have all day here."

"Yes."

The answer is sharp and jarringly concise.

He means it. It comes from his soul and valleys out into branches of verity, buried and unfamiliar truths. Even he's stunned with the fervor latched onto his answer, his eyebrows furrowing in thought. And, just as suspected, no jolts of electricity shoot into him. He's completely unharmed.

"You still think the same as when you and Mallory were friends? Do you still feel that same hatred?"

"Oh, c'mon. Don't make me say it again."

Vi glares at him, unflinching and unwilling.

He creates an indeterminable sound that is a mixture of clicking his tongue and his teeth. Almost like a disappointed sound. "Fine. Yeah. I . . . still feel that hatred. Same goddamn hatred."

Insurmountable excitement filters into my veins. *Good,* I think to myself. *This is significant progress. Now we can get to the even more imperative stuff, which is the secret drunk Jax almost revealed to me.*

I look around us and see that everyone's just as ecstatic as I am. This is a historic moment—of course people are pleasantly surprised. Jax Remington just told us that he hates the Rich. The government. His *father.* It may have been forced, but he said it. And he meant it. What's done is done. Irreversible and definitely undeniable.

I just need to know the details of his father now. Every single little plan he has set for D.C. . . . needs to be revealed. I am a hungry bear ravaging for prey, desperate for nourishment. And I will get my physical and mental closure.

Vi curls her lip up and slowly smiles. It's appalling to see something so rare appear on her face, something that definitely suits her, but barely reveals itself. "Damn, that wasn't so hard, was it? That's all you had to say." She presses her lips together. "Now, why *did* you take so long to say that? You could've just saved the trouble for yourself earlier on."

He narrows and brings his eyes to the ceiling, jutting his jaw forward. "I'm so used to shoving and hiding my feelings away that . . . I do it without thinking at this point. I can't come to terms with it sometimes either. So I'd rather just . . . not think about it."

She contemplates for a moment. "Okay. I get that." Silence. "Couple more questions. Do you—"

"Wait, Vi?"

Vi looks at me in slight irritation. "Yes, Blaire?"

I clear my throat, still hellbent on receiving my end of information. "Can you just squeeze one thing in for me?"

"What?"

"Okay, so, uh . . ." I suck in a sharp breath. "When I was monitoring Jax, he was drunk and told me that his father has one secret that he cannot tell a single soul about."

Jax closes his eyes for a long moment and whispers underneath his breath, "I'm never consuming a drop of alcohol ever again."

Vi disregards his statement and looks slightly intrigued. "Is that true?"

"Um . . ." Jax lets out a solemn chuckle. "Yes, um, unfortunately it is." He looks at me in great anger, and I simply shrug. *Sorry, Jax. Desperate times call for desperate measures.*

"Okay." Vi pushes her shoulders back, wordlessly turning the next knob up to the highest power. "What is the secret?"

"Oh." He raises his eyebrows. "Can't say, sorry."

"Why the hell not?"

"Because my father would literally kill me if I said a single word about it."

"Well, he's not here to do that now, is he?" Vi says. "And besides, I'm pretty sure you've said enough to give him motives to kill you."

"Fine!" He exclaims out of nowhere, his gray eyes widened in frustration. "I'll say it."

We all wait patiently, the humming of the lights the only sound occurring.

I almost go insane at Jax's long pause.

Soon enough, he opens his mouth to speak. Hesitation is prominent in his voice. "He's telling the entire Rich population false history of the Dark Ages."

There it unravels.

The loud, elongated shriek erupting out of him in just a short breath.

His hands spazz out as he jerks forward, the chair rocking to his direction as he wheezes. Electricity jams into his skin, veins growing on his neck, arms, legs, and chest. He is nothing but a silent storm of pain, convulsing in alarming manners.

"T-turn . . . it . . . o-off!" he gasps out, an animalistic growl escaping out his throat.

"Say the truth," Vi says, her voice showing no emotions. Her face is just the same.

He leans back now, the chair threatening to crash to the ground, and his growls, gasps, and yells never cease. His naked chest is red with anguish, marked in bulging blue veins. He could explode at this very moment.

Until he bellows, "H-he's killing them all!"

The torture immediately stops.

Extremely short, jagged, and rough breaths are all I hear from him. He's sweating profoundly, his entire face and body a burgeoning fire. His lips tremble, his eyes swarming with tears threatening to escape.

I stand here in encapsulating fear, my feet seeming to mold to the ground. Mal, Dylan, and Jeremiah have almost the same reaction as me.

This is definitely not what I expected Jax's answer to be.

"Excuse me?" The tone from Vi's voice isn't accusing; it's instead unnerving.

"Y-yes," he whispers so lowly that I have to physically crane my neck forward. "My father is planning to eradicate the entire Poor population."

MISSING

November 15, 2064
7:35 p.m.

ANXIETY CLAWS AT US.

Vi, Mal, Jeremiah, Dylan, and I are currently in the technology room, still trying to decipher what Jax had told us, strapped to the chair with distress clinging to his voice.

His father wants to murder us all.

To be frank, I had an intuition that this was going to happen —that Tobias would step his foot down and commit mass genocide. But he wouldn't call it that—no, mass genocide is way too much of a strong word. There's no way he would let his squeaky clean reputation be tarnished from such a heinous crime, so he would instead name it a purification, a cleansing. America's rebirth.

Which is exactly what Jax told us.

I could tell that he was immensely struggling to spit out information to us, only because he genuinely did not want to. But considering the dire situation he was in, he decided to swallow his pride and deal with the internal ramifications. He slowly, but surely, told us every detail of Tobias's plan. How he's going to set the act into order as soon as the new year begins, which no one will know of until the speech he makes at his annual celebration—the same event our original plan was going to take place. As soon as the clock strikes twelve, every single Guard in the vicinity will march into every Poor person's house and shoot them all, leaving nothing but blood and bones.

This will emerge America into the brightening horizon. America has spent enough time being weighed down by poverty; it is time for our beautiful country to rise above, to be the greatest country of all again. Poor people are not needed anymore either; their labor has provided enough for them over the years, and evidence provides that our environment is projected to grow and prosper tremendously over the years. Thus, we will be deemed as a waste of space. We will be killed, and D.C.'s environment and population will thrive, allowing the resuscitation of surrounding cities.

All stated by Tobias Remington himself.

I clench my fists, my breaths heavy and ragged. This bastard will forever be the bane of my existence.

Jax later went on to explain that his father never directly told him any of this; instead, he found out about all of this through eavesdropping on a conversation Tobias had with all of the members of the government several months ago. The bond the president has with the branches is too tight to even explain. That's why I just know they are hiding way more secrets between them. And that is why, when Tobias later saw his son eavesdropping on the conversation, he pulled him to the side and threatened to kill him if he said a word. Jax, furthermore, told us that he believes what his father said; he *would* actually kill him.

Hence one of the reasons why he struggled with the interrogation so much.

The interrogation was over by the time Jax revealed that

groundbreaking information to us because we were just so *shocked*. We knew Tobias was an extremely vile person, but only through his words and not through his actions. But finding out that he is striving to kill us all? To "purify" the country? To bring us back on the same level as the other countries?

It makes my mind spin.

"What are we going to do?" Mal's voice interrupts me out of my thoughts. "I mean, the interrogation is over now. We got what we needed. Does that mean we get rid of Jax?"

"No." Vi's voice is sharp as she shares a nonnegotiable look with her. "We're keeping him."

"But he's annoying," Dylan whines.

"So are you, but you're still here." She raises her eyebrow. As he pouts, she says again, "We're keeping him because he might still be useful to us."

"No offense, but in what way *can* he be useful?" Jeremiah asks, leaning against the wall.

Vi doesn't say anything as she gestures for Dylan to get up, since he's sitting by the main console. When he does, after lecturing her about speaking to others in a nicer way, she props herself on the chair, rapidly types onto the keyboard, and brings up a video on the large screen. My attention piques as I bring myself forward, alongside with the others.

She plays the video.

It starts off with a black screen with small white words on the very bottom. The music in the background is dismal, and when I read the words, I almost teeter back on my heels.

ON NOVEMBER 14, 2064, JAX REMINGTON DISAPPEARED.

The black screen transitions into a video of Natalie, the same reporter that interviewed Tobias, Isabelle, and Jax. She is in front of the Capital Center, where many people seem to be huddled around, mourning over their beloved missing individual. I notice that the sky is blanketed in dark hues of gray, meaning a storm is brewing.

The dead trees in the distance sway with very few crows perched upon the branches, cawing into the distance. I haven't been outside in so long that I've legitimately forgotten how the world looks like. And for a minute I've started to miss it too, but seeing the desiccated lands makes me rethink everything. It is just an Earth inundated in poignant remnants.

"I feel great despair to say that the president's son is missing," Natalie says. "That is why many citizens have gathered by the Center in order to commemorate Jax, who was set to do many amazing things in life."

As she continues to drone on about how important he was to society, the camera pans over to Tobias and Isabelle, who I can tell are faking their melancholy demeanor—especially after everything Jax told us, regarding how his parents treat him like scum.

"Is there anything you would like to say to the people, Mr. and Mrs. Remington?"

Isabelle steps up to the microphone and attempts to speak, but she immediately bursts out in tears and whimpers, "I-I'm sorry. I can't." She sniffles and stuffs her hands into her coat pockets. "I-I need to leave."

Dylan snorts beside me. "Someone should've hired her for Hollywood."

As she scurries away, Natalie solemnly nods and gestures the mic toward Tobias. "I can tell you and your wife especially have been scarred by this treacherous event. Is there anything you would like to say? There is no pressure, Mr. President."

At this very moment, the neutral expression plastered on his face conforms into a fabricated sense of solemnity and regret, and he brings his hand to his head, shaking his head slightly. "Honestly,

Natalie . . . I don't know what to say. I mean"—he removes his hand and reveals his eyes shimmering with tears—"my son is never one to disappear like this. He's always been such a well-behaved and distinguished man. He would never run away like this."

Tobias then gestures to two other people beside him, whose faces are blanched and smeared in despair. The first I see is a man, tall and lean, with light brown hair and oceanic blue eyes. He looks to be in his forties, yet his sunken and matured features point toward the fact that he may be older. Next to him is a woman, poised and frightening, her pale blonde hair reaching to her hips. Her skin is deathly pale, her lips dried and parched as well, and her hands tremble as she places a tentative hand on the man's shoulder.

Mal seems to stiffen beside me.

"Next to me I have Adam and Veronica Reaves, the parents of Mallory Reaves, who disappeared three years ago." Tobias looks over at the couple. "The entire community was and is still on a lookout for this wondrous lady for a very long and miser-able time. And it is unfortunate that we have not found her yet." He pauses. "That is why her parents and my wife and I will team up to find our children. We will not give up."

We all look over at Mal in a slow and concerned manner. All except Vi.

Mal's voice is thick with emotions. "Those are my . . . parents. Who I thought could care less about me."

"Well, looks like they do, huh?" Vi says.

"You knew about this, didn't you? That my parents and Jax's parents are teaming up to find us?"

"Whoa, relax." Vi pauses the video. "I saw this video this afternoon, when it went live."

"And you never bothered to tell us?"

"Because I wanted us to be focused on Jax before we looked at the outside world," she says, her face the exact definition of neutral. "Now that we've got him somewhat figured out, I decided to show the video to you all."

Mal takes a deep breath, attempting to consume both the video and Vi's words. "I thought my parents gave up on me a long time ago. I should've been dead in their eyes." She looks over at all of us. "My parents were highly protective of me before, but as soon as I started to show my actual thoughts and feelings to them . . . They immediately discerned me. Threw me to the side. That is why, when I ran away in the middle of the night, I was so adamant they wouldn't even care. But finding out that they're still on the lookout for me?" She scoffs. "I almost think of it as offensive."

Silence reigns. Dylan clears his throat. "Look, I'm sorry to hear that, Mal. But you know what?" He props his hands on his hips. "Screw your parents! Who cares what they have to think or say?"

Mal looks down at the ground. "Yeah, I guess you're right."

"He *is* right," Jeremiah says, walking up to her and placing a reassuring hand on her shoulder. "You're in a much better place now—with *us*. The past is meant to stay in the past, Mallory. Focus on your present. Build your future. And *destroy* what brings you down."

She smiles, very slowly but very thoughtfully. "I love you guys."

Vi clears her throat. "While they *are* very right, we can also continue on this conversation when we finish watching the video." She is uncomfortable, truly hostile to conversations deep with emotions.

"Yeah, you're right," Mal says. "Play the video now."

Vi resumes the clip.

"—a search party will be going out tonight in order to search for our missing children," Tobias says while standing next to Mal's parents. "All are welcome to join, as long as you bring your own flashlights and are acclimated to the cold and rainy weather."

"We want our daughter back," Veronica says, her long pale hair flowing against the shrieking wind. "It has been way too long since I've seen her. Adam and I miss her very much."

Veronica's expressions are masked and executed so well I can't even determine if they are fake or not. At least with Tobias I can pinpoint certain things about him that are falsified, but with this woman? It's certainly more difficult. Her body language is neutral, stable. Her eyes are not wavering. Her voice is calm and leveled. With the utmost concentration I'm still not able to decipher her movements.

Her husband, on the other hand, is nothing like her. While Veronica is menacingly nonchalant, Adam is shaking, his eyes moving in frantic ways. Veronica has to physically grip his arm when he starts to speak.

"M-Mallory, dear," he stammers, his thick eyebrows pushed together, "Your Mommy and Daddy miss you. Come back. Wherever you are. Please."

"C'mon, Adam, it's okay." Veronica's voice is as cool as the weather. "She will be back alongside Jax. We will be hand-in-hand together."

"But"—Tobias interjects, his gray eyes narrowed and equipped with threats—"if anyone is doing any sort of harm to them, then we will hunt you." He moves closer to the camera, nostrils flaring. "And we will most certainly find you."

Vi turns the video off. "That's all."

No one speaks for a good minute until Mal says, "We need to return him, Vi. We need to surrender."

"Why the hell would we do that?" she scolds.

"Didn't you just hear Tobias's threat?" Jeremiah says. "If and when he finds us . . . He is going to kill us for having both Jax *and* Mal in our presence. You and I both know that."

"You guys are a bunch of cowards." Vi lets out a cold laugh.

"Giving Jax up is just going to make life harder for us. I mean—he is in *our* grasp. And we can do whatever the hell we want with him, considering the second and final interrogation's success." Her eyes are burning with deep and buried passion. "He told us what we needed to know. But now he can tell his father what *he* needs to know."

"What do you mean?" I ask, breathless.

She gives me a half-smile and pulls out a camera from the open cabinet next to her. Her eyes gleam in pride as she says, "Time to blackmail."

EXTORTION

November 15, 2064
8:01 p.m.

"WHAT MORE DO YOU want from me?" Jax gasps out as we file into the underground room.

He's sitting on the ground, knees pushed up to his chest as his body still seems to be trembling from the electrocution. I'm surprised he's not paralyzed, or better yet, *dead* from the torturing. He's only shaking, his face is pallid, his eyes are strained, and his hands are still cuffed.

And he is still shirtless.

When we near, he shoots up to his feet in natural defense but immediately falls back down, flat on his back. His legs are shaking, still disoriented. He curses underneath his breath as he looks up at us in serious agony. His torso is marked with hues of cerise, faded blue lines running across his hard chest and down to his carved abs that tighten with every irregular breath. He looks like a lost puppy, encountering a pack of wolves that are determined to rip him apart.

"Hello? Are you not going to answer my question?" When we

don't respond, he takes an irritated breath in and says, "Look, you guys have tortured me enough—both mentally *and* physically. So I would much rather you leave me to drown in my misery."

"Don't be dramatic," Vi says. "We're not going to torture you."

His eyes narrow. "Then why are you here?"

"Our parents have teamed up to find us," Mal blurts out.

Jax immediately sits up, his lips curled into a frown. "What?"

"Yeah. We saw a video of them saying that they want to find us. Both of us." Mal clears her throat. "And judging by what you said barely an hour ago, I'm assuming you don't want to be with them anymore."

Jax is silent.

This time, his lack of an answer brings Vi to say, "And we need you for this crucial step."

He raises his eyebrows. "Aw, you need *me*? I'm quite flattered, Vi." When the word *Vi* comes out of his mouth, she flares her nostrils and starts to charge at him, but he hurriedly inches away from her and says, "Sorry, sorry! I meant Vienna!"

She stops in her tracks and growls. "You know, I would've knocked your teeth out if you weren't half-paralyzed."

"Well, thank God I am, right?" He lets out a nervous chuckle, idly touching the faint bruise on his jaw—the great result of Vi's powerful fist.

Once their encounter ends, she goes over to the wooden chair and scrapes it across the floor, stopping right in front of Jax. Then, she turns to him and says, "Sit."

He frowns. "I can barely get up, though—"

"—I don't care."

Moments later, he sighs and grunts as he propels himself to his feet, wobbling and swaying. Before he can face plant to the ground, he sits himself on the same chair he was tortured in. He looks up at the ceiling, taking steadying breaths in and out.

We huddle around him as I say, "All you have to do is sit and calmly read the script I give you." I bring out the paper stuffed into my pocket, folded approximately four times. Once I unravel it, I walk over to him, letting the paper fall onto his lap.

He looks down at it and rapidly shakes his head, fear latching onto his eyes. "Yeah, I don't like where this is going."

"You will be recorded as you read," Mal says, completely ignoring Jax's desperate remarks. "There should not be a lack of eye contact or confidence, and you must say these words like you believe it yourself. This recording will be sent to your father, and the rest will be up to him."

"Do you understand?" Jeremiah bellows, his expression cold and hard at once.

His breath catches in his throat as his eyes peruse the paper, now hanging limply from his tied up hands. "What if I don't want to read this out loud?"

That's when Vi brings something out of her pocket—something slicked in cool, black metal. The end of it is smooth but the front of it is packed with an instant death wish.

A gun.

She rests her finger against the trigger and points it at him—just a few feet away from him. His eyes are startled, and his voice is shaking as he stammers, "W-why do you have that pointed at me?"

"I will have this held up at you for the entirety of the recording," she says. "However, the moment you act like a dim-witted jerk and refuse to read the script—or even *dare* to run away—I will not hesitate to shoot you in the mouth. Do you understand?"

Jax's face visibly turns red. "Y-yes. I do."

"Good." She brings the gun down and looks at Dylan—nodding at him once.

He sends her an acknowledging glance and brings out the camera, which is packed with a gray exterior and intricate layers.

He stands in front of Jax, preparing to turn on the device, and exchanges a glance with Vi. "I'm ready."

"Great," she says, raising the gun to his face again. "Start the time now."

My heart-rate fastens.

Jax's eyes widen as he scrambles to read from the paper, steadies himself, and clears his throat. He looks at the camera, and says, "Hello, father. It is Jax, and I have been held hostage by the Subversives since November 14th, 2064. The Subversives are fighting for the abolishment of the social structure and want to form a new and improved society. The members and location of this organization is not to be revealed."

He takes a hesitant look toward the gun, and Vi is not daring to let it leave his proximity. His hands are shaking, the paper rattling as his voice tightens. "These members want to make a deal with you. In order to bring me back alive and well, you must step down from your platform and allow the Subversives to take over. However, if you do not comply, then the Subversives will . . ." His voice wavers as his eyes skim the rest of the words. They snap back to the camera, embellished in trepidation. "They will reveal that you are exterminating the Poor. I had told them of your plan under great persuasion. What you are doing is evil and vile and I"—he clenches his fists—"I agree with them. I secretly hate you and the government, which is why I will be under their supervision for as long as they deem fit. I may not seem like it, but I want to be here. I want to fight for equality for all."

Every word he says is perfectly read from the script . . . a bit too perfectly, at that.

His scar on his cheek is rough, jagged, and shimmers against the light as he says, "You have twenty-four hours to decide what you want, father. Make sure to choose wisely."

Immediately, Dylan says, "Done!"

Vi lowers the gun and Jax takes a relieving breath in, but his face is layered with endless frustrations. "Please, for the love of God . . . Tell me this is all over now. I've done what you wanted me to do. I gave you the information you wanted. I told you people shit I've never told anyone before. I know you won't let me be free, but at least let me get out of this dungeon already. I miss actual food too. Jesus, I'm so hungry. I can actually eat this chair right now—"

"We'll let you out of here," Vi says. We send her unnerving looks. "Relax, I'm only letting him out of this room itself, but he's still with us for however long we wish." She stuffs the gun back into her pocket. "And besides, the man is right. He's given us what we wanted. There's no need to act like a bunch of sadistic assholes and torture him just for the hell of it."

"And *you're* saying that . . . ?" Dylan asks.

Vi sends him a chilling glare. "It's the truth. Once the video is sent to Tobias, then we're just going to have to wait. Meaning Jax is free from this place."

"Yes, thank you." Jax sighs. "Also, can you take these handcuffs off—"

"No."

"Well, you're going to have to in order for me to climb out of here."

She rolls her eyes. "You can take them off while climbing up. Afterwards, you will be required to put them back on."

Jax shrugs. "I'll take it."

Seconds later, Jeremiah says, "And how exactly will the video be sent?"

"Dylan will send it to Tobias through an undetectable and untraceable file," Vi says. "This will ensure our incognito presence." And then, with one swift motion, she turns to Dylan himself and gives him a cold glare, her pupils nothing but icicles. "You do promise to make the file untraceable, right?"

"Of course I do, Vi."

"No, I need you to swear it. Swear that you will—or I will do very bad things to you if we get in the slightest bit of trouble."

Dylan, unwavering and completely still, brings his hand to his heart, his eyes pleading for reliance. "I swear on my loyalty and pride that I won't."

Next to me, Vi's face loosens with relief.

Silence finally weighs down on us, and that's when I realize just how much has happened in barely even a day. First, we kidnapped Jax, the man I've never once thought I'd be in the presence of. Second, he revealed to us, obviously with significant coercion, his true feelings toward his father and the government too.

And now, we are about to send a video to Tobias, and in the next twenty-four hours, we will know where this road may lead us—either to Heaven or Hell. Victory or loss. Contentment or eternal humiliation.

But the least we can do now . . . is wait.

22

PREMONITION

November 16, 2064

7:44 p.m.

IT'S BEEN NEARLY TWENTY-FOUR hours, and we've received absolutely nothing from Tobias's end.

We all are sitting around the dining table, apprehension so prominent no one even dares to say a word. The food in front of me barely budges too, only because distress seems to live in my lungs, making it hard for me to breathe. We've gotten so far already— more than we ever thought we would. And now, for almost a whole day, no progress has been made. To think Tobias would've done something about it, considering we have his son.

His son, who is sitting with us.

It definitely feels immoral and bizarre to have a man like him in our presence, not being tortured within our hands anymore. These puzzling feelings transpired when he revealed to us his confounding secret, how he despises his lifestyle and his father to this very day. Even though I could tell of his foreign personality during the inauguration, it still felt like my mind was befuddled when he told us, obviously against his will, about his true intentions. It makes me want to know more about his life. Why exactly would he would hate his father?

Jax is nothing but a book, each flipping page leading to startling revelations.

Suddenly, Jeremiah breaks the silence.

"I wonder what's taking him so long," he says, nudging his food with his fork. "How long does it even take to watch a video and reply to it?"

"How *can* he reply to us, though?" Mal asks, tucking one loose strand of her long and wispy blonde hair behind her ear. "Isn't it untraceable?"

"It is," Dylan says, "but I've made sure to add a falsified email address to the message we sent, so he can still reply to us, but he'll have no way to find us and won't even know who the hell it is."

"Great," I say, eating for the first time tonight. "That makes me feel a bit more relieved."

"Me too." Vi sighs, her tattooed arm reaching forward to grab the salt. "But anyway, enough of that talk. We need to discuss possibilities of what can happen now."

"Please tell me I'm not going to be tortured anymore," Jax says, his voice in great contrast to ours. His hands are not cuffed anymore, so he can delve into the food too, but his ankles are zip-tied to the legs of the chair, just in case he were to suddenly make a run for it.

I notice his body and legs are slowly healing, since he was able to climb up to the bunker, even though he did struggle a bit yesterday. We housed him with the men for the night, which Jeremiah claimed Jax did not associate with either of them at all, and for the entire day, he has been to himself. Just wandering around on his own.

He isn't shaking anymore, his original tan skin color returned, and, after eating and drinking water for the first time in the whole day, he looks a bit better too. And the clothes he wears are clean—black sweater with blue sweatpants. Honestly, I've been so used to seeing Jax in formal attire that him in casual clothes is slightly appalling.

And why do they suit him so well?

"You're not," Mal says. "You already gave us what we wanted."

Jax looks down at the ground. "So, now that I have . . . I'm just going to stay with you guys forever now?"

"Oh, God, no. Not forever," Dylan grumbles.

"Glad to see I'm welcomed." Jax scoffs.

"We're still getting used to the fact that you're, well, against your father," Vi says while taking a huge bite from the salad.

"I'm still getting used to do that too," he whispers underneath his breath.

"Has your father done anything to you to make you feel this way?" I blurt out, the question nagging at my mind.

His face hardens, his eyes rigid and burning, flames flourishing within. His fork clatters to the plate as he says in an eerily-leveled tone, "I don't want to talk about it."

'You've told us so much already," Vi says, "so, might as well tell us the reason why."

"I've already told you. They're disappointed in me. That's why I hate them."

"It's got to be more than that." Jeremiah scratches his firm jaw.

Jax pounds his fists against the table, his hair disheveled with every harsh movement he makes. "Why are you guys so invested in my life? Shouldn't you be grateful that I told you something I haven't told a single soul about in a very long time?" He glances at Mal for a split second. "I have never even dared to think about my feelings because I've taught myself to bury them away and deal with the life I have now. And you all may hate my father, but I can assure you no one hates him more than me. God, sometimes I just want to stuff a blade into that man's skull. But I can't. Because I am his son, and I would much rather live in peace and harmony than cause an uproar. Even though I've been wanting to leave that household and be my own person for the longest time."

His chest rises in and out. "So, please—for the love of God—I beg you to leave me alone. I don't need any more poking or prodding. I just need to be to myself." He leans back, his anger slowly subsiding. "Please."

Our mouths are hung open in shock, attempting to decipher the words that unraveled out of Jax's mouth. Pure passion and fury unveiled out of him, hurled at us before we could even blink. He's breathing fire, his hands clutching the ends of the table as he struggles to compose himself.

All he has done, though, is compose himself in front of his family for almost his entire life—judging by his desperate claims during the electrocution torturing. And I have no clue how he was able to do so—how he didn't succumb to his desires to be different.

To stand up to his parents.

There is still a lot I need to know about this man. But Jax is right. As much as he has caused us great trouble in the past few days, he's still done plenty for us. We forced him to say his deepest and darkest secrets in just a mere few hours, which he had successfully hid away for the past several years. So, it is courteous to respect his wishes and leave him be.

Even though all I want to do is pelt him with my never-ending questions.

"Okay." Vi clears his throat.

He arches his eyebrow. "That's it?"

"Yeah." She meticulously picks at her shirt's fabric. "We'll leave you alone and we will be cautious and mindful of your boundaries. Whatever you wish."

Jax is contemplating Vi's sudden compliance. "Seriously?"

"Yes."

"You really mean it?"

Her eyes narrow. "Now you're getting on my nerves."

"Okay, okay, sorry." A ghostly smile flickers on him. "So now that we're friends, does that mean—"

"I never said that we're friends."

He looks hurt. "What? I thought we were getting along."

"We're actually not." Her voice is stern. "I'm just granting you this one wish of yours. Doesn't mean that we're friends."

"Oh." He sits up straight and clears his throat. "That's fine with me."

A few long moments later, Mal anxiously asks, "What time is it?"

"Nearly quarter to seven," I say.

"Dylan, have you gotten anything from him yet?" Jeremiah asks, his large hands worryingly running across his forehead.

Wordlessly, he grabs his small and slick black device, takes a quick glance at it, and solemnly sighs. "Nope. Nothing yet."

"Goddamn, what's taking him so long?" Vi grumbles. "I mean, it's just straightforward shit we asked him."

"Well, to be fair, I did kind of tell him that he'll have to step down from his platform." Jax winces. "I just have a feeling that he will refuse our offer because my father is power-hungry and extremely desperate for societal validation. It's just who he is."

"Maybe we can offer something else to him," I say. "Something better." When Jax sends me a wounded look, I grimace and say, "No offense, of course."

He works his jaw. "None taken, I guess."

"What are you talking about, Blaire?" Mal asks.

"Well, I'm actually talking about you."

Jeremiah furrows his brows. "But I thought we were specifically avoiding Mallory being in this sort of situation."

"Yeah. We *were*." Vi looks at me pointedly.

"I know, but maybe we need to consider that, if we offer Mal just like we offered Jax, then imagine how much ruckus that would cause. Mal has disappeared from society for over three years. When people hear about her being alive and in our grasp —not to mention with Jax *too*—then Tobias will definitely be forced to resign from his position, let alone respond to us in the first place."

It gets so quiet that I can hear a pin drop. But suddenly, from the corner of my eye I see Dylan grinning brightly. "That is actually a great idea, Blaire."

"Really?"

"Yeah." He nods. "It just gives more of an urge to this situation. So we need to take the chance to show that we have Mallory with us in order to enforce the seriousness of this situation to Tobias."

"So you guys want to add her into the blackmailing too?" Vi asks, her eyes narrowed in concern.

"Sure, if she doesn't mind it," I say, looking at Mal.

She shrugs, her expression completely unreadable. "I wouldn't mind it at all. I just don't want to end up going back home. I don't want anything to do with my parents."

"You won't." Vi vehemently nods her head. "And look, how about this? Let's clean up the kitchen and go to the technology room to search for more updates and discuss adding Mal too. That way we are more professional and can think more clearly."

"Sounds like a plan to me." Dylan jumps out of his seat, grabs his plate, and runs to the kitchen.

When everyone finishes and proceeds to go to the technology room, Jax drums his finger against the table and murmurs, "Yeah, and I guess I'll just stay here, tied up to this chair and stare at the wall like a complete loser."

Vi's eyes slowly trail over to him, and as she sets to release his ankles from the zip-tie, I blurt out, "Wait!"

Her expression is hard as she glares at me. "You know, you've been interrupting me a lot lately."

I weigh in her words, realizing that I *have* been interrupting her a lot, and I start to wonder why I am not killed by her yet.

I clear my throat. "I'm sorry. I don't mean to do that, I swear. I just wanted to let you know that . . ." I look over at Jax in a hesitant manner. "I will untie him because I want to talk to him about something."

His spine suddenly straightens.

Vi raises her eyebrows, standing up and sharing a confused look with the others. "Um, all right. Just make sure to handcuff him afterwards, I guess."

And they all depart, leaving me alone with the man of the hour.

Without a word, I kneel down by his brought-out chair and begin to remove the zip-ties through the sharpened blade in my hand. It is moments later that he takes a sharp breath in, beginning to speak.

"If you want to confess your undying love for me, then I suggest you do it now."

I stop the removal process just to glare at him. His playful gray eyes make me feel irritated yet somehow . . . abnormal at the same time.

"Don't flatter yourself. I am here to talk to you about something else."

The zip-ties are removed. He lets out a breath of relief and stands up, his body towering over mine even when I bring myself to my feet. "What about?"

Our bodies are only two feet apart. The determination drawn into his eyes makes my heart stutter, and I mentally scorn myself for ever letting the gaze of a stupid man interrupt my thoughts.

I bring my shoulders back and engage in a mutual gaze with him. "About what you told us during the second interrogation."

His jaw constricts as his eyes swarm with utter chagrin. "I thought I told you guys to not poke and prod at me anymore."

"I'm not doing that," I say hurriedly. "I am instead, uh . . ."

"Instead *what?*" He takes one step toward me. For some weird reason, I feel my heart skip a beat.

I shove my hands into the pocket of my soft and warm jacket. I gulp and bring my eyes to the ground, finding eye contact to be too much for me right now. "I just wanted to instead . . . let you know that I am grateful for what you have done."

He snorts. "Is this a prank or what?"

My cheeks are burning as I look up at him, desperate for this encounter to be over. "No. It is not."

"Oh." His face slackens as he awkwardly scratches the back of his neck, amusement prominent in his facial expressions. "*You* are grateful for what I have done?"

"Yes."

"Why?" He cocks his head. "I thought you hated me?"

"I do," I say unflinchingly. "But that doesn't mean I can't be appreciative of someone who has clearly propelled us forward in our journey."

He raises his hands in defense. "Of course."

"Yep."

"Also, I hate you too."

I look up at him and cross my arms. "Glad to know the feeling is mutual."

He smiles, dimples forming on his cheeks. Again, I feel quite weird. Is it because of the food? Yeah. It definitely must be the food.

I clear my throat, reaching over the table to grab the gleaming silver handcuffs. Once I do, I gesture for Jax to bring his hands out.

Which he does.

My hands graze his, unintentionally running over his rough calluses. Something lodges into my throat as I clasp the cuffs around his red wrists, strained from being latched to these for the past few days.

I can just feel his smoldering gray eyes on me, raking over my apprehensive frame. He knows what he's doing to me, standing there so tall, so intimidating. It makes me feel something I've never felt before. I mean, I've been confined to my one-dimensional life since I was born, so I never interacted with men my age. I don't know what any of this means.

What I do know is that I hate this type of feeling—especially with this mind-numbingly irritating man.

I clear my throat and say, "Let's get going. The others might be wondering what's taking us so long."

"Yeah, you're right." Jax looks at me and points toward the hallway. "Ladies first."

I nod as I inch past him. He follows closely behind me, and I feel my breath hitch, adamant on not turning around.

Just a few seconds later, Jax blurts out, "Still waiting on that love confession."

I shake my head, chuckling. "In your dreams, Mr. Remington."

He laughs a deep and throaty laugh.

Now that I realize it, he must be very close to me right now. And it reminds me of that moment at Jax's party, when our bodies and faces and souls were so close that I could feel them almost merge. I couldn't feel any of my bodily organs working—except my heart, but it was beating way too hard where I began to feel it throb and pulsate at my neck. It's a bizarre feeling, whatever this is. And I am hellbent on ridding it.

Because I must now think about Tobias Remington and his possible response to us.

10:47 p.m.

We all climb into bed after the long and exhausting talk, which ended up going absolutely nowhere. We were all pooped, especially because we have been running after Jax for several days. Vi found it necessary to grant us this one day to relax and rewind, and then, early tomorrow morning, we will be back on track.

It is very concerning, however, that Tobias has still not said a word to us. Even with that thought remaining over my head, exhaustion is clinging to me like a leech, so right when my back hits the mattress, I feel my eyes drooping. My body sways, rising into the sleeping world and ready to rejuvenate for the mentally challenging days ahead.

But suddenly.

So very suddenly.

A loud yet distant crashing noise occurs.

My eyes fly open, and I shoot upright, my heart racing. I immediately rush over to Vi, violently nudging her awake. "Wake up," I gasp out.

She scowls and swats my hand away, her bright hair portrayed around her like a vivacious piece of artwork. "What the hell do you want?"

Another crash happens. Except it is louder.

This time, she alarmingly gets up and pushes herself out of bed, screeching to Mal, "Get up right now!"

Mal gets to her feet in an instant, an immediate worrying glance shared with the both of us. "What's going on?"

"I-I don't know," I stammer. "I don't know what's going on at all."

Another one. Louder. Scarier.

More follow after another. Dread is suffocating my lungs. I can't breathe.

Shortly after Vi grabs the gun right under her pillow, me and the girls run out the room, desperate to know about the terrifying crashes. I pinch myself, hoping this is all just a dream.

However, it is not. Because what I see in front of me is definitely, *definitely* real.

Rows of Guards are lined up in the living room while the others destroy every single remnant of the bunker. When they see us and eventually the boys beside us, first bewildered and eventually disappointed, they freeze in their spots and point their guns at us before I can even blink.

"Hands above your head and get on your knees now!" Their deep and dark voices terrify me to my core.

Everyone stops moving, and we share intense looks with each other. Our feet stay glued to the ground, not even trying to move from our spots. My hands are shaking so much to the point where my entire body starts shaking as well.

Slowly, we all get down to our knees, and not one word is exchanged. Everyone is speechless, not able to reel in these horrifying change of events. And everyone's faces are marked in great disappointment that grows at each heaving moment.

However, as I am here, knees digging to the ground and hands outstretched above my head, I notice something from the corner of my eye that makes my muscles stiffen.

Dylan smiling.

23

IMPOSTOR

November 16, 2064
10:50 p.m.

THERE IT ALL HAPPENS.

Getting up from his position. Chuckling to himself.

Swaying up to the front. Overlooking us all.

And putting his hands together, slow clapping.

"Wow, would you look at that?" His voice has changed, first light-hearted and pure, and now stemmed with malicious intent. "The people that are supposed to be many steps ahead of the government are actually way behind us all. We have been marking your steps. Notating your movements. And analyzing your behavior—your horrifyingly determined behavior—for longer than you could ever imagine." He lets out a cold-hearted laugh, encapsulated with victory. "And you fell right into my trap."

"Dylan, what are you talking about?" This is the first time I've heard Vi's voice trembling with fear. "Just a few hours ago you were talking to us about ways to add Mal into the plan. You are . . . a member of our organization. A Poor boy that knows how to code and hack into the most complicated of systems."

"Oh, Vienna." He sniggers, stuffing his hands into his pockets. "Think about what you just said. A *Poor* boy that can work with computers? Does that make any sense to you?"

I turn to her. Her face is hard with realization.

"All of you are complete idiots. To think you would've thought this through while recruiting me." Dylan studies us all. "But this was inevitable anyway. Even if you people never recruited me, then you would've been caught in the end either way. It's just the sad truth. For you, at least. But for us—the *Rich?* I mean . . ." He chuckles. "It's a great victory for us."

That is when I take the moment to reel everything in. The triumphant look on our traitor, someone we trusted with all of our hearts. Someone that we laughed with—even in the darkest of times. He revealed to us the interior of the White House, too. Shared his hatred for the government. And Tobias. And the world itself.

It doesn't make sense. None of this makes sense.

But then, it does start to make sense. How *can* a Poor boy ever be capable of working with technology? We should've seen this a mile away. Whoever recruited him in the first place should've realized that. This is all of our faults.

All of it.

What makes this situation worse is that the entire bunker is nothing but a heart-stabbing heap of mess. Papers and tables are strewn everywhere. Frames are torn off the walls and ripped into shreds. The dining table is broken in half, lying in a heap of misery. Lights are flickering. The food by the kitchen is barraged alongside the cabinets and drawers, and the TV is cracked and lying on the ground.

And the segment of the floor that leads to the secret weapons room is torn from its hinges.

Heartbreak is present, gnawing at our insides as we gape at

the mess around us like a gallery of some sort, almost as if it is mocking us. The years of hard work by this so-called *him* is thrown down the drain. It's over. It's all gone.

And my legs are numb and my mind is baffled, trying to decipher everything that happened in the past ten minutes.

I don't know what to feel. Should I feel hurt, frustrated that a close conspirator of the group was secretly plotting against us? Should I feel upset, where all I want to do is huddle into a ball and cry? Or should I feel angry, plunging my frustration onto Dylan as I strangle him with all of the strength that's left of me?

A silence is amongst us, heavy and thick with poison. It makes me want to cry, scream, wail, whine. I hate it here. I want to go back home. I want to go back to my family, to Em, to Nico. I wish I never joined the Subversives. I wish I never went outside my house that night.

I wish I never felt hatred toward the government because maybe my life would've been easier.

"What's up with the depressing expressions?" Our traitor sneers, making the overbearing extremity of this situation dawn on me again. "We're going pretty easy on you, y'know? Others would have been shot in the damn forehead for even thinking to pull any antics like these. Duh, that's obviously a no-brainer!" He lets out an uproarious laugh.

"But no, what's the fun in that? I want to make you guys feel tortured, feel hopeless. Because I, as a Rich person, want to see you guys in pain. *Endless* pain."

"Why did you do this to us?" I blurt out, my insides burning with fury.

"Because what you guys are doing is *wrong*," he seethes. "Did you forget that I am in control of all of the security cameras here and in the White House? That I know all of the where-abouts of this place? All those secrets you guys confided in me?" His eyes narrow into tiny slits. "You underestimated me, Blaire. All of you bastards underestimated me!"

He suddenly sits by the wine-colored couch, the only remnant of the home that seems to be intact. "You see, I was born into a Rich family. Both of my parents were lawyers, and my older sister was planning to be a lawyer as well. I was the only person in the family that wanted to go into the technology field.

"I loved to code, and not only that, but I was extremely good at it too." The curl to his lip hints toward excessive self-pride. "I was sixteen when I hacked into the White House's database. All of the security cameras and important electronic files were exposed to *me*, just an ordinary Rich boy."

We all are entranced by Dylan's story, eager to find out how and when and *why* he would ever do this to us. Befriend us and rip our hearts out without even a damn warning. Have us cowering underneath him, completely prone and exposed to any sort of unwanted violence. This is wholly unfortunate. A literal slap to the face.

"Eventually, the Guards had tracked me down and kept me detained in their prison. I would've been killed immediately if I was Poor. However, since I was a Rich person and my parents were well-known lawyers in D.C., I was dealt with not-so brutally. I guess that's nepotism right there." He barks out a laugh. "Anyway, I had spent two months in jail, not coding away and not hacking into more servers. It was my dream to hack into the greatest server out there and expose the truth about the rest of America, whether or not other people remained. I was dying to do whatever I could to get myself to the top.

"One day, my wish did get granted." A narcissistic sneer grows on his face. "The Guards ultimately let me out of prison. I, as a recently turned seventeen-year-old, was confused on how they let me out so early because my sentence was for three months. But, as they were letting me out, they took me to see the president. He was astonished by my impressive hacking skills, stating that they were unbelievable and quite flattering.

Now, I was taken by his compliment. I mean, the man I idolized for most of my teenage years was complimenting *me?* It was a dream come true.

"But, even more surprisingly, he declared afterwards that he wanted me to be on their IT team. *I* was wanted by President Remington. Obviously, I said yes—who in the right mind would say no to that kind of offer?" He adjusts his glasses. "So, I started working for them, and it was wonderful. I could finally delve into my need of coding again, to oversee many databases and dive into the technological world." Dylan's eyes darken as they center onto the ground. "One day, I was outside, looking for some decorations at a local store for my new home. And as I was walking outside, I ran into *you.*"

His eyes center onto Mal, who quivers and whimpers. "You had drugged and kidnapped me and led me to some dark place. There was Vi and Jeremiah in disguise, standing in front of me with venom in their eyes. You guys started to explain how you guys did a background check on me and saw that I had exemplary coding and hacking skills—someone you guys were desperate to have. Now, as someone who worked at the White House, I wasn't allowed to spread the word of me working there. So, as soon as I started my employment, the government changed my name to Dylan Faulkner in all my legal records."

"You changed your name?" Vi gapes at him. "You mean . . . ?"

"Yeah." He snarls at her. "My name's actually Zachary Everett."

Dylan's name is actually . . . Zachary Everett? He's been under this persona the entire time. I've been deceived.

We've been deceived.

And as I try to wrap my mind around everything that's been happening in the past twenty-four hours, Mal yells, "Your name's Zachary?"

"Yes, but I prefer being called Zach, though."

"Oh, shut your trap!" she hisses. "This has to be a joke!"

"Let me finish the rest of my story." He grits his teeth. "Otherwise, I will tell one of these Guards to send a bullet through your skull right now if you don't shut *your* trap."

Mal huffs and zips her mouth close, her body sulking with defeat.

"As I was saying . . . I was incognito as Dylan Faulkner, an astonishingly great coder and a Poor boy that could do no wrong, and I was especially perceived that way by these people —" He gestures toward Vi, Jeremiah, and Mal. "While they told me about the Subversives and the many things they had planned for people like me . . . Well, at the time, I found it as a perfect opportunity to go incognito again. While I was 'going against the government,' I was secretly and slowly exposing all of the rebels. And then came Blaire and Jax, our newest additions." He looks at us with a cold yet sarcastic glare. "This was an even better opportunity because someone of my kind was here, alongside a woman who genuinely hated my kind.

"And, as time went on, I was secretly noting everything I was told by you guys. I, of course, had to follow along and act just as crazy as you all. I even sacrificed sacred information from my side by exposing the White House cameras to you. No one has access to that, except me. So, now that you know, you of course will be held in jail *for life* with no outside contact."

"You're crazy," Jeremiah hisses between his teeth. "Screw you, Zach."

"Ah, I see you're getting acquainted with my actual name."

"Why would you ever do this to us?" I yell, my hands aching from being held up my head.

"Isn't it self-explanatory? I did it to serve justice to our hardworking president—justice that his own son should be giving." He sends a disgusting look to Jax, who I look over and see is not daring to move a muscle. His eyes are strayed to the ground, and his mouth is sealed shut, reeling in just as much as we are.

"You are a disgrace to society and your father, you know

that, right?" Zach tells Jax. "To think you could ever say those words . . . I still can't believe it. Your father can't believe it either, when I sent him the video the instant I recorded it. He immediately told me to lock you guys up for good—that an execution would never be enough to pay for the sins you guys made. An ever-lasting hell is on the way for you all." His jaw tightens. "And especially you, Jax."

My lungs are submerged into a suffocating tsunami.

He snaps his fingers. "Take them away."

Immediately, the Guards come to us, holding handcuffs ready to be latched onto our wrists. I close my eyes, ready to take in this heart-breaking moment and accept my unfortunate fate. We worked so hard to achieve our goals—just to have one of our close members betray us.

A cool tear drop rolls down my cheek. Nothing feels real right now. This has to be a sinister joke, some sort of a mocking nightmare. And as I kneel here, blood jamming into my veins and my heart pounding so hard I can feel it climbing up my throat, I feel my passion begin to fade away.

But then, a sudden cry of pain has my eyes flying open.

24

CHANGES

November 16, 2064
10:56 p.m.

VI GRASPS A GUN in her hands, and her breathing is ragged as she watches the Guard in front of her slowly fall to the ground, blood pooling around his chest.

It is eerily quiet.

A stray vein appears on Zach's forehead as he curls his fists, his jaw hinged close. "Enough of being nice, Guards. I want you to beat them senseless until all they can see is white." His rancorous brown eyes land on Vi. "Especially that bitch over there."

I glance toward her, noticing her defensive posture—her unmoving features. I know, deep down, she is fuming out of her mind. She never planned or suspected this to happen. Everything was in such great control by her, but now? It is all chaos. Nothing but a complete maelstrom.

Vi's finger still remains on the trigger as the Guards swarm over to us, each step heavy and painful. This time I keep my eyes wide open, unwilling to encounter this moment like a coward. I won't close my eyes. I won't live the rest of my life in shame. I *won't.*

Promptly, piercing through the air comes gunshots from Vi's firearm like a lightning bolt.

She shoots as many Guards as she can, blood splattering onto her clothes as several of them drop to the ground like dead flies. Her widened eyes land on us, and she yells, "Come on! Get up! Fight back!"

I immediately get to my feet, passion filtering through my veins, ready to take on these creatures. But the sudden realization of my very little combat skills punctures through me. The only skill I have is strength, due to me laboring with my parents, but even that is a bare minimum. I don't know how to fight against these muscled individuals. Hell, I don't even know how to stand my own ground without my knees buckling.

My overwhelming thoughts have me in the hands of an oncoming Guard.

He grasps my shoulder and brings his large fist back. Blinding and flashing pain filters through me as he punches me in the stomach. A strained wheeze trails out of my mouth, and as I start to fall to the ground, he pulls me up and pushes me back with great force, my rear hitting the hard floor and my head almost colliding into the hallway walls. My chest is rising in and out and in and out like a balloon almost about to implode. And as this man's enlarged eyes stare me down, he brings his foot back, ready to kick me until I cough nothing but blood and life slowly leaves my eyes—

Thwack!

I watch with amazement as Mal grips a large metal rod in her hand, a small dent from where it hit the Guard's exposed neck appearing on it. She sends me an acknowledging glance, her lips slowly curling up into a smile. My heart is filled with warmth, and I feel nothing but appreciation for her. *She saved my life.*

Before I can thank Mal, her blue eyes turn rigid with fury as she lets the rod fall to the ground and jumps onto the Guard's back, her legs wrapping around his waist. Unadulterated rage transpires through her as she smacks him across the head, leaving him stumbling back out of the hallway.

Near the entrance of the kitchen, Jeremiah gets up and brings out a large knife and slashes it into the Guard's neck behind him. The Guard roars in anger as he clasps his neck, blood oozing onto his gloves. Jeremiah finds that as the perfect opportunity to punch the guy in the face, leaving the Guard stumbling back onto the kitchen counter.

I notice from the ground that Vi is combating against the most muscular Guard here. They move in swift motions, and it takes up all of my energy just to keep up with them. The Guard tries to punch Vi in the gut, but she grabs hold of his wrist and twists it, leaving him wailing. Then, she yanks his wrist forward and makes him lose his balance, having him face-plant onto the floor.

Finally, from the wall I lay against, I see Jax standing by the wine-colored couch, cornered by the Guards that threaten to take him away. Not a single scratch is shown on him, since he refuses to fight back—let alone move a single inch. His face is drenched in confusion, his lips curled in thought. It angers me that he's so hesitant on this matter. He told us his intentions Why can't he do the same with the Guards that swarm around him like bees? Why can't he stand his ground? *Why?*

I look over at the others again, noticing that the Guards are overpowering the Subversives, only because they easily outnumber us. Large groups of them filter into the room, sending bullets everywhere. Everybody shields their bodies away, adamant to not die like *this.* Mal and Jeremiah are hiding behind the kitchen counter, holding onto each other for dear life. Vi attempts to shield her body, but Guards have started to shoot at her, since she is obviously one of the most dangerous individuals out of all of us.

And Jax clutches the couch, refusing to be admitted into the pervasive Guards' presences.

My body refuses to get up and enter the living room, where hell is being unleashed. My friends are being destroyed, and I am just sitting here like the coward that I am because I know the moment I step in there, I will be thrown around like a doll.

But is that really how I want this to go on? While everyone pushes past their own fears and conquers their enemies, I will be laying here, watching everyone slowly crumble to their doom. Is that really how I want this to occur?

So, I must push past my fears and at least attempt to fight back. While I may have no skills, I at least have a burning and raging and burgeoning soul. And I feel as if that will be enough.

I clutch my stomach as I get up to my feet, pain holding onto my sides with every breath I make. But before I can start walking though, I feel a strong pair of hands grab at my hair. I screech as I fail to snatch the hands away from my hair and turn around to see Zach gleaming at me in pure evil. "Thought I was just going to let you relax here?"

Normally I would let my fears overcome me and run away, but seeing the disgusting sneer growing on his face makes uncontrollable flames rise in me. All I want to do, at this exact moment, is punch him in the face over and over and over again until he is anything but recognizable. Blood will seep from every nook and cranny at his skin, and I will keep on going until he crumbles to the ground and perishes from my mind and sight.

I didn't realize it before, but I do have anger. It may be deeply buried within my veins, but all I need is a Rich person in front of me to beckon it forward.

That's when I pull myself out of his hands and grab his throat, all of my pent-up anger managing to seep out of my chest. He growls and claws at my face, and I decide that I must tire him out before I can properly strangle him. So, I prepare to brawl with him instead, hopeful to utilize whatever combatting knowledge I have.

My number one strategy is to defend myself, but if that doesn't work out, then I will just lash out at him with my raw wrath.

And, judging by his weak posture, I can tell it won't be that difficult for me to prevail. All this boy is capable of is being a mastermind behind a screen. But without a screen? He is nothing but a wimp.

Zach staggers forward and swings a punch at me, but I duck in time and try to kick his legs off the ground so he can fall to the floor. However, he only manages to slightly stumble instead. Frustration jams into my veins. Why won't he just leave me already? My mind racks with possible ways to have him crumbling to the ground—*something* to give me an advantage.

That's when I think about Jax's first interrogation.

I conjure up all my built-up ire and run my leg into his crotch at full-speed, and I watch his eyes crinkle together in pain as he howls. *But it's not over just yet.* I punch his face without a single hesitation, and he cries out as he grabs at his cheek, turning bright red profusely.

For a quick moment, great victory rushes through me, but my mouth opens in shock as he pushes me onto the hard floor with his free hand and grabs at my throat, squeezing it tightly. This time, *I'm* the one clawing at his face while he holds a strong grip on me. Soulless brown eyes drill onto my blanched face, his hands squeezing at every torturous second.

He growls at me like a remorseless animal. "Hello, Blaire Cohen. Looks like I won in the end."

I feel life leave my eyes in a slow, ghost-like manner. "Let . . . m-me go . . ."

He cocks his head. "And why would I do that? I finally have you in my hands. And you know what, Blaire? All this time I've been waiting to get my hands on you the most. Do you know why?"

I shake my head, tears streaming down my cheeks.

"Because there has been something I've been *dying* to tell you." He chuckles. "You honestly won't even believe what it is. When I heard it too, I was absolutely astonished."

"St-stop!" I gasp. White surrounds me.

His triumphant demeanor within the evilness in his eyes is predominant. The way his eyebrows curl together, lines amassing his forehead. He is nothing but of eighteen years, one year younger than me, yet he's already accomplished so much. He works for the government, utilizing his genius brain to his best extent—which has already gotten him so far. He's managed to coerce older and much more experienced people into thinking *he* would be the last one to betray us.

This bastard, I hate to say, had us wrapped around his finger.

And here he is now, dominating me and about to reveal something to me. I don't want to hear what comes out of his stupid mouth. I want nothing to do with him.

I think that, until he says this:

"I know the whereabouts of your brother."

The world stops. I am frozen in time. I feel and hear and see nothing but static.

But that is until the unforeseeable happens.

His voice ceases as he crumbles to the ground, a pool of blood forming by his chest as it then spreads onto the floor—so slowly and so mercilessly. I watch with hooded eyes as I notice Jeremiah standing behind him with a gun in his hand and two dead Guards sprawled around in his presence. He looks at me with concern and murmurs, "Come with me."

Without any hesitation, I grab his hand and pull myself up from the couch, my throat scratchy and aching. Another person that saved my life.

From the corner of my eye, I see Mal running toward the doors and Vi sticking her middle finger out at the two other Guards she beat up as she also does the same. Jeremiah and I run after them, noticing that only a few remain, but they are highly injured and barely able to sense anything.

"Are you coming, Jax?" Mal shrieks to him.

He is now around fallen Guards that seemed to have been killed by the others. But he looks confused, sharing indeterminable looks with us.

Vi scoffs, clearly impatient. "Look, we don't have time for this right now. Make your decision already before we leave you in this goddamn bloodbath."

He clenches his fists, his tan skin bathing in glistening sweat. Taking a sharp breath in, he closes his eyes, mumbles something underneath his breath, and opens them again. And then, he silently and abruptly nods.

There it is. The confirmation of him being a part of us now.

Something uneasy crawls into my mind.

"Come on then!" Jeremiah hisses. "Let's go—*now!*" And we run as fast as our feet can carry, speeding past Zach's limp body as well.

Before we can even make it out of the door, though, I feel a strong pain rip into my back as I plummet to the ground, my body convulsing. Everyone else seems to be in the same condition as me—in utter and extreme anguish as we scream for our lives. Among the unbearable torture, I notice within the blurriness of my vision that five Guards are standing in front of us with taser guns in their hands.

I try to let out a scream, a complaint, or even a mere cry, but I can't even breathe. My heart rate starts to slow as my eyes droop, darkness overcoming me, my mind numbing. And before I can even succumb to the obscurity, I feel my heart shriveling with disappointment as I am reminded for the umpteenth time that we have lost greatly against our enemy.

With that final thought, I manage to let go.

25

ISOLATION

July 13, 2059
4:40 p.m.

"WHAT HAVE YOU BEEN up to, Bumble Bee?"

I roll my eyes at the annoying nickname my brother gave me. Craning my neck to the right, I notice him leaning against the doorframe of the room, widely grinning at me with a teasing glint in his eyes. I gesture for him to sit beside me on the foot of the bed, which he does, his comforting presence intermingling with my desolate appearance.

"What are you doing here?" I whisper, my eyes trained onto the ground.

"I want you to answer *my* question first." I can feel his eyes boring into me.

I sigh as I play with the long dark strands of my hair—nervously, I suppose. "I just wanted to be alone."

Then, I manage to lock eyes with him, and his playful persona shifts into a soft and caring one instead. His dark locks fall onto his eyes as he pushes them back. "Why do you want to be alone?"

"Because I just do, okay?" I grumble.

He raises his thick eyebrows. "Okay, Bumble Bee. Something is obviously going on. What's the matter?"

"You know exactly what the matter is."

His deep brown eyes, the same one's he and Em inherited from my mother, sparkle instinctively as they fall onto the ground. "There's no need to worry about it, dear sister. I have reassured you plenty of times that I have it taken care of."

"That still doesn't make me feel any better."

Nico sighs and wraps his large arm around me, my head against his chest as I feel his heartbeat. *Boom, boom, boom.*

"Do you trust me?"

I don't even hesitate when I say, "Of course."

"Then there you have it. Just trust me."

I push away from his chest and force him to look me in the eyes. "Why would you do that? You do know that there are consequences to your actions, right?"

"Bumble Bee, what did I say?" he drawls. "Besides, I had to stand up for Em like that. The Guard was calling your little sister mean names. *Our* little sister. She is only seven. Wouldn't you do the same thing if you were in my position?"

"Yeah, I would," I mutter in defeat. "I'm just scared the Guards might hurt you now. You did something which many of us don't have the guts to do, which is talking back to a Guard."

"I know. But it's going to be okay." He suddenly leans back and cocks his head at me, as if he is studying me intently. "You know, you have grown up quite a lot. What are you now, eight-years-old?"

"Shut up!" I laugh, smacking his shoulder. "I'm twelve!"

He cackles and the room ends up drowning in our loud laughter. Suddenly, the door plunges open as my father's timid frame stands in the same area Nico initially stood in. "Everything all right here?"

"Yeah, we're fine." Nico grins at him. My father narrows his eyes at us, shakes his head while smiling, and closes the door. Trails of dust form afterwards, mingling into the air as the atmosphere starts to quiet down. I sit up and prop myself up against the foot of the bed again, bringing my knees up to my chest as I hug them tightly. Nico sighs as he sits beside me.

I furrow my brows as I watch his eyes land on the raggedy ceiling, swarming with a sense of despondency. He looks so vulnerable—which is the antithesis of how Nicolas Cohen, my amazing older brother, usually is. He's usually vagrant, mystifying, and courageous, all in one. But for this one second, I notice the aegis of his usual personality simmer down to his exposed self—the quiver in his lip, the sadness etched in his eyes, and the way he clenches his hands into fists.

Before I can speak, he starts to whisper into the emptiness: "Truth is . . . I am a bit scared. I did do something no one in this wretched society would even think to do. I stood up for my family—Em, specifically. A mere little girl was getting verbally abused by a Guard, just because she spoke a little too loudly when we went outside. *Just because she spoke a little too loudly.*" Nico shakes his head in disgust, his shoulders shaking with acerbic laughter. "Of course I got pissed. I am a nineteen-year-old man filled with anger! And of course I had to tell the Guard to leave Em alone. But, unfortunately, he managed to yell at me, and we disappeared into our home before anything could get worse."

He looks at me. "Don't tell Mama and Papa about what happened, okay?"

I shake my head. "No, they need to know—"

"No, Blaire. I'm serious." He *is* being serious because he rarely uses my name in an assertive tone. "If word of this ever got out to them, then they will never let me near you guys again. So, I need you to swear that you will keep this a secret. *Our* secret. You understand?"

I sigh in defeat as I nod my head eventually. "Yes, Nico. I understand."

"Okay. Good." He lets out a breath of relief.

I blurt out, "Wouldn't Em tell our parents what happened?"

He curses, but immediately composes himself with an abrupt grin. "Don't worry about Em; I will talk to her."

"Okay." A lump forms in my throat as I hug my knees even tighter. "Sorry if I seemed a little upset before. I was just afraid that the Guard might arrest you, due to what you did. You know what the Guards are like."

"Yeah, I know. But don't apologize for being upset—you had every right to be." Nico's eyes soften as his lips twitch into a broad smile. "Y'know, Bumble Bee? You care about me very deeply. And I know that if anything were to ever happen to me, you wouldn't *ever* give up on me."

"Don't say that!" I chastise. "I don't even want to think about anything ever happening to you. I wouldn't be able to live with myself."

His shoulders shake with laughter as he reels me in with his large arms, patting my head as his soothing touch caresses me, diminishing all of my worries away. "Don't worry. I won't be leaving you any time soon."

"Good." I smile into his arms.

And we sit there for what seems like several minutes. Just our hearts beating together, flourishing in the encouraging moment me and my brother share. I don't think I feel as happy as I do now, amongst our broken room, amongst our broken home, and amongst our broken society. But whilst the broken-ness around me is prevalent, I somehow manage to scour for some place in my heart that I reserved specifically for my brother.

Few moments later, he leaves. I beam at him as he saunters to the door, a wide grin splitting his face in half as he salutes me. I salute him back as he whispers, "Don't stay alone for too long. Okay, Bumble Bee?"

"Okay, Nico," I say. Moments later, he disappears behind the door.

Little do I know that a few hours later, he would be getting arrested, and not because he stood up to a Guard for reprimanding Em. But for something I, to this day, have no idea about.

November 18, 2064
2:53 a.m.

My eyes flutter open, struggling to adjust to the dimly lit atmosphere. My hands are bruised and scarred, shaking as I study them with narrowed eyes. My abdomen aches with pain, my legs feel heavy, and my face is itching with the scars I feel digging into my skin. Wincing, I bring a timid finger to my cheek, feeling a gash and hissing as a shot of pain occurs unexpectedly.

Whimpering to myself, I feel the hard floor digging into my rear. I curiously touch it, and my eyes travel further as I take note of the isolated place I am in. I sit alone, in an empty cell, with other large jail cells around me. There is a flickering light in the middle of the hallway, hissing instinctively as the humming of the AC rises into the room like a silent ghost. I shiver, the cool air tickling my skin as I hunch forward. The bright orange outfit I have on hugs me, concealing the hidden scars beneath it.

The ultimate realization of me being in jail and wearing clothes prisoners would usually wear has me shocked. The quietness makes me feel like I'm alone here, but me frantically looking around the room seconds later makes me realize that I'm *not*.

On the other side of the room are three other jail cells: an empty one, another one with Mal in it—who is sound asleep—and the one on the far corner with Vi sprawled across the floor, asleep as well. Hopefully, they are only sleeping—not anything worse.

And Jax and Jeremiah are on both sides of me, sound asleep just like the others. *So I am the only one that's awake.* A yawn overtakes me as I bring myself over to the back of my cell, wincing with every movement. My entire body feels like a weight smashed onto my ribs, a saw slashed through my legs, and someone punched my face about a hundred times.

Once my back hits the smooth wall, I sigh with relief. My heart beats erratically as I pray to God this day or night—whatever time it is—would go by fast. All I want to do is go back home to Mom, Dad, Em, and bring back Nico.

My lips dry as I remember the ambiguous statement Zach made to me two days ago as he strangled me to near death. What could he possibly know about my brother? Is he alive? *Dead?* Panic starts to pour into my lungs.

And to make my anxiety unintentionally worsen, I am reminded yet again that Dylan revealed himself to be a Rich computer extraordinaire that was secretly going against us the entire time. He concealed himself with a persona, made us believe that he was an innocent Poor guy that loved computers. Kudos to him because he landed all of us in jail—and only the universe knows what's in store for us next.

I don't know whether to cry or scream or sit in silence—but I decide to go with the latter as I take note of the desolate room and the numerous cells as I watch everybody sleep peacefully or with trouble. Mallory's chest rises and falls as I notice she's extremely beaten up as well. So is Vi, who snores, her colored hair spread around her like a masterpiece. Jeremiah, on the right of me, has his body in an upright sitting position on the anterior of the cell as his eyes are closed shut.

Finally, I notice Jax curled up on the left, his strong and bruised arms placed on the ground. His dark hair is disheveled, more than it usually is, and his trademark scar is gashed incredibly with dry blood etched onto it. Despite his bruised body and troubled expression, I somehow seem to notice his vulnerability, even when he's asleep.

Before I can evaluate him any further, he suddenly stirs around, and I gasp as I pretend to sleep. *Does he know that I was staring at him creepily?*

I close my eyes for a good minute, only to hear no more stirring from him. A few moments later, I open my eyes and see Jax shivering by the cell door that separates us, turning his head to look at me. "Cohen, where are we?"

Curiously, I inch toward him, every limb of mine aching as I sit by the door that separates us, leaving me and Jax only a finger's length away. "We're in prison," I say, watching his body harden.

I can feel the hypnotizing presence of his as his fearful gray eyes land on me. "Was this all a big nightmare?" He looks so vulnerable yet so hesitant with me. "Was me revealing to you guys all of my shit a nightmare, too? Revealing to my father to a damn video that I hate him? And running off with you guys after getting our identities exposed?" He looks at his hands. "Just to lose in the end."

My breath catches as I manage to whisper in a hushed tone, "Just because we lost this round, doesn't mean we lost the battle." My eyes meet his as I lean into the cell door even further, feeling the rigid poles interlocking together digging into my back. "Keep your chin up, Jax."

"I can't." His voice is pained. "I can't keep my chin up. I haven't been able to for a while, actually."

"Why is that?"

"Because of my father, Cohen. He ruined everything for me. And he . . . He did bad things to me." His eyes are irredeemably painful. "We lost. *I lost.*"

I manage to bring my hand forward through the spaces between the metal poles on the cell door and caress his shoulder, feeling the rough and rigid skin of his. "You didn't lose, Jax."

"Really?" he says, his stormy gray eyes not so stormy anymore.

"Yes, really."

Jax melts into my touch, his shoulders relaxing with ease as he leans back into me. I feel the strong muscles of his back—I feel *him* digging into my skin as I caress his arm, his soft breath on my shoulder. It is moments later that he falls asleep on me through the door that separates us.

He may have opened up to me because he was vulnerable at the moment, coming from a home filled with privilege and finding himself locked up in a jail cell alongside other rebels. It probably allowed him to plummet into a state of susceptibility.

Or maybe he genuinely felt like opening up to me about his father, in the vague way he did. Either way, it was the start of me figuring out the enigma that is known as Jax Remington, the one man I thought I would never hold respect for. But as I sit here, feeling his calm body beside mine . . . I start to realize that maybe I do hold respect for him.

And maybe there is more to him than I ever thought would be.

2 6

HOPELESS

November 24, 2064
12:24 p.m.

APPROXIMATELY A WEEK HAS passed since we've been in this hellhole, and all we've encountered so far are scornful looks from Guards—alongside brutal lashings afterwards. Zach wasn't lying when he said that we would be undergoing complete agony here. So far—ever since the night our bunker was destroyed and we were taken away—I've gained more bruises and gashes and cuts than I have in my entire lifetime. Before I would be in complete anguish over the tiniest of scars, but now? I've learned to live with it. And so have the others.

It is now lunch time, and the four of us are sitting at a table in a big and empty cafeteria with no one else around. There aren't many prisoners today, and I'm assuming that's because most of the people held here are being executed to this very moment. My stomach churns with disgust as I think of poor and innocent people being executed for shit that doesn't even make sense. And my stomach churns with even more disgust as I see the rotten burger and weird-tasting water in front of me. The food here is even worse than the food I eat at home, which is already ghastly to begin with.

Vi stabs her soggy salad with a fork as she hisses, "I want to get the hell out of here."

"We all do," Jeremiah whines as he stares at the rotten sandwich in front of him.

"This food is terrible," Mal grumbles as she sets her plate aside. "I'd rather starve to death than eat this crap."

"Ditto." I scrunch my nose as the grumbling of my stomach is not quite enough compared to the disgusting food that sits in front of us.

"I mean, is this one of their methods of torturing us? Making us eat food that smells like moldy cheese?" Vi gestures to the salad water dripping from her lettuce as she looks at it in pure repulsion.

"Probably." Jeremiah scoffs. His dark brown eyes seem to be emanating with fatigue as his large upper-body sulks in despair. "I would protest and demand for better food, but considering the stake we are held at . . . Well, the rational side of me is telling me to sit still and oblige. And also because the Guards staring down at us are making me feel quite nervous."

I take a quick look toward the Guards swarming around us, keeping a ten feet distance from us as they are spread around the cafeteria room. Since no one else is in the cafeteria except us, they decide to focus their attention on us, which really makes me feel pressured to breathe correctly around them, considering the fact that they will execute me right then and there if I did breathe wrong. However, they probably would not because our next torture session is scheduled for tomorrow morning, and God knows what it's going to entail.

Can they just shoot me now and get it over with already?

"Some part of me is hoping to be in Jax's situation right now," Jeremiah suddenly says.

"Because he doesn't have to deal with Guards being up his ass?" Vi raises her eyebrows in question.

"Yes!" he exclaims. "It's so nerve-wracking."

"Isn't he getting his sentence evaluated right now?" I ask.

"Yeah, he is—comes with the privilege of being Rich." Mal rolls her eyes in disgust.

"And being the president's son," Vi grumbles.

"Why didn't they ask you in there too, Mal?" I ask her.

"I don't know." She sighs. "That I am confused about too. Maybe they'll ask for me later? I honestly have zero clue."

"Maybe you're right," Jeremiah says. "And besides, weren't your parents dying to reunite with you?"

"They were," Mal says, brushing her long blonde hair to the side. "That's what confuses me. If they really wanted to see me again, then they should've asked for me the moment they found out. But who knows."

"I guess we'll just have to wait and see how Jax's evaluation goes." Vi clenches her jaw.

"I just know they're going to go easy on him," Jeremiah says.

She sighs. "It's definitely his privilege that is going to come in handy for him."

As Vi's remark seeps into my mind, I just can't help but wonder how exactly Jax's sentence evaluation is going right now. It personally repulses me to even think of the fact that they might be going easier on Jax, only because he's the president's son. *Only because he's Rich.*

"Can you guys believe that Jax decided to come with us, though?" I ask. "He easily could've stayed back with the Guards and beg to join his father's side again. But he didn't." I scoff with disbelief. "I can't believe it."

"Me neither," Mal says. "The Guards and Zach himself treated him well, too. He had every reason to leave us."

Vi snorts. "I guess that electrocution interrogation really changed him."

"How did you do it so effortlessly, though?" I ask. "He told you everything in a day. That's absolutely amazing."

She stops and thinks. "Persuasion and messing with his childhood fears. That is the key."

"And also kicking him in the crotch," Jeremiah adds.

Vi clicks her tongue, her expression full of pride. "Also known as the perfect way to weaken a male figure."

"Didn't you do the same to Zach?" Mal asks me. "I saw that you were under attack by him."

"Yeah," I say, "mainly because he saw me not getting manhandled by any Guards. I guess he found it as a great opportunity to have me in his hands. And guess what?"

"What?" Jeremiah asks.

"He told me he knows about my brother's whereabouts. Can you believe that guy?"

"Wait, seriously?" Vi looks surprisingly intrigued.

"Yeah." I nod. "He told me while he was choking me to near death. By the time he was about to say more, Jeremiah shot him. He should be dead—hopefully."

"Shit," Jeremiah says. "I'm sorry to hear that, Blaire. But what happened to your brother, if you don't mind me asking?"

I close my eyes and explain everything. The moment where we had that life-altering conversation to when I screamed for my life, clinging to my mama's side as Nico was hauled away.

"Oh no." Mal frowns, her blue eyes glassy with tears. "That's so terrible. And it's been five years too?" I nod my head. "Gosh, I'm so sorry."

"I mean, it's whatever," I say, forcing my emotions down my throat. "I just want to avenge for him. That's all."

"And that is why we are all here," Vi says, her pale eyes deep with relatability. "To avenge for the hell the government put our family members through."

"And what Zachary put us through, too," Mal whispers.

"Goddamn Zach." Jeremiah shakes his head. "Now I was

honestly not expecting *him* of all people to dupe us. How could we possibly not recognize that?"

"I don't know." Vi looks disappointed as she shoves her food aside. "I hate to say it but that boy did a great job tricking us all. He actually made us think that he was just a sweet and innocent Poor boy that could code." She chuckles to herself in a disdainful manner. "And he was also right: How were we so dumb that we completely disregard the logistical error in a Poor boy being able to work with technology? *How?*"

"Vi, don't dwell on it too much; it's okay." Jeremiah tries to console her.

"But it's not okay," she says, her eyes burning with fire. "This is our fault. We are the reasons why we ended up in this rotten hell."

"No, we're not," Mal says. "Everything was going great before Dylan revealed himself to be our traitor. So, in reality, it's his fault. *Not* ours."

Vi bites her lip and looks into the far distance, not convinced.

As we continue to sit and talk amongst each other, chaos ensues near the posterior corridor to our west, where an open-ended hallway anchors off to the cells.

Near the entrance of this corridor is a man fighting against a large number of Guards. The man starts to run off to the northern side of the corridor, screaming at the top of his lungs, but five Guards come running to him and pound him senseless. His echoing screams resound into the room. My lips wobble in fear as one Guard rams the butt of his rifle into the bottom of the man's chin as they pull him to his knees and bring both of his arms behind him. They hold him in place, and his entire face and body is oozing blood.

Two Guards come behind us and aggressively pull us to the cafeteria exit. "Prisoners number 203, 204, and 205, follow me, *now!*"

We follow them halfheartedly, the sounds of our footsteps echoing down the corridor. The Guard's hands digging into my wrists make me wince in pain as I try to look behind me and see the man manhandled by the other Guards. They ram the gun into the front of his skull as the man continues to let out guttural cries. His eyes are drowning in tears as he peels them open, suddenly meeting mine.

My heart lurches to a stop as he shouts, "Get away from this city while you still can! Save yourselves!"

Seconds later, he gets shot between his eyes.

VERACITY

November 24, 2064
12:38 p.m.

WE ARRIVE AT OUR jail cells. My nose scrunches up as the sudden smell of puke overtakes the entire room, and I gag as I notice the pile of vomit laid out by the entrance. A Guard comes over to wipe it up as the prisoner in front of us looks guilty as she is escorted away by three other Guards.

Once we pass the entrance, we see Jax sitting in his jail cell, slouching forward as he fidgets. I notice the forlorn look on his face—etched with utter disdain.

Two Guards stand by our cells. I've noticed the layout of the prison is bizarre, almost shaped in a pentagonal pattern. In the center is the check-in area and cafeteria, each post on the side containing five cells. Ours is held in the far corner, amongst the other cells that point out to different directions. Even the bathrooms are held in interlocking areas.

"How did it go?" Jeremiah whispers as we huddle into Jax's cell. The two Guards suddenly straighten themselves and rush to where we are, but Jax sends them a threatening look that makes them sulk and rush back to their posts. I raise my eyebrows, astonished by how successfully that went for him.

Once we situate ourselves around him, the iron-pad locked door slams shut. Jax takes a deep breath and says, "It went pretty well."

"That's it?" Vi raises her eyebrow. "Now, something doesn't sound so right here, Rich boy."

"Can you not call me that?" He raises his gray eyes to her.

She narrows her eyes at him, her expression becoming more frightening at every passing moment.

Jax runs his finger along the concrete floor. "Sorry for bursting out at you like that. I just hate being referred to as my father's son, let alone a Rich boy."

"I don't care about what you feel," she says. "But what I do care about is knowing how your interrogation went."

Jax leans back against the wall as we huddle around him, the cool air making the hairs on my arms rise. "Well, first of all—I walked into a blindingly white room and and saw five Guards. I sat and asked why I was there. The Guards told me that my sentence was going to be evaluated separately. I asked why, and they said, *obviously because you're the president's son.* So, in the first hour of the interrogation, I tried to persuade them to let me get the same sentences as you guys."

"What was your sentence?" I ask.

His eyes widen slightly as he shakes his head. "Um, I don't know if I should tell you. It's really going to piss you guys off."

"Well, now you *have* to tell us." Mal crosses her arms over her chest.

"Yeah," Vi says and Jeremiah echoes her words as well.

Reluctantly, Jax sighs and forces himself to tear his eyes off the ground and onto the ceiling. "I was going to be let out immediately and sent back home."

"What?" our voices clatter together, and the alarming looks in our directions by the Guards has us lowering our voices.

"Yeah." Jax winces. "They were willing to let me off the hook at that moment and forget I was a Subversive. And get this! My father was willing to pay one million dollars to bail me out. Can you believe that?"

"Hell no," Vi grumbles.

"And what did you say?" Jeremiah asks.

"I said no," he says.

"Okay, I'm glad to hear that." Mal breathes out a sigh of relief.

"I guess this means you're loyal as hell to us. Zach could learn a thing or two from you." Vi scoffs as she quickly ties her hair up into a low ponytail.

"I still cannot believe he was against us the entire time," I say. "I really trusted him. *We* really trusted him. And then he just . . . betrayed us."

"We're relying on each other now," Vi says. "And we are in a crucial part of our journey too. We may be stuck here for God knows how long, but we are still together no matter what. And Jax . . ." She looks over at him. "You know you're a Subversive too, right?"

His face is unflinching. "Yeah. I do know." He works his jaw as he says again, "I honestly don't mind being here. I just want to be away from my home because I hate being a part of the Remington family. Thousands of Rich people were expecting future President Jax Remington, but they instead received quite the opposite." He lets out a shaky breath. "Everybody in the entire city knows of my genuine reputation. My father knows too, and I know that whenever I see him next, he won't hesitate to kill me, even though he wants to let me off the hook easily. And do you guys know what's so shocking?" We shake our heads. "It's the fact that I don't regret doing this thing. I don't regret wanting to destroy my own kind. I don't regret being here. And as freaky as it is . . ." He lets out a deep and rumbling laugh. "It also feels kind of good."

Vi takes in everything he said. "I'm glad to hear that." *Is she being nice to him?* I just have to pinch myself to make sure I'm not dreaming this.

"Thanks." Jax nods his head and then smirks. "Does that mean I can call you Vi now?"

"No."

He winces. "Ah, well, it was worth a shot."

"It's never going to happen, you know that, right?"

"You say that, but we all know it's going to happen."

"Shut the hell up. It's never going to happen."

"Yeah, yeah. Whatever floats your boat." She scowls at him, but all he does is smile.

9:00 p.m.

Hours pass by in the blink of an eye, even though all we do is sit in our individual cells and contemplate to ourselves. Sure, we had bathroom breaks and mini interrogation sessions, but mostly it was just us sitting, batting an eyelash to each other and pondering to ourselves eventually.

And bedtime, which is at nine, soon arrived.

I scramble back to my cell and lie down on the cold, hard floor. I place my arm underneath my head in order to use it as a cushion, and I dig my eyes close, trying to find some solemn peace amongst this raucous place—before our next torture session is tomorrow morning.

Which Jax does not have to partake in.

It feels weird knowing that we are in prison now. And it feels even weirder also knowing that Jax decided on his own that he doesn't want to reunite with his parents and revel in his luxurious lifestyle. He instead wants to be with us.

All of the thoughts running through my mind are hard to decipher. Hard to formulate. Hard to recognize.

But it seems as if that maybe, one day, they will be easy to decipher. Just like this unfortunate life.

November 25, 2064
1:29 a.m.

BANG! BANG!

My eyes widen as I lunge from my spot, looking around to see where the loud noises came from. Everyone else has shot out of their sleeping spots too, and we gawk in disbelief as we notice our jail cell doors are wide open. And everyone, as in Mal, Jeremiah, Jax, and I are in our spots.

Except Vi, who stands in the corridor with two dead Guards beside her.

"Vi?" Jeremiah screams.

She grins for the first time in a while as she puts her gun into the pocket of her jumpsuit. "Are you guys coming, or am I going to have to drag your asses out?"

2 8

EQUAL

November 25, 2064
1:30 a.m.

I FORCE MY BLEARY eyes open as we all run out the door, following Vi. Something in the corridor catches my eye, so when I squint, I notice the faint display of an ID in Vi's hand. Whirling around, I see the two Guards Vi had killed, their bodies exhibited with pools of blood spreading around them. *It must be theirs.*

Vi leads us out of the iron-clad doors and into a door by the far corner that has a sign displayed on the top, which reads: EMERGENCY EXIT. It was the same exact sign that was exhibited on top of the door in which we led Jax out of—when we kidnapped him.

Suddenly, a Guard appears by my side. Before I can freeze and cower, Jeremiah goes and thrusts his fist into the Guard's heavily protected abdomen. He doubles over, allowing his rifle to fall to the ground too. Jeremiah's eyes latch onto the fallen rifle, and he grasps it tightly, as if it were a prized possession.

Without even thinking twice, he presses the trigger, an ear-splitting *bang* ringing into the air.

I take a shaky breath in as I notice the Guard splayed out on the ground, just like the other Guards Vi killed. Blood pools around his head, and that is when he screams, "Let's keep going!"

Everybody nods their head . . . and then we run. Faster than the wind itself.

My lungs ache as I let out hefty breaths, my heavy boots thumping against the floor as we run out of the emergency exit door. A loud blaring sound initiates, and Jeremiah curses to himself as we stand in the cold November air. "Shit! We need to keep on going!"

But if we keep on going, we'd be running into the forest. It creeps above us, like stalkers in the night.

That's when I realize that this is the first time in a while that I'll be stepping foot into the outside world—the first time I'll be encountering fresh air. Where I'll be standing on grass digging into my feet, where trees will tower over me and shade me from any possible harm. I haven't seen or felt nature in such a long time.

But not as long as compared to the others.

Mal shakes her head. "We can't go into the forest. It's an ultimate death wish."

"Well, it's better than dealing with *this,*" I urge, pointing at the building, where the faint blaring sound still seems to be going. Mal sighs halfheartedly and nods . . . and that is when Vi sprints.

The way her eyes dart back and forth, analyzing her surroundings—it astonishes me. And her feet work just as fast, moving like lightning bolts as she makes her way into the forest. The rest of us follow behind her, with Jeremiah catching up to her—which I am astonished by, due to his amputated leg—Jax following right behind him, and Mal and I running alongside each other. I haven't run this fast in my entire life, and my lungs could explode at this exact moment.

My breaths come out as rough and jagged as I squeeze my fists tightly, wanting to not do anything except go *forward*.

We make our way into the abundance of trees deprived of leaves. I would usually find nature to be calming and beautiful, but this forest is anything but. It screams danger and reeks of the unknown. And it makes me want to freeze in fear, go back to my family, and bask in their warmth and comfort. But, instead, I go forward alongside my comrades, not looking back once.

The distant blaring seems to dissipate with every inch we make closer to the dark forest. Birds caw in the distance with a melancholy edge. I can barely breathe as my legs pound against the weaving grass, trying to trap me beneath the earth's core. Sweat beads trickle down my forehead, and I wipe it incessantly, my breaths coming out ragged.

"We're almost there!" Jeremiah yelps as he makes his way into the forest that looms over us like a steel cage, ready to envelope us.

We follow them, bushes and trees and grass and wildlife forming around us. However, a large weed growing from the side causes Mal to trip and plunge to the ground.

"Mal!" I scream. I look over to where we entered, and there seems to be silhouettes of large bodies in the near distance. *Let's hope they don't find us.* I urge my hand forward to Mal, feeling her matted and long blonde hair tickling my arms as she struggles to bring herself up.

She lets out a gasp. "Sorry about that. I didn't see the weed there."

"It's okay." I try to catch my breath. "But we need to catch up to the others." I point toward the bodies of Jax, Jeremiah, and Vi, as they continue to run. Mal doesn't even think twice before she starts running again, clutching her sides at the same time.

I follow her, my dark hair falling in waves around my shoulders as I notice the band of my hair-tie has broken. Grumbling to myself, I push my hair to the side and keep on running, hoping we will lose the Guards' sights.

I don't know whether it's been five minutes or five hours, but we somehow have found a place for us to settle.

My serrated breaths come to a steady rise and fall as I lean onto a giant tree trunk. The bark digs into my orange-jumpsuit as I notice the others sitting around me. Mal lies on the ground, closing her eyes as I can tell she's trying her best to not think about our unfortunate situation. Jeremiah doesn't even sit—all he does is simply stand against the tree beside me, placing his hands on his hips. Jax is sitting on the ground beside Jeremiah, pushing his knees to his chest as he drags his fingers through his exceedingly tousled hair.

Jeremiah faces Vi, scoffing. "Now do you mind telling us why the hell you would do this without our permission?"

"I knew this would happen." Vi rolls her eyes. "You all would think it's too risky and not worth a shot, like you just said."

"Yes, of course I would! Because look at the goddamn hell we are in now!" His deep and baritone voice courses throughout the woods, for he immediately lowers his voice. "You still have yet to explain to us where the hell you got that idea from. Care to enlighten us?"

Vi grouses to herself and purses her lips together. "It came through my mind before I fell asleep that night, okay? I knew I could not tell you guys about it because the Guards were standing *right there.* So, I decided to keep it to myself."

"And then?" Jax asks as he lets out a quick yawn afterwards.

"I woke up in the middle of the night. I told a Guard that I had to use the restroom—*politely,* that is—before he growled at me and told me to go back to sleep. Then, I used a bit more force in my voice. He got pissed at me and came over to my cell to give me a lecture on not creating chaos, or some shit like that. Right when he came over, I grabbed his wrist through the opening of the cell doors and twisted it with all of my might. That unfortunately brought the attention of the other Guard. I then tried my best to rummage for the keys in his pocket, but the other Guard came and raised his gun to my face. I was freaking the hell out.

"As the other Guard shot the bullet at me, it clanged against the metal keyhole and ricocheted back to him, lodging into his neck. He was gasping for air as the other man looked at him in alarm, and that's when I found the perfect opportunity to go for the keys. I was able to grab his keys since they sat quite idly in his pocket—stupid ass Guard." She snorts and continues to speak. "He was yelling at me as I opened the door, and then I head-butted him. He stumbled backwards as I grabbed hold of his arm and pulled it as hard as I could. Man fell to the ground as I placed my foot on his neck, making sure that son of a bitch loses oxygen.

"Unfortunately, the other Guard came and wrapped his hands around my neck. I was gasping for air as I had my foot placed on the first Guard's neck and tried to get out of the other's wrath. Somehow, I did, and I found that to be the perfect opportunity to grab the gun he had in his hands. Then, I punched him across the face as the gun fell to the ground. I reached for the gun, but I face- planted onto the floor as the Guard grabbed my foot and lifted it off the ground. My face hurt like shit, but I ignored all sorts of pain as I was reaching for the gun like there was no tomorrow. Few moments later, I was able to grab it, and as soon as I made sure the safety was off, I shot the bullet right into the other Guard's forehead. He died right on the spot, which was kind of hilarious. And then, last but not least, I shot the other Guard in the mouth and then in the forehead afterwards. Ain't that kind of badass?"

"So, you're telling me," Jax starts off, "while you were fighting two Guards, I was sound asleep?"

"What can I say?" Vi shrugs, smirking afterwards. "I work with stealth."

And then, we lie here for at least a few minutes, talking to each other and relishing in each other's presence. Then, we talk about Zach, the one person we had learned to rely on and trusted with all of our hearts. But the guy we had sought out to be the witty and technological Dylan Faulkner turned out to be the furtive and back-stabbing Zachary Everett. I felt a knife slashing through my heart at the exact moment Zach decided to out us to the government. At that exact moment is when I knew we were *screwed.*

The night sky wraps around us like a comforting blanket, stars twinkling distinctively. I find myself captivated by the beauty and simplicity of the night, how calming yet so ambiguous it is. When I was in the bunker with everyone, I became so used to the underground environment that I honestly forgot what it's like to breathe in fresh, naturalistic air and feel encased within the layered sky. I'm not able to enjoy it much right now, since there are far more harrowing thoughts in my mind, but maybe when life slows down,

I can sit back and gaze at the stars, hopefully D.C. being a better place by then.

The cool air starts to rush around me as I huddle in my prisoner clothes, wanting so badly to tear them off my body. I don't want to be labeled as a nuisance in this society. I want to be labeled as an equal. I want to be labeled as a worthy individual, someone worthy of love and appreciation.

And as I sit here with Mal, Jax, Vi, and Jeremiah, I realize that with them, I can accomplish my dreams. I can accomplish it through hard work, cooperation, and respect. With those aspects, I will be unstoppable. The Poor will be unstoppable. *We* will be unstoppable.

Someone's voice suddenly interrupts my thoughts. I jolt upright as I realize the voice is not coming out of my friends—it's instead coming from the sky.

"What is that?" Mal asks.

"It's an announcement from the government," Jax mutters, and the look on his face tells me that this night might just end badly.

"What for?" I whisper, but a deep and masculine voice cuts through the air again, as if they were sending deadly daggers down to us.

"This is a message authorized by the Government of the United States of America. I repeat, this is a message authorized by the Government of the United States of America."

Pause.

"On November 16th, circa 2064, five rebels were arrested for the act of treason. As stated in the Constitution of the United States of America, the act of treason can be subsequent to the life sentence with tortuous acts. These rebels have been articulating a plan to destroy the government for approximately eight months, led by an individual of an unknown name. The rebels present in this group are Jeremiah Morgan, ex-Guard, aged twenty-five, with dark skin, strong build, and brown eyes. Vienna Powers, Poor, aged twenty- two, with pale skin, strong feminine build, and brown eyes. Jax Remington, Rich, aged twenty, tan skin, strong build, gray eyes. Mallory Reaves, Rich, aged nineteen, pale skin, feminine build, blue eyes. And Blaire Cohen, Poor, aged nineteen, olive skin, feminine build, green eyes.

"This group consists of two well-known individuals, Jax Remington—the son of President Tobias Remington and First Lady Isabelle Remington—and Mallory Reaves—daughter of established surgeon Adam Reaves and his wife Veronica Reaves, otherwise known as the Secretary of the Department of State. We believe these people are held against their will by the three rebels. If you see either one of them, please do not hesitate to report your sighting to the government. We need to preserve the future of America, the children of the Rich. And we will rise back to power and let the world know of who we are. Long live America . . . Amen."

29

AMITY

November 25, 2064
1:49 a.m.

WE SIT HERE IN stunned silence. The sky reverberates with the echoes of *amen,* and all I feel like doing at this exact moment is screaming until my voice is hoarse.

Jax's expression is forlorn. "I can't believe they would say that."

"Me neither," Mal replies, her blonde locks falling in front of her eyes as she tucks a few strands behind her. "The reason why I left my parents was to not let my place in society label me for who I am. And it seems as if the universe completely looked over my wish because here I am now, hearing that I am still granted the luxury of coming back home, even when I explicitly show them I want nothing to do with them."

"Reputation." Vi's voice is sharp and thick like a blade. "That's what all these Rich parents care about . . . their kid's reputation."

"What reputation do I have left, though?" Jax says. "My father heard me say and clarify that I want nothing to do with this life

—let alone *him*. I mean, does he not get the hint? Does he not understand what I'm trying to convey here?"

"I'm guessing that your father kept the video to himself and assumed, when you said that, you were saying it under great coercion," Jeremiah says. "He's preserving your true personality from himself and society."

"How screwed up can one person be?" Vi mumbles underneath her breath.

"This is our fault," Mal blurts out. "We should've just stood up for ourselves when we had the chance."

"This is *not* your fault," I say. "You didn't ask to be put in this position."

"I don't know." She sighs. "I'm just tired of being associated with *them*. I don't need a pity party for me, and neither does Jax."

"It's all right, we'll show those bastards what is up," I whisper into the air. "Together, we are unstoppable. All we have to do is remain out of their sight, focus on our goals, and stick together."

"Wisest words I've heard," Jeremiah says, grinning.

Afterwards, Vi clears her throat and says, "Well, let's at least get some rest before the sun rises. Shall I assign shifts?" We all nod. "Great. First shift can be Jeremiah. You don't mind that, right?"

"Nope." He grins. "I'll just think about my family the entire time."

"Wonderful. Second shift can be—"

"Me and Jax will do it," Mal says.

"Both of you?"

"Yeah." She clears her throat. "I need to talk to him anyway."

"Um, okay . . . Works for me," Vi says. "You guys can do your shift for as long as you can—but don't stay up too long." She takes a quick glance toward me, a short and sharp breath leaving her. "And I guess me and Blaire will be the last shift."

For some reason, I feel great apprehension pour into my

lungs. It was already awkward enough staying with Jax *alone* for one whole hour, but with Vi? I am genuinely terrified. And seeing the cold glare in her eyes makes me think that she might just rip my head off.

However, for the past few weeks, I feel like the "partnership" I have built up with her has been pretty great. I mean, I may have annoyed her at some points, but hasn't everyone? Jeremiah and Mal are an exclusion from that, though. It seems as if they can insult Vi without getting a slap in the face. But me? I don't even know her that well. When I first met her and her past was brought up, it was like she brought up an invisible shield and ever since then she refuses to say more than two sentences to me.

Maybe during my shift with her, I can somehow get closer to her because, I don't exactly know why I feel this way, but I think we can be great friends. We're both Poor. We both hate the Rich. We both hate this world. And we both hate Tobias.

I can surely do this. As long as I don't get on her nerves.

It is minutes later that my eyes decide to give in on me, feeling like hundred-pound weights as they close. My head falls on the trunk of the large tree behind me, my legs stretching forward as the aching of my body doesn't seem to go away. Nothing seems to go away.

3:03 a.m

My wild and untamed hair itches my neck as my eyes slowly flicker open. The sky seems to be aglow with many stars still dazzling and radiating with energy.

It takes every muscle in my arm to move it and anchor myself upright, my back aching with every movement. A small groan escapes me as I pull myself forward, hoping that I won't break any essential limbs. Then again, pretty much every limb is essential.

I look around my surroundings, noticing the still-sleeping figures of many—well, just Vi and Jeremiah. Jax and Mal seem to have disappeared, meaning their shift is happening at this very moment. My curious self begins to search for them with my wandering eyes.

Seconds later, I catch them by the far corner, their bodies across from each other as they seem engaged in a conversation. My bleary mind is at first unable to decipher their words, but the more I wake up, the more I am able to.

"—kind of freezing my ass off right now." Jax lets out a chuckle.

Mal bursts out laughing. "My ribs hurt so badly. That probably means laughing isn't a good idea right now."

"Probably." Jax sighs.

Mal is across from Jax, her back turned toward me. Jax, on the other hand, I can see very clearly, his body anchored to her as he continues to beam. It was just barely two weeks ago that Mal was slapping him across the face, reprimanding him for not revealing his true self. But life has changed plenty now—*especially* Jax, too. And, the more I look at them, the more I realize that their energy together is so calm, so comfortable.

"How are you holding up?" Jax scratches his jaw.

"Not so great. You?"

"Same. It really sucked to hear that announcement."

"I know, and I can't even imagine how the others felt hearing that. They are actually Poor—and they grew up like that as well. Well, kind of for Jeremiah since he wasn't exactly Rich or Poor. But me and you? We grew up Rich, so we have no idea how much they struggled."

"Exactly." Jax sighs. "I just think it's so stupid on why the Rich even bother with dividing the country."

"It's because they want to be better than everybody else." Mal snorts. "My parents were especially like that too. They constantly belittled the Poor, only because they lived a not-so ideal life compared to us. I always sympathized with the Poor, hoping to give them a better life . . . I just didn't know how to."

"And you know my parents are like that too—especially my father. I felt so infuriated hearing how he talked about the Poor. And you know that because we shared our deepest thoughts with each other."

"We could relate so much."

"I know." He smiles. "We were so young and innocent back then. All we wanted was *everyone* to be happy, not just a selected group of individuals. And now . . . We're not so young and not so innocent anymore. We're fending for our lives right now, right in the middle of the forest with people that actually dealt with shit in their lives. We were privileged, so we never understood. But now we're experiencing it first-hand . . . and finally realizing the constant torture Poor people are put through."

Mal leans back against the tree trunk, and I can see a sliver of her face now. "You know, the night we kidnapped you . . . I was really upset when you acted like you had no idea what I was talking about."

He winces. "I got to admit, I was a bit of an asshole back then."

"You *were*."

"But that was only because I am so used to shoving my feelings away," he says. "And imagine how frustrated and pressured I felt when you guys were forcing me to open up. It obviously took a while for me to open up—I understand that. But you have to understand where I come from, too. And I'm especially not as brave as you, Mallory. I mean, c'mon!" He chuckles. "Running away from your parents? *Willingly?* That's kind of badass, if you ask me."

From this distance, I see Mal's cheeks flushing. "Oh, stop it."

"It's true, though." Jax grins.

She quickly changes the subject, leaning forward in great interest. "Remember when me and you used to swing on the swings and talk until three in the morning?"

"I remember." Jax chuckles. "We did that every single night."

"And our parents used to get mad at us for staying out for so long." Mal grins. "Those were the good old days."

"Tell me about it."

Silence.

"Hey, Mallory?"

"Yeah?"

"Why did you leave without me? And why didn't you tell me you were planning to?"

Mal sighs. "I couldn't because I knew you would stop me. You always discouraged me from running away from my problems, and I knew that if I even brought up the mere notion of running away, then you would not approve of it at all. So . . . I did it on my own."

"So, that's it? You just left without looking back?"

"I had to, Jax!" She gnaws at her lip.

"No, I feel like there's another reason why you left all of a sudden, but you're not telling me."

"Fine, you want to know?" Mal looks at him angrily, deep and raw emotion threatening to escape out of her. "It was because I liked you. *More* than a friend."

He sits there in shock, his mouth agape as he tries to understand what Mal had told him. Even I'm sitting here, a shocked expression on my face as I listen to the conversation escalating in front of me.

Mal continues to speak. "I didn't know how to tell you of my feelings. I myself wasn't able to realize it as well. So, I found it best to just keep it to myself. And besides, it didn't seem like you reciprocated what I felt for you too. Not once did it seem like you held romantic interest in me. I felt so miserable, so much to the point where I just *had* to leave. So, I left—for my sake and for yours."

"Mallory . . ."

"Don't worry, I don't like you anymore. It's in the past now, y'know? I left and was happy being alone, fending for myself. I learned how it was like to be Poor in the hard way. And sooner or later, I forgot about my feelings for you. I didn't forget about *you,* per se. I just forgot about how I felt for you, that's it. So, it wasn't exactly you that made me leave: It was the memories we shared and how I felt about it—how I felt about you. So, there are no hard feelings."

"I'm so sorry."

"No, don't be." She smiles. "It's in the past now."

"Still! I . . . I feel so bad. I shouldn't have overlooked you like that."

"It's okay, trust me. And besides, I'm telling you—I'm over it now. I only think of you as a friend now, okay?"

"Yeah, me too." He looks a bit relieved.

"Okay, good." She clutches onto his hands afterwards. "I'm proud of how far we've come."

"Me too." Jax grins, his scar glinting against the moonlight.

"Hey," Mal whispers, "I keep on forgetting to ask, but . . . where did that scar come from? I know it's pretty recent because it wasn't there when we were friends."

I wonder about that all the time, too.

"Um . . ." Jax shakes his head. "It's a long story."

She cocks her head. "I have all the time in the world."

He lets out a sigh and adjusts himself. "I really don't feel like talking about it."

"Why not?"

"I don't know—it's just . . . associated with pretty bad memories. And talking about my scar and where and how it came from honestly makes me feel sick. It's nothing against you, Mallory, but it's honestly only to do with me."

Mal looks a bit disappointed but regains herself with a quick smile. "Don't worry about it, Jax. I understand where you're coming from."

He beams at her, relief flooding through him.

As they continue to talk, I bask in the beautiful darkness of the night and feel the strained muscles of mine slowly relax. I find it great to hear that Jax and Mal are rekindling their friendship and realizing their great moments together. Especially because Mal felt so dejected about leaving him in the first place, but she had to do it for her own good.

I can't even imagine leaving my family like that, even though I did leave them, just not willingly.

And I grew up in a place where it was desolate and depressing. I didn't know how to communicate with people my own age. Never did I think I would be here right now, with these people that share the same goals and aspirations as me. And never did I ever believe I would be content with leaving my family, just to make sure they have a good life in the end.

But I am learning every day as I venture through this hapless life. I will continue to grow as life goes on, and the Subversives has taught me morals that I will carry on with me for the rest of my life. And somewhere amongst the dark world, I find happiness peering through my soul.

I have always found some way to be cynical, but in the mere distance, I can find some light peeking past the dismal holes. I rise like the sun, sitting in the unknown and then merging into the known. Maybe I will be able to accomplish what I want in life if I am more optimistic, less snarky, and able to figure life out with a clean slate of mind.

Maybe I will.

30

PURPOSE

November 25, 2064
3:03 a.m.

SOON ENOUGH, MY SHIFT with Vi begins.

The air is cool, rigid, and stiff, and each movement I make to the tree several trees away from us makes me shiver instinctively. Vi is already there with her knees pushed up to her chest, and all I can really think about right now is how mortified I am to spend a significant amount of time with her.

And *alone,* too.

I decide to not dwell on it much and instead quickly make my way over to her. It seems as if she's staring straight at the sky, biting her lip as she doesn't bother to say anything, or even look at me.

Which is honestly fine with me. Whatever she prefers.

Luckily there is a tree right ahead of her, not so far away either, so I lean against the tree trunk, sitting exactly in front of her. From here I can clearly notice the hardness in her expression, and the way her eyes are anything but welcoming. Her skin is pallid, just as usual, but this time it's even more pale because of the biting cold atmosphere. Her body is angled in a strict and taut posture, and she rests her hand against the gun in her lap, prepared to shoot at someone if necessary. I sometimes wonder why she is the way she is. Something horrible must've happened to make her so closed off—so *abrasive*. Something truly life-changing.

"Why are you staring at me like that?"

Her tone cuts through the air like a knife. She raises her eyebrows and looks at me, her intense glare making all sorts of air leave my lungs.

"S-sorry," I mutter. "I was just wondering what you're thinking about."

"What *I'm* thinking about?" She leans forward, her distinctive features shimmering against the night. "Do you really want to know?"

"Sure," I say, shrugging.

"Well," she says, "for starters, I am extremely upset by the way our journey is going. Only because everything was going so great until a close companion of mine decided to reveal himself as a Rich person who works for the government." Vi purses her lips. "Also, my sudden decision to escape prison has landed us in this cold, wet, and disgusting jungle that leads to God knows where—meaning that we currently are on the government's watch list. Oh! And not to mention that the government is specifically searching for Mal and Jax because they, of course, are the worthy individuals." She straightens herself. "So, based on hearing that, I think you can conclude that I am not in the mood for any sort of conversation with you right now, right?"

I press my lips together. "Right."

It is suddenly quiet, except for the very few crickets chirping around us. I sigh, intertwining my fingers as I rest my head and body against the hard bark of the tree, glistening sweat bathing underneath my clothes. Even though it's almost been two weeks since the disaster in the bunker occurred, I weirdly feel as if it happened months ago and we've been in prison for weeks on end —when, in reality, we were not. I'm guessing I feel this way due to the lashings we underwent in jail, but maybe it's also because of how much we've been through in almost a damn month.

Something heavy settles onto my stomach as I realize that *so much* time has passed by ever since the inauguration. That was the last time I saw my family, and judging by how this journey is going so far, I feel as if that was my last time seeing them in general.

I don't like that feeling.

My entire life has revolved around them. My mother has educated me on every single aspect in this dying country. My father tells me funny jokes and lifts my soul up whenever I dwell on the negative aspects of this society too much. My sister is someone that I can hug and caress after a long day at work, and I can't even imagine not seeing any of them.

Because it's been five years since I've last seen my brother. And I'd lost all hope on seeing him again for a while now.

That's when I am brought to reality again, weighing in the unfortunate situation I am in—both in entirety and my extremely quiet shift so far with Vi, too.

Something clicks inside of me. I cannot spend our entire shift sitting with this woman in this dark and murky place and not exchange a single word with her. I want her to know that I just would like to be friends with her. That is all I want.

I clear my throat, my voice shaky as I say, "Hey, Vi?"

She slowly looks over at me, her expression flat and frightening. "What did I just tell you?"

"That you don't want to have a conversation with me," I say. "I know."

"Okay." She nods. "Then I suggest you stop talking before I—"

"But why, though?"

When the words escape from my mouth, I begin to prepare for my eventual death.

It is horrifyingly silent—except for the noises that occur when she adjusts her position. "Excuse me?"

"Why do you not want me to talk to you?" I gulp.

She narrows her eyes. "Because I just don't. End of discussion."

"Did I do something to you, though?"

Seconds pass by. "No. You did not."

"Then why don't you ever want to talk to me?" I am slowly becoming desperate. "I've been nothing but nice to you. I mean, yeah, I may have interrupted you a couple of times, which is ill-mannered on my part. But never have I ever done anything bad to you—intentionally or unintentionally."

She lets out an exasperated breath. "Jesus, you really want to talk to me, huh?"

I almost smile. "Yeah. Of course I do."

"Why?" She scowls. "There's absolutely nothing interesting to know about me."

"Just say something," I say. "I won't judge."

"You won't judge?" She rephrases, not seeming convinced.

"Of course not." I shrug. "I just want to be your friend, Vi."

Her shoulders begin to shake with silent laughter. Her bright grin is radiant, even in the consuming night. "Damn, you're a pushy woman." When her laughter dies down, she sighs and extends her legs, stuffing the gun into her pocket. "Fine. Go ahead and ask me questions."

My eyebrows fly up to my forehead. "Seriously?"

"I am always serious."

I smile. "Oh my God, thank you so much."

"You know, my patience is wearing very thin right now."

"Okay, okay—*sorry*," I mumble. Excitement is coursing through my veins. "So, uh, when's your birthday?"

She looks unimpressed. "That's the first question you want to ask me?"

I frown. "Just wanted to start off with something."

Moments later, she grumbles to herself and says, "July 23rd, 2042."

"Okay. Um . . . Tell me about your family."

Her face is like a block of ice. "And this is where we stop."

Disappointment filters through me. "Vi, c'mon, I told you—I am not going to judge."

"I don't care." She crosses her arms. "This is none of your business."

"But—"

"No!" Her voice is singed with venom, dropping to a low baritone. Her eyes are raging and flourishing with deadly flames. It feels as if something huge lodged into my throat.

I sigh with defeat, embarrassment washing over me as I look away in shame. "I-I'm sorry. I shouldn't have pushed your boundaries like that."

She doesn't say anything.

I press my lips together, incredibly frustrated with myself and Vi. I know I shouldn't have annoyed her like that, but there is nothing more I want than to be her friend. I've always wondered about her childhood and the memories she made, too. I don't care if she has the worst past in the world—that will never change my perspective of her. I just want to get to know her, especially because we are all in this together. And it's just not fair to me that these people know every nook and cranny of my life while I know nothing of them.

Vi surprisingly speaks a minute later.

"The last time I opened up to someone, they revealed themselves to be a traitor."

I look up at her, studying her pained expression. I know exactly who she's talking about.

She continues speaking. "He knew about my past because I thought I could trust him." A heavy pause. "Key word is *thought.*"

"You can trust me, though."

"That's exactly what he told me, too." She takes a deep breath in. "Do you see what I'm trying to say here?"

"You think I'm going to backstab the group?"

"No," she says almost immediately. "I just have major trust issues."

Another long and heavy pause.

"But you and Zach are two different people."

Her eyes are suddenly bathing in a completely different emotion as she says with a low tone, "And I shouldn't do that to you."

Did *the* Vienna Powers just . . . speak to me nicely? I am absolutely appalled.

I sit here in silence, watching her push her shoulders back and letting out a long sigh. My hands are shaking—from the cold and from the extreme anxiety jamming into the veins that run in and out of my system.

And she speaks.

"My father, Isaiah Powers, was white, and my mother, Jessica Zhao, was a Chinese immigrant. They fell in love with each other and immediately got married in D.C. Life was going pretty great for them . . . until 2038, though, when the new society emerged. My father at the time was working at a low-level job at some sort of firm, and my mother was unemployed because her English wasn't the best, not to mention she had very little education, too. Of course, they were immediately placed in the Poor category."

Vi adjusts her jaw. "A couple years later, my mother was pregnant with me. And then four years later, she was pregnant with my little brother, Matthew. It was a nice little family we had, despite the many societal issues that were going on. The situation was just so tense back then, especially because our president wasn't the nicest. And honestly speaking, all of the presidents throughout the years didn't show a sliver of sympathy toward the Poor. I'm starting to think these bastards were 'elected' just to shit on us in the end.

"But anyway, uh . . . As I was saying, the situation was bad. The poverty was unbearable—it was starting to be as bad as it was during the Second Great Depression. Maybe even worse. And, um, it got so bad to the point where the president began to issue orders to the Guards because he was so desperate to rid of anyone that not only looked Poor now, but also looked as if they were international spies hellbent on destroying America's reputation even more.

"The number one competitor with America was China before the Second Great Depression. That is why, when it happened, they believed China was also a reason why it occurred, but they didn't really take the idea into motion until the poverty was extremely uncontrollable."

She pauses.

"That's why the president issued an order to kill all Chinese people. It was a truly heinous and obviously racist decision to make, but he never thought or mentioned it as that because he wanted to keep his flawless reputation in check. That's why he instead called it an imperative act to commence the advancement and rebuilding of America." She lets out a sad chuckle. "What a terrible time it was."

Vi bites her lip, her voice suddenly strained. "That's when my father issued me, my brother, and my mom to remain inside our shack at all times. My father was safe because he was, well, *not* Chinese, and he knew that too. He didn't want us all to be in the hands of the Guards.

"But one day . . . That did happen.

"I was fourteen years old when the worst night of my life happened. My father was at work, obviously, and we were all at home, just like we were supposed to be." She laughs a sad laugh.

"Let me tell you, I was extremely close with my family. My parents were my role models; they were the hardest-working bunch I knew. And my brother, he . . . He was an amazing little man. Super smart and super amazing. God, I really loved them so much.

"But yeah, we were just sitting there in our small living room, laughing and smiling and trying to find the good within this shitty ass world. It was several minutes later that I had to use the bathroom all of a sudden, so I went and did my business. But, uh . . . as I was leaving, I suddenly heard the most terrifying gunshots in my own goddamn house. I was shaking out of my mind, and I was curious to know why that terrible noise happened.

"So, I opened the door a tiny bit and I felt my heart ripping into shreds at that very moment. I-I couldn't move because my mother and my brother were on the ground, dead, blood coming out of their chests and"—her eyebrows pinch together, her voice becoming frantic—"I just stood there like a coward, so mad at myself, so *pissed* at myself that I couldn't defend them. That I just had to use the bathroom at that exact moment.

"And, as if it couldn't get any worse, my father came home seconds later and screamed when he saw his wife and son on the floor, dead. I thought they would spare him since he was white. Even fourteen-year-old me knew what the loathsome president was up to." Her breath catches in her throat. "But they didn't. They shot him too because he was associated with these 'Chinese spies' that wanted to destroy our country."

She brings the gun out of her pocket, looking at the cuts and edges of the black and shimmery metal. "And, like the great coward I was, I ran away. I ran out the open window in the bathroom with absolutely nothing on my hands, and ever since then, I've been an orphan. No family members left alive. Nothing and no one to love. And nothing and no one to look forward to."

Her eyes are filled with years of misery. "But I can give justice to my family members. I can fight for them the way I should've eight years ago. And while the president we have now doesn't follow the same path as the president we had during the worst night of my life, I still think that the entirety of these privileged folks should be punished and brought down from their reign. They shouldn't have authority over America. They shouldn't excuse their behavior by calling it a purification or safety measure when we know that it is most definitely a mass genocide."

Her body is firmer than I ever imagined it to be. "I don't dwell on my past anymore either. What's the point of torturing myself with that terrifying night, y'know? So I decided to just make mind of it and move on. Of course I'll never forget it. Jesus, I have nightmares about it even to this day. But the world we live in, Blaire, you still have yet to experience the most traumatizing parts of it. And God forbid you ever do because it will scar you for life."

My heart is nothing but heavy.

No words seem to formulate in my mind or out of my mouth. I feel my lungs constrict, air leaving and entering through elongated measures.

Vi told me her entire past, and now? I know why she's always closed off. Why she has trust issues. Why she refuses to be kind to others.

Because she's endured hell.

She's survived the deadliest of fires and came back stronger than ever, more than willing to destroy anyone in her way. She wants to provide justice for Matthew, Isaiah, and Jessica because she loved them. They were the *only* people she loved.

And now she has nobody. In her eyes, at least.

That's why I hope that, one day, she realizes that she does have people to love and rely on, such as me, Jeremiah, and Mal.

Jax is a bit volatile, though. But she does have supporters. She definitely does.

She speaks moments later. "You are to never bring this up ever again, you hear me?"

I rapidly nod my head.

"No, I'm serious as hell. If you bring any of this up in front of the others or even in front of me, then I will—"

"Chop my head off." I give her a small smile. "I understand."

"Good," she says, squaring her jaw. "Glad we're on the same page."

Vi turns and looks the other way, angling her body to the side as she rests the back of her head against the nook of the trunk. Her beautiful eyes are nothing but inventories of her past that shapes her to be the woman she is today. And as she clutches the gun in her hand, truly defensive and truly determined to accomplish her goals, I can't help but feel an immense amount of respect for her.

31

MOLLIFY

November 25, 2064
6:12 a.m.

I GO DOWN TO the lake near where we slept last night. The calm waters rush in and out of the bank, trickling to my toes as I step near it. I shiver to myself as the water touches my feet, and I let out a sharp wince as I reel it back in. That is when I decide to sit by the bed of grass adjacent to the lake, the soft blades digging into my rear. The sun is rising right now, and I can't help but stare at its beauty as it awakens from its slumber.

I haven't noticed this before, but the early morning is truly beautiful just because of how peaceful it is. The only noises that seem to be around me are the constant cawing of birds and the soft noises of the water trailing in and out.

Suddenly, I hear someone trekking behind me. Curious, I swirl around to see Jax, purely haggard. I gulp as he makes his way beside me, keeping a considerable distance between us.

He presses his lips together as his tired gray eyes lock onto me. "Hey."

I answer a few moments later. "Hi."

Jax clears his throat, looking at the lake in front of us, the smooth coating of it shimmering against the radiating sun rays. "This view is beautiful."

"It is." I look at him. "How have you been holding up?"

"Well, I barely got any sleep last night, I'm starving my ass off, and I just want to take my clothes off."

"W-why do you want to take your clothes off?" I say, heat taking over my face.

"Because I hate these prisoner clothes," he says in a slow manner, sending me a lopsided smile afterwards. "Did you think I meant something else?"

"Uh, no."

"You sure about that?"

I send him a death glare.

He laughs lowly. "Relax. I'm just joking."

I grumble to myself, eager to change the topic. "Anyway . . . I feel the exact same way as you. Just wearing these bright orange prisoner clothes makes me want to puke."

"Same." He scowls. "It constantly reminds me of how screwed up the American government is."

"That you got right."

A few seconds of silence passes over us, for he clears his throat. "Also, uh . . . about the other night."

I furrow my brows. "What other night?"

"The night where I was highly upset and, um, kind of slept on you."

The night that we were first jailed. "Yes, what about it?"

"Well . . ." He awkwardly gesticulates. "Can we just forget about that?"

"Why?"

"Because I was being really vulnerable. And I hate being vulnerable." He winces. "Especially in front of women."

"There's nothing wrong with being vulnerable," I say.

The look he sends me is filled with irritation. "There's actually a lot of things wrong with being vulnerable."

"Yeah, for you, maybe."

"What the hell do you mean by that?"

I let out a sharp breath. "Because you are a man with an over-inflated ego."

He scowls. "I am not."

"Didn't you just say being vulnerable is wrong?"

"It is," he says. "And I'm not saying that because I am supposedly a man with an over-inflated ego. I am saying that because it is just morally wrong on so many levels."

"Whatever." I scoff. "I'm done having this conversation with you. Besides, why are you even here?"

"Because I can't sleep."

"So you had to come and follow me?"

"Yeah, why not?" His eyes are suddenly playful. "I thought I could charm you with my overwhelming beauty."

"And there's your over-inflated ego coming into play."

He frowns playfully, nudging my arm with his elbow. "Damn, you got me there, Cohen."

I smile. "Now that we got your ego established . . . How was your encounter with Mal last night?"

"You should know." He smirks. "I saw that you were awake."

My spine almost snaps in half. "H-how did you know?"

Jax merely shrugs. "The joking answer would be that I have eyes in the back of my head. But the serious answer would be that you're loud as hell when you wake up. Seriously. I could hear the leaves rustling quite loudly when you were eavesdropping on us."

"God, I'm so embarrassed."

"Don't be." He runs his fingers through his overly-disheveled dark hair. "I would want to eavesdrop on a conversation like that, too. But anyway, let me answer your question." He takes a deep breath. "I think our conversation went really great . . . except the fact that she told me she used to like me."

"Yeah." I wince. "Do you, uh, have feelings for her?"

"No," he says. "She is most definitely a very beautiful woman, but I've just not seen her like that in *that* way, y'know? She used to be my closest friend in the entire world. I wouldn't even dare to complicate our friendship like that."

For some weird reason, I feel a great amount of relief coming through me.

"I understand that."

"Why'd you ask?" He grins. "Do you have secret feelings for me and just want to confirm if I'm emotionally available? I don't blame you, though; I am quite an attractive man."

"And he's back."

He laughs, dimples creasing into his cheeks. I can't help but chuckle, too.

Silence falls between us, but only for a second or two because Jax leaps to his feet suddenly and lends me his hand. "You want to hunt with me? I bet the gang is wanting some food right now."

I take a look toward his hand and feel a grin playing at my lips. "Why not?" I place my hand in his, warmth filling my insides as he pulls me to my feet. My body feels like it got run over multiple times, and I find it appalling to see that I am on my two feet without crumpling to the ground.

Once Jax lifts me up, we trek farther from the group, and as I start to ask Jax about what we're going to hunt with, he grabs a stick lying on the ground. It is long and jagged, and he carries it in his hand as I follow him wordlessly.

The tall and lanky trees loom over us and cover us like protective blankets, almost as if they were shielding us from the bright sun. I forgot what day it is, but judging by the cold and brutal weather, it's probably nearing December. And my body is so used to the cold to the point where it has no reaction to it—it is simply numb.

Soon enough, I find myself getting annoyed by the constant

crunching of the fallen leaves due to our heavy steps. Eventually, though, the crunching stops as Jax and I cease our trekking.

He leans in to me, his breath tickling my ear. "Look over there."

My eyes trail over the innocent and hapless rabbit hopping from one place to another, seeming to have no care in this world.

I rip my eyes away from the rabbit as Jax gestures towards his stick. He lowers himself to the ground and digs the butt of the stick onto the surface of the hard dirt. Then, he wraps both of his large and strong hands around the stick and rubs it, grunting as the stick maneuvers around the ground. I watch with an open mouth as, a few moments later, the butt of the stick is finally sharpened. There is a jagged point appearing from the end of it as he shows it to me, grinning with pride. "See?"

"How did you do that?" I ask.

"It was something my dad taught me when I was younger. He used to take me hunting when I was eight years old, and I found it as a great way to release some steam. I used to hunt with my father before he became president. I stopped hunting then, but I definitely did not forget all of the useful skills he taught me. Now, I only plan to hunt in emergencies such as this."

"Wow, that's awesome," I say breathlessly.

"Well, the awesome part is just now coming." He sends me a smirk and narrows his eyes onto the innocent rabbit who nibbles on a fallen leaf. Jax pushes his dark hair back as he adjusts his position, his right foot forward and left foot back as he fixates his vision on the small rabbit. Then, he lifts the spear right next to his ear, the pointy part forward as he slightly brings it back and forth.

Finally, he shoots it forward, flying with great speed as it pierces into the rabbit's body.

I let out a gasp as I watch the animal stumble and plop onto the ground. "Jax, you killed the poor rabbit!"

"Yeah, that's the point." He raises his eyebrows.

I take a deep breath as I try to say another complaint, but my words come to a stop as I realize that he is right. We have no other food to eat. And how long can we actually live on berries? They might be poisonous too . . . .

The both of us walk over to the dead rabbit, blood seeping out of its torso as I continue to feel bad for it. Jax, with no hesitation, rips the spear away from the rabbit's torso and holds it up in his hand. "Let's go back. The other's must have awakened by now."

We walk back to our spot with the others. Jax clears his throat after a few moments. "Y'know, I completely understand if you were weirded out."

"Honestly, I was—a little." I sigh.

Jax snorts. "It's a bit ironic that the Rich person hunts, and the Poor person is weirded out by it."

"Honestly, you're right." I chuckle. "But anyway, yeah, I obviously don't support you killing the rabbit for fun, but in this given situation, I support you with all of my heart because I am dying over here." My stomach grumbles just at that moment.

He laughs. "It's all right, and of course I don't kill animals for fun. Just like I told you, I only planned to use these skills for survival shit. I'm not a weirdo, Cohen."

"Oh, well, that's a relief." I laugh as he nudges me playfully.

As we continue to walk even farther, I take a quick look toward Jax. My body starts to warm as I notice just how close we're walking together, his arm touching mine every now and then. His strong muscles, still covered in bruises and cuts, stand out within the prisoner uniform. And his dark hair is not short and cut concisely like before; instead, it looks wildly untamed. His scar still glints hauntingly, gashed painfully. He looks a bit wise, too.

The walk is very peaceful before I laid eyes on the dead rabbit held in Jax's hand, its eyes still wide open, but not holding a single sense of life. There's something about the way it is so *dead* that bothers me, how Jax was so quick to kill the rabbit. It sort of reminds me how Guards treat the Poor: killing them with no hesitation and no explanation required as well.

My stomach grumbles again, loud enough for Jax to hear. He nudges me again. "Don't worry, we're almost here."

I send him a hesitant grin and look ahead, immediately hearing commotion from where we set camp. Jax and I share a frightened look as we run toward our friends. All I want is to protecting my friends from any harm. I know they don't need protection, but sometimes even the strongest of people need help at some given moments—even from the weak.

My heart lurches to my throat as we near the camp and see Guards roaming around Mal, Jeremiah, and Vi. Rifles are cocked at them, and when they see Jax and me beside them, some of them lift their guns at us now.

Simultaneously, the dead rabbit in his hand falls to the ground.

3 2

DANGER

November 25, 2064
6:36am

WE STAND IN COMPLETE silence, hearing nothing except the swaying of the trees. It's only been a few seconds, but it feels like forever standing here, looking back and forth . . .

Before Vi throws the first punch.

She moves at lightning-speed, bellowing a war cry as she jabs her elbow into a Guard's exposed neck. I think of her melancholy story, something she revealed to me in the middle of the night. I still can't seem to swallow that whole ideal. And I begin to understand why she refuses to speak or hear of her past . . . It makes dread and ire smash into her lungs. So she would rather carry her family members in her heart and dedicate every decision and movement of hers to them.

That is when I get the message that I shouldn't hold back and be civil anymore. I should instead fight back, fight like my life depends on it, and fight like there is no tomorrow.

The others seem to have gotten the message too, as I see Mal ripping the mask off another Guard and ramming her fist into his face, his nose blotched with blood instantly. I've never seen this much rage coming from her before, except the time our bunker was raided, but I guess in this given situation, I should just be grateful for her sudden wave of anger.

On the other hand, Jeremiah grabs the ankle of another Guard and sends him flying to the ground. There, he yanks out the rifle upholstered in the Guard's hands and sends a bullet flying into his left eye. Blood splatters everywhere as his pitiful screech echoes into the air like a dying bird.

My stomach tightens in disgust, and before I can react to the situations unraveling in front of me, one Guard suddenly comes behind me and pulls me into a chokehold. A warbled gasp escapes out of my throat as I try to pry the Guard's strong arms away from my neck, but he continues to hold on tightly, growling into my ear as he slams me onto the ground. It reminds me of how I was choked when Zach outed us to the government. How I felt so lifeless. So helpless.

My back hits the forest floor, pain shooting through my spine. I groan as I try to console myself physically, but no single limb seems to work. However, I still try my best to get off the ground and run after the Guard that smashed my body down, but Jax beats me to it by body slamming him to the ground and punching his stomach repeatedly. Trails of blood escape out of the Guard's mouth like a stream, his lips turning pale blue as Jax sends another painful punch to him—except it goes to his mouth instead.

A huge wave of appreciation rushes through me as Jax finishes off the Guard—the same one that attacked me. And he seems really great at combat, which is bizarre, considering how he's had zero combating skills. However, there's still so much more I need to know about this man, so he may as well be extremely talented at fighting. Maybe more than Jeremiah.

Which, seeing how Jeremiah's fight is going, I begin to doubt that incredibly.

He rises from the ground after snatching the Guard's helmet, bullet proof pads, and other armor from him, also holding guns in his large hands. Jeremiah looks frightening, nothing but seventy-eight inches of muscle and steel. He's angry at these people for separating him and his family away—his family that he hasn't seen in *years*. He's angry beyond his mind that revenge starts to seem like child-play too.

We all have reasons to be angry, but Jeremiah's seems to be reaching from his blood and bones.

On the other hand, Mal seems to have taken care of her enemy quite well by smashing the Guard's face into mere pieces by the butt of the rifle, for I can't even tell his features anymore. She grunts and groans as she pushes the dead Guard to the side and goes and fights the remaining one. The other scariest person in this group *has* to be Mal. She may seem sweet and kind from the outside, but if someone does her wrong, she will not hesitate to rip them to shreds.

I look over to my right and see Mal jumping onto the Guard's back and snatching a knife from his pile of weapons. Without any hesitation, she slashes the sharp blade across his neck, blood spurting from his skin as the Guard screams, his deep voice rattling throughout the atmosphere. As he waves his hands through the air violently, trying to get Mal off him, I feel the sudden urge to get up off my back and be useful for once. I want to fight. And I *will* fight.

So, I get up.

Grab the gun lying beside me. And aim it at him.

But I don't even know how to use one!

Panic sifts through me as I rack through my mind, desperate to remember any conversations the other's had about using a goddamn gun. I know I should press the trigger and let it be, but I heard it's super loud as well—so loud to the point where my ears can split apart. My mind is running around with thoughts and—

"Keep both hands on the gun, keep your balance and breathing steady, and pull the trigger!" Jax desperately says to me, going off to fight another Guard.

"Okay!" I yell, aiming at the Guard who flails around with Mal on his back.

I force my breathing to slow and plant my feet onto the ground firmly. Both of my hands grab the gun tightly, and it takes forever for them to stop shaking. Once I feel as if I am ready, I let out a low exhale and press the trigger. *No more wasting time anymore. I am just going to do it.*

It all happens in a matter of seconds.

An earth-shattering *boom* escapes from the gun, alongside a tiny bullet that finds its way into the Guard's throat. I wince, my ears ringing from the piercingly loud sound, but I do not allow my eyes to waver from the dying Guard. Mal looks at me victoriously as she unlatches from him. "You did it, Blaire! Your first kill!"

Immense disgust unravels into my stomach as I see the Guard laid out on the ground, blood spreading in a slow and daunting manner from the center of his neck. My hands waver as my eyes begin to water, wondering if it was the right thing to do to murder a breathing and living human being. It definitely does not feel right to have blood on my hands.

But then I realize that this is my life now. This is who I should be now—a cold-hearted revenge-seeker. And honestly, hearing from Mal that this is my first kill makes all of my remorse dissipate into thin air.

Now we have four down, one more to go.

However, while we were fighting our enemies, it seems as if Vi was still struggling with her's.

The massive Guard has her pinned down to the ground, and her screams pierce through the air as she goes and head butts him—*hard.* He flies back, his back hitting the tree bark next to them. Groaning, he starts to pull something out of his pocket, and my eyes widen with fear as I shout, "Vi, watch out!" I get up from my spot and start to run toward her, but the gun in the Guard's hand lets out a *bang!*

Hot tears blur my vision as Vi lets out a deafening wail, clutching her right forearm as blood pools out of it. Jeremiah looks like an untamed bull with his nostrils flared, and he runs toward the Guard and beats him senseless, which he finally slams the Guard's body onto the tree trunk, his bloody face and body crumpling to the ground.

We run toward Vi, her forearm gushing blood at an alarming rate. Mal holds it in agony as she shouts, "No, you have to stay strong!"

Her mouth is agape, and she tries to breathe, but all that comes out is a dry gasp. I place my hands on her pulse, two fingers on her wrist and the side of her neck as I try to hear any sound of life. I feel a very faint beating, and I clamor, "She has a heart rate, but it's very slow!"

"Shit!" Jeremiah gasps, his eyes filled with heavy tears as he grabs a hold of Vi's face. "You're not going anywhere! Not on my watch!"

"What are we going to do?" Jax wails, his gray eyes filled with worry. "We need her! Without her, we're doomed!"

Tears spill down my cheeks as I try to compose myself, but I can't. I'm losing it. And there's no way we can lose Vi—no way in hell.

Suddenly, Mal comes running toward us with a white box in her hand that has a bright red cross on it. "Move aside, please," she whispers, her blue eyes rimmed with concern. "I got this."

And we do, allowing Mal to kneel beside Vi. She tears open the box, revealing tons of materials such as bandages, gauzes, alcohol, medicine, and so much more. *It's a first-aid kit but bigger. Guards usually have those, so she must have gotten it from one of them.*

Mal rips open a section of the pouch to reveal a stethoscope and another machine curled up inside. "My father is a surgeon, so I am well aware of this. All I need to do is regain her vitals through this defibrillator. This will resurrect her, so I can go on with the next step."

"What's the next step?" Jeremiah whispers.

Mal completely ignores his question and gets the stethoscope out and adjusts herself. She places the bottom end right where Vi's heart would be and gasps out loud. "Crap, she has no heart rate now!"

After telling Jax to put pressure on the wound, Mal rushes to grab the defibrillator and places two hefty pads to the side and gets the machine running. She moves at such a fast pace that it is extremely difficult to tell what she's doing. Soon enough, she tells Jax to let go, so she can begin the process.

She situates herself and lets out a shaky breath as she leans down onto Vi's chest, clutching the pads in her hands as she presses them onto her. A distinct zapping noise occurs as Vi's eyes open for just a slight moment, her body convulsing with energy—but then is seemingly lifeless again. Mal curses to herself, shocking her again. Jolts then run into Vi as she shoots upright immediately, her eyes widened with panic.

"What happened?" Vi rasps, her eyes landing on us as her chest rises in and out.

"Well, I think Mallory just brought you back to life," Jax says breathlessly.

"Really?" she whispers. Mal nods her head. "Thanks, Mal."

"Of course, but . . . I don't think you're going to thank me for this next part."

"What part?" Mal winces as Vi looks over at the huge wound on her forearm, blood continuing to pour out as she screams with horror. "Shit, no!"

"It's okay." She reassures her. "I can fix this."

"How the actual *hell* are you going to fix *this?*" Vi screeches, her eyes filled with absolute terror. "Might as well leave me to die here."

"No!" Jeremiah hisses. "We're not leaving you! We need you!"

"Exactly," I say. "You're staying. And Mal will help you with this."

"Yes, I will," Mal whispers. "Except, um . . ." She shuts her eyes tight as she stammers, "You may or may not be fond of what I'm about to do."

"Do what?" Vi looks at her suspiciously.

Mal breathes in as she grabs something from the huge first-aid kit. I hear clatters as she brings out . . . a knife. Or a sword. Or an axe. Whatever it is, it is very able to cut something—or someone.

"Oh, hell no." Vi looks at the knife in Mal's hand with fear. "Get away from me."

"Jeremiah, take this cloth and stuff it into her mouth," Mal whispers. "She's going to need it."

"No, Mallory." Jeremiah shakes his head. "You're *not* chopping Vi's arm off. We can fix this in a much better and less gruesome way."

"I am not cutting her arm off. I'm taking the bullet out," Mal corrects. "She is bleeding a lot. By the time we try to fix this in another way, she will be dead. Trust me, my father has told me plenty. I have also lived in the wilderness for a very long time. I'm just going to take the knife into her forearm, search for the bullet, take it out, apply some healing alcohol, and seal it with a large bandage after stitches are added. Trust me. I got this."

Finally, we allow Mal to carry on. Vi is still reluctant, but then she notices the severity of her situation—how much blood still seems to be pouring out of her forearm and how much her breaths have become much more erratic. I notice the imminent terror in her eyes, realizing just how risky this situation really is. But she trusts Mal, she trusts her with her entire life. So of course, she nods her head afterwards.

Jeremiah brings a dark blue cloth and places it into Vi's mouth as she leans back onto the tree behind her. Once Jeremiah sits beside me and Jax, Mal sighs and brings the blade to Vi's forearm. Vi sucks in a deep breath, and so do the rest of us as we watch and prepare for whatever's coming next.

Seconds later, Mal digs the blade into the bloody part of Vi's skin. A sick feeling rises in my stomach as the blade enters the interior of her forearm roughly, rummaging around for the bullet. Vi lets out a muffed shriek as Mal forces it in even more—

Bile rises at the back of my throat.

I find myself running over to a tree diagonal to where we are and deposit my insides by the grass there. I clutch my sides, puking every single remnant out of my stomach and onto the ground. I've seen terrible and mortifying things as a Poor person. But what I just saw . . . up front and personal . . . I could not deal with it anymore.

I push my tangled hair back, and I turn around to see the others still engrossed in Mal digging into the inside of Vi's forearm to scavenge for the bullet. I dare not to see it because who knows what I would puke next—I pretty much threw up everything in my goddamn system.

Vi lets out a bloodcurdling scream, even from the cloth stuffed into her mouth, as Mal digs into her skin like a buccaneer scavenging for treasure. "I'm almost there," she murmurs, the bloody blade in her hand moving back and forth. Jeremiah and Jax, on the other hand, watch almost mesmerizingly as Mal continues to forage and Vi continues to scream. *How are they not puking their guts out too?*

After a few agonizing moments later, Mal beams as she brings the blade up in one hand and a tiny bullet in another. "Finally!" She gasps, chuckling.

Vi, right beside her, moans as she clutches her arm. Mal places the bullet right next to her and digs around in the huge first-aid kit. As I sit beside Jeremiah and Jax, once I regain myself, I see that she brings out a small alcohol bottle.

Mal clears her throat as she says, "Now, one last painful moment left, okay?"

Vi, who is beyond tired and just wants this to be over with, ruefully nods her head and squeezes her eyes shut. Mal, without any hesitation, pours some of the alcohol onto the gaping wound, and Vi jabs her teeth down onto the cloth, screeching. Her wound is sizzling with the alcohol, and as Jeremiah comforts Vi, Mal quickly yet painfully sutures her wound and brings out a roll of bandages and wraps it around her forearm. She has wrapped it so many times that the roll is almost finished.

At that time, everybody is calm, including Vi, who has unclenched the cloth and let it fall to her thighs. She lets out deep breaths, not erratic and compulsive ones, and also allows Jeremiah to side-hug her, who seems to cling onto her worryingly.

Some moments later, we decide to keep on moving farther into the forest. The decision was not really spoken. Sure, our bodies were aching, and we felt like we were on our last breaths but sitting around and waiting for the universe to take us would lead to imminent death—whether by the Guards or nature itself.

As we leave the bloody and beaten Guards behind, our footsteps trek against the forest floor, the sun continuing to taunt us with its bright rays. How ironic it is that the weather is beautiful and gleams with delight, yet the events that just occurred were instead quite the opposite.

I notice Vi clinging onto Jeremiah, her injured arm hanging to the side as Jeremiah has his arm slung around Vi's shoulder. He has asked her plentifully if she wants to be carried, but she disagrees every single time, saying that being carried is for "ninnies."

"Where are we going now?" Jeremiah breaks the silence several minutes of our trek later.

A few moments later, Mal answers. "I have no clue. Just walking wherever my feet lead me."

"Aren't we walking away from D.C.?" Vi asks.

"Don't know." Jax shrugs.

I sigh, scrunching my nose as I try to look farther from where we are walking. To be honest, it seems as if we're walking around in circles, not seeing anything different. It sort of makes me feel pissed off, knowing that we've made zero progress in the past thirty minutes we've been walking.

My throat feels scratchy, and my hands are shaky, still reeling in the events that unraveled like a scroll. Not to mention the overwhelming rush of pain filtering through my back. However, it seems as if I'm not the only one that's in pain.

Jeremiah struggles to walk as he clutches some materials that he stole from the Guards in his left hand. Vi has a few gashes on her neck and that one big injury on her right forearm, trying very hard not to move it. Jax has the same scratch on his cheek, still incredibly fresh and sort of bloody, and the rest of his body is scattered in bruises. And finally, Mallory is sort of limping as she carries the first-aid kit in her left hand, looking around to see if there are any new changes to our environment.

Soon enough, we do find a change. A very significant one, actually.

Vi stops walking. "Wait, that looks familiar."

"It doesn't look familiar to me," Jax murmurs, narrowing his eyes to get a better look.

"Hold on . . ." I whisper, a spiel of memories hitting me like bricks. "I know what that place is."

It's the Poor villages. My family is here.

33

BETRAYAL

November 25, 2064
7:20 a.m.

TEARS BLUR MY VISION as I survey the Poor villages in front of me—frayed roofs, cracked sidewalks, trash on the side, and people displayed on the streets like litter itself.

"Are these the Poor villages?" Mal asks.

"Yep." Vi's body seems to stiffen. "They sure are."

We stand here, soaking in the silence while the entire extremity of the situation weighs down upon me. I am not that far away from my family. I should go check up on them, hug them, kiss them, just be there in their presence. I want to go back to them.

However, my feet stay stuck to the grass like glue, not even wanting to run past the trees and into the opening. My mind wants to run toward my family and never leave their side again, but it seems as if my feet have a mind of their own.

"You know what I just realized?" Vi says to me. "We are the only Poor people here. Like, the ones that were Poor from the start."

"Seriously?" I ask.

"Yeah." Vi snorts. "Funny how there's more Rich people in this group than Poor."

"*More* Rich people?" Jeremiah frowns.

"Yeah, you're technically Rich too because you were a Guard at first," Vi says.

"Uh, no. I don't want to be classified as Rich."

"You were at first, though."

"*Were.*" Jeremiah emphasizes. "I'm not anymore."

"I know you're not anymore. I am saying that you were at first, so you are technically considered Rich."

"That makes no sense at all."

"Guys!" Mal hisses.

"What do you mean it doesn't make sense? It makes perfect sense to me."

"God, Vi, I am not in the mood for an argument right now."

"Guys! Please listen!" Mal bellows but not loud enough where she can garner the attention from the Poor outside.

"What?" Vi and Jeremiah both hiss at the same time.

Mal grumbles and gestures for all of us behind a large tree and several others, where we can easily mask ourselves for the time being. It takes forever for us to sit around the trees because our muscles are aching so much we can barely even move. Our shabby clothes and messed up hair, alongside the bruises and rashes running along our skin, is enough to exacerbate the fact that we are exhausted.

Once Mal finally brings us all together, she points at the Poor sector and whisper-yells, "Guards are over there scolding some Poor person!"

"What? Who?" Vi's spine shoots upright from her relaxed position.

"I don't know. It was some little girl."

"Little girl?" I murmur, my heart beginning to race. "What did she look like?"

"She had, um, I don't know . . . dark hair, I think? I couldn't really see her from where we were. But I know she had sort of a small and skinny figure, and she was sobbing because some Guard was yelling at her. I don't know who it could be, though, and I wasn't able to hear in on their conversation because Vi and Jeremiah were having a yelling session."

My hands start to shake. "Is it my sister?"

Mal's face turns alarmingly red. "I-I don't know. I don't know what your sister looks like."

"Shit," I whisper, my head peering past the large tree behind me. I can barely make out the figures by the villages, but I can see two large figures hovering over a little girl whose face is covered in tears, and she wails loudly.

"B, where are you? I need you!" she sobs, her face crumpling in misery.

I don't think twice before I stand up and begin to run, disregarding the pain shooting through my limbs. I ignore the yells of my companions behind me and follow my instinct . . . which is to protect my sister.

"Em!" I shout, my breathing frantic as I get closer to her.

She wipes her cheeks with an abrupt swipe of her wrist and looks up at me, her lips quivering. "B? Is that you?"

I start to revel in her appearance, not seeming to believe my sister stands in front of me, breathing and alive. This entire time I was afraid something had happened to her. But here she is now, her eyes big, her hair tousled, and her body quivering. And I am now determined to lash at anyone who dares to lay even a finger on my Em.

My upcoming words are converted into screams as I feel a hissing pain spread across my back, my chest suddenly thudding to the hard ground as I groan miserably. I slowly look behind me and see one of the Guards hovering over me with a whip in his hand. "You're Blaire Cohen, aren't you? One of the rebels?"

I try to say something, but the pain in my body is too much to even bear. Instead, all that seems to come out is, "Get . . . away from my sister!"

"B!" Em shrieks as the Guard pulls me up to my feet by anchoring his gloved hand into my underarm and throwing me back down to the ground, even more pain hitting me like a brick wall. No sounds of agony come out of me this time; instead, I sit here in pregnant silence, the echoing wails of Em seeming to be the only sounds in this atmosphere. My vision is bleary to the point where I can't even make out the large crowd that formed around me, looking at me so curiously and whispering amongst themselves. My face is throbbing, my lungs are aching, and my limbs are shriveling. Is this it? Is this the end?

"Hey, bastards!"

With the little movement I can make, I crane my neck to the left to see four blurry figures by the edge of the forest, limping and in misery, but still intact.

The two Guards behind me cock their guns and aim. "Are you the other rebels?"

There is a loud silence. "Yes. We are."

Murmurs erupt. I gasp out for air, trying to reach for Em, but I can barely move. She seems to have reached me, though, her touch like birds beautifully chirping into the rising sun. Her breaths are short and succinct as she wraps her arms around my neck. "B, where were you? Who are those people? Why did you leave me?"

I can't answer. I can't speak. And I want to answer her, but I just can't.

One of the Guards starts to shout, "Knees to the ground, now!" The four blurry figures, with no hesitation, dig their knees into the ground. Thousands of emotions are plastered on their faces, painted with misery and humiliation. Immense guilt begins to throb at my veins, and I feel my face crumpling with defeat as my knees begin to weaken. This is it. It's all over now.

Suddenly, something unanticipated occurs.

A large group of Poor people charge at the Guards like angry bulls with no control, their minds racing with anger as they bellow war cries. Bodies run into bodies, blood mixes with blood, and limbs break with others. They beat them senseless after throwing the guns away, and then continue to pound at their bodies and faces. I stay here, lifeless, watching the Poor beat the two Guards victoriously.

At this moment, I feel a smile slipping onto my face. Despite the increasing pain I feel while slowly grinning, it is well-worth it.

And I find myself lifting my broken body from the ground— slowly but surely. And that is when Em hugs me, her face digging into my ribs as she sobs with delight. "Please come back, B . . . Please . . ."

Tears blur my vision as I lean down to say to her, "I wish I could. And I wish I can explain everything to you. But . . . I can't. Not now, at least."

"What? Why?" she whines.

I take a deep breath in as I force her to look at me in the eyes. "You'll find out really soon. Okay?"

"But . . ."

It takes every part of my heart and soul to say what comes out of my mouth next. "I know you're frustrated. I know you want to know why I left that night and never was to be seen again. And I know you want to know who those people are. But I promise that in due time, you will find out. Just not right now because I have to go back to them." I gesture toward the pile of Poor people on the beaten-up Guards.

"You really have to?"

"Yes, I do."

Em frowns and whimpers. "These days have been so miser-able without you. Even Mama and Papa miss you a lot."

"And I miss them too—so, so much." God, it's so true. "I'm

doing this for us, though. I'm leaving you guys for now, just so you can have a better future. Aren't you tired of being home alone while our parents are at the mines?" Em nods her head. "Exactly. So, I'm leaving you for now because I don't want you to live that life anymore. Let me go—just for now. I promise I'll be there for every moment of your life then. But as of now, I have to go. Okay?"

Em thinks for a moment, and I can tell my words hurt her a lot.

But I have to do this—for my family's sake.

Finally, she nods. "Okay, B."

I pull her in for a tight hug, not wanting to let her go. Her tears soil into my prisoner clothes, and I sob as well, my heart aching and shriveling.

"Also," I say afterwards, "tell Mama and Papa that I miss them a lot. And that their daughter will be back soon and won't be gone forever. All right?"

I feel Em's head moving up and down against my chest. "All right, B."

It takes me a while to rip away from her and walk away, not looking back because I know that if I did, then it would hurt so much more. I feel my heart shredding into pieces as I hear the screams and cries of my beloved little sister. But there's no looking back now because I have to join the others.

Limping and wincing, I reach the others and see that their usual optimistic expressions are replaced with anger—especially directed toward me. I was afraid that this might happen, that me running to my little sister would upset them. But I had to do what I had to do. If I didn't interfere, then my sister would've been dead instead.

"Let's go," Vi snarls as she turns around to trek into the woods. The others look at me with disappointment too as I feel my heart shattering into even more pieces, lying in a hapless pile of depression. Jeremiah tuts and follows behind Vi. Mal frowns and follows after him. And Jax's desolate silver eyes scan over me once before he shakes his head and follows behind the others as well.

I start to follow behind them too, aching to give them an explanation, even saying sorry for what I've done, but I soon feel a harsh pulling on my elbow. I turn around and see three new batches of Guards in front of me.

"Hey, you five! Stop right there!"

Jax, Jeremiah, Mal, Vi, and I stop in our tracks as we look at the Guards in fear. "Now . . ." one of the other Guards snarls afterwards, "where do you think you're going?"

10:03 p.m

The heavy door slams shut behind us as we sit together. The Guard sitting in front of us clears his throat, his slimy green eyes tracing over each and every one of us.

"You do know what is in store for you imbeciles, right?"

Due to our lack of response, he chuckles to himself—and not with humor. "You rebels are rash for thinking you could escape us. And when we found out you all left your cells and killed two of our most well-valued Guards . . . Well, we were astounded, to say the least. But most importantly of all"—he snarls, slamming his large hands onto the table—"we were pissed!"

Everyone continues to remain quiet. I am sitting on the far corner of our line of seats, and I turn to the side to make eye contact with Mal, since she is sitting right beside me. However, all she does is keep her blue eyes glued to the ground. I know she, including everyone else, is pissed about what I had done this morning. And now, because of me, we are held in the same interrogation room we were in last time, and now we have no clue of what lies ahead of us. The Guard narrows his eyes into tiny slits as he clenches his hard jaw.

"Someone very special has requested to meet up with you very soon."

"Who?" Vi pleads. I can see from the corner of my eye that she is preventing eye contact with me the most since her body is angled towards Jeremiah. She looks tired, her brown eyes masked with eye bags underneath, and her tall and skinny body can barely seem to sit in the little chairs we are in. Her right arm is still encased in the bandage Mal made for her, and I can tell from the strenuous expression she has plastered on her face that she is struggling to deal with it.

Guilt starts to dawn upon me. If it wasn't for me and my sudden instincts to protect my sister, then we would be safe and sound in the forest still, away from the eyes of the government. I should've conversed with the others and made my intentions known—not run off to Em. And all I want to do is go back in time and wish I never went outside my house that night. I wish I kept on sleeping and never dared to stand by my porch.

I close my eyes for a split second as I start to delve into my thoughts, but the Guard speaks again, his eyes lightening with amusement. "It's someone Mr. Remington knows very dearly. Think. Who could it be?"

Jax sits upright, alarmed. The answer dawns upon me too, my lips suddenly drying as worry overcomes me.

"My father? No, it can't be."

"Oh, yes, it can be." The Guard chuckles. "President Remington has been very eager to meet you all and . . . discuss."

"Discuss what?" Mal asks.

The Guard raises his eyebrows, and I feel hot tears forming in my eyes as he says, "Why, to discuss your execution, of course."

34

GUILT

November 27, 2064
6:03 p.m.

I STAND BY THE entrance of the prison, trying my very best to ignore the two Guards standing behind me. The reason why I'm not even daring to move an inch is because one of these Guards will shoot me if I do so. So, I decide to stand here, ramrod straight, and try very hard not to burst out in tears.

Because we are about to meet Tobias Remington.

Two days have passed by since we were caught by the Guards again. The rest of the group is still not on talking terms with me, and what makes this situation even worse is that all of our cells are together, just like the first time we were in prison.

The past few days have been aggravating, trying to get everybody's attention and let them know that I am sorry for what I have done. I *had* to run after my sister. Or else, she would've been killed. If their family member was held in that position, then they would run after them too. And I love Em; just the mere thought of seeing her held by those Guards makes me want to scream in fury.

However, I shouldn't have run after her like that without letting the others know. Where we are now . . . is solely my fault. And I will forever have to live by that.

The heavy double doors creak open by the far corner, and my eyes widen as I try to see who is coming. I am the only one standing here, ready in the formal outfit I was forced to wear—which is a pleated and short-sleeved navy-blue dress, jet black heels—while having my hair tied into a low bun.

I see Mal come out of the doors, her face etched with disdain. Her long blonde hair is coiled into a braid that runs down her back, tiny strands framing her angelic face. Her aura seems to reek of weariness, judging by the bruises on her face, arms, and legs that are accentuated by her tan-colored dress. The two Guards behind her follow very closely and have her arms held together by silver handcuffs. Just like me, and probably just like everybody else as well.

Then comes Jeremiah, his hefty muscles encased beneath the light blue dress shirt and ironed gray dress pants he has on. He's frowning too, and he looks troubled, walking past what was his own kind. Jeremiah's stormy eyes make me want to crawl into a hole. I know he's thinking: Blaire. *How could you do this to us? How could you ever put us in this situation again?*

I look down at the ground, not knowing what to think.

Then comes Vi. She wears a short red dress and heels that she appears uncomfortable in, her bandaged arm also slung across her chest. To my unfortunate avail, she looks at me for a few seconds, her brown eyes rimmed with rage, and I feel a lump growing in my throat as she settles in beside me and gives me the finger.

And to think that I had *just* gotten closer with her.

And finally, out comes Jax. His freshly shaven face makes me raise my eyebrows in surprise because now it clearly shows his sharp jawline. It also seems as if he trimmed his over-growing dark hair slightly. His eyes portray a sense of hesitation, which I assume it's because he's about to meet his father after a long time. I can't even imagine what he's feeling right now.

He never looks at me once, by the way. Just like everybody else.

My heart cracks into pieces, and I try to ignore the overwhelming need to sob. I need to make it up to them, somehow.

But how? How will I ever redeem myself? Before we end up being in the hands of the government? Before we are killed? *How?*

My chest heaves with anxiety as the Guard behind me lugs on my handcuffed wrists. "Let's go." I nod my head once as we are led outside of the main corridor doors.

The cold air smacks my face as my eyes narrow into slits, trying to block out the harsh wind. It's probably near freezing right now, and judging by the overcast sky, my gut tells me it's going to snow very soon.

In front of us are two large black SUVs. The Guards push all of us into one of the vehicles, and I sit by the window as Jax reluctantly sits beside me, Mal beside him, and Jeremiah and Vi facing us on the other side. Two Guards sit in the front. Simultaneously, four other Guards sit in the SUV in front of us.

My heart thumps.

The car starts to roll forward as soon as the vehicle in front of us departs. I prop my hand up on the arm rest by the window and gaze at the city that zooms before us. In the far distance, I can see the Poor villages beneath the large city buildings. I feel my chest deflating as I think back to what happened a couple of days ago when Em was almost killed by those Guards. God knows what she had done to piss those Guards off. And God knows what would've happened if I hadn't stepped in.

Guilt still seems to be following me around like a shadow, something I can't seem to quite get rid of. I want to rip it off my veins, throw it into the far distance, and forget the past few days ever happened. Forget the past *month* ever happened.

And now? The four people who trusted me with their lives despise my entire existence. I screwed everything up for them. I screwed everything up in general.

I don't know how to redeem myself. I really don't.

Rich people chatter around us, walking back and forth on the sidewalks as they commute to either work or their luxurious homes. Suddenly, something on the far distance of the streets catches my eye. And it seems as if my companions have the same reaction as me, too.

There are large screens hung across several street-lamps longitudinally, and the pictures and words formed on those screens are what makes my eyes widen with fear, shock, and anger combined.

ATTENTION CITIZENS OF WASHINGTON, D.C.!

IT IS WITH GREAT SHOCK AND DESPAIR TO SAY THAT THERE ARE REBELS PRESENT IN THIS COUNTRY. THESE PEOPLE HAVE DARED TO REBEL AGAINST US BY INITIATING A PLAN TO DESTROY THE GOVERNMENT OF THE UNITED STATES OF AMERICA. THESE ARE VILE ACTS PERFORMED BY THESE ANIMALS, AND THEY MUST BE PUNISHED GREATLY.

TODAY, PRESIDENT REMINGTON WILL DECIDE THEIR FATE. WILL THEY FACE IMMINENT PAIN AND TORTURE FOR THE DISTRESS THEY HAVE CAUSED FOR THIS COUNTRY? OR WILL THEY INSTEAD DIE IN THE HANDS OF THE GOVERNMENT, WHICH WARNS OTHERS OF WHAT IS TO COME IF THEY EVEN DARE TO GO AGAINST OUR WELL- ESTABLISHED COUNTRY?

WE MUST PRESERVE OUR NATION. IF NOT, THEN WE ARE DOOMED. AMEN.

What the hell?

I feel my face burning with fury as I read the words plastered in front of us. In fact, they are *surrounding* us, hanging on possibly every single streetlamp out there.

Vi scoffs, leaning back in her seat. "Glad to see their way of dealing with a bunch of rebels is embarrassing us by showing our pictures to the entire Rich sector. What's next? Stripping us naked?"

"Probably." Jeremiah snorts, then lowers his voice suddenly. "Am I the only one that's nervous to meet President Remington?"

"Oh, trust me, it's not just you," Jax whispers, rolling his eyes afterwards. "I'm nervous as hell seeing him, but at the same time, this is my perfect opportunity to show him my true intentions. I don't want to be a president like him. In fact, I don't want to be a president *at all.* I don't even want to be Jax Remington: I just want to be Jax. I'm just so tired of having the name *Remington* following after me. I hate being labeled as one."

Silence.

I clear my throat, hoping this will lead to something good—in some way, also leading to me getting on everybody's good side. "I'm sorry to hear that, Jax. And don't worry, you will make your intentions known, and your father is going to have to accept you for who you are."

"Why are you talking, Blaire?" Vi narrows her eyes at me. "No one asked for your input."

"Vi." Jeremiah glares at her.

All she does is scowl at him. "You're seriously defending her? The woman who got us involved in this mess in the first place?"

"I'm not defending her. I'm just making sure you don't cause a scene." His eyes dart toward the Guards in the front.

Vi shakes her head, letting out a prickly laugh. "Don't worry, I'm not causing a scene. I just wanted to address the elephant in the room." She looks at me, her eyes filled with deadly intentions. "Because of your heroic stunt you pulled a couple of days ago, we're all here, slaving for your mistakes. We had to step in to pull you out of there because if we hadn't, you and your sister would've been killed." She pauses. "You know that the number one rule of the Subversion Act is to stick together, no matter if the other person is acting up. But I swear, Blaire, I lost all respect for you. And it's going to take a hell of a lot to gain it back."

"I'm sorry," I say, pushing my tears back. "I know I made a huge mistake, and I don't know how to repay everything to you all. It's just that . . . my sister was there, begging for my help. I love her with all of my heart, and I already lost my brother, so losing another one of my siblings . . ." I shake my head. "I can't even imagine losing Em. So, I ran after her. I was running on my instincts, not common sense. I didn't even think of the consequences at the time."

"That's not how it works here," Vi seethes. "In the real world, you're going to have to think of consequences. And I know you lived a one-dimensional life for a long ass time, but now you're in a group that's fighting for social justice. And we're fighting *together*. Just because you see your family member struggling, doesn't mean you run after them *immediately*. You first talk to us about it so we can work together as a team. That's how things run in the real world."

"How would I know that? I've never been in the real world before."

"And that I won't hold against you. But it's purely common sense. The stunt you pulled back there? You must've been out of your mind. You really caused all of that shit just to lead us back here, except the consequences are even more dire."

"I don't know," I mumble. "I feel so bad."

"I'm pretty sure Blaire has learned her lesson by now," Mal says. "We don't have to ignore her."

"I'm not letting her off the hook that easily." Vi glares at her. "She almost got us killed, Mal."

"Yeah, I know. But we were all naïve and innocent at one point, especially when we first entered the Act. This is Blaire's moment to be naïve and innocent, so I think we should grant her a second chance."

Vi disregards her statement. "What don't you guys get about the real world? The real world doesn't grant people second chances! Blaire needs to understand the extremity of her mistake because it cost us a shit ton—more than we expected. And we're about to be executed!"

"Hey!" The Guard driving snarls. "Keep it down back there, you rebels! Before we shoot you and drag your dead bodies for the public to see!"

And with that, we finally become quiet. Reluctantly, of course.

35

REIGN

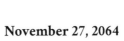

November 27, 2064
6:24 p.m.

THE WHITE HOUSE HOVERS over us, its prominent structure taunting me. The SUVs roll to a stop when we hit the pavement, tires screeching, and silence prevails.

Until the Guard that is driving starts to speak. "Guard Robert over here will escort you guys to the President inside. Face forward at all times, remain in your single-file line, do not attempt to break out of your handcuffs, and do not speak a single damn word. If you fail to follow any of these rules, then you will be killed immediately. Understand?"

We nod our heads.

The other Guard pulls himself out of his seat and comes over to my side, ripping the black door open. I try to get up, but it's hard to do so when my hands are tied together by uncomfortable metal cuffs. Guard Robert becomes impatient and pulls on me, my heels hitting the hard pavement as I try to regain myself without making a sound.

I would do anything to not be in this ill-fated situation right now.

As Guard Robert leads me forward, the others start to form behind me. "I order you to follow behind this rebel at all times," he bellows. "And remember what Guard Uriah said up there: Any sort of foul movement or actions will result in your eventual death."

Then, he mutters something underneath his breath. "If President Remington hadn't ordered us to bring you animals alive and well, then you all would've been dead a long ass time ago."

I try to ignore his hurtful remark and continue to walk forward.

We climb up the marble steps, and I am simply envious of how beautifully President Remington and his family get to live. Not a single speck is found on these steps, walls, columns, or roofs, and it takes me by surprise.

Guard Robert pushes the heavy door open with his gloved hands, and my breath catches in my throat as I take in the dazzling surroundings bathed in luxury. I've seen the White House basking in the distance, but never have I been inside of it, especially with my feet touching these prestigious grounds. And with its glorious flooring and intricate designing, it is pretty safe to say that the Americans, before the Dark Ages, had labored extensively to form this beautiful work of art. I've heard this palace has endured multiple wars and battles, and even through it all, it has still reigned.

We make our way through the massive entrance as Guard Robert leads us into what I am assuming is the West Wing. There is a large dining room over to the left, which is exactly where he finally leads us to.

He stops and turns around to speak. "Please take your seats. The president will be meeting with you shortly." Suddenly, his voice becomes hoarse as he reluctantly says, "The president also instructed me to release your handcuffs to form the most welcoming dining experience." Every word he says is cinched in distaste.

Some part of me thinks Tobias is making us feel "welcomed" only to make his son join his side again.

Once our handcuffs are released, the five of us take our seats around the twelve-seat dining table, and I almost gape at the expensive silverware and dishes placed around. Seeing all of these fancy materials makes me feel . . . jealous. And completely pissed off.

As I sit, I notice the large painting of Abraham Lincoln portrayed above the marble fireplace. My eyes then land on the chandelier twinkling above us, tiny lights anchored by golden arches that connect in the middle. Finally, I make note of the decorations around us: the priceless vases filled with pretty flowers, a stainless mirror affixed by the door that leads to God knows where, and golden lights located every few spaces away from each other on the wall. This makes me feel a bit over-whelmed, knowing that we are in this state-of-an-art room where we will soon meet the man we've been planning to kill for about a month.

The suffocating silence breaks as soon as Mal says, "So . . . we're here now."

She sits right across from me, in the center of the table, and right next to her is Vi, who speaks next. "Yeah, no shit."

"I'm just trying to break the awkward silence here." Mal frowns.

Jeremiah, who sits a few seats away, shrugs. "I'd rather sit in silence than try to alleviate our worries away by chatter."

"Me too," Jax whispers.

"How are you holding up, by the way?" Jeremiah questions, looking at him with concern. "I know it's rough to be here because, well, this was your home after all."

"Not so good, honestly speaking," Jax says. He sits a couple of seats away from Vi. "I'm getting horrible memories just sitting here, acknowledging this place . . . and I am scared to see my father again. I don't even know what to say to him.

Should I be a normal son? Should I be rude? Or should I not talk at all?"

"Look," Vi says, "you need to let your father know that this is where you want to be—with us. Because the entire Rich population, including him, thinks that you don't want to be here, that you are being held hostage or something. You need to stand up to him."

Jax closes his eyes for a bit. Seconds later, he opens them and sets his gray eyes onto the chandelier. "I've tried so hard to stand up to him. I really have. But it always backfired on me. So, I found it easier to pretend I liked being Rich and wanted to be like my father. I did despise my lifestyle with all of my heart. I just did not know how to escape it.

"And now I'm here, waiting for my father to appear so he can determine a sentence for us, including *me* . . . I don't know. I feel scared, not knowing how he's going to be around me, but I also feel relieved, knowing I won't be in his clutches anymore. I am my own person, and I don't need my father telling me what to do." Jax pauses and shakes his head, chuckling sadly a bit. "My birthday is also on the 13th. I bet he doesn't even remember that."

Jeremiah frowns. "It's okay, Jax. We will celebrate your birthday."

"Thanks." He smiles halfheartedly.

"And just know that if your father doesn't accept you for who you are, then that is his loss." Mal's lips tug into a grin.

"Yeah, I know," Jax shrugs. "I just really want to make me known. Make my father know that this is who I am, and there's no way he can change that."

"Now, that's what I want to hear." Vi smirks.

I start to notice how tired he looks, tired of being named as the president's son. And as I have learned for the past four weeks, he is much more than that. He is a man with a big and loving heart, he just doesn't know how to use it. And, for some reason, I feel my stomach churning as I look down at the ground, trying to understand these weird feelings that erupted in my stomach.

"We are really about to meet Tobias Remington, huh?" Jeremiah sighs, taking a quick look towards the gaping door on the other side of the other closed door. There stands Guard Uriah and Robert, their backs turned towards us as they stand ramrod straight. "How come they aren't looking at us?"

"I think they just want us to think that, since their backs are turned toward us, we will have more chances for escaping, or something." Vi rolls her eyes. "It's utter bullshit, how their thinking works."

"Tell me about it." I snort.

Vi cocks her head at me, my heart ramming against my chest as I know what exactly is coming up. "Hmm, Blaire . . . how does it feel, knowing that *you* are the reason we are in this situation in the first place? You must feel like shit, huh?"

"Vi, enough!" Jeremiah furrows his eyebrows. "Can you just grow up for once?"

"Grow up? I'm just stating facts, Jeremiah."

"I'm sorry for what I have done," I blurt out. "I know this is all of my fault. I will admit the fact that we are here because of me, and I won't try to digress from it. But I didn't mean to do it. I never once meant to cause you guys any harm. But . . . my sister was in trouble. So, I will take the blame for all of this.

"I just . . . I don't want to be hated by the only people I trust right now. It's my dream to destroy the government, and now I'm finally here, except I'm not alone. I don't ever want to lose you guys. And I know I made mistakes that you all may or may not be willing to forgive, but I have never talked to people my age. The only people I ever talked to were my family. I don't know how friendship works. I don't know how real life works.

"I'm not making excuses, by the way." I dare to look Vi in the eyes. "I am stating the truth. I'm learning, and I'm growing, and

I'm especially evolving. So please . . . keep all of this in your mind. Know that I am trying my best. And know that I will *never* do what I did before, *ever* again."

For a single moment, I notice Vi's expression slipping into pure forgiveness. It makes me feel relieved, almost weightless, knowing that Vi will finally forgive me. Or if she doesn't, then that is okay too, because I will continue to work toward being on her good side. I will do whatever it takes to have Vi on my side again.

But the door creaks open to our unfortunate avail. And, with bated breath, I watch as a very familiar man steps toward us with a broad and irritating grin on his round face.

HOSTILITY

November 27, 2064
7:00 p.m.

"GOOD EVENING, EVERYBODY." TOBIAS Remington's deep and dark voice radiates into the room as his gray eyes, similar to his son's, slither onto us. "What do you think of the White House? Pretty gorgeous, right?"

No one speaks. We sit here in fear and anger combined instead.

Tobias looks at us with amusement and laughs, tugging at his red tie slightly. "Cat got your tongue? C'mon, I don't bite."

Before anybody can even respond, he looks over at Jax, who cowers in his seat and avoids eye contact with his father. His dark hair covers a good portion of his face as he drops his head low, and the scar on his cheek glinting against the light makes my throat constrict.

"Hello, son." Tobias speaks again, attempting to get Jax's attention.

All Jax simply does, though, is hiss at his father, "What do you want?"

"Ah, so he speaks!" Tobias lets out a wheezy laugh. "I really missed you, son. Me and your mother want you to come back."

"I don't want to come back."

Tobias seems surprised by Jax's reaction as his eyes widen in bewilderment. "Is this about the bullshit video I was sent?" He laughs. "You know, son, I didn't believe a single word you said from there. Sure I was highly upset when I found out that you told these people of the secret I trusted you with, but I realized that maybe you were forced to say it, which I will forgive you for. You are just being forced to say these things by these people, right?"

Jax rolls his eyes as he clenches his fists. "I am not being forced. I say it because that's what I think."

"Because that's what *you* think?" He looks at his son in utter surprise as he pulls out an elegant seat to sit in—of course at the head of the table. "This has to be a joke, son."

"It is not a joke."

"What is wrong with you?" Tobias yells, slamming his large hands against the oak dining table. It shakes slightly, the silverware clattering as the glasses filled with champagne rattle back and forth. "Do you really want to be a part of this rebellion? You are out of your mind, Jax Remington. Out of your damn mind!"

Jax, just a couple of seats away from Tobias, bites his lip and raps his knuckles against the shaken table. "I am sick of your shit, Tobias. So sick of it."

"Oh, so we are on a first-name basis now?" Tobias furrows his bushy eyebrows. "I am your father. Never forget that."

"With all due respect, President Remington," Mal interrupts, "I believe we are here for other matters, such as those not involving reprimanding your son."

Tobias looks at Mal and snorts. "You used to be my son's best friend and are the daughter of Adam and Veronica Reaves. Ah, I am still dear friends with them. And I hope you take into consideration what I'm telling Jax and return to your family as soon as possible. You are just like my son—valuable and worthy —so you deserve to go back. Not be here with these rebels. You guys are troubled and don't belong here.

"So, here is what I'm trying to say. We, as in the Rich, want Jax and Mallory back." Tobias's expression makes my insides knot. "We believe that we need to preserve our two most valued members of the Rich community and sentence the others simultaneously."

"That's not fair!" Vi screeches, shooting out of her seat.

The two Guards from the outside send her dangerous looks.

She rolls her eyes and sits down hesitantly, pushing her body forward into the edge of the dining table. "President Remington . . . we, as in the Subversives, believe that your sentence is unjust. You are favoring two Rich people over us."

"Well, what did you expect? That I was going to hold sympathy for a bunch of Poor people?" Tobias snorts. "You rebels are invaluable. And face it—we all know damn well what your sentence is going to be."

"That is enough!" Jax growls, leaning forward in his seat as he glares at Tobias. "I am tired of how you have been treating the Poor! It is inhumane and immature of how you guys think, and it needs to be stopped. *Now*."

Tobias starts to whisper, looking at Jax with irritating care. "You need to get out of that group because they are feeding you nonsensical information. I care very deeply for you, son."

"Don't call me that!" Jax grumbles. "I don't want to be known as your son, or even a Remington. I am ashamed to be a part of this family."

"Please. Come back to us. Your mother and I miss you a lot."

"No, you don't. You only want me so you can form me into a mini you," Jax says. "You only want me back so your reputation will prosper."

"Enough of this!" He growls. "I did not come here to argue with you, son. I am here to talk about their execution."

My heart pounds as I feel myself edging on the chair with anxiety. Tobias's eyes pan over us, which he then smirks, wrinkles forming on his forehead. "As the President, it is my duty to provide happiness to others. I have to think long and hard when it comes to making decisions for this country, and I *really* have to think long and hard when it comes to deciding sentences for rebels. There are many Poor people that have been sentenced for life, or even death. All executions are private, but none have been public."

I feel my lungs constrict and my eyes bulge as he says next, "Public and formal executions are rare here. But when it comes to those that purposefully plan to destroy the government and valued individuals that revolve their life around America . . . well, they must be punished greatly." He pauses. "And with that said, it is hereby declared by me, as the President of the United States, that the execution for radicals Jeremiah Morgan, Vienna Powers, and Blaire Cohen will be held on December 4th at six in the morning."

My breathing ceases as I feel my knuckles whitening against the armchairs. I don't even feel angry, upset, or sad at this point. Instead, all I feel is disappointment.

This is the end. This is the end of our journey.

"It's okay if you all hate me; I'm just doing what is necessary here." He clicks his tongue in thought. "You rebels will be punished greatly for your unreasonable actions."

"I want you to include me," Mal spits out, her lips curled into a deep frown.

Tobias barks out a laugh. "Are you out of your mind? No, it will be just these three rebels."

"No!" Jax bellows, slamming his hands against the table. "I will not follow what you say! I want to be executed too!"

My eyes widen with surprise. *Mal and Jax are standing up for us? And even more perplexing . . . they want to be executed with us?*

"No, Jax, you and Mallory will come with us while these three rebels are being executed! It is final!"

Jax's eyes are rimmed with terror and rage as he storms over to his father and looks at him dead in the eye, his lips formed into a straight line. Tobias doesn't seem fazed by his son's sudden demeanor, but the hardness beneath his expression seems to crack like a fragmented vase.

Although, his pride sticks to him like a clinging shadow, forcing his face to remain neutral.

"What do you want, Jax?"

"I want you to allow me and Mallory to get executed with the others."

"Why do you guys want to be executed so badly?" Tobias asks with desperation. "Jax, do you really want to be executed? Die in the hands of the government just for doing something stupid? Or do you instead want to come back to your warm and welcoming family again, where you can then pursue your dreams?"

"Do you even know what my dreams are?" Jax's voice cracks with agony.

Silence swarms around the place like a ghost as Tobias cocks his head at his son in question. "What do you mean, son?"

"Enough with calling me your son—I already told you that."

"Jax, please. Tell me what you mean."

He sighs as he starts to pace around a small portion of the dining room. "You think you know me, when really . . . you don't. You never tried to. You always assumed that I wanted to be President, like you, so you made me follow along. I didn't say much because, honestly, I was scared to fight against you. I didn't want to create tensions within the family as well because you and Mom were all I really had.

"But deep down . . . I hated being Rich. I hated every ounce of it. And because of how I felt, I constantly yearned to escape this place. I wanted to explore what used to be the amazing country known as America and learn more about our place before it perished due to the Dark Ages. That's really all my dreams were, and you never knew because you never even bothered to ask."

For a second, I think that Tobias will slip up and reveal the concerned side of him, where his personality is not masked and filtered due to his excessive ego. And the way he looks at Jax with such vulnerability, willing to forgive him and wanting to let this whole thing go . . . I think that is what's going to happen.

Until he goes and slaps his son.

The harsh sound of Tobias's hand hitting Jax's cheek reverberates into the atmosphere. It rings into my ears, and I wince as I notice the dark red mark on his skin. Anger forms inside of me, anger for Jax, and anger for those who are forced to hide and shove their dreams away.

"That is utter bullshit, Jax Remington. Do you know why?" Tobias squares his jaw and levels his eyes onto his son, who dares not to look at him. "I hate to break it to you, but dreams don't exist. They are simply a myth, nothing else. People who believe in dreams are a bunch of ninnies, and they deserve nothing but eternal punishment. And for that, I am embarrassed to have you as my son. I thought that, maybe one day, you will come out of this stupid teenage boy phase and realize the strong and smart man you are. But honestly? I believe anything but, Jax. You are meant to do nothing. You are nothing but a pathetic loser, and you are not my son. That is it."

I think it is over, until Tobias speaks again. "And you know what? You want to follow your dreams? Then go and get executed. When you kneel there at the Capital Center, hanging in chains and not wanting the Guards to shoot you in the back of the head while thousands of people watch, then you'll realize how pathetic dreams truly are because they land you absolutely nowhere. Keep that in mind, Jax."

As Jax clenches and unclenches his jaw, deciding what to say,

I notice something from the corner of my eye that makes my veins pound.

Vi has grabbed a butter knife from the plate in front of her and has placed it on her palm. The look she and Jeremiah share afterwards is self-explanatory, and it has my throat drying with apprehension.

They're going to try to kill the president.

NUMB

November 27, 2064
7:11 p.m.

THE OPPORTUNITY IS PERFECT. Sure, we may have two Guards patrolling our environment, but it's us versus them— and we've already fought dozens of Guards. We've been through it *all*.

This is the perfect chance for us to accomplish our number one goal for the Subversion Act—which is to destroy the president. And he's here, unarmed and completely vulnerable, allowing the clearest shot to us.

So, within a blink of an eye, Vi growls and jumps up to the table, attempting to plunge the knife into Tobias's heart.

But the Guards are too fast since they have started to shoot at us. Bullets fly at the silverware like lasers, and Vi immediately ducks and rolls off the table, her breaths heavy. She exchanges desperate looks with us and says, "Let's do this!"

When Guards Uriah and Robert aim at us, I shield my body behind the chair, desperate to do something about this situation. They are the only ones armed. All we have is our silverware and plates and—

Wait.

I quickly eye the plates and send acknowledging glances to everyone. They immediately understand.

So, we grab as many plates as we can and hurl them at the Guards, glass shards flying everywhere. It may not pierce through their skin, due to their heavily-armored selves, but it is enough to distract them, as I can see their aim is going haywire now.

Soon enough, we run out of plates, and we panic. But, thankfully enough, the Guards have run out of ammunition as they throw their guns to the side and prepare to jump at us. But Vi, who would never allow anyone to win against her in *anything,* jumps on top of Uriah—and she doesn't let her bandaged arm stop her—and plunges the butter knife into the side of his neck. He screams out and attempts to reel the knife out, but she climbs down his back and kicks the back of his legs, leaving him falling forward.

Allowing the knife to plunge into his neck even more as his neck makes contact with the floor—leaving him completely dead.

As we set to destroy the last and final Guard, Tobias gets up from his seat and wheezes, "Enough! I've had it with you all." He frantically taps his wrist watch and yells, "I need fifteen Guards with me, ASAP!"

As soon as he finishes speaking, though, Jeremiah grabs the butter knife near him and starts to throw it at Tobias, but it eventually clatters from his hand since Robert has him in his grasp, pushing him to the ground as he begins to overpower him. Jax and Mal go to help Jeremiah, leaving me with the butter knife.

"Blaire, throw it!" Vi says as she holds Tobias in her grasp. She wraps his arms behind his back.

The president hisses, "Get your hands off me, rebel!"

As he continues to yell at her, I grab the knife and climb on top of the table, heading to where Tobias is sitting. His startling gray eyes scrutinize me, his matured face heavy with stress. Lines amass his forehead as he grumbles, "Blaire Cohen. The youngest of the Subversives. And the little sister of the notorious Nicolas Cohen."

I stop in my tracks. "How do you know that?"

He lets out a wheezy laugh. "How do *I* know that? Your brother was the most wanted criminal we had, and we arrested him the moment we laid eyes on him."

A weight is crushing my body. The words coming from his mouth intrigue me, but I must carry on with my actions. I must follow through and kill this son of a bitch already.

But as I raise my knife back, he says breathlessly, "Have you ever wondered why your brother was arrested?"

Ignore his words, Blaire. Just stab him already.

"He was arrested for a dire act." Silence.

"He threatened to go against the government." "Stop."

"He was hauled away by Guards and was tortured daily."

"Shut up!"

"Oh, you're going to want to hear this next." Tobias smirks.

I shake my head. "No, I don't want to hear you talk anymore."

However, he disregards my desperate request. "Then, he escaped."

I feel my lungs deflating. The muscles in my face loosen. My hands feel numb. I feel numb.

"He escaped the prison and formed a group to destroy the government."

"Blaire, just stab him already!" Vi says, hurriedly looking over at the others that are struggling to kill Robert, but have slowly looked up at my altercation with Tobias.

"He created an underground bunker filled with other rebels, such as Vienna Powers, Jeremiah Morgan, and Mallory Reaves."

Vi is eerily quiet now.

"They planned to destroy the government. And, due to our great technology, we found out who the leader was."

My lips dry.

"And so, we killed him." I close my eyes.

"You're lying. You didn't kill Nicolas."

"Or is that you trying to convince yourself that I am lying when I am not?"

"You *are* lying!" I hiss, hot tears invading my eyes. "My brother is alive!"

"You want to see his body?" Tobias snarls. "He's buried underneath the plantation where we shot him! The plantation near the underground bunker!"

My chest heaves up and down. *He's not dead, he's not dead, he's not dead!* "Stop lying! Shut up! Stop it!"

From the corner of my eye, I notice Jeremiah, Mal, and Jax get up from a now dead Robert. Their expressions are unreadable—truly enigmatic.

I frantically make eye contact with them. "Is it true?"

They stare at me, almost lifeless. *Nothing.* I want to scream, unleash my pain and fear and terror and frustration everywhere. I'm tired of going through this shit. I'm tired of *being* tired.

I scoff. "Why did you hide this from me? I thought we told each other *everything*."

"Blaire . . ." Vi says. "We had to keep it a secret from you."

My heart pangs as tears plunge down my cheeks, my breaths heaving with pain. *"Why?* Why did you keep this big of a secret from me?"

"Because Nicolas told us to," Jeremiah speaks softly.

"Why?" I screech. "Why would he want to do that?"

Tobias's harsh words make me come back to reality. "Nicolas

hid secrets from you too, Miss Cohen. Just like you found out now."

"Why did you tell me this?" I snarl at him, digging my nails into my palm. "Why do you ruin *everything?*"

"If I didn't, then who would?" He challenges me by raising his eyes to mine. "Obviously your so-called friends didn't even bother to tell you the truth."

"Because Nicolas ordered us not to!" Mal hisses.

"Why?" I sigh, turning to her. "Why would he ever order that?"

I promise to never keep anything from you Bumble Bee. And you know I always keep my promises.

"He wanted to keep you safe. He thought that if you knew about him being the leader, then you would've been too busy looking for him. And if anything happened to him, then you would blame yourself the entire time." Jeremiah takes a deep breath in, after explaining. "His words, not mine."

I turn around as I try to make sense of the words pelted at me. "So . . . he lied to me for . . . my own good?"

"Your brother did love you, Blaire." Vi clears her throat as her neutral brown eyes simmer onto me. "He loved *all* of us. And what he did . . . was for the good of our country."

I just want to fight for us, for our people.

"For the good of our country?" Tobias reiterates, snorting afterwards. "That imbecile went against our country. How would that do *any* good? It's a good thing we killed him. He was turning our country into a shame, that little rascal. He deserved to be killed. And all of you are next when you will be executed on the 4th. Mark my words."

Something instigates inside of me, almost like a light switch. It is as if Tobias's words truncate my patience and lead me to utter abhorrence, where I solely rely on my emotions. I am just a human soul, and he is a demon, trying to possess me with his ideals and notions.

But I will persist.

Without thinking twice, I take a quick look at Vi. She catches my eye and tries to decipher what I am thinking. And then, a few seconds later, she nods her head. She understands me. She knows me. She approves of me. She forgives me.

And she also allows me to do this.

Moving at the speed of lightning, I tighten my hold of the butter knife in my hand and yell at the top of my lungs as I turn around in one swift motion and allow it to ram into his eye. Blood spurts out from his eye as he screams in shock and pain, flailing around and crashing into the decor. He falls backwards onto the floor, trying to pull out the knife.

And as I go stab him in the heart, right in that sweet spot, a mass of Guards come trampling into the room and shoot at us, but they are not bullets. They are instead lasers incised with a heavy and distasteful feeling. Before we can all hold cover, we are hit in one swift movement, our bodies hitting the ground.

Darkness overcomes us all.

38

DISTRAUGHT

November 28, 2064
12:05 a.m.

I WAKE UP IN a strange environment.

It is absolutely dark and smells like wet cobblestone here. There are a few dingy lights illuminating the vast space with a tiny hallway leading to an iron-clad door. But, other than that, it is just empty darkness.

As I awaken, I see that the others have began to wake up, too. We seem to be changed out of our formal clothes into casual clothing, nothing more than beige shirts and pants. And everyone seems pretty distraught as well, adjusting to this foreign atmosphere. Vi's hair is wild and untamed, her body covered in nothing but cuts and bruises. Same with Jeremiah and Mal. And Jax looks frightened while awakening, his gray eyes widened in horrible realization at the depressing chamber we are in.

Dry tears cover my face, and my eyes ache as well, my heart clanging as I am reminded of the horrible news Tobias told me. I try to push away the thought that my brother was the leader of the Subversives and died in the hands of the government. I really do. But I just can't help but think of how unfair it is for him. He's buried by our destroyed underground bunker, for God's sake.

My stomach churns with disgust and sadness. *He deserved so much better.*

The anger that riled up in my veins at that exact moment was enough to tear down the entire city. It was like a disease that took over, and the only way to get rid of it was to unleash the hell inside of me onto the demon that wreaked havoc upon D.C. And the satisfaction I felt while jabbing the knife into Tobias's left eye and watching him wail with agony, knocking into decorations while crimson blood gushed out of his eye . . .

Let's just say the sadistic side of me gleamed in delight.

But suddenly, we were ambushed by the Guards Tobias had called over, pelting us with stray bullets that weren't meant to kill us, but were instead to soothe us. To weaken our knees. And to send us falling to the ground, great slumber overcoming us.

And here we now, in this isolated dungeon that honestly has my veins pulsating with fear.

I shiver to myself, the feeling of us getting executed still thrashing at my mind. We will be executed publicly, which many executions have occurred, but ours is a formal event, something the entire city would be required to attend. And just like that we will be gone. Right in front of the Rich, and right in front of the Poor.

And right in front of my family—knowing that another one of their children is gone.

Vi's voice interrupts my thoughts. "What the hell is this place?"

"I-I don't know," Mal says. "It looks to be like some sort of—"

"Torture chamber?" Jax says, raising his eyebrows.

"Why would they put us here?" I ask.

"Um, do you not remember stabbing Jax's father in the eye?" Mal looks astonished. "I think that may be why."

"So, they're going to torture us now . . . because of that?"

"I don't know." Vi looks around the place. "I'm assuming they're going to keep us in here until our execution and starve us to death or something. Who knows." Her voice is soft now as she looks at me. "How are you . . . holding up?"

I've noticed she's holding sympathy for me now, and the others too, judging by their solemn expressions—which I find to be a bit appalling. I guess it's because they feel guilty for not telling me about Nico being the special *he* that led the Subversives, so now they are trying to make up for it by being extra kind. Is this why they were kissing up to me before? Since Nico was my older brother, they felt as if they had to treat me like a princess?

One other thing that runs through my mind is the notion of Nico escaping from prison and creating a group that wants to destroy the government. How did he even have the time to come up with that? I know he talked about hating the government a lot with me, but never had he brought up the possibility of him forming a group to destroy it. And never in a million years would I have ever guessed that it would've been him.

My heart sinks a little as I am reminded for the umpteenth time that he is dead. And there's nothing I can do about it now, except die in the hands of the government—just like he did.

I gulp. "Do you want me to lie or be honest?"

"Be honest," Jax says. I crane my neck toward him and notice his gray eyes are on me, his lips curled with thought. I whirl my head back and stare at the ground, despondently noticing the rough edges to the flooring.

"Okay, well . . . honestly, I am dying inside. I am dying inside from figuring out that my brother is dead and that he was the leader of this group the entire time. There. That's my answer."

Jeremiah clears his throat from the front of the room. "You

do know we had a valid reason to hide that from you, right, Blaire? Because Nicolas specifically told us not to."

"I mean, I do know," I mutter. "I just don't understand the fact of him protecting me from it. Did he really think I'm not capable enough to focus on the group when he was there? And wait . . ." Another question peeks into my mind. "Where was he when we were together? And did you guys know when he was killed?"

"Okay, we might as well explain everything then," Mal says. "Vi, do you mind doing the honors?"

"Okay," Vi says. Silence fills the air for just a few seconds, and I feel my heart thudding as she speaks again. "About a year ago, when I was still on the run, I ran into this guy. He had long dark hair reaching to his shoulders, cuts and bruises on his tan skin, a scruffy beard, and a very deep and commanding voice. It was your older brother, Blaire." A huge lump forms in my throat. "I met Nicolas by the Poor markets, and we became very close friends in a matter of several weeks. I could trust him with my entire life. And, soon enough, he spilled a secret to me. He told me he had recently escaped from prison for conspiring to destroy the government, and now he was planning to destroy it —except he needed people to help him.

"I first thought Nicolas was crazy as hell. I mean, *destroying the government?* Of course I had thought about the idea itself hundreds of times, but I didn't think anybody would have the balls to actually do it. Turns out he proved me wrong by asking me straight up if I wanted to join him, after two months of being best friends. I, of course, said yes.

"Then, he took me to the outskirts of D.C. in this government vehicle I am pretty sure he had stolen. Nicolas took me to this forest, which had an entire open space of greenness, and brought me to that exact space. I was intrigued by his ambiguity, his determination to have me as a part of his team."

Vi lets out a chuckle. "The ground started to sink beneath

my feet, and I was scared shitless. But all of my fear soon disappeared as I saw the underground bunker appearing in front of my own eyes. And one thought ran through my mind as I walked through this place . . . *how did he build all of this?*

"Sooner than later, Nicolas answered all of my questions. He told me, when he escaped out of prison, he befriended a Guard and found this underground place with him. Turns out, it was Jeremiah Morgan, the infamous Guard himself."

Jeremiah grins, a sliver of his amputated leg appearing from the end of his creased sweats. "I met Nicolas by the forest I had escaped to, when I ran away from the Guards that infiltrated the hospital. The entire time I was thinking about my wife and the beautiful baby girl that she was pregnant with, but I knew that I had to stay alive *just for them.*

"He eventually told me that he was willing to start this Subversion Act, which would have people in it that share the same hopes and dreams. I agreed with him immediately."

Jeremiah shifts around in bed, furrowing his dark eyebrows together as his skin shines against the warm lights. "And so, we got to work. We disguised ourselves as the Rich, which wasn't that hard—all we did was pickpocket Rich people walking by, steal their clothing, and mimic their language. We walked through the streets with not even a second glance toward the Guards wandering around, which weren't that many because most of them guard around the Poor sector. And then, we went into the prison and stole a black SUV government vehicle. And it was mostly him who did all of the stealing. I was fending off the other Guards, while he miraculously started the engine *without the keys* and gestured for me to come inside. And so, I did, with other specific tools and materials he told me to steal from the Guards.

"He took me to the outskirts of D.C., to the same place he took Vi. Nicolas had a map of D.C. displayed to him in prison and said that he studied it intently. He was planning the Subversion Act for years. Eventually, Nicolas brought me to the empty green expanse and told me to stand near him. I was so damn shocked when the ground sank. I was greeted with a home—an actual home—that I hadn't seen in so long. Since I was a Guard, I had a home by the Rich. But ever since I was on the run, I hadn't seen an actual home in so long.

"I asked Nicolas what was up with this home, and he had explained to me that Rich people in the 2040s built this extremely secret underground bunker to formulate tactics to destroy the Poor. He ventured out here alone by himself, before I met him, and discovered it by clicking on the stray remote control there on the ground, almost like an artifact. Then, that is when the idea struck through his mind, to house the Subversives here.

"Time went by, and we were acquainted with the facility there. There was some technology we had to refurbish there, which we were hoping to find someone that would be skilled enough to do so.

"Eventually, Nicolas decided to recruit someone who held the same fiery spirit as us. That is when he left for the Poor markets and befriended a raunchy woman with colorful hair and thousands of piercings."

Vi sends him a scornful look.

Jeremiah chuckles. "Anyway, we had our third member now. And we explained everything to her. Vienna Powers was more than willing to join. That was what made us happy."

Vi begins to take over Jeremiah's explanation. "For a while, it was just us three. But we realized we needed somebody else that would lower the tensions in the group since all three of us were hot-headed. That is when I decided to venture off into the Poor markets as well, and Nicolas had ordered for me to kidnap the person in a vulgar manner, to emphasize the severity of this situation. And so, I did. I found Mal by the Poor markets, completely starving and malnourished. And I also noticed this fire in her eyes . . . which emphasized her anger toward the Rich." She clears her throat. "Mal, care to take over?"

"Of course." Mal chuckles. "I was homeless and living on the streets, as all of you know. Vi had kidnapped and brought me to this underground home where the two men were. They introduced themselves to me, checked my background, and made sure I wasn't a spy for the Rich. If I was . . . they would have killed me. Nicolas knew I was Rich, but he didn't tell Vi and Jeremiah because I told him not to."

"Seriously?" I hear Vi shuffling around and Jeremiah looking up at Mal with widened eyes.

"Yeah, I wanted to hide it from everybody. The only reason Nicolas had to know was because he was the leader. I told him that I left my home and was wanting to be a part of anything the Poor held. I just didn't want to be labeled as a Rich person anymore. Fortunately, he believed me, so I was soon accepted into their humble abode.

"Our group became very close, and we realized that we were missing one other person . . . someone I wish we never had recruited . . ." She drifts off with bitterness edging at her tone. "We needed someone to implement security cameras that exhibited *all* the places around here. Nicolas had hoped someone like that existed, and, well—they did."

It gets silent to the point where we can even hear a pin drop in the room.

Mal speaks again, her voice wavering. "We had recruited Dylan Faulkner, just about four months ago, and he was the light in the darkness that was our group. He was funny, sarcastic, and light- hearted. He was just what we needed, besides his insane computer skills. Nicolas did make sure to do an extreme background check on Dylan because no Poor person would have skills like he did. However, Nicolas saw no trace of Dylan possibly being Rich all over his records. Dylan himself even begged and swore that he was willing to do anything.

"Nicolas gave in and allowed him to join because no one on our team had technology skills at all, especially not like the ones Dylan had. He was willing to take the risk because he needed a better leeway into the system, to hack all of the cameras there, so we would've had a better idea of where to trickle into and hold initiative in certain places.

"For a few months, everything was going great. Then this happened three months ago . . . Nicolas stated that he wanted to bring Blaire into the Subversives as well." My eyes widen as I feel my heart pound louder and harder. "He said that you were turning nineteen very soon, so he was willing to have you join as well. He mentioned that you were brave, determined, and courageous, and also had so much hatred for the Rich. He said that he just knew you could encounter any obstacles thrown at you like a boss." *He really said that about me?*

Hot tears start to form in my eyes as I force them to go away. *Nicolas wouldn't have liked it if you cried at the mere thought of him. Instead, he would have much more appreciated it if you laughed and smiled at the thought of him. He never would have liked it if the memories of him brought pain to you.*

Mal continues. "Of course, we agreed with him. We were more than eager to allow you, the sibling of the man we praised, into our group. And Nicolas was probably the most eager of us all. He couldn't wait to hug you, love you, and be near you like he was before. That's how much he loved you."

I am still not able to reel in the fact that he's dead, not with us anymore, and not breathing either. *I really want him back. I can't bear the thought of him being gone.*

"And then?" I whisper, hoping it was loud enough for Mal to hear.

"And then he . . . He left to go to the Poor villages to take you and bring you here. It was a few days after your birthday . . ." Mal pauses, struggling to let out whatever she has to say next.

"He left that day—I remember it was a warm, August day.

We were so excited to bring you here, alongside your brother—reunited as well. We were thrilled. But . . . looks like fate had different plans for us."

"He didn't come back, did he?"

A few seconds of silence pass by before Mal rasps, "Yeah. He never came back. And after what Tobias told us, that he was killed on the way there . . . it made me feel infuriated. We already dealt with the horrible news of Zach betraying us, and now we just learnt of the fact that Nicolas was killed by Tobias and his men. And for that, I will forever resent the government."

Three beats of silence go by.

My mouth starts to dry. "Okay, uh . . . Things start to make sense now. But what I still don't understand is why you didn't just *tell* me the moment I walked into the bunker. If Nico was gone and certainly not able to enforce his opinions, then you should've just told me and not have me find out from Tobias instead."

"And that is our faults," Jeremiah says solemnly. "We should've told you but we couldn't because . . . Well, you just reminded us of him so much. From your looks to your personality, you guys were just so similar. So it pained us to even bring up Nicolas. And we didn't want to pain you with the terrible news, too."

I bring my knees up to my chest, my eyes feeling heavy with weariness. Everything Mal, Vi, and Jeremiah just told me . . . Well, my tired mind is not able to conjure up all and make mind of it.

My body aches, my mind aches, my heart aches, and *I* ache. I am here breathing, but even breathing seems to ache, too.

"Wow," Jax says. "So this was the guy who was the leader of the Subversives—Cohen's older brother?"

"Yeah." Mal frowns.

"Damn," he curses, biting his lip. "He seems like a cool guy."

"Yep," I say, "he was."

As soon as those words escape from my mouth, something rings into the air. I wince, feeling the ceiling vibrate with the intense reverberations.

"Hello, rebels." An indistinguishable voice booms into the overhead speakers. "You are inside the White House's underground chamber where you will be held until your execution. Here you will be monitored alongside your peers, and twice a day, several Guards will come by to punish you for your wrongdoings. Each person will be tortured by the Guard's desired liking. There is no way out of here except the steel door that can only be opened by a Guard. Any attempts to kick, punch, or destroy the door will result in your eventual failure and an increase of your physical beatings. I highly request that you remain civil to make this process as . . . *pleasant* as possible.

"Food, which will be stale bread and a cup of water, will be brought once a day, since we believe the proper preserving of the human body will allow the most desired reactions to your lashings. Your sleeping places will be on the floor with no blankets, pillows, or mattresses provided. However, if you feel as if your injuries are more painful than you'd like them to be, a Guard will hand you the necessary medical supplies for which you will tend to yourself. While we want you to think about your horrible decisions thus far, we also want your bodies to be in great condition before the execution on the 4th.

"In just a minute, three Guards will be coming in to initiate your first session. They will treat you however they wish for the fifteen minutes they will be there. Once they leave, you are free to roam in the cellar with no suspicious activity involved. Remember, there are cameras around you."

There is a long pause. "This is for America, who has suffered enough. Your abominable behavior shall not be excused. Amen."

Right when the voice finishes, three Guards filter into the room, holding no weapons in their hands. All I see are their fists emblazoned in brass knuckles, curling into their palms in a slow and apprehensive manner.

My heart lodges into my throat.

They stand before us, and we cower, freezing in our spots. Even Vi doesn't think to fight back because she knows that there is no way out of here.

There's no way we can win this battle.

And so, I brace myself as the metal clashes into my jaw, suddenly feeling a blinding flash of pain jolt through me.

39

INTIMATE

November 28, 2064
1:47 a.m.

MY MUSCLES ARE ACHING and pounding. I take ragged breaths in, feeling fresh scars gashing at my skin, and wincing when the brutal injuries burn vigorously.

It's been more than an hour since our first torture session ended, and we have been expected to fall asleep now—which I don't know why they would ever expect that out of us after pummeling us alive with their metal knuckles. They left our dying bodies heaving in blood, and ever since then we went to different areas of the chamber, drowning in our painful sorrows.

I clutch my sides, my bones fragmented and my heart cracked. We have to deal with this twice a day? Until the 4th? I can barely even compose myself after the first time.

Movements from the corridor leading to the iron-clad door has my interests piqued. I look over there and see Jax grabbing supplies from the medical kit and seeming desperate to heal himself. The others are dead asleep, which I am astonished by because I haven't been able to sleep a wink. Maybe I can go over there to tend my injuries, too, hoping that once I am finished, I can somehow sleep in this depressing hell.

With elongated breaths, I hold onto my stomach, my face numb with bruises as I struggle to make my way over to the corridor. My legs don't seem to be working very well, so I instead drag my body against the rough flooring, each movement causing me significant and ground-breaking anguish.

Few minutes later, I reach the corridor and clear my throat so Jax can notice my presence. He looks over at me in shock, eyes widened and chest rising at irregular periods. "Cohen? What are you doing here?"

"I-I need to tend to my injuries," I stammer, making my way beside him. "And I also need someone to talk to."

In any normal situation, Jax would joke that I decided to talk to *him* of all people, but this time, regarding the severity of our situation, he thins his lips into a straight line and sends me a desolate look. "Me too."

As I sit next to him, I notice just how concerning his injuries are. His face, first of all, is marked with bruises and scars, yet they are nothing compared to his thin and jagged trademark scar that travels down his right cheek. And he is completely shirtless, revealing his muscular chest that has many red and gashed lines running across. He's trembling, confused, and desperate to fix his injuries so he can rest. But he's too worried about what's to come on the 4th. And the situation he's placed himself in.

"How are you feeling?" I ask him.

He scoffs, his legs outstretched now. "I feel like shit—both mentally and physically. What about you?"

"Same." I let out a sad chuckle. "I mean, I stabbed your father in the eye because I heard my brother is dead *and* was the leader of the Subversives—oh, and not to mention we're getting executed soon."

He hands me the medical kit. "Well, if it makes you feel any better, I will be dying as per my father's request and he still refuses to acknowledge the fact that I want nothing to do with him."

I frown at him. "God, our lives are so shitty."

"Tell me about it." He groans.

I notice his breathing is still erratic, sweat clinging to his torso in concerning ways. His soft and flawless skin is brazen with dry blood and agonized in red, and he struggles to push past his injuries, groaning and wincing to himself.

"Here, let me help you," I say, rummaging through the medical kit.

"No, you don't have to do that," he says hurriedly. "Besides, I think you should take care of yourself first."

I shake my head. "You're out of your mind, Jax. I can at least breathe; you, on the other hand, look like you're about to pass out." As he begins to protest more, I hold my hand up at him, looking at him earnestly. "Let me help you."

His expression softens, his gray eyes raking over me. "I don't want to be an inconvenience to you."

I sigh. "Just because I find you highly annoying, doesn't mean you're an inconvenience to me."

At that, he grins, portraying his beautiful smile that has intense knots growing in my stomach. "Wow, we're making progress here; first you completely hated my guts and now you just find me highly annoying."

I roll my eyes at him, a smile slipping onto my lips. "Yeah, I've learned to tolerate you over the past few weeks."

Seconds later, I find gauze pads, tiny cotton balls, several bandages, and a large bottle of rubbing alcohol, which should be enough to not completely get rid of his injuries but at least alleviate the pain. Oh, and also make sure he doesn't get any life-threatening diseases from having his gaping flesh wound out in the open. Especially in this murky environment.

"I don't know much about tending injuries," I say, "but I'm just going to go based off how Mal tended to Vi's arm."

"It's fine, I don't know much either." He looks desperate. "Just do your best."

"I will." I nod my head.

I gently grab a cotton ball, douse it in the rubbing alcohol, and get closer to Jax so I can apply it on him more easily. My heart-rate increases, enamored in his overwhelming presence. We're so close to each other, since I am slightly leaning over his legs and inches away from his face. My thigh grazes his, and I realize that if I move any more to my left then I will basically be sitting on his lap.

He sucks in a sharp breath.

I place my left hand on his shoulder and dab the cotton ball against the bruise on his forehead in a very gentle manner. He winces, reeling away from me but I hold him in place. "Hold still," I say in a stern voice.

"I'm trying," he grits through his teeth.

As I very tenderly run the cotton ball across his face, residue of the rubbing alcohol simmering into his wounds, he grits his teeth the entire time, his eyes squeezed shut and veins appearing on his biceps. He lets out a strained yell as I move my left hand to his jaw, grazing my hand against the sharp and meticulously formed angles of it and place the cotton ball there.

His hands unintentionally grasp my hips. "Cohen, that, uh . . . That really hurts."

"I know, Jax," I say, "Just a few more seconds, okay?"

"All right." His voice is raspy, fingers digging into my skin.

I press my lips together, cursing at myself for ever letting his touch affect me in *any* sort of way. He's only in pain—that's why his hands are grasping my hips. He needs something to grab, to hold onto, just to ease himself.

My throat tightens. Did it have to be my *hips,* though?

Finally, I finish and place one large bandage on the underside of his jaw since there seems to be a gaping wound there. Other than that, his facial injuries are pretty manageable. As his hands slowly leave my side, I deliberately gaze at his trademark scar, gashed furiously and threatening to unleash its terrors. I send Jax a confused look. "What do you want me to do about your scar?"

His eyes fly open, his hand hastily touching it—the same one I've wondered about for a while now. "This one?"

I nod.

"Oh, uh"—he nervously chuckles—"don't worry about that. It's been there for a while."

"Why?" I blurt out. When the word leaves my mouth, I wince to myself. Maybe I *am* a nosy woman.

He raises one eyebrow. "I'd rather not talk about it."

I let out a disappointed sigh. "Jax, you need to open up about your scar one day at least."

"Why are you so worried about it?" He sounds defensive, his eyes suddenly rimmed in rage. "It's just a scar."

"I noticed it during the inauguration," I say. "I noticed lots of things, actually."

"Like what?"

I take a deep breath, contemplating. "For starters, you didn't seem engaged in your speech at all, you ran off randomly, and you seemed scared out of your mind." I pause. "Also, one of the cameras zoomed into your face, and I saw your scar. I hadn't seen it before, so that's what intrigued me. Obviously I am quite curious to know how it happened."

Jax looks absolutely amazed. "Are you sure you're not a detective?"

I snort. "I'm not. But the least you can do for me is just tell me about your scar."

"Yeah, but what if I don't want to talk about it?" He frowns.

I sigh, looking at the wall he's currently leaning against. Words begin to fly out of my mouth. "I have a mother, a father, a little sister named Emilia, and an older brother named Nicolas. I was torn away from my family when I was kidnapped on November 5th by the Subversives, and I unwillingly lived with them for the time being. However, as time passed by, I started to enjoy staying there. But it is unfortunate that I later found out by *your father* that my brother led this entire group and died in his hands. I didn't even get to say good-bye to him." My voice is wavering. "And now, I'm here in this shitty dungeon, expecting my near death, just like Nicolas received his." I send him a cool and nonchalant gaze. "If I can open up to you, then you definitely can, too."

Jax is speechless.

Moments later, he purses his lips. "Fine, you want to know? I'll tell you." His silver eyes land on me, making my insides broil. "Only because I know I have no way out of this." Jax adjusts himself, and as I sit diagonally to him, I prepare myself to hear the story I've been *dying* to hear . . . How he got his scar.

The air is thick, heavy with stillness. ﹀

"I haven't told anyone this," he says. "Well, I'm suspecting Mallory knows because she's known me for a very long time."

I wait patiently, fidgeting to myself.

"As you are aware, my father expected me to step up to the 'throne' after him. He made me participate in events that he hosted, made me talk to others, made me do speeches on television, you name it." He looks at the ceiling. "My father tried his very best to make me the ideal golden boy, the son that followed his every word. I was very well-behaved in front of television and in front of the entirety of D.C. as well." His voice starts to waver while he starts to embrace himself against the chilling weather. "However, things at home were a different story."

My lips dry. "What do you mean?"

His silver eyes meet mine once again, telling a story of their own. "What I'm about to tell you, Cohen . . . It's going to be disturbing. And it haunts me forever just merely thinking about it."

Before I can even think about what I'm doing next, I run my fingers over his red calluses and place my hand on top of his. They feel warm still, even amongst the cold and desolate atmosphere. "Take your time. I am here for you and will be listening the entire time. I promise," I whisper.

A small smile takes over his lips, causing butterflies to form in my stomach. "Okay," he whispers.

He starts to speak again, his voice lowering to a few notches to the point where I have to lean in to hear him properly. And, with bated breath, I wait for him to start speaking.

"As I was saying . . . Things were quite different at home. I didn't care about what I said to my father—I had no filter. And I think, the more I grew up, the less I cared about what he thought. Unfortunately, that came with consequences."

He pauses, closing his eyes. Finally, he curls his hand around mine and places it against his scar. I cup his warm cheek with my hand, feeling the jagged scar that I have wondered about for years. The rough edges feel bizarre underneath my fingers, almost like a catalytic alchemy.

My hand is still on his cheek as he turns to me, his eyes an inventory of buried pain. "My father caused this scar, Cohen."

My jaw drops, and I feel my throat drying with worry. "What? Really?" *I don't even know what to say right now.*

"Yeah." He gulps, shaking his head. "He used to hurt me."

I think, trying to wrap my mind around what I just heard.

He chuckles, sort of in a pitiful way. "Whenever I disagreed with him, he would slap me across the face. Whenever I yelled at him, he would punch me. And whenever I insulted him, he would . . . beat me up. Call me insulting names back, except his was more scarring. I was a teenager, Cohen. I was hurt for *simply* expressing my opinions."

"You don't deserve that at all . . ." I whisper, caressing his scar.

His breathing is erratic. "Last year, uh . . . We got into a really bad argument. It all started because I didn't want to attend one of his parties. He got pissed and told me that I was the worst son ever. Then I pushed him . . . which is all that it took for him."

"Don't tell me he . . ."

"We were right by the kitchen, so out of anger, he got a knife out of the drawers—it was thin, but very sharp—and brought it to my face." He shudders, forcing his tears back. "I was trying to rip away from his hold, but he held on tight to me and . . . dragged the knife against my cheek. It was a brutal cut . . . I remember that I was crying and screaming and blood was pouring out of my skin, and all my father did was scoff and bring out a napkin to me. He told me to clean up and to get ready for the event. And you know what made this situation even worse?"

I shake my head, speechless as ever.

"My mom was standing there the entire time, watching my father drag the knife against my cheek. She heard her son scream yet did not do anything about it. And that is when I knew that I was not a Remington. That is when I decide that I'll never acknowledge myself as a part of the prestigious Remington family ever again."

I can't even help it anymore. I have to do this.

I embrace him, pulling his body toward mine. Our bodies are perfectly combined, and all I can feel and hear is his soft and irregular breathing. He wraps his hands around me, planting his chin onto my shoulder, his torso sulking against mine. *He deserves so much better.*

I pull away from him. "You are so strong, Jax. And you should not have gone through that at all. You were just expressing your feelings, and your father should not abuse you for that. He should not even lay a hand on you. You are your own person, never forget that."

His soft gray eyes gaze into mine. "Thanks, Blaire. Your words mean so much to me."

I feel my heart racing as something settles in my mind. "You said my name."

He cocks his head at me, amused. "You noticed that I only say your last name?"

"Yeah, of course, I did. So, tell me. Why don't you ever say my name?"

Jax presses his lips together, his eyes a smoldering fire, all comprehensible thoughts leaving my mind. We're so close to each other, and if I leaned in any further we would be—

I gulp.

He grazes his fingers up my arm in a meticulous manner, the energy in my body startlingly vivacious. There is no space for me to breathe because this man's beautiful face is right in front of me, and frankly, breathing seems to be the last thing on my mind.

He brings his hands to my hips again, gradually trailing them up to my waist. "Saying your beautiful name makes me realize that it is associated with a beautiful woman like you." He brings his face even closer to mine, his soft breath tickling my neck. I can't breathe. "And I wouldn't be able to control myself if I said your name . . . Blaire."

And he leans in.

But that is until he curses out loud, reeling his hands away from my waist and placing them on his rigid torso where blood seeps out from his gaping wound. He looks at me in over-whelming embarrassment, cheeks bright hues of red. "Shit, I completely forgot that was there—"

"It's okay," I say, wholly flustered and embarrassed as well.

Were me and Jax about to kiss? I was so caught up in the moment that the entire situation didn't really dawn on me. We were just so close to each other—so *intimate*—that I was unable to register everything. He's just so addicting, his presence making my mind swirl. I normally would scorn myself for allowing him to affect my state of mind . . . but now?

I don't mind it so much.

I quickly grab the bottle of rubbing alcohol and the cotton balls, douse it before I can even blink, and rub it on his skin— his lower torso. The flesh wound is concerning, blood dripping down to the entrance of his pants. He tilts his chin up, growling like a pained animal.

When I finish, I grab a roll of gauze and wrap it around his lower torso, adamant to conceal his injuries. His breathing evens out, and he lets out a huge sigh of relief. "Can they just kill me already?"

I frown as I conclude my tending to his injury. My hand grazes over his covered wound, feeling the slightly rough fabric of the gauze. "They obviously seem to get more pleasure torturing us than killing us right off the bat."

He scowls. "They're sick people. I hate them. *All* of them."

I look up at him, the anger washing away from his features as his soft gray eyes graze over me. He brings his hand to my cheek, lightly trailing over my injuries. "Let me help you, too."

"No, Jax. I got it."

"But I feel so bad that you've been taking care of me this entire time and you're here, dealing with your own injuries too." He looks adamant. "Please let me help you."

"I'm telling you," I start to say, "you don't have to help me—"

"And what's going on here?"

Jax and I almost jump to our feet in shock as we turn our heads around to see Vi standing at the entrance of the dimly-lit corridor, a smug look on her face. My face warms up as I realize that I am almost sitting on his lap, his hand on my cheek and mine by the lining of his pants.

This is surely a very compromising position.

"Uh, no," I mutter underneath my breath, "you are not interrupting anything. I-I was just . . . helping Jax with his injuries."

She raises her eyebrows. "Sitting like that? And touching his chest . . . like *that*?"

"I know it looks really bad." Jax winces. "But I swear to you, she was just checking up on me."

Vi crosses her arms, leaning against the wall. Her body is heavily bruised, not to mention the horrible injury she received while we were in the forest, too. But that doesn't seem to bother her at all. In fact, she's acting just like she normally would.

"All right." She nods. "I believe you."

I breathe out a sigh of relief. "Thank you."

She almost smiles. "Well, you kids carry on then. I just came over here to check up on the commotion happening here, but I see that, uh . . . You guys are pretty acquainted with each other." Before any of us can answer, she says again, "I will be going to sleep now. Good night. And try not to, um, do anything indecent. Remember"—she points to the ceiling—"there's cameras."

Vi salutes us, walking away with a ghostly smile on her. And Jax and I lay here in the narrow hallway, our bodies still slightly intermingled and our faces still heavily flustered.

40

INCONCEIVABLE

December 3, 2064
10:55 p.m.

AFTER SEVERAL BEATINGS, WE have somehow found some way to remain in one piece. And breathing, too.

During the first few days, we were barely able to hold ourselves upright. The lashings were just so merciless, so *demeaning*, that we fell to the ground each and every time, breaths wheezing and veins throbbing. Our bodies were drenched and ravaged in cuts and bruises gashing in bright red blood, and if it weren't for the medical kit, we would've been dead on the spot.

The only reason the Guards even bother with allowing us to heal after the torturous sessions is to, as they've said multiple times, "preserve the bodies before the ultimate execution." If they had refused to allow us to tend to our injuries then there wouldn't be a public execution—which they don't want; they want as much raucous and untamed energy as possible.

Now we are sitting here in this same old chamber, dripping in intense draftiness. The dark walls are cool and hollow, and whenever I prop my body against it, I feel a huge wave of chilliness sift through my nerves. It is genuinely a very uncomfortable feeling, so that is why I steer away from the walls as much as possible. But the floor isn't any better either; the roughness of the planks makes it hard for me to sit anyway. So I stand, ignoring my knees buckling due to the intense lashings I've received.

I want to get out of this place so badly. And we all are slowly going insane, eating the same old food, being surrounded by the same old people, and living in the same old environment. We all want to leave—*now.*

Jeremiah sighs from the other end, pacing back and forth. "One last session. And we will be done." His words are clipped, finding significant pain to even speak. "I can't take this anymore. Why can't they just kill us already?"

"I think that every single day," Mal says while laying down on the ground, her blonde hair displayed around her like a piece of art. "I'm tired of getting beaten up like this."

"At least we will be able to deal with the execution." Vi snorts as she leans against the wall, her legs outstretched in front of her. "Since we've been through so much already."

"I mean, if you think about it," Jax says, "there is one positive thing in this entire situation."

"What?" She glares at him, who's sitting diagonal to Mal.

He gives her a pointed look. "We get *bathroom breaks.* You've got to admit, that's pretty generous of them."

"Are you kidding me?" Vi scowls.

"What? You know it's true."

She rolls her eyes. "I don't have any sort of patience left in me to deal with your annoying voice. I've become absolutely insane in here, having you next to me all. The damn. Time!"

"Well, it's not easy for me either." He scoffs. ·

"The hell do you mean by that?"

"You're always so *pessimistic!* Like, relax. Take a deep breath. Everything's going to be okay."

"Did you just call me pessimistic?"

"Yeah." He works his jaw. "Somebody had to."

She jumps up from her feet, her nostrils flaring with intense anger. "Listen here you asshole. I am going to—"

"Guys!" I yell, holding onto my knees for dear life. "I know that we are all super tense right now and just want to get the hell out of here. I know that. But turning onto each other like this isn't going to alleviate anything. In fact, it's just going to make our situation worse."

Vi shoots Jax one last disdainful look and grumbles as she sits down, rapidly tapping her foot against the floor. "God, I really need a cigarette."

And so we all sit here in loud silence, weighing in the enormous situation we are in. It was just two weeks ago that we successfully kidnapped Jax and were on track to successfully force Tobias to resign from his position. Everything was going so well.

Until Zach turned on us.

I hope that son of a bitch is still there, lying in a pool of his own blood. I hope he's nothing but a decaying corpse, disintegrating into what is left of the bunker, which may be absolutely nothing at this point. He's caused us enough damage. He's caused us enough turmoil. And he's caused us enough hell.

Because we are all stuck in this claustrophobic dungeon, feeling both hopeless and helpless.

I find myself looking at everyone, studying their every movement. Jeremiah is still pacing back and forth, gnawing at his nail as his dark skin is bathed in dry blood and bright bruises. Mal is still flat against the ground, bringing both of her hands to her chest and closing her eyes, letting a tear trickle down her cheek. Vi is still tapping her foot, but not so rapidly as before; and her eyes are trained onto the wall ahead of her, filled with venom and deadly intentions.

And Jax.

My heart squeezes as I notice him looking at the far distance, his gray eyes contemplating and melancholy. His knees are pushed to his chest, and he bites his lip, his disheveled hair falling onto his eyes. I think of the mind-boggling and hair-raising moment we shared a couple of nights ago, when I soothed his wounds. When I was so close to him that I could feel his torso digging into mine. When he shared the story of his scar, how his father was the cause of it.

And when we almost kissed.

Heat rises through my skin in a slow and tantalizing manner. Never would I have imagined Jax and I to be that close in the first place, so intimate and so delicate with one another. Just two weeks ago I wanted to rip his head off. But now, things are very different. We were forced to like one another because of the extremity of the situation we were in. But that forcing led into genuine appreciation for one another. I may not be fully fond of Jax and who he is as a man, but I do respect him. I respect him for the hell he's been through. And I respect him for having the guts to stand with us, when he could very easily slip into a life filled with privilege again.

So, if I only have respect for him, then why does my ability to breathe always vanish whenever he's in my presence? Whenever his deep voice rumbles into the air? Whenever his soft fingers graze my skin? Whenever he shows off that beautiful smile of his? And whenever his mesmerizing eyes land on me, casting some sort of uninterpretable spell on my soul?

This complex and enigmatic man, I hate to admit, has left me utterly enraptured.

Suddenly, noises occur outside the heavy and stiff door. "Who's that?" I say frantically.

"Our next torturer, I think," Jeremiah says. "And our last one ever."

I brace myself as the door flies open, revealing a tall and skinny figure on the other side.

My heart drops to the bottom of my stomach.

The boy steps forward, pushing his thick-rimmed glasses to the bridge of his nose. His overly-messy brown hair is now combed neatly, just one strand of hair poking out. His strides are precise, marked with purpose and an irritating attitude. He smiles a face-splitting smile, nothing but a sadistic appeal smeared across his impish features.

And as if life couldn't get even more inconceivable, I notice his torso is encased in a white layering, revealing just a glimpse of clotted blood transpiring from his chest.

My lips remain glued shut as I cower against the wall, the coolness of it not bothering me anymore.

Because Zachary Everett is standing in front of us.

41

DEMISE

December 3, 2064
11:01 p.m.

"WELL, WOULD YOU LOOK at that?" Zach says, his gleaming brown eyes raking over us. "We meet again."

No one speaks.

"Why is everyone so quiet?" He laughs, standing by the corridor. "C'mon, everyone. Let's talk. Let's catch up!" He gesticulates wildly, grinning so much his face almost splits in half.

"H-how . . . How are you still alive?" Mal's face blanches.

"Ah." He crosses his arms, tapping his finger against the sleeve of his dark green sweater. "Well, I was quite surprised when I was alive, too. I thought, when Jeremiah shot me in the chest, it would pierce through my heart and kill me immediately. But, as soon as the Guards tased you and took you to the prison, I was brought to the hospital and was revitalized through their exceptional surgical skills. And do you know who did my surgery?"

Mal's mouth is agape. "My father?"

"Yes." He chuckles. "Doctor Adam Reaves, the finest surgeon in D.C. Your father removed the bullet which was *very close* to plunging into my heart. But I guess the odds were in my favor because little to no harm was done to me." He shrugs. "And now I'm back and better than ever."

My mouth dries as I take in the information Zach told us. First of all, my muddled mind is barely able to grasp the fact that our traitor is right in front of us, smirking and seeming quite pleased with our reactions. And as if life couldn't get even more torturous, Zach also told us that Jeremiah's attempt to shoot him had failed and now he's here in the damn flesh.

Jeremiah's pacing has stopped long ago. "You're telling me that I didn't kill you? Are you shitting me?" His expression is livid and truly terrifying, fists outstretched in front of him as his gigantic figure charges at him. "I will get the job done *now*—"

Zach brings a gun out of his pocket and points it at him. His face is unflinching, but his knees buckling tell a completely different story. "I knew you guys would not be happy with my appearance. So I made sure to be armed, just in case things were to go awry." His finger rests against the trigger, pointing the jagged tip at Jeremiah's temple. "So I suggest you remain civil, Mr. Morgan."

A few seconds later, the enraged man huffs and stands by the far corner, sending Zach a look that is lethal and unnerving at once.

"Wh-why are you here?" I stammer, my insides gnashing with perturbation.

"Oh, Blaire." His grin widens when his slimy eyes land on me. "I almost didn't see you there. How are you doing?" He suddenly winces and pretends to look sorry for me. "I was so deeply saddened when I heard about your brother. I'm sure he's in a much better place."

"Go to hell," I snarl.

"Well, that's not very nice to say." He frowns. "I've been absolutely nothing but nice to you so far. And, in all honesty, I think you all will be the ones going to hell, not me."

"You lied to us," Mal says. "You betrayed us. You *broke* us, Zach."

"Ah, don't be so dramatic. I only did what was necessary for the betterment of the country. I swear it's not anything personal."

"I don't care about what you have to say," Vi says, pointing an accusing finger at him. "I only want to know why the hell you are here."

He sighs, adjusting his glasses. "I mean, if you guys really want to know . . ." Zach pauses. "I'm here to torture you all."

She scrunches her nose up at him. "*You* are going to torture us?"

"Oh, Vienna, you really underestimate me." He holds a hand up to where his heart would be. "I am capable of quite much, actually. Like, for example, I duped all of you guys into thinking I was some innocent guy named Dylan. And, because of that, you fell into my trap that I meticulously planned for months on end. So, if you think about it, I am more dangerous than all of you combined, meaning I am perfectly capable of torturing you."

"But torturing has to do with physical strength," I say, "which we would indefinitely overpower you in."

At that, Zach chuckles to himself, shaking his head. "All right, well . . . What if I told you this torturing session has nothing to do with my physical strength?" As we stare at him wordlessly, he gestures at us with the gun in his hands, still pointed at us in defense. "Get up, everyone."

Jax speaks for the first time in a while. "You can't tell us what to do."

And in the fraction of a second, Dylan points the gun at him and releases the trigger, allowing a bullet to whizz by Jax— barely grazing his left ear. The bullet slams behind him, creating a small crack in the cobblestone wall. It formulates a resounding sound, reverberating and shaking our surroundings. My heart almost leaps out of my throat, thinking that this entire chamber may as well collapse, but all that occurs is the mere crack on the wall, and nothing else. I'm guessing this entire place may have been built from the Earth's core itself.

Jax curses underneath his breath, gently touching his ear. "Well, at least we know the gun is definitely loaded."

Moments later, Zach walks toward us, his eyes gleaming victoriously. "Do you want to rethink your stubbornness now?"

We all share uncertain looks with each other, confused if we should put our pride above all else or allow Zach to win this round, just so our lives aren't at risk. And, judging by their conflicted expressions, I start to think that we are going with the latter.

My notion is solidified when Vi walks over to the middle of the quasi-tenebrous room, defeat clinging onto her features. The rest of us follow her, standing in a strict single file line with depression nagging at our insides. We have no other choice but to comply because we know that Zach won't hesitate to shoot us all.

"Wonderful." He beams, standing in front of us all. A harsh breeze filters into the room, causing the hairs on my arms to rise. "See, life is so much easier when everyone gets along, right?"

No one says anything.

"Okay, well . . ." Zach doesn't even bother to hide the excited look on his face. "Let's get started, shall we?"

Four beats of silence go by, the unsteady beating of our hearts colliding together.

"Mallory, please step forward."

Since she is beside me, from the corner of my eye, I can see her body stiffen, her face dropping in substantial terror. Her feet are like weights drawn to the ground.

Zach impatiently taps his foot. "You know, I don't have all day here."

Several grueling seconds later, Mal sighs and slowly steps forward, her long blonde hair flowing down to her hips as she refuses to look him in the eye. Tears are threatening to spill down her cheeks, desperate to unravel all of her buried fears. But she sucks in a sharp breath, adamant to not reveal her emotions in front of the enemy.

Something uneasy crawls into my stomach.

And, it is with great shock as I see Zach reach into his pocket and pull out another sleek gun, shining against the dim lights. He beckons it to Mal and says:

"Shoot Vienna."

My eyebrows fly to my forehead. Everyone clamors around me, absolutely shocked. Mal, on the other hand, is shaking, furiously shaking her head. "I-I can't do that."

"If you shoot Vienna"—Zach ignores her desperate remarks—"then I will let you go. But if I don't, then somebody else will step in your place."

Mal is strict, her lips thinned. "I will not shoot her. And I want nothing to do with my parents." Her voice is trembling very instinctively, but she has her feet grounded. Her knees aren't buckling as much. Her big blue eyes are ferocious, filled with nothing but enraging sorrow.

"Okay." Zach nods once, aiming the gun at her. "Looks like somebody else will step in instead."

"Wait!" Vi interjects.

His jaw ticks. "What do you want?"

"What is the point of this?" she hisses. "Why are you telling her to shoot me when we are going to get executed tomorrow anyway?"

"Nobody said the execution has to happen live in front of everyone tomorrow," he says. "It can most definitely happen now. As long as there is recorded proof of the execution, we can show it to everyone on screens tomorrow, so it'll be much better for them to watch from the comfort of their homes."

"And where will it be recorded?" Vi glares at him.

Zach doesn't say a single word; he instead points up at the ceiling.

The damn cameras.

"You are a sickening little boy." Jeremiah's voice is raspy.

"Little boy? I must humbly remind you that I am an adult." Zach smiles. "And I am not sickening either. I am only providing justice for this country that has been embarrassed plenty by you rebels. And we have already been through enough. Our damn president is in the hospital because of you"—he sends me a seething look—"and the last thing we need is a bunch of stupid people determined to destroy our government that took years to build."

"You're younger than us, Zach!" Jeremiah yells desperately. "What can you possibly know about the government?"

"That it has provided great relief for us."

"For just the *Rich*, you mean?" I snarl.

"Look, I am not here to argue with you all! I am here to get my job done before your execution tomorrow. That is it."

"Do whatever you have to do," Jax says, "just don't put Mallory in that position."

"Okay, fine." He shrugs, nodding at him. "You come in instead."

Jax's jaw drops. "Excuse me?"

"Didn't I say somebody else will come in for her if she is unable to execute the job?" He sneers. "So you step in instead."

He slowly shakes his head. "Yeah, you're absolutely out of your mind."

"I do not want to chatter with you any further," he says. "I want to make this as quick and easy as possible. So step forward *right now* before I actually shoot you this time."

He contemplates to himself, eyebrows furrowed and expression conflicted. It is seconds later that he nods once and goes to take the gun from Zach. "Fine. I will do it."

We all exchange worried glances with each other. *What the hell is he doing?*

Even our traitor looks surprised too, chuckling nervously to himself. "All right." He hands the gun to him, and Jax studies it in his hand, looking at it intently.

Zach's voice is venomous as he says, "Now, shoot Blaire."

Jax's neck almost snaps by how fast he looks up at him. "What?"

"You heard me." He smirks. "Shoot Blaire Cohen."

He stammers, weighing the gun in his hand and biting his lip. My feet are melting to the ground, and my heart is now wedged between my throat, allowing no air to enter or exit my system. I shouldn't be worried, though, right? Jax and I bonded over that conversation we had a couple of days ago. We almost kissed for God's sake. He would never turn on me like that. I *trust* that he won't.

But he does.

He turns around.

His gray eyes meet mine.

And he points the gun at me.

Zach lets out a loud laugh. "Wonderful! This is simply wonderful!" He grins, almost starting to jump up and down with excitement. "Now shoot the damn woman!"

"Jax, what in the actual hell are you doing?" Vi grits through her teeth. "We thought you were on our side!"

He, unfortunately, doesn't say a single word. He instead unflinchingly keeps the tip of the gun pointed at my temple, not blinking the entire time he looks at me. I first found his eyes to be mesmerizing and simply ineffable, but now they are nothing but empty soulless pits lacking remorse. I would pounce at him, yell and scream and taunt him, but my feet are too numb. My muscles are weakening at the moment.

Maybe this is where my journey ends: not tomorrow, but instead today, in the hands of Tobias Remington's son, who I thought to be different. But he is actually *just* like his father— maybe even worse.

Another person to betray us.

Jax rests his finger against the trigger, faintly trailing over the curve of it and threatening to pull back. Zach grows impatient and hisses, "What are you waiting for? Get it done already, or I will do it myself!"

He presses his lips together, his extremely disheveled hair framing his sharp masculine features carved from the most meticulous designers of the universe. He is startlingly beautiful, but only on the outside.

On the inside, as I've just learned, he is assuredly conniving, gaining my trust out of nowhere and ripping it up into shreds by holding the gun up at me.

Trust is nothing but a figment of my imagination.

I wait for this painful moment to be over, so he can just shoot me and get it over with. I can't stand it any longer. I just want to vanish already. I just want to get out of this situation already. I just want to—

He turns around faster than lightning. And shoots Zach instead.

My hands fly to my mouth as blood spreads like a bacterium at his chest, right where his bandaging is. It most definitely passed through the white fabric and lodged into his chest, hopefully at his heart too.

He falls to the ground, his breathing heavy and thick with agitation. Fresh crimson blood drips from his bandaging and stains the floor around him, and he grits his teeth, angry and painful tears escaping at an alarming yet satisfying rate.

Jax drops the gun to the floor, lets out a sigh of relief, and turns to me. His eyes are gleaming. "You really thought I was going to shoot you?"

I can't help but laugh, relieved tears escaping out of my eyes. "O-of course I did! But I didn't know that you were going to shoot—"

"Zachary?" He cocks his head.

"Yes!" My hands flail around as I grasp my mind for the necessary words. "H-how did you turn around so fast? And shoot him so . . . perfectly?"

He suddenly smiles. "I used to hunt. Remember?"

The realization hits me like a hundred pound weight. *How could I ever forget?*

As I go to give him a limb-breaking hug, Vi goes and unexpectedly smacks Jax across the face. He yells, grasping his cheek where a stinging bright red color starts to form. "What was that for?"

"For scaring the living shit out of us!" She shrieks. "Why would you ever point that gun at her like that, huh?"

"I'm sorry!" He winces. "I wanted him to think that I was finally joining his side or something. And I guess it did work."

"Well, he is right." Jeremiah sighs, looking over at us.

"What do we do with him now?" Mal asks, still traumatized by this entire encounter.

"We don't do anything with him . . . not *yet*, at least." Vi raises her eyebrows.

"What do you mean?" I ask.

At that, Vi walks to him, her heavy footsteps pounding against the floor. She kneels beside him, and we all crowd around her, wondering what she's going to do.

Zach still seems to be alive, unfortunately, since he's twitching to himself still, but the life is most definitely draining from him in a slow and careful manner. He's huddled into a ball, desperately clutching his wound that is overwhelmingly pouring out blood.

When he sees us cowering over him, he gasps out, "W-what do you guys want?"

Vi cracks her knuckles. "How do we disable the cameras?"

In the midst of his twitching, he freezes and glares at her, his brown eyes marked in acrimony. "Like I would ever tell you."

In the blink of an eye, she rams her fists into his torso—right where his bloodied wound is.

He screams a guttural scream. "Want to try that again?" She sneers.

He's sobbing uncontrollably now. "Y-you disable them with my fingerprint through the console panel. The console panel is hidden beside the iron door. Y-you'll see a very faint black button there. When you p-press on it . . . The console panel will show."

She nods once. "Okay." Then she gestures toward his hand. "Now, I don't think you'll be able to get up and disable it yourself, so we will have to . . . compromise."

His eyes widen to the size of saucers. "What are you talking about?"

Moments later, Vi turns around to us, still kneeling. "Do you guys have any sharp objects on you?"

We all shake our heads.

Next, she looks at Zach again. "Do you have any sharp objects on you?"

His refusal to answer has her searching through his pockets, violently rummaging through every nook and cranny of his pants. He yelps in surprise. "Stop this immediately!"

But as soon as those words come out of his mouth, she holds up a decent-sized knife in her strong hand, one eyebrow arched in question. "Was this also going to be used for self-defense?"

His lack of response answers her question.

She sighs and looks at us again, sending us an acknowledging glance. I don't know where Vi is going with this, but I'll do anything it takes to destroy Zach—both mentally and physically. So I kneel beside him, holding him in place with the others.

He grits his teeth, his pale face turning bright red at each passing moment. "If you're trying to escape, then I will honestly just let you know it's not going to happen. The door can only be opened and closed by the Guards. I was able to enter because they admitted me here. Other th-than that, there is nothing on me that can help you guys get out. I swear on everything I own."

Vi grips the knife in her hand, her expression completely unreadable. "That's perfectly fine with me."

"Oh." He gulps.

Before silence can weigh down on us, she says, "Which hand? And tell me honestly because if you don't, then I will shoot you five times in the face."

From where I hold onto his left leg, his torso convulses in fear and crumbling pain. "Left."

Great. That means I'll be getting a front row seat for this.

Vi goes over to his left hand, just a few inches from me, and says again, "Which finger?"

"Pointer," he says almost immediately.

And I expect her to wait a couple of moments before slashing the knife down to his pointer finger. I expect her to bring her thoughts together before bringing imminent doom to Zach's hand.

But she doesn't wait at all.

She brings the knife down with indecipherable speed, blood splattering her face as Zach lets out an animalistic screech.

The sight is absolutely gruesome . . . but absolutely satisfying as well. Watching our enemy's eyes flash burning white and his body coil up makes unimaginable contentment crawl up my veins. And when Mal was tending to Vi's wound in the highly disgusting way she did, I could barely watch it.

But this time? I watch with no guilt. I watch with a bright grin on my face.

Vi lets out a sharp breath as she holds the bloodied finger in her hand, wiping away any excess blood with the cloth of her shirt. "I'll be right back," she says.

She walks away from the scene, and comes back two minutes later with a small smile on her lips.

"It worked," she says quietly. "The cameras are disabled."

We all jump up to our feet, excited. But the reason for why she would want the cameras disabled is still unknown.

It seems as if she can read my mind because she says next, "I wanted him to disable the cameras so the Guards wouldn't feel the need to check up on us. And we can spend our last painful moments here in great peace that we won't have people watching our every move."

"I aspire to be you," Mal says breathlessly.

Vi shrugs and throws the finger to the far corner of the room. "We still have one more thing to complete."

We watch nervously as she saunters over to the gun beside Jax. She gives him an honorable look. "Shall I finish what you started?"

He nods, grinning. "Of course, Vienna."

She sighs, turns to a cowering and unresponsive Zach—

And shoots him five times in the face.

42

REVELATION

December 4, 2064
5:30 a.m.

THE COLD AIR SWARMS around us like a deadly poison as I try my best to swallow the overwhelming feeling of gloom gnashing at my insides. My hands are tied behind my back in handcuffs that dig into my wrists, and the growing agony in my mind claws at me, for there seems to be no way I can escape from this never-ending hell.

Today is execution today. Today is the day where history will go down. And today is the day when we, as in the Subversives, are no longer existing.

My eyes are trained onto the ground, refusing to look at the Guard that stands in the front. He continues to bellow orders at us, as if we were mindless puppies.

I just want to get out of here already. I don't want to be here anymore.

However, my feet are stuck to the concrete like glue, for my limbs are so numb, so weary. All I want to do is escape this place and run into the unknown, where a better life for me possibly awaits. I want to go past this place and go wherever the wind takes me because, at this point, any place is better than D.C.

My mind aches for rest while my heart yearns for unrest.

I let out a gasp as I feel the skin where I dug my nails into seep out blood. Immediately unclenching my nails from the back of my palm, I straighten myself and feel my body tightening with worry.

My dark hair falls in waves against my shoulders, framing my beaten face as I push a few strands behind my left ear. All of us, pretty much, have been beaten up so much we are barely able to stand on our own two feet. We're barely able to breathe, for the air around us is filled with the inevitable. Because, so far, our entire journey as the Subversives brought us nothing but harm.

It was just yesterday night that Zachary Everett surprised us with his presence in our dimly-lit torture chamber. And it was just yesterday night too that Vi brutally murdered him with five consecutive bullets to his head. His head was nothing but demolished, a disgusting portrayal of the bits and pieces of his brain. And the entire night we stayed there, huddled in one area and refusing to step any closer to the clearly-dead Zach. We were traumatized by the way he made us shoot each other which, thankfully, we did not. Although Jax's eyebrow-raising actions had my heart plummeting to the bottom of the stomach, it was thankfully revealed that he was aiming for Zach instead. It took many tries to kill that bastard, but eventually we did.

The Guards came trampling into our room at five in the morning, curious as to why the cameras were deactivated, and were simply speechless by their companion's entire body obliterated in blood and remnants of his brain. They did attempt to kill us, but as soon as they realized our execution is today, they composed themselves and told us to get ready for our inevitable demise.

We are all in a horizontal line with Guards standing in front of us.

On the right of me is Jeremiah and Mal, who are wearing the same black short-sleeved romper as everyone—with the United States flag engraved onto the right breast pocket. Both of their heads are hung low as they also seem to be avoiding eye contact with their designated Guards.

And then on the other side is Vi and Jax—him being next to me. We all stand four feet apart in this small room, but the distance between Jax and me makes me realize just how close we were that night. When I took care of him and he told me the story behind his scar. The utterly melancholy story behind his jagged and haunting scar.

From my peripheral vision, I notice that Jax is standing ramrod straight, his eyes trained on the wall next to his designated Guard. Tufts of dark hair fall onto his eyes as he doesn't even bother to push them back. It seems as if there's something more harrowing on his mind.

Something crackles into the air.

My eyes widen with intrigue as I hear the Guard in front of me say, "Shall we take the rebels into the Center now?" I look up at her for a split second and see that she has a walkie-talkie held up to her mouth.

Seconds later, the walkie-talkie crackles back. "Yes, take them outside now."

The Guard nods once and stuffs the device into her pocket. Then, she walks over to the heavy double doors in front of us and tears them open, the outside air sifting inside. I shudder as we turn to our left and are escorted outside.

Vi is first in line. Her colorful hair is tied up into two French braids, and her eyes are cast onto the ground, her mouth closed as she follows behind her Guard. *She has accepted her fate too . . . just like everybody else.*

Next is Jax and his Guard, following behind and not daring

to shift his vision anywhere—or so I think until he glances at me. I feel my heart lurching to a stop as he studies me for what seems like forever. Suddenly, there is a slight curve to his lip, his eyes gleaming with delight. It makes my insides warm like a scorching hot summer day.

However, his light-hearted expression ceases as the situation we are in dawns upon him. As a result, his eyes darken, his mouth forms into a straight line, and he shifts his sight over to the double doors.

Then comes me.

My heavy combat boots thump against the hard floor as I feel my heart rate increase the more I near the double doors that have outside light peering in. The Guard in front of me turns around constantly to make sure I don't run off, even though that is the stupidest thing anyone can ever do because there are dozens of Guards surrounding us . . . the act of escaping is an utter death wish.

How ironic, since we are walking toward death itself.

As we step past the double doors, light strains my eyes as they struggle to adjust to the early morning. The entire sky is basked in thick white clouds, leaving no space for the sun to shine its rays upon us.

Taking a deep breath in, I turn to where the line is moving and move in long strides, which makes my calves hurt twice as much. The gravel path we are traveling on reminds me of the one Nico and I used to sit on—in front of our tiny shack. We used to share the juiciest of secrets, the funniest of jokes, and the best of advice with each other. There was never a dull moment with my *hermano* . . . There never was.

And the constant reminder of him being gone makes my heart deflate. The torturous voice of Tobias yelling that Nico is dead run in my mind over and over again, and I don't know how to get rid of it. It's as if my own mind has turned against me.

I just want to be happy. I do wonder about how it feels to have full exhilaration running through your body like a drug. I wonder how it's like to grin ear-to-ear—and not fake it. And I do wonder what it's like to live in a society where people are allowed to be happy. I really do wonder about that.

The distant buildings of the Rich sector become less and less distant the more we approach it. And it seems for once that the city is quiet because they are still reeling in from the shocking news they heard . . . hearing that six people planned to destroy the government.

But the more we approach the Rich sector . . . the more I realize that this city is anything *but* quiet.

My mouth is hung open with shock as I see people running toward us but are stopped by oncoming Guards. The furious looks engraved on their faces makes me realize that these people were bound to murder us before we even stepped foot in the Center.

Their words, to begin with, are infuriating, and it takes every bit of me to restrain myself from killing them with my own bare hands.

"What you have committed is a sin!"

"You rebels are tarnishing our reputation!"

"I hope you die before you even step foot in the Center!"

"You are embarrassing our founding fathers!"

"President Remington will forever reign on!"

"Jax is a disgrace to the Remington family!"

"Burn in hell, imbeciles!"

Objects are thrown at us as well. Somehow, the Guards manage to get us out of here without a scratch, and I feel confused as to why they are protecting us—but then I realize they only are because they want to see us get executed in front of the 7,030 citizens that live here.

Bile rises at the back of my throat, and I immediately force it back down. *Now is not the time to lose your composure, Blaire. Get it together.*

Once we escape the large crowds of angry Rich people, we arrive at the Capital Center, which stands tall amongst the city. Large screens are embellished everywhere, cameras are set on the large stage, seats are placed in front of the stage, and the national anthem plays in the background. Horrible memories of the inauguration begin to flash into my mind.

We are near the huge stage of the Capital Center. There are already citizens gathered here, sitting in their seats and talking amongst themselves. And just like the inauguration, the Rich are on the luxurious side while the Poor are on the desolate and dreary side.

I try to look for my family, but they are nowhere to be seen. Among thousands of people, it is quite hard to pinpoint a couple of family members. So, as a result, I force myself to look forward and ascend the stairs, following the line as we set foot upon the well- known stage.

I gulp as we are instructed to stop. The Guard in front of Vi steps out in front of us and pulls down his mask, revealing a man with dark skin and cornrows that reach to his shoulders.

"Spread out near the front of the platform. Make sure to kneel and remain in that exact same position the entire time."

We spread out over the front of the stage, shadowed by a Guard that orders for us to sit in a specific position. The distance between each of us is about four feet, which makes my heart ache with pain because we won't even be able to embrace each other before we are executed, however we are killed. We will be gone, just like that.

On the far-right side, where the stairs are, is Mal, who looks down at the floor with despair. On the other side is Jeremiah, who clenches his jaw, his dark eyes leveled onto the Rich side of the audience. Next to him is Vi. Her arm is still encased in the cast— and it must be uncomfortable for her, regarding the handcuffs—and her entire body sags forward as she tries her best to compose herself. Despair settles in my stomach, remembering that nobody in her family is alive.

And then, next to Mal is Jax, who takes a deep breath in and out. His entire body is tarnished, considering the bruises on his arms and his scar being even more noticeable than how it was at the inauguration. Tobias hurting Jax makes me feel angry, and I am glad that I stabbed the son of a bitch. He deserved it after what he had done to Jax *several times.* And Jax didn't deserve that.

We are all the same yet different in our own way. And for that, we should cherish our differences—not chastise and separate others.

I feel my face warming as Jax looks at me, his silver eyes gleaming against the overcast sky. He looks tired. Upset. Angry. For all I know, I am glad that we shared our moment that night because now I know what it's like to *feel.* Even if it was for that exact moment, I still *felt* something—something I have never felt in my entire life. It felt strange yet endearing.

And we both know we aren't going to make it. But knowing that we have each other is all that matters. It is enough to keep me satisfied, just for this single moment.

Suddenly, someone's voice pierces through the air. The chatters in the crowd settle down, the Guards stand behind us, and my breathing slows as I wait with bated breath.

Someone emerges from the right side of the center.

I see Tobias Remington coming up the stairs, wearing a large brown coat with brown pants at the bottom, squeaky clean dress shoes, a scarf that embodies his neck, and black gloves that encase his hands. I feel my ears burning as I watch the wretched man come up to the stage, a smile tracing his lips.

He has a black eye patch on. I didn't expect him to be dead, but I definitely did not expect him to be back on his feet so suddenly either. And he doesn't seem affected by his injury at all

—he keeps on smiling, his gray hair shimmering against the lights.

"Good morning, America," Tobias says into the microphone, turning toward the crowd as he stands right in front of Jax, his *son*. "I apologize for the ugly eye patch—my left eye has been quite irritated for a while now." He shoots me a glance, which says it all. *You caused this, you little shit.*

He continues to speak. "Today is the day that will go down in American history because we are now set to execute five rebels that dared to go against our government—the same one our founding fathers constructed with their bare hands. These said rebels are Jeremiah Morgan, Vienna Powers, Mallory Reaves, Blaire Cohen, and Jax Remington . . . my son.

"This execution is a warning to those in the future that dare to go against our well-established government. America will rise back to where it was before, and in order to do that, we must exterminate those who are our enemies—even those who come from our own blood."

His eyes land on me, and I feel my insides lighting with fury. "Let's initiate this execution, shall we?"

43

IMPACT

December 4, 2064
5:50 a.m.

MY HEART BEATS FAST.

"In front of us," Tobias begins to speak while wandering back and forth, "are America's biggest enemies. These creatures have *dared* to go against our country, the same one that has tackled many issues throughout history. We are number one and will forever remain that way until my last breath. However, these people of our own blood found it convenient for their liking to form a group called the Subversives, where they secretly planned to destroy the government."

Murmurs of disgust erupt in the crowd, and I feel my stomach churning. "Can you believe it?" He stops pacing and looks toward us, his eyebrows furrowing. "It's scary to think that some Americans themselves would execute this stupid plan. Even those that you've known and lived with your entire life." His gray eye shifts to Jax, who stares at the ground with a blank expression.

"My son Jax was loved very dearly by me. I showered him

with riches and showed all of my love by giving him whatever he wanted. All I wanted in return was him becoming just like me—a powerful and intelligent man. And he complied, for a little while, at least. He went to rallies with me, spoke profoundly, and let others know that he was bound to become president . . . just like me." Tobias's hard and demanding footsteps echo across the stage as he comes toward Jax, who kneels beneath him, refusing to look his father in the eye.

"Look at me, son," Tobias pleads. Jax shakes his head.

With an irritated sigh, Tobias kneels down and places his hand onto Jax's shoulder. "C'mon. It is me, your father."

Silence settles in around us as I, with bated breath, watch as Jax finally looks him in the eye. His jaw is clenched as he frowns, fury etched onto his face. I know the anger Jax feels because his father *abused* him. Tobias didn't appreciate him He exploited him. He used his son to his advantage and told him lies, such as him loving Jax. But he didn't. It was all lies. Just for his benefit.

"Wonderful," Tobias whispers into the microphone in his hands. "Now, repeat after me I am sorry for what I have done, father. I do not want to be executed and am willing to come back home. Please take me back."

Jax shakes his head, no sense of regret in his eyes. "No."

"What do you mean, *no?* This is not a choice, Jax. This is mandatory."

"I don't care, Tobias. I don't want to be affiliated with you."

Tobias sneers. "Make the right decision here. Do you want to die at an early age and ruin your chances of being powerful, like me? Or do you want to change your mind, come with your parents, and become the successful man you are destined to be?"

I see Jax's eyes sifting over to the entrance of the stairs that lead up to the stage, and I notice that over there stands Isabelle Remington, Jax's mother. Something irks inside of me when I notice her beseeching eyes land on Jax. "Come on, son! Join me and your father. We can end this. You can go back to normal. Just don't make the wrong decision. Please."

Jax looks down at the ground again, ignoring his father kneeling in front of him. Finally, he looks up and says, "I would much rather die early than live a life I am not destined to live."

With that said, Tobias snarls as he goes and slaps Jax across the cheek, the harsh *smack* resonating against the atmosphere. A large red imprint of a hand is embellished onto Jax's cheek, but he pays no heed of it.

"You want to be executed? Fine, go ahead with these rebels. But you will regret it, Jax Remington. You *will* regret it."

Before he can answer, Tobias gets up from his spot and marches over to the front of the stage, clutching the microphone in his hands. "My son has affirmed that he wishes to be executed alongside these rebels. My son was independent and strong- minded, but it seems as if he can be easily influenced. If he wants to be executed, then that is all right."

Isabelle breaks down in tears as she flees from the stairs, her high heels clacking against the stage. Tobias hangs his head low, biting his bottom lip with thought, and all Jax does is look up at the sky with almost a smile on his face. He finally got what he wanted.

Tobias starts to speak, grinning widely. *Why is he grinning? Isn't he at least the slightest bit upset that his son is about to be killed in the hands of his own people?* "Today is execution day. These five rebels will be shot in the back of the head in approximately seven minutes. This will go down in history as the day people were publicly executed for co-conspiring subversion.

"And we, as Americans, have obviously come so far. We've overcome the Dark Ages. The United States went through a gloomy and depressing time because of rebels that were upset with the way America worked. If they didn't like it, then why didn't they leave? It was as simple as that!"

Even though we are in a dire situation, I just can't help but chuckle. *Sometimes, it astonishes me how inane Tobias can be.*

"They caused unnecessary chaos in this country. They disrupted the calm in our motherland and decided to wreak havoc upon it—simply because they couldn't pay their bills." Tobias snorts. "Rich is Rich, and Poor is Poor. Some people need to escape their personal fantasies and realize that life is filled with labels. You are expected to be in your designated category and live your life based on that. If you're Poor, act like a Poor person. And if you're Rich, then act like a Rich person. Stop chasing after dreams that aren't even attainable in the first place."

Tobias's jaw tightens as he looks at all of us. "It was also unfortunate to find out a young and prodigious member of the government, Zachary Everett, was murdered by Vienna Powers, one of the rebels here." My hands begin to shake. "He was incognito under the alias Dylan Faulkner and was determined to get information out of these rebels. It is fortunate that he did dupe them and without him, we would not have them in our hands in the first place. So, in honor of Mr. Everett, the young adult genius, we would like to commemorate his significant loss and pay our respects to him."

Silence weighs down upon us like a thick and suffocating blanket, and I look around at the others, hoping to see their reactions to this grim circumstance. Mal is slumping forward, still kneeling as she heaves out silent cries. Jeremiah continues to clench his jaw and trains his eyes forward, his back ramrod straight as he refuses to reveal his emotions. Vi is rolling her eyes and rapping her fingers against the floor of the stage—well, that is until the Guard behind her tells her to *knock it off.* And Jax looks at the ground miserably, his muscular body slouching forward as his lips fall into a deep frown.

And I, as helplessly as ever, think that this is the end. There is no way out. If we tried to escape, then not only will we be attacked by thousands of Rich people, but we also will be shot by the Guards behind us.

Sometimes, you can't escape what is inevitable. Not even death.

A thought appears in my mind, and I gasp as my eyes graze throughout the large crowd surrounded in front of the stage. I try to search for my family, but it is no use. The entire city is gathered here, half of them eager to see us dead. There's no way I'll be able to spot my family. I will have to die without being able to see their faces—one last time, at least.

And then, Tobias speaks again. "It is nearly six in the morning, approximately four minutes before the execution. At this designated time, these rebels are more than welcome to share their thoughts on this current situation." He looks toward us, his acerbic eyes landing on us for protracted times. "Any last words, rebels?"

For a while, no one seems to speak up. I look toward my friends beside me, and they all shake their heads with no hesitation whatsoever. *It seems as if they just want to get this over with.*

But I don't. I want to make sure I say what I feel to Tobias because, frankly, I have a lot to say to that son of a bitch.

My voice rips out of my throat. "I have some things to say." It feels weird, saying that to the unknown . . . but I have to. Because I don't want to die feeling unsettled and unsatisfied. I want to die happy, knowing that my haunting words will forever stay in Tobias's mind.

"Go ahead." He sneers, trying to taunt me with his arrogant smirk. "We only have three minutes left, though, so you might want to hurry it up."

I nod my head once, look down at the ground for a split second, and look back up—just to stare at Tobias. *Time to say what I've been holding back for the past nineteen years.*

"This country was first founded with the signing of the Declaration of Independence by many infamous men." It's hard to get my voice across thousands of people, but I don't care. I just want Tobias to hear it. "Their main goal was to establish a country with *independence* for all, hence the title of the document. I know not all received independence, but throughout history, though, everybody started to receive equal rights. Sure, there were systematic issues prevalent, but we still overcame them."

"I'm pretty sure we all know American history, rebel," Tobias chuckles as half of the crowd bursts out laughing.

My cheeks burn red with embarrassment. "We overcame many issues and followed our country's name—The United States of America. The name is an oxymoron itself, isn't it? All fifty states were separated, yet we were all still somehow united. Weird, right?" I take a deep breath in. "How come we aren't following that name anymore? There aren't fifty states anymore —there's just one. We are the only ones here, so we have to be united. Why separate people based on their financial statuses? That is rash. While we could be working together on building our country back up to the top, we are instead tearing each other apart.

"And you are completely wrong, Tobias. Nobody is supposed to act like a Poor, or a Rich. Instead, we are supposed to be *ourselves.* We are supposed to follow our heart, not society. And what is the point of living life to other people's likings? Then it is not one's life anymore . . . It is simply a predicament.

"This is America, for God's sake! Land of the free and home of the brave! Instead of having a nationalistic pride and separating each other based on class, why don't we all *unite* and embrace each other's differences? Then we will truly be able to reach the top again. Then we will truly be able to explore the unknown and see if there are other Americans out there."

I look over at Tobias, whose face fumes from aggravation. "And I don't believe a single word the government has to say. Don't you think it's a bit suspicious that *every single* American died during the war? Either this totalitarian government is lying through their teeth about this statement because they want to enforce their strict policies upon the Poor, or they eradicated the rest of the American population themselves—just so they could have a hold on us.

"But in terms of eradication, our beloved president was determined to wipe out the entire Poor population." Confused murmurs erupt in the crowd. "He was going to induce an act that will be initiated at the start of 2065, where all the Guards will march into every single Poor home and kill all of the Poors. You all need to realize our president is not the man you determine him to be! He is a conniving and manipulative man set to commit mass murder in hopes to cleanse America of all dirt, when in reality, he just wants to have the upper hand."

My voice increases in both volume and force. "Screw you, Tobias Remington because you have ruined this country's chance to regain itself—only because you were blinded by your reputation. *You* need to get a reality check and realize that we need to unite. Life is not based on labels. It is instead based on *living,* and we are not living if we are not loving each other."

My last few words echo into the speakers, and my heart beats anxiously as I look over at the audience. The Rich side is mixed—some seem to give in while others are still like the same cold and judgmental Rich people.

But the Poor? The entire side starts applauding, their cheers drowning into the iridescent morning. A smile that reaches to my eyes grows on my lips, and I feel satisfied. I can die happy now, knowing that I got my words across to this wretched society.

However, Tobias declares, "It's six o' clock . . . and you know what that means." His expression is still livid from my speech.

Groans and protests erupt from the Poor side and some from the Rich side, and Tobias interjects by demanding, "Guards." He looks over to them. "On the count of three."

336

We hurriedly make eye contact with each other, the severity of the situation now dawning upon us. We can't hug each other. We can't embrace each other before inevitable doom occurs.

"Three . . ."

You have finally gotten your words across.

"Two . . ."

You can die satisfied now.

"One . . ."

You can be with your brother now, forever and always.

"Now—!"

BAM!

My body plunges to the ground.

44

FAMILIAR

December 4, 2064
Unknown Time

MY EARS ARE RINGING, hundred-pound weights strapped onto my convulsing figure.

Why am I still alive?

I heave out elongated breaths as I struggle to look around me, and when I get a glimpse of the environment I am in, I feel my heart lurching up to my throat.

The entire Center is ruined, decorations scrambled everywhere, and the set lights strewn upon the ground with electricity crackling by them. The entire view is fuddled and covered in thick clouds of fog that make it hard for me to breathe.

What makes my eyes widen with surprise is seeing piles of bodies on top of one another. I feel my heart racing as a thought dawns upon me . . . *Is my family dead too?*

I wail out a cry as I realize there are people fighting each other by the foot of the stage. It is Rich against Poor, letting out war cries while piling on top of each other. Some are dead. Some are alive.

A revelation forms in my mind as I look over to the others beside me, who are also sprawled out and unconscious, just like the others. Tobias in the front of the stage is also just like the others, his eyes rolled back as his head lolls against the edge of the stage.

I see the Guards behind us dead or passed out as well. That is when I know the execution did not occur.

If not the execution, then what caused this? What caused the entire Center to get destroyed within mere seconds? Who could have ever done this?

Ultimately, from the very little I can see, I notice a large and familiar figure trekking past the stage beneath the fog, long hair grazing his shoulders and olive skin gleaming against the sun.

His eyes meet mine.

He smiles and mouths something to me.

And walks away.

45

EXECUTION

December 4, 2064
Unknown Time

I PULL MYSELF UP.

I ignore the pain shooting through my spine. I ignore my arms shaking by my side. I ignore the ringing in my ears. And I ignore the unfortunate need to scream until my throat aches.

Nothing affects me anymore. I am lifeless . . . inside and out.

Grunts escape out of me as I limp over to where Vi lies. Blood pools out of her nose as I struggle to bend down and shake her awake. "Vi," I say, my throat hoarse. "C'mon, get up."

No response.

I crawl over to Jeremiah. He should wake up. But as I try to shake him awake with heavy tears tumbling down my cheeks, I notice that he isn't responding either.

Same goes for Mal. Her long blonde hair is sprawled out, slowly getting stained from the blood escaping out of her mouth. I wail out, "Mal, please! Please wake up!" Nothing occurs.

Finally, I try Jax. And as I try to crawl back to where he is, I notice his gray eyes are open but have no life present in them. My body heaves as I slap his arm repeatedly. *Please wake up.*

But it's no use because they are all dead. Something has killed them, and I am bound to know what.

I try to study the Center and seeing the Rich and the Poor continue to fight makes anxiety claw at my chest. *So, some are dead, and some are alive? How is that possible?*

A thought forms in my bleak mind, and I gasp as I pull myself up to my feet, still trying to ignore the intolerable pain forming inside of me. Then, with no regrets, I steadily make my way down the stairs, wanting to see what's happening up close.

And it's a bloodbath down here.

There are Rich and Poor people dead, their bodies splayed out on the ground while waiting for nature to take care of them. War cries screech into the air as I see everybody letting out their true animalistic tendencies. They don't care about the rules of society anymore. And the Poor are the angriest because it's *their* people that are getting killed. And these people were fighting for *their* freedom. Meanwhile, the Rich are fighting them because they always have to be better than them—in some way or another.

My heart cracks as I notice children are fighting too. Their bodies are also limp and lifeless, displayed on the ground. Children are hating each other too. Not just adults . . . *children.*

This is the type of hate where there are no limits. In this world, not many opinions and actions are allowed—we're all supposed to follow the preconceived standards of society. But now? The president is possibly dead, unconscious by the foot of the stage, so now these people don't feel restricted anymore.

Also, as the thought dawns into my mind . . . who was the mysterious man that trekked along the Center? Why was he smiling at me? And why did he look so damn familiar?

Before I can evaluate my thoughts any further, I hear a familiar voice.

"B, we're over here!"

I whirl my head around to where I heard the voice, and I breathe out a sigh of relief as I see Em running toward me with her arms out. *My beloved little sister.* Once she hugs me, I feel my heart slowing down to a calm rate, and tears spill down my cheeks as I whisper into her ear, "I am so glad to see you are okay."

"I am glad to see you are okay too," she murmurs, patting my back.

"Where's Mama and Papa?"

My ears perk up as I hear them speak from the side. "Over here."

Still hugging Em, I crane my neck to the right and see my parents standing next to each other, wearing tattered clothes, their eyes gleaming with tears. I gesture for them to come, and as they make their way toward me, I suddenly feel protected, loved, and comfortable—all in one. Me and my family. *Finally.*

Their arms wrap around us, engulfing me into a pleasant group hug. Warmth fills my heart as I lean into my parents' shoulders while gripping Em's back. It would've been better to have Nico join us, but the constant reminder of him being dead makes my heart sink to the bottom of my stomach. *How am I going to tell my family about him?* I decide that maybe I should fight off all my thoughts and enjoy the time I have with my family as we hug like the world's about to crash on us. I never want to let go of them ever again.

However, the unfortunate realization of the Rich and the Poor fighting in the Center beside us makes me realize that I need to let go of them. Just for now.

I pull away from my family, and I wipe my tears as I say to my parents, "It feels good to see you guys. I've missed you so much."

"We've missed you too, *Mija,*" Mama whispers, her eyes watery. "Where did you go? Why did you leave us? What is a . . .

Subversive? And planning to destroy the government with a bunch of strangers?" Papa asks while his dark green eyes bore into mine.

"I can't explain right now," I say, looking toward the middle of the Center. "We are at the risk of being attacked. Everybody is losing control and the Rich won't hesitate to kill us when they set their sights on us." I take a deep breath as I study the stage. "No one is daring to fight on the stage as of now—which is why I order for you guys to stay here and *not move.*"

"What about you, *mija?*" Mama wonders. "We are not leaving you out here!"

"Somebody has to protect you guys."

"But we cannot afford to lose you, Blaire," Papa says. "Not after what happened to Nicolas."

I want to tell them about Nico being dead because they deserve to know. But I know that this is not the time to say the bad news. Instead, I need to keep it hidden for now, and once all of this dies down, then I can tell them the news. Only because my parents have been worried sick since day one, and hearing that their son didn't make it would crush the absolute life out of them.

And I know that my parents don't want me gone too, but I have to protect them. And Em has to go with them because I need her to be safe beside them. I have some experience fighting ... which means that I can defend myself and my family.

But when I realize that my entire body is aching, my limbs are crumbling, and the weird feeling of blood is seeping down my legs, I conclude that I *need* to stay safe. My parents cannot afford to lose another one of their kids.

I take a deep breath in, bracing myself for what's to come. "I need to go. And I will stay safe, I just have to protect myself and you guys."

"No, B!"

"I have to, Em." I look down at her. "You guys go over to the stage, okay? Trust me."

Silence encompasses us for a few moments. And then, my parents sigh in defeat. They bring themselves in front of me as my mom says, "Please stay safe. I do not want anything to happen to you. We have been worried sick, ever since you disappeared, so we don't want to put you at risk."

"But . . ." My dad looks down at the ground. "We do trust you."

"Thank you." Relief floods through me. "I promise I will stay safe."

"Okay, *mija*." My mom pats my back.

And with that, they leave, their footsteps pounding against the metal stairs.

However, as I watch them go up the stairs, I feel somebody grabbing my waist, lifting me in the air for a split second, and throwing me back on the ground with me landing on my back. I groan as I try to regain myself, but the person is too fast for me as they throw a punch into my jaw. Pain shoots through me as I grimace, and I blearily look up to see the Guard that was about to shoot me for my execution—before everything went to hell.

The Guard's mask is off, revealing her green eyes and pale skin. And the scowl on her mouth says everything there is to know about her and what she feels about me.

She wasn't able to shoot me then, so she wants to do it now. "Well, hello," she seethes, grabbing onto my neck with her strong left hand. I let out a raspy breath. "Did you really think that I was going to let you win this battle?"

"Let . . . me go!" I rasp out while trying to push her hand away from my throat. Black spots dance in vision as I try to understand what is going on, but what I *can* only see is the Guard's furious look and raging green eyes.

And her reaching into her pocket, just to pull out a sleek black gun.

She turns off the safety and cocks the gun at me, pressing it to my temple. Sweat beads form on my forehead as shaky breaths escape out of me. I would fight back, but I am tired to the point where I just cannot.

"Goodbye, rebel," she snarls. I keep my eyes wide open, challenging her with my unwavering eyes—but at the same time, I am scared out of my mind. *Is this really it?*

But as she starts to press on the trigger, I watch with relentless shock as I hear a loud *bang* echo into the air. A few seconds later, blood trickles down the back of the Guard's neck as she lets out a grunt, falling to the ground. Her hand unlatches from my aching neck, and from the back of her skull, I can see just exactly where the blood is forming.

From the corner of my eye, though, I see a figure in front of me, and I bring my eyes up gradually to make eye contact with them.

Vi stands in front of me, smirking as she tucks in her gun into the back pocket of her jumpsuit. "You really thought I was going to let you die?"

"Vi, I thought you were dead." I can't seem to unmask the shock in my voice. As I look at her incredulously, I pull her down for a quick hug. Her arms refuse to hold me, but it's okay. I am just glad to see that she's alive.

"Really? I was only unconscious."

"Oh. Then is everybody else unconscious too?"

"Well, Jeremiah woke up." I look over at the stage and see him standing in front of my family, on the lookout for those that dare to fight against him.

"When he woke up, he saw that there was a family huddled in the far corner of the stage, so he decided to protect them."

A smile forms on my lips. "That's really sweet of him. When did he wake up?"

"He woke up a couple of minutes after I did, due to me

prying him awake." Then, she points over to the center of the stage. "Mal and Jax haven't woken up yet, unfortunately."

"Shit," I curse while trying to pull myself up to my feet. "Do you think they could be dead?"

"I don't know." She frowns, her brown eyes grazing over me. "Let's try to think positive and stop all this fighting, okay? I don't want any more Poor people to die because it seems as if there are more Rich standing, at this very moment." I look over at the middle of the Center, where chaos continues.

However, to my unfortunate avail, the mob seems to be coming closer to us too. They move in a synchronous motion, almost like a poisonous wave. Any interaction will result in death.

My veins begin to constrict as I say, "I don't have any weapons on me."

"I do."

Shockingly, I see a very familiar girl walking toward us with her long blonde hair let loose and her bright blue eyes gleaming with victory. *Mal woke up!* I notice she is limping and wincing with every step she takes while carrying loads of weapons in her hands.

"I borrowed these from the four Guards still unconscious there," she says while handing them out to us. I have a gun and a pocket knife, Mal has a blade and a small pistol, and Vi has a rifle and her powerful fist to accompany her.

"Wait, so are we going to kill as many Rich people as we can?" I ask. "But I thought the goal of the Subversion Act was to unite everyone—not eradicate our enemies."

"It *was*," Vi says. "But that notion is nearly impossible because we have hoards of angry Rich people around us, and there is simply no way we can bring them on our sides." She balances the gun in her hand. "We have to kill them, no matter if the Subversion Act is against it."

I gulp. We have to kill as many Rich people as we can? A wave of terror ripples through my veins.

While we get acquainted with our weapons, we see a Rich man nearing us. "Kill them!" he bellows. All at once are dozens of Rich people charging at us, their faces contorted into fury.

"Okay, ladies," Vi says, "remember everything we have learned and who the hell we are. This is not child's play anymore. This is the real deal. Understood?"

"Yes," Mal and I say, our voices filled with pride.

"Good." Vi clears her throat as she cocks her gun at the Rich man just a few feet away from us. "Now let's kill these sons of bitches."

As soon as she finishes speaking, the bullet from her gun escapes with an echoing *bang* and lodges itself into the tall Rich man's chest. He falls to the ground, blood oozing from his torso.

Then, we charge forward.

PRIDE

December 4, 2064
Unknown Time

I TARGET A LARGE woman running up to me, and I begin to remember everything I have learned in the past month, even including how to shoot a gun.

Without hesitation, I stand guard, aim, and fire. *Bam!*

Her body falls to the ground with a heavy thud, her face drowning in blood as her eyes roll back.

Then, I kill another. And another. So many until I lose count. Some with my gun. Some others with my knife. Sure, I'm injured a bit—probably from a knife lodged in my arm for a split second before I pull it out. But I don't let *any* of these people win against me. And there is only one thought running in my mind the entire time:

I feel satisfied.

Watching all these Rich people fall to the ground due to me, Mal, or Vi killing them is probably one of the sole reasons I have decided to keep on living. I have been waiting for this moment for my entire life.

As soon as I start to kill another one of the Rich, Vi pulls me to the edge of the Center. I look at her in confusion while she says, "Go try to wake up Jax."

My heart starts to race. "Why?"

Vi gestures toward the stage, looking terrified for the first time in her life. "Because Tobias is starting to wake up, and he looks angry as hell."

Anxiously, I look over at the stage and see that she is indeed correct. And I need to get Jax out of there before something bad happens to him.

I make eye contact with Vi. "Okay."

"Good." She nods once. "And kill that son of a bitch as soon as you can."

"I will." And with that said, she leaves, leaving me to take care of the man I can't stop thinking about.

I start to run—or try to, at least, because my lungs are bursting with every movement. But I don't care because I need to get to Jax. I need to save him from that stage.

Ignoring all sorts of pain shooting through my body, I limp toward Jax while keeping a close eye on Tobias. I notice Jax's eyes are wavering—closed at one point and open at the other. He looks at peace for once, but I must wake him up. I *must*.

"Hey, Jax." I nudge his shoulder. "We need to leave right now." He doesn't stir awake at all. Instead, all he does is flutter his eyes open and close.

I grumble and try to pull him up, but his muscled figure is accursedly too hefty. Sighing in defeat, I decide to push and pull his body violently.

"Please, Jax, get up right now. Don't let your father win this round. Prove to him that you are the dominant one, not him. And remember those times that he abused you and you felt powerless? Well, now is your time to win. Now is your time to show him what happens when anybody messes with you. C'mon, Jax, please!"

And then, to my fortunate avail, his eyes flutter open . . . and remain that way.

He shoots himself upright, his expression frenetic, and then he makes eye contact with me. His eyes soften as he whispers, "Where are we? What happened? Why aren't we dead?" Before I can even respond, he brings my hand into his, holding it tightly. "And you're here with me, Blaire. You are here with me."

I gulp, feeling my cheeks flush. But I ignore all incoming feelings and say, "We need to get up, Jax. Right now."

"Why?" He looks up at me, his face inches to mine. "I want to stay here with—"

He never finishes his sentence.

Instead, his breath catches in his throat as his upper body falls onto my torso, his jaw landing on my chin. I gasp with horror as I see blood spreading out near his shoulder, staining his arm-sleeve, and flowing down his arm. I scream out loud as I grasp the blood in my hands, while looking at Jax anxiously. *It's only his shoulder that was shot, so he should be okay . . . right?*

He rasps out elongated breaths as he clings onto me. Then, he looks back, his eyes glossed with angry tears. And I look ahead, my body fuming as I see the man that has caused us so many issues, so many *troubles.*

Tobias Remington . . . who stands there with a pistol in his right hand.

"You asshole!" I snarl, going up to attack him.

Jax pulls me back down. "No, Blaire. Don't go."

I look at him, confused. "Why not?"

Jax's eyes latch onto his wretched father, and he snarls, "Because it's time that *I* give him a taste of his own medicine."

I start to hesitate, but the passionate glint beneath Jax's eyes allows me to let him go. But before I do, I whisper, "Stay safe."

He nods. "Of course. Anything for you."

Then, he leaves. I notice by the stage is Vi and Mal, watching Jax striding toward his father, and before Tobias can start to shoot his son again, Jax goes and kicks him in the stomach, sending Tobias flying back. He goes to him and looks to us in desperation. "Help me pin him down!"

The Subversives come running over and help, and Jax glares at him, towering over him while clutching his left shoulder, stained with blood. "You have hurt me plenty, Tobias."

Tobias grunts and spits on Jax's face, his expression livid. "So, this is how it's going to be, son? You seriously want to kill *me?* I raised you! And you're not appreciating me!"

"You hurt me." Jax wipes the spit from his face. He speaks with a neutral tone, but his eyes are hooded with anger as he takes the large knife from Mal with his right hand. "You made me feel worthless and very small next to you. So . . . Why would I appreciate you for that?"

Tobias snarls, his matted gray hair falling onto his forehead. "These rebels are brainwashing you, Jax. You need to come back to me and your mother."

Jax, with no hesitation, shakes his head, ignoring the blood seeping down his arm. He ignores his father shooting his shoulder because . . . he's about to do something even worse to him.

"I'm never coming back!" he shouts, his deep voice laced with rage. "I'm tired of being in that damned household. I'm tired of being controlled by *you.* Remember when you caused this?" Jax points to his scar. "You dragged a knife through my cheek because of my goddamn opinion! A father is supposed to let his son be different and unique! You are so blinded by society's ideals of the Rich and the Poor that you would sacrifice your own son for your stupid reputation!"

Jax brings his knife back and plunges it into the ground of the stage, right near Tobias's neck. Tobias's eye widens in fear as he says, "Please, son. Forgive me. I'm sorry for what I have done. I will accept you as who you are. Just please come back." *He's only saying that because he doesn't want to be killed. That bastard.*

The weather is still gloomy, except bright white snow simmers to the ground, kissing the earth. And the snow even lands in piles of blood, melting with the liquid.

"I will never forgive you, Tobias. You need to be taught a lesson for the mistakes you have made—the *many* mistakes you have made."

And with that said, Jax lifts his father's eye patch up, revealing his bloody eye and his discolored pupil. Jax, as carefully as ever, grasps the knife in his right hand and places it by Tobias's cheek. With bated breath, we watch him graze the knife through his cheek, and then, he digs it in deeper.

"Son, please stop!" Tobias pleads, his stabbed eye almost bulging out of its socket. Blood spills out of his skin as Jax draws a thin and jagged line running through Tobias's cheek . . . one that is very similar to his own scar.

Then, Jax brings the knife down to Tobias's chest. "You have caused us enough pain and suffering."

"No, Jax, please! Don't do this! You will regret this!"

All Jax does is smirk, strands of his dark hair decorated in snow. "No. I won't."

And then, he thrusts the knife into his father's chest. But he doesn't stop there.

He stabs another time. Then another.

And then so many times the knife is drowning in Tobias's blood.

"You . . . hurt me so much!" Jax screams, slashing the knife into the president's chest repeatedly. "You hurt me so much! You hurt me so much!"

"Jax, I think he's dead now," Mal says. The others seem to agree.

Let him get his anger out, I think to myself. *He deserves to, after all the shit he's been through.*

And finally, he stops—just a few seconds later.

The knife clangs to the ground as Jax continues to clutch his bloodied arm. I watch Tobias's eyes flutter close as his head droops to the side, blood pouring out of his cheek and chest. *He's dead. He is finally dead.*

I see from the corner of my eye that a tear seems to fall down Jax's cheek, and he wipes it away, sniffling afterwards. I go over to him, wrapping my arms around his neck. He starts to sob, his shoulders shaking as his rugged hands grasp my back. Soon, Vi, Mal, and Jeremiah join us. We hold each other for that single moment, our hearts beating together and trying to reel in what just happened.

"We did it," Vi whispers.

But then, the roars from the Rich by the Center makes us jump up in surprise. "It's not over just yet," Mal grumbles.

Quickly, we help Jax up to his feet, leaving Tobias's corpse to nature's liking. Then, we make our way down the stairs, trying to avoid the Rich that run toward us. My family trails behind us as well, and while I hold onto Jax, I make sure that no one gets to them.

Watching Tobias die in the hands of Jax made my insides bloom with happiness. We can finally get out of here now, not worrying about the Rich and the very few Guards that are still alive.

However, as we all start to run toward the Rich sector, trying to escape the completely destroyed Center, a huge blast transpires around us, similar to the one that happened before we all passed out. Before, I heard my ears ringing and the faint beating of my heart . . .

But this time, I hear nothing at all.

2:58 p.m.

My body convulses with shock as a gasp escapes from my throat. *Where am I?* I look around, hoping to find some sort of clue, but everything is blurry. The only thing I can make out is the white-clad ceiling with bright lights flickering instinctively. Other than that, I am mostly clueless, and any small movement makes me wince in pain. Even clenching my fists causes my veins to constrict with soreness.

After blinking several times, I make out the fact that I am in a room that is blinding white. I look at my body, which is laid out on a white bed itself. My hands and feet are tied down to the bed in cotton straps, and just a single movement of them makes me curse to myself. *Why does my body ache so much?*

The last thing I remember is attempting to escape the Center with Jax, Mal, Vi, Jeremiah, and my family—but then an unexpected large blast pierced through the air. Just thinking about it has anxiety filtering through my veins because it makes me wonder if everybody else is okay. They *better* be okay.

My matted and sweaty hair sticks to the white pillow beneath me, and I realize that I have cuts, bruises, and especially burns covering my entire body. They are mostly pigmented with a bright red color and seem to be ravaging with pain—which is why I decide that I probably should *not* touch them.

So, what now?

The white door is shut, so I know that screaming for help is not going to do much. There is a closed window by the side of the room, yet it does reveal the snowy weather that is tumbling into D.C. right now. When Jax killed Tobias, white flakes showered on his head as he stabbed and stabbed and stabbed his father, fountains of blood spurting out of his chest.

Just thinking about Tobias being dead makes a weight lift off my shoulders. Now, the only things I have to worry about is making sure everyone's okay and eventually telling my parents about Nicolas being dead. I don't know how to accomplish those certain tasks, but hopefully I will.

Suddenly, I hear a concise knock on the door. My eyes

widen as I start to say that they can come in, but the door opens anyway.

I sit there in complete shock as I watch Vi peer inside of my room. "May I come in?" she says, her voice thick with emotions.

"Sure," I try to say, but all that comes out instead is a warbled version of what I was initially going for. *Why is my voice so hoarse?* I try to speak again, but it barely comes out this time. My throat is dry and aches with every word I say, and I grab my throat outrageously, feeling even more pain occur.

"You can't speak?" Vi asks while closing the door behind her. She takes a seat at the foot of my bed, undoing the straps that hold me down. I breathe out in relief as I try to sit up straight, ignoring the pain that shoots through my spine.

That is when I evaluate her too, seeing that the front portion of the left side of her hair is completely singed off, revealing short hairs underneath. Otherwise, the rest of her bright and colorful hair is left. And she doesn't have that many cuts and bruises on her body like me, but she does have a lot of burn marks.

"I can speak," I say. "But . . . it's just kind of . . . difficult."

"That's okay." Vi sighs. "I'll be doing most of the talking anyway."

Silence. Vi speaks again.

"I know you're very confused right now, so I'll explain everything to you to the best of my ability." She clears her throat. "Let me start off by saying that we obviously did not get killed when Tobias was counting down to our execution. We heard one horrendous-sounding *boom* instead of five separate ones. That meant that something even bigger interjected—and it was a bomb blast.

"I don't know who did this. The only thing I do know is that we were going to get executed and that is it. There was no backup plan, *nothing*. But it seems as if some mysterious individual out there had bigger plans conjured up for us."

"That's really all you know?" I croak out.

"Unfortunately, yes." She sighs. "What I do know is that someone out there had tendencies to kill the Poor, the Rich, or maybe even both. Someone out there is three steps ahead of us, and I don't know how to catch up to them."

Gears begin to churn in my mind. "How were . . . some people dead and some alive?"

"Not everyone was affected by the blast. Some took it horribly and died on the spot, but others were able to only be unconscious and get up some time later. I'm glad we were only unconscious—I can't imagine losing any one of us."

"How are they?"

"Well—they *are* recovering, just like I said before. Everybody is dealing with their separate injuries, but at least they survived. And your entire family survived as well."

I smile, but even doing that hurts. "That's g-good to hear. I just can't . . . grasp the fact that Jax killed his own fa-father."

"Yeah, I can't either. Jax really got passionate there for a moment."

My breath catches in my throat as I think about the night Jax told me his deepest and darkest secret, right before we *almost* kissed. I still feel butterflies roaming around in my stomach whenever my mind wanders over to what happened that night, hoping something would happen again . . . but *more*.

Suddenly, someone knocks on the door again.

Vi and I straighten up with alarm, but she then shrugs, getting up to get the door. "It's probably just Mal."

I nod my head, feeling at ease that Mal might be at the door. It'll feel good to have at least somebody accompanying us.

However, when Vi pulls the door open, the person standing by the door is definitely not Mal.

And the person beside them too.

My heart stops beating as those two people step forward. The man on the left and his familiarity makes my stomach churn with nervousness, but the woman beside him is completely unfamiliar to me.

The woman has dark skin, large and voluminous curly hair, and a strong body that stands out from her ripped jeans and large sweatshirt. I notice that there is a toddler standing by her side, her dark skin—like her mother's—glinting against the white lights.

And then, I notice the large and tan man beside her. With his gleaming and kind brown eyes that are too familiar to my liking, the scar that runs across his throat, the scruffy beard glued onto his face, and his tall and large body . . .

No. It can't be him.

Finally, the man speaks. And the words he says makes my limbs loosen.

"Hi, Bumble Bee . . . It's me, Nicolas. I know you might be wondering what is going on, and I promise I will explain everything. But first, I need to introduce this woman to you. Her name is Layla Morgan, and the girl next to her is her daughter, Tamia. Layla is the leader of the refuge in the Midwest, and she wants to bring us there."

47

UNRAVEL

December 4, 2064
3:08 p.m.

ALL I DO IS blink in surprise.

I can't seem to comprehend that my long-lost brother is in front of me, in the flesh, with a hesitant grin on his lips. His long and unruly dark hair, the same color as mine, reaches to his broad shoulders, and his entire torso is hidden beneath the black military vest he has on. Weapons line the pockets of his leather pants, and he walks over to me, his combat boots pounding against the hospital floor.

I feel my breath hitch in my throat. Here I thought he was dead, and now I see him approaching me. This must be a dream.

But it's not because his large and rough hands suddenly grasp mine, which shake by my sides. He clutches them, his warm skin sending cordiality into my deprived soul, and I feel a smile slipping onto my lips.

I study his eyes. They shimmer against the lights, and I know that behind those eyes is a story of his own. Behind those eyes is the answer to everything I've been craving to know. Behind those eyes are his sorrows that have been buried away as he does whatever it takes to prevail.

And behind those eyes is the brother that I dearly missed, the same brother that I never gave up on. The one I never *dared* to give up on.

He towers over me, his muscles bulging underneath the black shirt he has on underneath the black military vest. Nicolas looks like he just came from a battle itself, considering the scar running across his throat and several others scattered across his arms as well.

His mouth twitches as he speaks. "I've missed you, Bumble Bee." Before I can even answer, he pulls me in for a hug. I feel my heart crying with happiness and my veins pulsating with energy as his comforting arms encase my worn-out body. At this exact moment, I feel nothing but contentment. It's still difficult for me to wrap my mind around the fact that my brother is *alive,* but then again, I could care less.

At least he is alive.

And then, he releases from me, tears falling down my cheeks, and Nicolas pushes them away as he says again, "I've really missed you. So much."

I sniffle as I grasp his hand tightly. "I missed you too . . . *hermano.*" My throat hurts with every word I rasp out, but I just had to say it out loud. If my brain can't seem to decipher Nico standing right in front of me, then maybe I need to speak for me to fully believe.

"What's wrong with your voice?" he asks, his eyes darkening with worry.

"The blast made her lose it." Vi speaks from the corner, her face masked with thousands of emotions. Nico notices her and runs toward her, embodying her in a heart-warming hug as well. Vi laughs, almost tearing up, but she brushes it away quickly by releasing from him and smacking him upside the head. "What's wrong with you, you idiot? Everyone and especially your sister has gone crazy thinking that you were dead, but here you are, standing right in front of us!"

"I know it's a lot to take in. That's why I'm going to explain now." Nico gestures for us to sit back down on the bed, wincing while he clutches his head. Vi and I sit while Nicolas sits at the foot of it.

Meanwhile, I look over to the right of Nico and see the beautiful dark-skinned woman he was talking about—Layla Morgan. Her daughter stays glued to her mother's leg, and her big brown eyes wander over the room as she murmurs to herself.

That is when I realize something.

I gasp as I breathe out, "You're Jeremiah's wife . . . aren't you?"

Layla smiles. "Yes. I am his wife—for over five years now."

Five years? She has been separated from her husband for such a long time, and I know how much that impacted Jeremiah. Every single day, in the bunker, he would talk about her and say that he misses her dearly and would do anything to reunite with her and their beautiful daughter. I can't even imagine how happy he would feel, seeing his wife and daughter after such a long time. Jeremiah deserves to be happy. He really does.

"Holy shit," Vi murmurs, staring at Layla with astonishment. "I—I've been dying to meet you."

"I've been dying to meet *all* of you." She chuckles, her eyes grazing over me and Vi. "Hearing that my husband's in a group to destroy the government was definitely a shocker. But I bet him hearing that me leading the refuge several hundred miles from here is going to surprise him too."

"Yeah, what the hell is up with that?" Vi raises her eyebrows at Nico. "You two barging in here is amazing and all, but it's about damn time we get an explanation."

"Okay, I'll explain." Nico sighs, his eyes meeting mine. I

smile, my heart warming while the realization of Nicolas being back reels into my mind, and I usher for him to begin.

And so, he does.

5:01 p.m.

A white yet gruesome landscape is portrayed amongst the ruins of D.C. The tattered roofs with smoke billowing out of its crevices, the walls torn like delicate pieces of paper, the blood splattered on the streets decoratively, children crying in the near distance, and the crows cawing into the grayscale sky makes my heart heave. D.C is… gone. Demolished into thin air. Just like that.

But the thought of D.C. being gone settles in my mind, and that is when I smile, rather satisfyingly. D.C. may be gone, including our homes, but that does not mean we don't have a place to live now.

Because in approximately one hour, we are going on a train that leaves for the refuge in the Midwest, the one Layla Morgan leads.

In the far distance, I can see the silhouette of the Rich sector, and it's not exactly beaming with lights and raucous noises—it's actually replaced with ambulance sirens and the distant crackling of fires.

The Poor sector wasn't meant to be destroyed in Nico's terms, but it was anyway because the Rich had rioted here. They burned the houses down, hurled large objects at our delicate shacks, and inscribed cruel insults on our ripped-out walls with bright neon coloring. We had retaliated against them, so of course they had to fight back. *Of* course *they did.*

But little do they know that the Poor and only the Poor are leaving for the Midwest. We will leave the remaining Rich to fend for themselves in this hell, trying to scour for food in this limited environment. And we know that the Subversion Act's goal was to unite the Rich and the Poor and create a better society for everyone, but life took a wide turn. We kidnapped Jax. Zach betrayed us. We killed Zach. Our execution turned into a mass of bomb blasts. Nico is unexpectedly alive. And Jeremiah's wife is bringing us to a refuge in the Midwest, where I've always wanted to go. So our plan to unite everyone was impossible; our situation was way too complicated, meaning we had to resort to violence. We had to stand our ground and assert our ideals. We *had* to.

And the Rich might prevail for a little, but as time goes by, their bodies will perish into thin air, leaving nothing but their carcasses strewn onto the ground—mixed with snow and blood.

I walk upon the grass intermingled with the oncoming snow, which falls so gracefully onto the land. The crunching of the snow underneath my new combat boots emanates a harmonious sound, and I zip up my coat at the same time, shivering. It must be near freezing right now, but the thought of leaving this shitty place makes me push away all thoughts of potentially freezing to death for now.

My heavy footsteps trek across the pavement covered in snow, and I let out a gasp as I see my home. The entire roof is torn apart with smoke peering out from the holes of it and the walls are ripped open and covered in offensive words that make my insides boil with hatred.

Compose yourself, Blaire. You are only here to pick up your belongings. Or rather what's left of them. That is it.

Before I step inside, I immediately remember the interaction I had with my brother back at the hospital, when I had found out that he was alive. He had explained his entire backstory, which left my jaw clanging open—unable to close.

He first started to describe his feelings toward the government, how they always mistreated us and never seemed to take our feelings into account. He said that his hatred was getting out of control—so much he lost it one day. Started yelling at a Guard by the Poor sector. Said that it was unfair of how the Poor are treated and threatened to take each and every one of the Rich folks down. Thought that since no one else was going to stand up, he might as well.

Unfortunately, that led to him being on the most wanted list. They were on the lookout for him, and that is when he knew that he had to go somewhere—just to protect us. That is also when he saw Em getting reprimanded by some Guards that morning. He was pissed and didn't hold his feelings back. So, he stood up for her, making things worse. He was only an angry nineteen-year-old that thought of no ramifications to his actions. Nico knew at that moment he had to leave as soon as he could. He stated that he couldn't live with us because that would be too dangerous, too risky. So, he packed the very few items he had left and spent his last moments with everyone, especially me. He wanted to emphasize the importance of standing up to those that dare to question me.

As soon as Nico went outside, he was cornered by Guards and was violently led by them to the government vehicles. He was upset by how much his intentions failed. As he was pushed and shoved into the vans, he saw me and Mama screaming for him on the side, and he knew that Papa and Em were inside because he didn't want to let her know what was going on. He said that seeing me and Mama outside, looking at him so desolately . . . tore him to pieces. Made him feel empty. Lifeless.

He then attended prison for a long time—a couple of months. The Guards decided that a death sentence, which is a regular sentence for any Poor person who either pickpockets or commits homicide, was known as being "too easy" on him. So, they decided to have him tortured in prison for a whole year. If he was still alive after that entire year, then they planned to hang him.

However, during his entire time at prison, he came up with

an idea. It was to destroy the government. He said it was absurd, risky, and downright stupid, but it was something he was willing to try.

And he knew, right then and there, that he had to escape out of prison. He was aware of the Guards watching him, even when they reached for their pistols as soon as Nico made any suspicious movements. But the only time he had a shot for escaping was when he went to the bathroom. The Guards would usually wait outside, so when he went one day, he saw a vent—and made a run for it, not even thinking twice.

He ran like never before. Like hell was chasing him.

Nico had studied the maps in prison, which showed the entire layout of the city. It outreached all the way from south Maryland to north Virginia, so it had pretty great distances to it. He was willing to escape to the northern Virginia area because that was where the Potomac River was, and if something were to happen, then he could easily escape by swimming away.

Then, he mentioned meeting Jeremiah afterwards, which Jeremiah told me himself. They met while he was running away too, and that is when they came across the bunker that Rich people built during the Dark Ages. He then met Vi, and they became the best of friends. He told her about me and how he was doing this to create a better life for his family. Next, Mal and Zach came into the picture. He had to recruit Zach, or Dylan, because they desperately needed someone with exceptional computer skills. He didn't know about Zach being, well, *Zach*, but seeing the news made him up to date on everything that was going on. He claimed that it was his fault. Said that he should've known better.

One day, he then went outside to fetch some materials. But as soon as he left, Nico saw a swarm of Guards forming around him. They completely cornered him, and that is when he saw Tobias Remington step forward. He taunted Nico and said that he would die for the terrible crimes he had committed. So, multiple injuries later, Tobias shot Nico by his collarbone. The wound he has now is purple-red colored, and I remember wincing seeing it.

Zach would've ended the Subversives journey right then and there, and he had the perfect opportunity to do so, but he was waiting for me to come since he was aware of all the plans. He let the government and the president know of the plans and let the Subversives blindly go through their day, just so I could come. And just so *he* could be the one to out us right when Nicolas Cohen's little sister came into the picture.

He was knocked out for a good amount of time, so the Guards took it as an opportunity to bury him. They dug some portion of the grass—luckily not the one where the bunker was —and threw him in there and concealed up the area.

That is when Layla came into the picture.

She explained her backstory, how she was a Poor woman that fell in love with Jeremiah seven years ago, who was a well-known Guard back then. He loved her too, but he knew he couldn't fall in love with a Poor woman because a Guard and a Poor cannot be together. However, he disregarded all of those rules and decided that he wanted to be with her. They dated secretly for around two years and got married shortly after-wards. A year later, Tamia was born.

But one day, Jeremiah had to go out on duty. He left . . . then never came back.

Layla eventually found out on the news that Jeremiah had to execute a Poor old woman but refused. One Guard shot his leg, and he ran away to God knows where.

They lived alone for a year. Layla tried to move on and accept the fact that he was never coming back, which she was grateful that he didn't because if he did, then he would've been shot and killed immediately. So, that's when she decided that maybe she could search for him. She deemed it as a risky and a horrible decision to make, but she was determined to find him.

Jeremiah still had his government vehicle, so she went at night and drove all the way to West Virginia, hellbent to find some sort of revived environment. Then, she went north and kept going forward and forward and forward until . . . She saw a completely different city.

She was intrigued, so of course she explored the depths of this metropolis. Layla thought that maybe Jeremiah came here, so she was willing to go farther. But as she went into this beautiful and extravagant city, she slowly got acquainted with it. She was still determined to find Jeremiah, but she felt so loved in this city. She said there are no labels. No totalitarian government. No restrictions. Just a peaceful and wonderful life there.

Turns out this magnificent city held a refuge for those that suffered during the Dark Ages, so this city was housing them and helping them recover. Three years soon passed by, and she got involved with the community work there. Tamia grew up; Layla grew into this new world. Life was changing for them.

Sooner than later, Layla found herself wanting to travel back to D.C., in hopes to bring some Poor people along. She drove back to D.C. but saw someone getting buried alive. As soon as the government vehicles had left, she ran toward the spot, dug everything up, and saw the large man cooped up in that tiny area. Once she cleaned up the area after lugging him out, she drove him back to the city. No way was she going to leave him in D.C.

She brought Nico to a hospital there—in the new city—and he started to recover. And, for about a couple of years, Nico lived there and became very acquainted with the area as well. He also revealed to her that Jeremiah was part of the Subversives he created which she reacted very surprisingly toward. She wanted to see him, but he claimed that it was too dangerous, and that they would only go back around December of 2064 when he planned to recruit me. He wanted to recruit me when I was his age.

And then, Layla and Nico came here, just in late November of 2064. They disguised themselves and hid in the forest but still kept close note of all the things happening in the city at the same time. Nico knew that all five of us were wanted. He knew that we were imprisoned two times. He knew that we were going to be executed.

That's when Nico came up with a plan. Something that could either save our entire nation or wipe it out entirely within seconds.

Blasts. He caused the blasts.

He went on to explain that he was the reason the blasts occurred, the ones that affected a majority of the Rich and a minority of the Poor. The only reason why he would take such a risk is because we were about to get executed by the Guards. He had thought that these blasts would go off right before the bullets went through our head, and those that were the targets of the blasts—otherwise known as the Rich—would either be unconscious or die on impact. Depends on how close they were to it.

On the other hand, not many Poor people were affected by it, but there were still a few. Even though the blasts weren't centered on them, some of them still took the hit. And some were even murdered by the rioters that went into the Poor sector and shamelessly demolished the entire area.

I force my tears back, trying to avoid seeing the horrifying display of Poor bodies right in front of my house. In order to move forward, we have to sacrifice. And in order to sacrifice, we must take risks, for risks allow us to open up the gateway to achievement—whether it be physical or emotional.

Nico prepared the bomb blasts by sneaking into the governmental area of D.C. and pretending to be a Guard. Layla had also helped by acting Rich and using her daughter to emotionally manipulate those Rich people that are willing to act kind for once. Once that happened, Nicolas set the bombs up and formed a tactful and flawless plan—and it most definitely was. We prevailed in the end . . . because of *him.*

After Nico explained his entire backstory and plan, everybody had walked into the room, including Jeremiah, Mal, and Jax. The hospital we stayed at only housed them because we managed to get away from the Rich crowds, so we had no issues dealing with security. But when everybody came inside . . . It was very emotional especially because Jeremiah and Layla were reunited. Seeing them hug and kiss each other made me smile deeply because seeing family reunited is a feeling like no other. And seeing him pick up his daughter and drowning her in kisses as well made me realize that Jeremiah accomplished his dreams too. Just like me accomplishing my dream of being reunited with my brother. The accomplishment that Jax gained when he killed his father and left his mother behind, not knowing whether she's alive or dead.

Afterwards, Jeremiah and Mal reconciled with Nico while Jax met up with him for the first time. When everybody met up with Nico and caught up, we hugged once again. I still feel his arms wrapping around me, making my heart grin with happiness. I have finally accomplished one of my dreams. Now it's time to accomplish the other.

Getting the hell out of this cursed place.

48

LIBERATION

December 4, 2064
5:16 p.m.

I PULL OPEN THE raggedy door that seems to be on the verge of collapsing from its broken hinges. It creaks open, and spurts of dust burst into my face, and I hack out a cough, aggressively swiping the poisonous remnants away. Finally, I step inside, my feet aching with every step I take.

The entire home is demolished.

The couch in the living room has its cushions ripped out, and the small TV is cracked with weird colorful lines appearing on the screen every now and then. In the kitchen, the light above the small dining table keeps flickering. Everything in this small but nostalgic home is ruined. The Rich marched into *everybody's* houses and tore up everything their beady little eyes laid upon.

After we left the hospital, we were advised to scour around and find any of our belongings before we leave for the Midwest. We were hoping there would be some things left over even after the riots, but it seems as if there's little to nothing left.

What can I even bring? I think to myself, wandering around the home. But as soon as I look at the door that leads into our one and only room, I feel something settle inside of my stomach. And it's a good feeling.

I meander inside the room, gradually opening the door to reveal almost the same environment as the outside. Our bed is the most destroyed—the same bed that we all slept on. The comforters are ripped open, the pillows are torn apart, and the legs of the bed are removed from it itself.

Worry runs through my mind as I pace inside the tiny closet of our room and pull open that door. I breathe out a sigh of relief once I see the small library of books my mother kept since the initiation of the Dark Ages. They seem untouched, almost as if the Rich had not even bothered to grab a boring pile of books anyway.

I kneel by the rickety bookshelf and slowly pry all the books out, including *The Catcher in the Rye, Animal Farm,* and *To Kill a Mockingbird.* Just the collection of pages that taught me so much about life. So much that school would've taught me.

A small smile grows on my lips as I cup the books in my hand, admiring the smooth texture of them. Books are precious items, and they must be cherished. They've been there for us humans since the very beginning, and without them, life would not be the same. I value books especially because they taught me so much about life and the various outcomes it holds. I'm grateful that these precious objects exist.

Once I stash the books into the small duffel bag I brought, I perk up in fear when I hear a small knock by the closet door. I turn around, eyes widened, expecting to see a Guard ready to shoot my brains out—

But I let out a breath of relief when I see Jax standing by the door, a comforting grin on his face.

"Hey," he whispers, kneeling beside me. He's wearing a long black coat with a blue sweater underneath, and he also has black pants on with winter boots on the bottom. His dark and messy hair falls onto his eyes as he says again, "Nicolas told me you were here."

One side of my lip curls up, attempting to smile. "Are you . . . guys waiting outside?" My voice has slightly healed, but it still hurts to speak. Shit, it hurts *so* much.

"Yeah, but it's okay. Take your time." He pauses. "And how is your voice doing now? It's sounding a bit better."

"Eh," I whisper. "It's improving."

"That's good." He beams, pulling himself up to his feet as he extends his hand out to me. I accept it, and Jax lifts me up, our eyes simultaneously meeting each other.

My heart-rate ceases as I notice how close we are.

I open my mouth to speak, immense gratitude pouring through me. "Thank you, Jax."

He cocks his head, clearly confused. "There's no need to thank me."

"No, there is." I shake my head. "You did a huge favor for the Poor. You killed . . . Tobias."

"I wouldn't have been able to if it weren't for your brother, though. Thank God that bomb happened because if it didn't, then *we* would've been dead, not Tobias. I just had to do what I had to do."

I smile sadly. "I know. But thank you, Jax. Thank you so much."

"What did I say?" He smirks, encasing my left cheek within his soft hand. "There's no need to thank me." I stand here, stunned, watching his eyes waver to my lips. "But there is another way you can . . ."

My face is set aflame. "What can I do?"

Jax's eyes are suddenly hooded with desire, and his lips twitch with amusement as he whispers into my mouth, "Kiss me."

That is all it takes.

It's a weird feeling, whatever this is. Being so indeterminably close to someone, and especially someone you've never expected. And our lips are desperate for each other, desperate to know how they feel and taste. Desperate for what was inevitable.

I stand on my tiptoes and run my fingers through his unruly hair whilst he wraps his arms around my waist, kissing me so hard I start to see stars. Right now, Jax and I are in a completely different world. Right now, our bodies are molded, our lips intermingled with frenzy. And right now, there is nothing else I prefer to be doing except this. Nothing else.

Finally, we release from each other, panting and out of breath. His eyes meet mine, masked with an emotion that makes butterflies roam around in my stomach. I wrap my arms around his neck, pulling him in even closer as I graze my nose against his jaw, right below his scar.

And we kiss again.

5:29 p.m.

The sun starts to drown against the horizon, hues of orange and red fading with the blue sky. The snow had stopped, meaning that a beautiful and naked sky is finally revealed. However, the snow that had fallen before does not seem to be melting, mainly because the temperatures are almost below freezing.

Everybody, which I mean the remaining Poor population, is currently scrambling to get inside the fifty-car train that awaits us on the railroad tracks. The train is located about ten miles south from where our bunker was, so all we had to do was stack up on government vehicles and drive over to where a snow-sheathed plain was located. On top of the plain is a large train, and Layla had informed us that this was the exact train that would take us to the refugee.

And now, due to the rear-biting cold air, all 3,000 men, women, and children are ushering to find a seat in the train that stands ominously against the blood-red sky.

Once everybody settles in, the Subversives, Nico, our family, and Layla and Tamia step inside. The first three cars are supposed to remain empty for us because Layla decided that we deserved some time to ourselves.

The cool air converts to warm as we trek forward into the top three cars. We push past the people sitting on the seats in the cars below us, and food is immediately offered to them by hostesses, and they don't even think twice to desperately grab the food.

Once we reach the third car, we exhaustively sit on the seats attached to the sides of the train. My legs ache as I press the back of my head onto the wall, feeling the engine slowly rumble to life.

The seats we are currently sitting on are only two per row, so beside me I have Em, who grins at me. I smirk at her and bring her in, hugging her tightly.

In front of me are my mama and papa, who are so tired that they immediately fall asleep as soon as their asses hit the seats. Seeing their son after a long time has made them super excited, and tears poured out of their eyes when they saw him emerging out from the shadows after we left the hospital room. It makes me so happy to think that my parents are at ease now.

Then, behind me is Jeremiah, Layla, and their daughter, and they are laughing and smiling together. It's weird to see Jeremiah look so happy because he mostly had a calm demeanor when we were in the bunker. But now? He's grinning ear-to-ear, his harmonious laugh resonating into the air. Being with his wife and daughter probably made him feel so relieved.

Then, in the aisle next to us is Jax and Mal sitting together, laughing with Vi and Nico, who are right behind them. My heart warms as I notice *everybody* is united and loving each other immensely—just how our society should have been. It's a damn good thing we left the Rich behind. It definitely is.

It wasn't hard leaving them behind, though. They were too busy worrying about themselves to the point where they didn't even notice more than half of the population left. The Rich are fending for themselves now.

Finally, Nico stands up and starts to speak into the intercom that reverberates into all of the cars. "Hey everybody! We are now leaving to go to the refuge. Hopefully we can get there before tomorrow morning, but if it gets too late, then you are more than welcome to sleep. The train is about to depart, so I'd advise you to remain seated. Thank you." Nicolas decides to hang up the intercom, and he rubs his hands together as his long hair falls onto his eyes.

"I can't believe we made it, guys." Vi looks at everybody incredulously. "We are all alive and well. We made it."

"Amen to that!" Jeremiah says, and everybody cheers, laughing and smiling excitedly. I continue to hold Em, clapping as I watch everybody's expression filled with great delight and contentment.

Once that settles down, Jax suddenly clears his throat. "I can't wait to get out of this place. It's about damn time that we did."

"Definitely," Mal grumbles, pushing her long blonde hair to the side. I notice the conflicted look settled on her face, which most definitely resulted from her leaving her parents behind— just like Jax did. "How many people are there?"

"A lot," Layla says. "Probably around 50,000."

"50,000?" I echo. "That many people are in the city?"

"Yeah." She nods. "The government lied to us the entire time."

"Honestly, I'm not so surprised about that," I say, looking out the window as I notice the train has started to depart.

"We're moving!" Em claims happily. I grin as I notice the train's speed is increasing, blurs of white trees whizzing by.

"Bye, D.C. We ain't gonna miss you!" Vi snorts as she waves at the city.

Jax chuckles. "Y'know, now that we are friends . . . Do you think I can call you Vi now?"

Vi lets out a long sigh, sending him an irritated look. "Fine, you can call me Vi. But easy there with the *friends* bit . . . You have lots to work on to receive that title."

Jax snorts out a laugh, seeming greatly accomplished now.

Mal asks suddenly, "Where is your mother?"

He says, "I left her behind. I felt terrible for a split second when I did, but as time goes by, I will feel nothing at all. *Nothing.*" And the expression on his face reveals it all—reveals that he's saying the truth. He doesn't regret leaving Isabelle behind, which she's probably surrounded by dead bodies, including her husband's. But she deserves to stay there in the ruins of D.C. Because she didn't help Jax, her own son, when he needed her help. His mother's help.

Amid all of my pondering, I find Jax's eyes meeting mine. They linger for a bit, and I feel my heart racing as I recount what happened in my closet today. The kiss we shared was absolutely incredible, and I keep thinking about *him* every five seconds. His lips, his eyes, his hair, his body, his smile, him . . . Everything about him is unforgettable.

Finally, I try to listen to everybody's conversation, but their voices start to drown as my eyes start to droop close. I lean my head against the wall, which shakes with every movement the train makes, but at this point, even sleeping on a bed of nails is enough for me. I am tired and just want to sleep my troubles away.

And soon enough, my tiredness overcomes me, making me enter the unknown.

December 5, 2064
7:44 a.m.

"How was your time with the Subversives?" Nico asks me.

I speak, the hoarseness in my throat seeming to have decreased. "I loved it so much. I made such amazing friends, and I also learned such valuable lessons. There were very stressful moments, but I learned the hard way how to overcome them." I turn to him. "I couldn't stop thinking about you, Nico. I couldn't stop thinking that you could be dead at that moment. When I learned from Tobias that he had killed you . . . I lost it."

His eyes are somber as he pulls me in, his hand on my shoulder. "I'm sorry, Bumble Bee. You know I had to do what I had to do. But hey, at least we're together now. Correct?"

"Yeah," I whisper. "Correct."

We are currently standing inside of the topmost car that is right behind the conductor's car. This means that we are able to overlook the beautiful scenery in front of us, mountains covered in specks of snow with the beautiful bright sun beaming with energy. The train rumbles with every movement, but it's a soft and soothing movement that causes my mind to enter a euphoric state. I look at my brother and notice the calm expression on his face.

His eyes are narrowed slightly as he studies the outside.

I clear my throat. "How many Rich people died?"

"Around 1,500," Nico answers almost immediately. "That's half of their population."

"Seriously?"

He nods. "Yeah. Those blasts really affected them."

"Good," I grumble. "I'm so glad to hear they were mostly affected by them."

"Me too." He grins.

I look out the window, bringing in my blanket tighter around me. "What is the city like?"

"Beautiful, that's what it is."

"And there's no societal divisions?"

"Nope." He shakes his head. "This city is class-free. There are no labels."

"That's good to hear." I breathe out a sigh of relief. We continue to gaze at the outside, acknowledging the wondrous and breath- taking scenery.

Suddenly, a silhouette of a distant city appears. I gasp with excitement. "Is that . . . ?"

"Yep. That's the refuge."

"It looks like an entire city," I murmur incredulously.

"Well, it's a refuge inside of a city. The city is called Detroit."

"Detroit," I say, seeming familiar with the name. I continue to gaze at the large skyscrapers poking out like enormous monsters. It's so much more intimidating than D.C., but Nico telling me that everybody is accepting of others there makes me feel a bit less anxious.

"We made it," he whispers, grinning at me.

"We did." I gulp, tears almost forming in my eyes as I take in the oncoming city one last time. "We really did make it."

And as the city comes closer and closer to us, standing tall and proud amongst the outside ruins of America, I realize one thing that makes my entire body shiver with awareness. I've felt a huge round of emotions in my entire life. I've felt angry, sad, tired, frustrated, or lonely at some points. Never did I feel happy. Sure, I've had moments where I grinned ear-to-ear and forgot all of my gut-churning issues, but I never felt ground-breaking happiness that reached into my soul and soothed me.

But I feel it now. I feel this happiness escaping into the valleys of my soul and filling me up with desire, wanting to go into this city and feel at peace for once. Feel as if I belong somewhere.

And standing here with my long-lost brother, who stares at the city looming in front of us, I also realize that I have never felt free before. Liberation was never a part of my life, but it is now. Because I feel it calling for me. I feel this city calling for me, desperate to extend its ever-lasting warmth.

Home. Home is calling for me.

ACKNOWLEDGMENTS

Throughout my entire writing of this novel, I've endured many moments of writer's block, lack of motivation, and second thoughts. I sometimes thought that writing this book wouldn't be worth it, that I am wasting my time writing something that wouldn't have much of an impact anyway.

But seeing the great uproar caused by Subversion . . . It made me feel as if my words mattered to others. And that is why I am so indebted to all of these people that helped me throughout my writing journey, just a young and innocent teenager traversing through the rocky paths of writing and publishing a compli-cated dystopian novel.

I would first like to thank my wonderful readers. Your dedi-cation to read and cherish my words will never go unnoticed by me. You are the reason why I write. So, thank you so much. You mean more than the world to me.

Next, I obviously would not be here without my editor Amy Vrana, who I can most assuredly tell you is the bravest person on earth for reading my extremely chaotic manuscript. If it weren't for her, then my writing wouldn't be nearly as good as it is now. I thank you tremendously for your patience and belief in me.

I would like to thank my mother and father too, for trying their best to understand the indecipherable elements that go into publishing a book. Thank you for believing in me and helping me accomplish my dreams. I love you more than words can ever explain.

My family has helped me plenty with this, too. My grandpa, for one, who I've written my first story about. Chhotu Bhai, for helping me gift wrap the ARC copies for my advanced readers. My amazing cousins for being there for me no matter what. And everyone else in my family, who supports me and believes in me. I love you all.

Certain friends can never go unnoticed, too. All of them are incredibly amazing and supportive, but there are two that have been there for me since the very beginning: Mahi and Antra. Thank you, Mahi, for reading the truly bland and one-dimensional stories I wrote in freshmen and sophomore year. Your support for me is so appreciated, and I know I can count on you for absolutely anything. And thank you, Antra, for being my well-appreciated motivation buddy. You always lift me up and push me to write, and I am absolutely certain I would not be this far in my writing career if it weren't for your great belief in me. I love you both so much.

Lastly, the final piece goes to me. I don't mean to be narcissistic, but honestly, the work I put into this novel is mind-boggling. This story is something that's been buried in the vast corners of my mind ever since I was thirteen-years-old, and I finally dug it out with a significant amount of planning and a concerning amount of mental breakdowns too. Subversion wouldn't have been Subversion without me, so I'd *especially* like to thank myself for writing this in the smack dab of junior year and writing until three o' clock in the morning while aggressively chugging down energy drinks. It is truly great to see how far I've come.

I hope you all have enjoyed this story of mine. And remember, this is not the end of the story just yet; in fact, this is only the beginning.

DISCUSSION QUESTIONS

Warning: There are spoilers. Read with caution!

1. The story opens up with a line that delineates the coldness of the room. Why do you think the author wrote that as the first sentence? Does it contribute to the general theme/ambiance of the story?
2. What are your thoughts about the main characters introduced in this novel? And since this is a series, how do you think their personalities will grow/evolve in the other books?
3. Why is Blaire's overall anger/frustration so imperative to the story line? How do her emotions shape the novel?
4. What were the main themes of this book? How were those themes brought to life?
5. While Blaire and Nico are well-educated and mature, Em is described to be "below" her age's average education and maturity level, hence making her seem younger than she really is. Why do you think the

author incorporated this certain characteristic of her's?

6. Dylan Faulkner/Zachary Everett revealing himself as a traitor to the Subversives was the turning point of the organization's journey. Did you find it to be believable? Shocking? Or necessary?

7. Think of Jax's decision to draw an identical scar of his on his father, right before killing him. What are your thoughts on that? Do you think his decision to do that will affect him in the future? And in what way?

8. Silence is mentioned frequently throughout the novel. Why do you think that is? How does that tie in to the general ambiance/environment of the book?

9. What is the main message of this story? What do you believe others can gain from this novel?

10. Judging by how the story ended, what do you think will happen next? Will their lives actually get better? Or will they get worse?

Printed in Great Britain
by Amazon

12175770R00226